Lessons on Love

4 Schoolteachers Find More Than They Bargained for in Their Contracts

Susanne Dietze
Rita Gerlach
Kathleen L. Maher
Carrie Fancett Pagels

BARBOUR BOOKS
An Imprint of Barbour Publishing, Inc.

Print ISBN 978-1-64352-184-8

eBook Editions:
Adobe Digital Edition (.epub) 978-1-64352-186-2
Kindle and MobiPocket Edition (.prc) 978-1-64352-185-5

Cover photograph: Sandra Cunningham / Trevillion Images
Interior line art illustrations by Jensine Eckwall

Published by Barbour Books, an imprint of Barbour Publishing, Inc., 1810 Barbour Drive, Uhrichsville, Ohio 44683, www.barbourbooks.com

Our mission is to inspire the world with the life-changing message of the Bible.

Member of the Evangelical Christian Publishers Association

Printed in Canada.

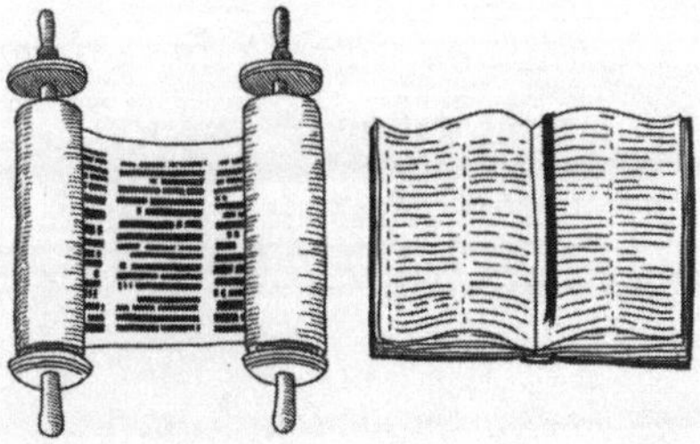

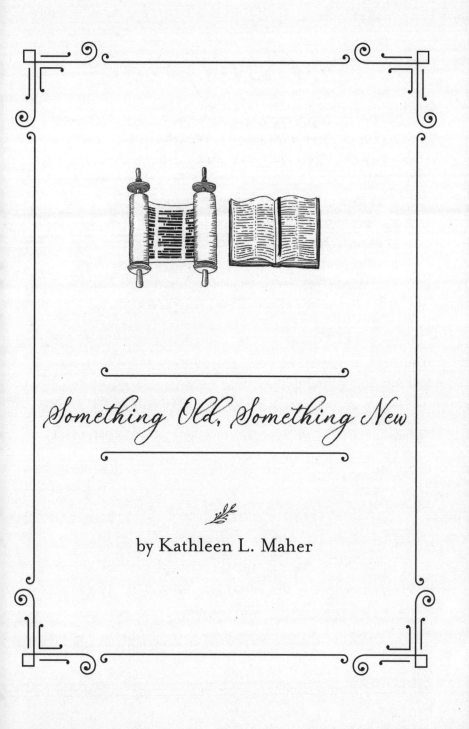

Something Old, Something New

by Kathleen L. Maher

Acknowledgments

Without the help of mentors and critique partners, the creative process would grind to a halt. I am incredibly blessed to have two amazing and talented women to whom I can turn. Debbie Lynne Costello and Carrie Fancett Pagels have been more than professional writing resources; they have been the kind of friends that come one in a million. I am twice blessed. Thank you for your help, prayers, and devotion. And having the loving support of my husband, John, humbles me. He makes me laugh even when I don't realize I need to. Thank you for being you!

Glossary of Hebrew and Yiddish Terms

Aruk ha-Shalem: a gift, token, payment

chuppah: the wedding canopy. In traditional Jewish weddings, there are two stages: the betrothal, or ketubah, and the marriage under the chuppah.

El-Shaddai: the Sovereign One, God Almighty

G'mar chatima tova: "May you be inscribed (in the Book of Life) for good." Yom Kippur greeting. Tradition teaches that one's fate is written on Rosh Hashanah and sealed on Yom Kippur.

Hashem: literally "the name [of God]"

kaddish: prayers for the deceased

kippah: yarmulke, or head covering worn by Jewish men

Mazel tov: wish of good luck or congratulations

mikvah: the washing of the bride—a time of separation and preparation of the bride

minyan: a meeting of public Jewish worship, traditionally consisting of a quorum of ten men

mitzvah (pl. mitzvoth): a good deed done from religious duty

Oy vey: exclamation indicating dismay or grief

Rosh Hashanah: Jewish new year

shalom: literally, "peace"; a blessing at greeting or departing

Shalom aleichem: "Peace be upon you."

Sheva Brachot: "the seven blessings," also known as "the wedding blessings"

shiva: the seven-day period of mourning for Jews following the death of a loved one. Evening minyan for mourners to say kaddish (the mourner's prayer), followed by anyone who wishes to say something about the deceased. Sitting shiva is when the immediate family does nothing for seven days but sit, often on the floor or on a low stool, to receive those who wish to come and pay respects.

Shloshim: thirty-day period following burial in which kaddish is said. If the deceased was a parent, the mourning period is extended a year.

tenaim: the conditions of a Jewish marriage, such as the wedding date, or the dowry, arranged by the parents or family of the betrothed upon their engagement

Yahrzeit: commemoration of a loved one, especially on the anniversary of the person's death. In addition to lighting a candle on the anniversary of the death, the Yahrzeit candle is also lit on four other designated days of the year, called Yizkor dates. Yom Kippur is one of those dates.

Yeshua: Hebrew name for Jesus

Yom Kippur: Day of Atonement; the most solemn religious fast of the Jewish year, the last of the ten days of penitence, or Ten Days of Awe, that begin with Rosh Hashanah, the Jewish new year.

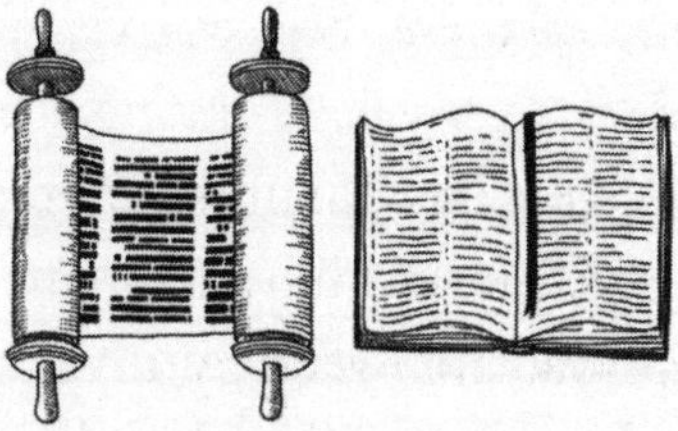

Chapter 1

Cortlandt, Westchester County, New York
September 1840

"Hadassah, hurry, it's almost sundown."

Gilda turned from the stairwell, cupping her hand in front of the taper as she moved so the flame wouldn't sputter out. Keeping one ear attuned for her younger sister's response from the upper floor, she set her focus on her other sibling.

"Hannah, do you want to be late for Papa's *kaddish*?"

It had been a month since Papa had died, but after this first year of loss ended, only four *Yizkor* dates on the Hebrew calendar provided for mourning. Would it be enough to memorialize Eliezer Jacobs—to light his candle and commemorate a life that had shaped her entire world? Papa deserved more than that. He deserved a lifetime with Gilda following his sterling example.

She passed the looking glass hanging in the dining room and

instinctively faced it, but a white sheet met her gaze rather than her appearance. Of course, mourning customs. The looking glasses were all covered. Every one of them. She was certain hers would have been a disheveled reflection anyway, running around and making all the preparations for Mama and giving no thought to vanity on this day. At least, not much thought.

Mama sat, as she had for weeks since Papa's passing, in her rocking chair by the hearth. The rockers made a rhythmic sound over the polished wood floor as she rocked slowly, enshrouded both in silence and by her black shawl.

Gilda set her candle in its holder next to the *Yahrzeit* mourning candle on the lampstand and approached Mama softly. "Would you like to conduct the *minyan*, Mama, or should I?"

Deep brown eyes shuttered, and a long sigh escaped her mother's petite frame. "You say it, Gilda. I have no breath to recite."

Gilda fixed the shawl that slipped from Mama's shoulders and nodded assurance. "I'll do it."

The click of hardware and tread of boots announced a guest entering the front door. It had been a parade of late, as the community continued to come and pay respects for Papa. Both Hebrew and Gentile, many throughout the county admired him. A sigh similar to Mama's threatened to pull from Gilda's chest, but she cleared her throat and attended to her *mitzvoth*, her sacred duties.

Her youngest sister, Hadassah, joined Hannah on a settee near Mama, and Gilda brought another chair from the dining room to accommodate the arrivals, as not one, but several gentlemen stepped in and removed their hats—and their shoes. Her pitcher and bowl, set by the door, was employed by each in turn.

"*G'mar chatima tovah*" Gilda said to Rabbi Rothstein, who led several men with familiar bearded faces into their parlor. The sun dipped low on the horizon, and following its sloping path toward the start of *Yom Kippur* at sundown, her eyes burned. Her eyes never ceased to burn these days.

She blinked away the hot tears and steeled herself with the strength her family needed from her. Poor Papa. He hadn't a son to say his kaddish. She would have to do.

"*Shalom*, Miss Jacobs."

"*Shalom aleichem*, Mister—"

She looked up from her woolgathering to meet a piercingly blue gaze. This man she'd never met before. Startling and yet heartwarming that a stranger to her thought enough of her Papa to come. His tailored waistcoat of slate blue fit his trim figure, accentuating a narrow waist and broad shoulders. He could not have been much older than her own age of twenty-one, mayhap a year older. This man was not of great height, apparent once he removed his top hat, nor did he have the rough hands of a laborer. He was neither neighbor, schoolmate, or synagogue congregant. Was he a business associate of Papa's?

Surely she would have remembered this man. She swallowed.

With his blond hair and bright blue eyes, she couldn't mistake him for anything but a Gentile. Yet he seemed to know her customs. She was at a disadvantage, not knowing his name. And worse, not knowing what her appearance presented.

"Mr. Blake," the handsome young man replied with a courtly bow.

She lowered her eyes and nodded a solemn, wordless response, hoping her blushing cheeks did not betray her unbidden thoughts.

The procession of guests took their chairs. Gilda followed them in, giving one more assessment of her preparations. With adequate seating in place, she approached to light the Yahrzeit candle.

Rabbi Rothstein stepped to her side and patted her arm. "Allow me, my dear." His kindly eyes shone with affection behind his spectacles, and she could have wept with relief at the small mercy.

Gilda made way and took the last available seat—a footstool, low to the ground, in keeping with mourning customs.

Words—comforting, familiar words, in soothing and predictable cadence—tumbled in the rabbi's accented voice for long moments while she struggled to keep her focus, as all that Papa had left unaccomplished stretched before her. He'd left a small savings for his widow and children. At fifty-five, he was still young and vital. Until the sudden end. There should have been plenty of time to rebuild his investments after paying for Uncle Mortimer's passage. Fine expense that turned out to be. He had never arrived. So, as it was, there was little to live on for four hungry mouths.

Fortunately, Papa had left detailed lesson plans for the school, a syllabus with which Gilda was intimately familiar. She would be ready as head schoolmistress instead of as Papa's assistant, when the month of *Shloshim* ended, to resume where Papa had left off. The position would help make ends meet and give Mama some peace of mind, though women teachers were paid only a fraction of men's wages.

The kaddish ended sooner than she realized in her state of distraction, and friends and neighbors were already paying respects to Mama, Hadassah, and Hannah. Gilda needed to rejoin her family. She gathered her black taffeta skirts and eased through the rows of chairs to the front near the hearth.

Pieter Van Brugh, a prominent merchant from one of the oldest families in the county, took Mama's hand in a gesture of sympathy. "Eliezer was a brilliant man and will be greatly missed, Mrs. Jacobs. I don't know how we will do without him at the common school this year."

"My Gilda knows exactly what is required. Her father prepared her well."

"Yes, yes, she has been a faithful assistant to your husband. Very faithful indeed." His smile included Gilda, and he stepped to the side to make way for the next in line, the mayor.

"My dear Mrs. Jacobs. You know how fond we all were of your husband, so I hope you don't take this the wrong way. But managing unruly pupils requires a man's strength and stature. Gilda is barely out of school herself."

Gilda fixed her face to match the smile of the politician. "You are quite right, Mayor Roelantsen, in stating that I've grown up with these boys all my life. The experience has given me a unique ability. I can handily whip any boy who dares to challenge me."

Hadassah and Hannah chortled behind their gloved hands. Mama appeared as though she might swoon.

"Now, Miss Jacobs, with all due respect. . ."

They would *not* take the position from her. Gilda squared her stance. "It is true. Brute strength can accomplish certain things. An ox can plow a straight furrow, sir, but it takes intelligent direction to plot its course."

A few of the elders from synagogue chuckled, and Rabbi Rothstein patted the mayor on the back. "The young lady has a point, Cornelius."

Mayor Roelantsen waved off the gesture. "Miss Jacobs, Mrs. Jacobs, I'd like you to meet my nephew. I've brought him with me today so you could become acquainted. It is my hope that, with his oratory experience and study under the esteemed Reverend Charles Grandison Finney, he might be useful to our school."

The handsome blond man with the piercing blue eyes stepped alongside the mayor. "This is Joshua Blake, my wife's brother's son. I believe our common school will benefit greatly by the unique qualifications he brings."

Gilda's heart had dropped into her stomach, and she clutched Mama's hand discreetly behind the folds of their skirts. Her mother's grip was equally firm, communicating solidarity. This man would take away her ability to provide for her family? Not if she had any say.

A bit flummoxed at his uncle's timing, Josh grinned sheepishly. This family grieved their patriarch, not a month gone. And here his uncle had announced that Josh had come as the deceased's replacement. More to the point, to take the position out from under the feet of the man's daughter like the tapestry rug on which she stood. And what dainty little stockinged feet they were. He shook himself from the distracting thought and met her gaze. The spritely and quick-witted Miss Jacobs skewered him with her dark eyes rimmed in gold. And what beautiful eyes they were. He swallowed, not accustomed to being at a loss for words.

Josh folded his hands behind his back and lowered his head in deference. His uncle was a determined man but not the most sensitive to others' feelings. What the community needed was not an ambitious politician, but a minister. If teaching gave Josh a segue into their trust, he would gladly be their shepherd.

"I am afraid Mr. Jacobs leaves impossible shoes to fill, Uncle. If I can be of some small comfort or assistance, it would be an honor to help bring healing to a bereft community."

The atmosphere, and Miss Jacobs's posture, tangibly shifted.

Uncle Cornelius cleared his throat. "I propose Miss Jacobs start on a trial basis as headmistress, with my nephew as assistant teacher. If she will make amendments to the curriculum to include Christian instruction in moral character, if she can succeed in improving attendance among the farmers and lumberjack camps and all the while maintain discipline, she may retain the position. If, however, she fails on any of these points, I propose my nephew be appointed headmaster."

The rabbi waved at the air. "Can this wait for another time? Consider the grieving—"

"I agree to those terms!" Miss Jacobs's voice rose high but not shrill above the gentlemen's negotiation.

A half grin spread from one corner of Josh's mouth as Miss Jacobs shook Uncle Cornelius's hand. The young lady certainly had what her people called *chutzpah*.

"In fact, if Mr. Blake can begin Monday, I see no reason to delay. Our students mustn't wait any longer." She folded her arms over her chest and gave a tilt of her pert little chin that spoke a challenge equal to a man removing his gauntlet and striking him. Josh closed his mouth, which had dropped agape, and offered a bow to Miss Gilda Jacobs, interim headmistress.

"I look forward to the challen—that is, the opportunity."

Her gold-rimmed brown eyes glittered, her gaze unwavering. Josh drew a deep breath and expelled it slowly. The mission with which his mentor, Charles Finney, had commissioned him would go a lot smoother if he held the community's trust. He could build that from the platform of schoolteacher. And no matter how compelling Miss Jacobs's reason for needing this job, he mustn't let it stop the work of the Gospel. He must not let her drive him out.

Chapter 2

A brisk breeze blew in from the Hudson on Josh's early morning walk, and he drew in the earthy scents of river and pine. With the sunrise the town sawmill commenced its industry along his route to the schoolhouse, its workmen in muslin shirts, busy feeding logs into the jaws of iron-toothed blades. The workers exchanged rough words with one another in the talk of the common class—the sort of people among whom he had grown up. Salty. Mayhap they too could become the salt of the earth. God had reached even the likes of him, after all—a man of unfortunate breeding and cast away as a newborn upon the mercy of his aunt and uncle.

It was a pleasantly appointed town in which he found himself. So much opportunity to teach. Uncle Cornelius had extended the invitation a few years ago for Josh to come and live with him after Josh had concluded his formal schooling. Schooling for which the pious Dutch reformer had ungrudgingly paid. Without his uncle's intervention, only God knew where he would be. He would not disappoint the man.

Whistling a hymn, Josh continued along the tree-lined lane. A whitewashed picket fence framed the schoolyard just ahead, and already pupils congregated at the steps leading up to the building. A girl of perhaps six years, wearing a pinafore and cotton dress, met him at the gate and flashed him a gap-toothed smile.

Josh tipped his top hat. "Good day, miss."

"This is my first day of school. Are you my new teacher?"

"Indeed, I am one of your new instructors. I am Mr. Blake."

"I'm Aggie Willard."

Several of the others gathered round, most a few years Aggie's senior. A boy in tailored britches and suspenders appraised him with head tilted back.

"You're shorter than Headmaster Jacobs."

An older girl corralled the boy in the crook of her arm. "Mind your manners, Steven. Pa will tan your hide for impertinence."

Josh bit back a chuckle but kept his expression temperate. "It's true I am shorter than some. Comparison is a tricky thing. I'm taller than you, for instance."

The boy folded his arms across his chest and frowned. "That's 'cuz you're all growed up."

"Grown up," his sister corrected him.

"You have a solid grasp on your grammar, Miss. . . ," Josh said.

"Miss Elizabeth Beckwith. Thank you, Mr. Blake. I sometimes help with the younger children."

"I'll keep that in mind."

A clacking sound drew Josh's attention away. Swaggering up the path and drumming a stick against the picket fence slats as he went, a ruddy-faced and sturdy-framed adolescent made his arrival known.

Elizabeth Beckwith cut her eyes at the boy. "That's Oliver Simms."

Josh nodded, her huff inviting him to draw conclusions. Her brother pulled out of her grip and ran to meet the approaching boy, who was roughly twice his size.

"Hi, Oliver. I caught a butterfly this morning. Got him in my lunch bucket. Wanna see him?"

Oliver paused, gave Josh a once-over from head to toe, and took Steven's pail. He lifted the book off its opening, and orange-and-black wings fluttered up into the air, gone.

"Hey! You let my butterfly loose!"

Oliver shoved him aside like a weed blocking his path. "No, I didn't. You're the one who let me see it."

Elizabeth stomped her foot. "You're such a bully, Oliver Simms!"

Josh stepped up and patted the girl's shoulder as he strode toward the boys. "I'll handle this."

"Mr. Simms? I'm Mr. Blake."

"So?"

Josh's grin broadened. "So I'm the new teacher. One of them, anyway. I'm here to help us all start the new year together on the right foot."

"More than one teacher?" The boy's nose wrinkled, and his plump cheeks grew darker red.

"That's right."

"Miss Jacobs can't manage without her father?" A few of the boys congregating at the steps laughed.

"There will be none of that." Josh turned and faced them all. "Your first lesson is to learn the Golden Rule: 'Do unto others as you would have them do unto you.' "

"You sound more like a preacher than a teacher."

"And do you know what that rule means, Mr. Simms? It means that if you want to be treated fairly, you have to be fair to others."

Oliver smirked. "You mean, I should get his stupid butterfly back?"

"That would be a good start." Josh snagged his thumbs on his belt.

Aggie tugged on his cutaway overcoat. "Are we going inside, Mr. Blake?"

"Uh, the keys I believe are with Miss Jacobs. She should be along momentarily."

"Can I sit next to you?"

Josh peered down the avenue for any sign of the headmistress. He withdrew his pocket watch, and the face showed five minutes past the hour. He excused himself and slipped past Aggie. What could be keeping Miss Jacobs?

A trio in dark skirts and shirtwaists sashayed up the road. One taller, two shorter. If they were Miss Jacobs and her sisters, he would not have guessed they'd arrive on foot. Hadn't she a carriage at her disposal? Her home was nearly two miles away.

"Boys, I want you to line up on the left, and girls on the right."

The children picked up their slates and primers, lunch pails and belongings, and formed two lines. Miss Jacobs would arrive to see that he had everything in order.

The girls stood serenely like Greek statues with the autumn sun falling on the folds of their skirts. The boys were a bit fidgety, but Josh supposed that was to be expected. Steven Beckwith stood behind a couple of quiet brothers, Oliver at the tail end.

Conversation drifted to Josh while he waited for Miss Jacobs and her two sisters near the gate of the schoolyard.

"Look, Stevie, it's your butterfly."

A loud thump sounded, like a book dropped from a height.

A growling, angry cry ripped from the younger boy. "You! You killed it! Aagggh!"

"Oomph!"

Josh swung around to the sight of boys fighting, Steven on top, punching and yelling, Oliver on his back trying to knock him off.

"Break it up!" He covered the distance and pulled both boys to their feet by their shirt collars and suspenders. "Enough!"

The older boy shifted his weight, knocking Josh off balance, and he lost his grip on them. Oliver commenced to pummel Steven.

Elizabeth joined in the fray to defend her brother. Josh grabbed at the three of them and came up empty-handed. The students toppled over someone's pile of belongings left on the grass.

"They broke my slate!" Aggie wailed.

Josh gathered the littlest student away from danger and turned back around to end the fight.

Before he could, another voice broke through the chaos.

"I see we're off to a fine start, Mr. Blake."

Josh froze and mopped his face with his hand. Miss Jacobs couldn't have arrived at a worse time.

Gilda watched from her stance by the gate, her arms at her hips, her toe tapping as Mr. Blake attempted to restore order. What a fine mess! Is this what she could expect the rest of the year?

Hannah and Hadassah gathered around little Agatha, consoling her over her broken slate. Elizabeth slinked away from the fray, her cheeks blazing, possibly with chagrin to be caught in a boy's brawl. What must have transpired to make the mature young lady snap? Oliver backed away from Steven, assuming a cherubic expression of innocence. Steven glared at Oliver but thrust himself into picking up the scattered books and belongings.

Outwardly, Gilda made sure to look the part of disappointed schoolmarm, but inside she fought ironic laughter. Joshua Blake, the one who had been sent to maintain order and discipline, had allowed the worst behavior she'd ever witnessed, and the day hadn't even begun.

She walked calmly to the entry, turned the key in the lock, and opened the door. "You may take your seats, class."

None made a peep as they filed into the single room and sat on pine benches.

Mr. Blake brought up the rear and stood toward the back of the classroom.

"Come up here, Mr. Blake," she beckoned.

In a few quick strides, he joined her by the large slate board mounted to the wall. He folded his hands behind his back and looked out over the class.

"I assume everyone has met our new instructor whom the school board has sent us. This is Mayor Roelantsen's nephew, Mr. Blake. I hope you will give him your undivided attention and your best manners today."

The students murmured agreement.

"I needn't remind you all that at the end of the day, there are floors to scrub, firewood to carry, and water to pump from the well. I will have no choice but to mete out chores to anyone who disrupts the progress of our learning.

"But for the one who excels, shows earnest effort, and finds ways to be the most helpful, I have incentives." Gilda paused and met each curious gaze. "I hope to give out many merit awards this year."

Mr. Blake's expression also filled with curiosity, and perhaps a hint of admiration. Her stomach did an unexpected flip as his azure gaze trained on her.

"Please take out your Blue-Backed Speller and open to the first chapter. Mr. Blake, if you would, please find Agatha a spare slate in the cloak closet."

She looked away before her staid exterior crumbled to the smile begging to show. How on earth would she maintain order over her rebellious thoughts, much less a classroom with divided authority? She would give no quarter to any of it—his interference, the children's boundary testing, and least of all, her foolish fascination with those piercing blue eyes.

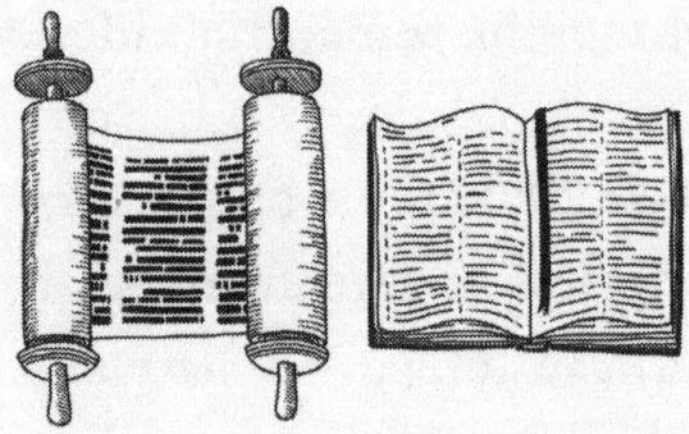

Chapter 3

Josh had gotten the wind knocked out of him. He paced the perimeter of the classroom to restore equilibrium, taking in the enormity of his assignment. A wry grin creased his face. In his unprepared state, he couldn't hope to earn one of Miss Jacobs's merit awards. And what sort of favor might she offer him if he did? He sighed, shuttering his natural instincts around such a pretty young woman. No, he must make no provision for the flesh. And tomorrow he would have to bring his best efforts, even if this job was just a means to fulfill a higher calling.

He'd said little throughout the day but remained in a posture of observation and an attitude of humble prayer. The remarkable young lady had instilled order and cooperation seemingly with no effort. Even Oliver had sat diligently, bent over his slate, working out a difficult arithmetic problem with her encouragement and praise.

Now, the day over and the children departing with smiles, his mind brimmed with questions. Miss Jacobs's trim figure stood silhouetted by the afternoon blaze of sun at the door. He approached her with shuffling boot steps.

Her gold-rimmed eyes shimmered in the light, and a hint of a smile played on her lips. "Have we made you reconsider your appointment, Mr. Blake?"

He couldn't help but grin. "It'll take more than a rough start to scare me away, Miss Jacobs."

"Good. Because we haven't seen the full size of the student body yet. These are just the regulars. Wait until after harvest, when the farmers' sons show up. And wait until the lumberjack camp wives and children return to town."

Josh nodded. "Would you be willing to go over the curriculum with me? I have a few questions."

Miss Jacobs crossed back through the room to her desk and gathered her materials. "Certainly. I can spare a few minutes now."

"That's a good start. Thank you. I'm curious that the syllabus does not include the new McGuffey Readers. They seem to be quite popular."

"Mr. McGuffey's work is relatively new to the scholastic scene."

"I've seen his material put to good use, with great effect."

"Your uncle and some others on the school council had been after my father to incorporate his work. My father preferred the tried and true, Blue-Backed Speller."

He lifted her worn copy of Noah Webster's primer and held it with a gesture of consideration. "This has no doubt served here for many years."

"Yes. Papa was a great admirer of Mr. Webster's ecumenical approach to schooling. Mr. Webster believed in universal toleration, where all religions and opinions are accorded equality."

"I see. Very admirable from the standpoint of the scholar that

I have been told your father was. But I am also told in no uncertain terms that the community demands religious instruction. It is one of the hinge pins of my appointment, to introduce lessons on Christian morality to their sons and daughters. I realize this is a delicate subject, Miss Jacobs, and I must assure you that I have no intentions of stepping on your toes. . . ."

Her eyes were all gold-rimmed fire. She stood unwavering, her feet—those delicate, lovely feet he had glimpsed in her home just a few days prior—squared beneath her billowing skirts. He softened his tone. "I desire a partnership, and nothing more. I don't wish to usurp the good work you're doing here. Only augment it."

He brought his boot up onto the nearby chair and leaned across his knee.

"Would you permit me to take an hour of class time for the McGuffey Reader, and introduce various passages of scripture, while I remain poised to assist you in anything you might require out of your curriculum the balance of the day? And if it suits you, perhaps, I might arrange oratories of memorized portions and passages, to recite for their parents, every quarter?"

Miss Jacobs pressed her lips into a hard line. Josh's heartbeat kicked up a notch, surmising her displeasure. And in the pity of her hiding what soft lips they were.

"I find that an acceptable compromise, Mr. Blake. You may tell your uncle he has prevailed in this matter."

"And one other thing, Miss Jacobs?"

She raised one brow, but her lips had softened considerably again, as she gazed on him awaiting his next request.

"May I drive you and your sisters to and from school in my uncle's landau? We live on the same side of town, and it might be wise if we arrived before the students, so that there are no more unattended students on the grounds, nor opportunities for trouble as we had this morning."

Gilda drew a gasp of air. The audacity of the man! Dictating to her when she should arrive at the school she had served for a decade.

Footsteps approached, and she recognized her sisters returning with a bucket of water from the well. "Oh Gilda, my feet hurt so! Could we? Please?" Hannah pleaded.

Hadassah joined the chorus. "Yes, please, could we take the carriage with Mr. Blake tomorrow? My boots are chafing my heels."

Gilda closed her eyes until she could employ a tone devoid of the rebuke the girls deserved, then fluttered them open. "I will discuss it with Mr. Blake, and you may wait on the steps outside."

The girls obeyed, whispering together as they departed. Mayhap it was time to hang a hickory stick at the front of the classroom. Indeed, tomorrow she may well take the class on a field trip to find the very one together. Just like Papa, she would never use it, but its presence might provide sufficient deterrent.

"Your offer comes as a surprise, Mr. Blake. Forgive me for not thanking you for your consideration before my sisters imposed their opinions."

How did the man know she had arranged to sell Papa's carriage to provide wiggle room in the budget? They would need wood for the stove this winter, and other expenses loomed. She realized it was a lot to ask of her sisters, to walk the mile and a half each way while carrying books and bundles—especially when the weather turned cold and snow and ice lined their paths. Bad enough they missed their papa, but now they should be expected to live like paupers and walk? Guilt and worry tightened double cinches about her stomach.

She let out a sigh.

"Then, you'll allow me to drive you?"

Gilda nodded. "Thank you, Mr. Blake. There's no reason we can't form a partnership, as you say. Arriving together might benefit our desire to present a unified front and discourage the students from attempting the old divide-and-conquer tactic." She smiled, and his blue eyes danced with pleasure.

"May I walk you and your sisters home today? I'd be pleased to carry your books for you."

Gilda's face prickled with the blush that threatened to steel over her cheeks again. What a sight that would be in her black gauze mourning dress, rose-painted cheeks like a maiden turned out on a dance floor. *Oy vey.*

"Does that mean you will assist me in scrubbing the pine floors and washing the slates first?"

"I am your humble servant." He bowed, and her head swam. What a ninny she was being. But she fought the smile that found its way to her lips, begrudging any display of her secret thoughts. As maddening as this young Gentile could be, he was also rather endearing.

Elohim ya'azor li.

God help her, indeed.

"Another thought I have," Mr. Blake began as he hefted the wash bucket and carried it to the slate board. "You mentioned that the farmers' children don't attend until after harvest."

"They're needed to help their parents bring in the crops for survival."

"Yes, of course. I wouldn't deny them their livelihoods. But I was thinking. What if instead of waiting for them to come to us, we went to them?"

Miss Jacobs had just gathered her skirts and sunk to her knees with a scrub brush. She peered over her shoulder at him with an expression that suggested he was daft. "You mean to go to every farm and lumber camp? Who has time for that?"

"I already have plans to go. I preach in the villages and hamlets in my spare time, and I would be happy to carry materials to them from the school when I go."

She frowned and faced her work, sending the scrub brush vigorously over the pine boards. "And what would be the incentive for them to come to school? If we cater to them, they may find no reason to go the distance to town."

"Well, what if we hosted a social? A harvest festival, with open enrollment?"

She ceased her scrubbing. Hadassah and Hannah forgot their tired feet and jumped up and down in the entryway. "Oh yes, Gilda! Can we? Please? Can we?"

Gilda struggled to her feet and slapped her tousled skirts down over her stockinged legs. "Here's what you can do, you troublesome little mice. You can take a broom and a rag and get busy."

"Yes'm." Hadassah went to the closet and retrieved the straw broom.

Gilda blew a bit of her hair that had come loose from her chignon and wiped her hands on a rag before handing it to Hannah.

"A social? I'm in mourning, Mr. Blake. I'm not sure I can be of much help with—"

"Oh no. I didn't mean to volunteer you. I can put together a committee myself. I just wondered what you thought of the idea." He flashed his perfect smile, and her insides quivered.

She tilted her head to the side as she weighed his spontaneity against her own stodgy, responsibility-driven routine. Either he was an impetuous, reckless oaf, or he was a brilliant strategist. She hated to admit it, but this charismatic preacher's ideas just might work.

"Let's discuss it along the walk home. If we don't get the schoolroom cleaned up soon, we'll be walking in the dark."

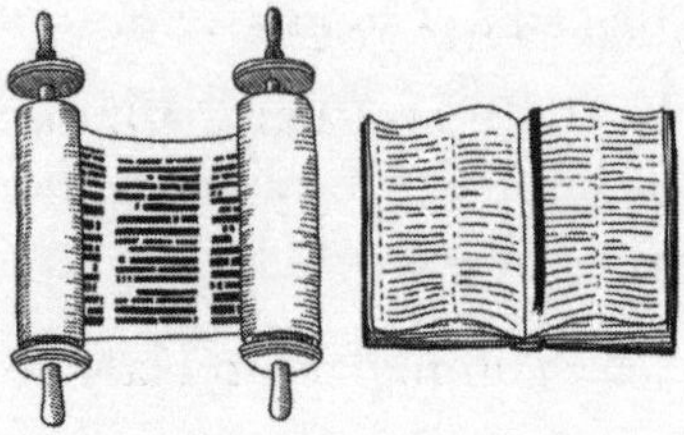

Chapter 4

"Gilda, can you go to market? We're low on stores."

A pang of angst riffled her belly at her mother's simple request. She hadn't told Mama she'd sold the carriage, and that the cart was on loan to Mr. Diller who was paying her in milk and butter when he returned from market with his dairy surplus. He'd had more to sell than his own cart could handle. How wonderful for him.

She hoped she could stall Mama until Mr. Diller delivered payment. Perhaps that would satisfy her mother's shopping list. But they were low on everything. Her poor sisters were eating porridge for their supper again tonight. Something had to be done. Her efforts were falling short to manage the household until Mama came out of her malaise. Mama had sat in her rocker by the hearth day in and day out until today. This was the first meaningful exchange she had engaged in with the family beyond her corner of the sitting room.

Gilda was heartened that Mama finally had taken an interest in affairs, yet it troubled her at the same time. Now Mama would have financial burdens added to her grief.

How did Papa do it on his salary? Of course, his had been a bigger wage than hers.

"Write me a list, Mama."

"Why is that Gentile coming around lately? What does he want with you, Gilda?"

"Mr. Blake is my business associate."

"Yes, and that means he should come by here every morning and evening?"

Mild amusement played on her thoughts. Her mother, such a biting wit. "At least he's respectful. And Hannah and Hadassah adore him."

"And you? What do you think of him?"

Gilda opened her mouth to speak, and her mother cut her off. "I'll tell you what your father would think. He'd roll over in his grave!"

Gilda shook her head. "Don't be so dramatic, Mama. Mr. Blake is helping me keep my position. The mayor told me I must do three things: First, offer Christian curriculum, and Mr. Blake is overseeing that. Second, increase enrollment, and again, Mr. Blake is reaching out to the outliers, to draw them in. More students could mean higher wages—"

"For him!" Mama's frown deepened. "Don't be so naive, girl. You're handing over the position to him. Mr. Roelantsen has no intention of hiring you if his nephew has his foot in the door. *And* making all the changes he requested."

"But he still can't manage the classroom. The third condition is discipline, and he failed miserably at that the first day. Besides that, I'm teaching the majority of the curriculum. I'd say it's a fair distribution of the workload."

Mama scoffed. "Fair? You expect fairness from the mayor and his nephew? He'll tell Cornelius that he's doing it all. He'll take credit, and you'll be out of a position."

Gilda grinded her teeth, wishing she could refute those predictions. But she'd seen it with her own eyes, how those in power made the rules to suit themselves. And she had two strikes against her. She was Jewish, and she was a woman.

A fatherless woman, at that. With no man to speak up for her in a man's world. Well, she would make them hear her.

"And when were you going to tell me you sold your father's carriage?" Mama's words came softer, the pepper gone out of her tone. She sounded grieved. Which she had every right to be on a number of scores. "You should have come to me."

Gilda sat by Mama's side and took her hand. "I'm sorry. I should have. But you have so much weighing on you already, much less to worry about what we're going to do about the coming winter. It was an expendable asset. How else are we to get by?"

Mama cupped her elbow. "You take on too much, my girl. It's enough that you have to earn the living now." Mama's sigh expelled the tension between them. "I suppose I would have done the same thing in your shoes."

Tears burned at her eyes, and Gilda wished her mother would have scolded her. Instead, her tone resonated with disappointment. "I'm so sorry, Mama. I overstepped my bounds. But I truly wished to spare you worry."

"Worry?" Mama raised both hands with shrugging shoulders. "What else is new? Worry we will always have."

There would be fewer worries if Papa hadn't used his entire savings on Uncle Mortimer's passage. But Gilda left that thought unspoken.

"Mr. Levy owes your father from last spring when he borrowed money for seed. You go and collect when he returns from market, and that should cover our winter stores."

Gilda nodded, a tear rolling down each cheek and one dripping off her nose. She missed Papa so much. Even if he had made unwise financial decisions, his heart was bigger than his business sense. Mama lifted her lace handkerchief and dabbed at Gilda's face. And she was smiling, the first smile in a month.

"There, now. Don't take the whole world on your shoulders. You're still young, and life won't always be so hard. I hear there will be a social. You should go. And Abraham is back from Europe."

Abraham Herschel. Tall, accomplished. From a wonderful family. What was not to love? Yet something of her recollection of him had lost its luster. Through no fault of his. Something in her had shifted.

"Do you think I should go to a social, Mama? I don't want to disrespect Papa's memory."

"Of course you should go. It's for the school, is it not? You *must* go."

Gilda nodded. "Mr. Diller will be returning our cart—"

"Tomorrow, yes. I know. Do you take me for dead? I know what goes on in my own home, Gilda. He's a good man and will take care to keep his word. It was a shrewd deal. Too bad you didn't *lend* our carriage as well."

Laughter, gentle and healing, tumbled from them both. Mayhap the future needn't be so frightening after all.

Except where Mr. Blake was concerned. Had she figured him wrong? Was he using his charm and charisma to seek advantage in the community only to oust her? A worry, seated in her bosom, settled and spread to her gut. She had let down her guard with the handsome and charming Gentile, but no more. She would be the shrewd businesswoman that her kind Papa had never had the heart to be.

"It's a clean break in the axle. Looks like this rig is going nowhere fast, young man."

Josh mopped his brow in the Indian summer heat. He straightened his back from being bent over Uncle Cornelius's carriage and absorbed the blow of the farmer's words. It was a long way back into town, and no place was open on a Sunday to repair it.

"I'd best be about unhitching the horse then. Can I leave the carriage here until I make arrangements?"

"Of course you can, Son. I'll lend a hand, and we'll move it into the side yard. No sense in risking parts of it walking away."

Traffic on the Hudson brought all kinds. His uncle's vehicle could be somewhere along the Erie Canal come morning. Josh thanked the man, and they both heaved at the horse and carriage until the obstinate rig was moved into the cover of foliage.

"Would you do me a favor in return, Son? Could you hitch your horse to the Jacobs's cart and return it to them for me, since you're heading out that way? I have some produce and dairy for them, and a package from Mr. Levy for Mrs. Jacobs."

"Of course," Josh replied. It would be a blessing to have something to ride back in, since he didn't think the trotter was broke to ride. If he took it easy, the horse could probably manage the heavier cart without mishap. "I'd be pleased to."

"You see the family more than I do, I daresay. How are they getting along without Eliezer?"

"They seem to be managing." Josh's brows rose, and the thought struck him with chagrin. It hadn't occurred to him to ask. Of course, Miss Jacobs was mighty proud. She wouldn't take to anyone nosing in her affairs, much less a newcomer like him. He should have had discernment. Of course, the family would need someone looking after things. It was only the Christian, neighborly thing to do.

Once Diller loaded the last jug of milk and sack of produce onto the cart, and Josh looped the last of the trappings about the harness, he turned to thank the man once again. "God bless you for being a good neighbor and sending along these provisions."

"It's a shame you never met Mr. Jacobs. He was a fine man. His widow is a fine woman."

A knowing smile wended its way to Josh's face. "Are you coming to the social next week? I can see if the widow Jacobs might venture an outing. . . ."

Diller laughed and waved his arm in dismissal. "Off with you, Blake, and your crazy notions."

Returning the chuckle, he waved goodbye and slapped the leads over the trotter's back. He couldn't wait to deliver the goods to Miss Jacobs and recount to her the successes of the day. Of course, he didn't expect she would care to hear of his preaching or of the many who seemed eager to hear God's Word. All in due time. First, he wished to get to know her and see if he could be of true usefulness to her. How else should he expect to deserve the right to be heard if he wasn't willing to serve?

But she surely would want to hear the good news about the interest generated in the school social and in the concept of itinerant lessons. Perhaps with the money raised at the event they could purchase extra primers and readers. Excitement buzzed in his veins like a hive of honey bees. He was eager to pollinate the world with glad tidings.

Along the road, he waved at passersby, some of whom he already knew by name. Oliver Simms strolled with a fishing pole over his shoulder, and Josh slowed his trotter to call out. "Catch anything good?"

"Hello, Mr. Blake. Got me some catfish."

"Let's see."

The boy held up his basket for Josh to inspect. A few plump

specimens lay inside, occasionally flapping their tails and gaping their mouths.

"Your folks will be pleased. Fine catch."

"Eh, they don't care. Figured I'd take these to Stevie and Lizzy."

"That's a very nice gesture, Oliver."

"Reckon I can't give back his butterfly, but I can share these."

"That's keeping the Golden Rule. I'll be pleased to tell Miss Jacobs and recommend you for one of her awards."

The boy smiled and waved as the cart pulled past. "Thanks, Mr. Blake."

Joy expanded in Josh's chest until he felt it would bust his shirt buttons. The Good Way was already leaving its mark on the people. What a thrill to behold the transformation. Like bottled sunshine.

Whistling a hymn, Josh slowed his uncle's horse to a stop and set the brake outside of the Jacobs's house. The low, slanting roof of the Dutch colonial gave the home a sleepy look, like heavy eyelids drooping over peeking windows. A solid structure, it still could use a fresh coat of paint and a few shingles nailed back into place. Perhaps he had found his inroad to her through service.

He hopped down from the driver's seat and strode to the door, the bundle for Mrs. Jacobs in hand. Before he could knock, Miss Jacobs opened the door.

"Mr. Blake, to what do I owe this unexpected visit?"

He stopped in his tracks halfway up the walk. By the tilt of her chin and the way she peered down her nose at him, she might have said *intrusion*.

"I hope I haven't disturbed your household. I came to deliver your cart from Mr. Diller. My uncle's carriage broke, so he lent me this, to bring to you." He approached again, his stride more reserved. "He sends his regards to you and your mother and sisters. He also sends a few bushels of potatoes, and milk and butter too. Oh, and this. From Mr. Levy. For your mother." He held out the bag, which rattled with coins as he shifted it into her hand.

"All of this? Are you the new courier in town as well, now?" She raised her brow, surely to make sport of him. Or was it suspicion that tweaked her fair face?

He laughed. "I just happened to come from Mr. Diller's farm. He allowed me to use his property to hold Sunday meeting."

She seemed surprised. Both brows had risen over her gold-rimmed gaze now. "In exchange for what?"

He shrugged. "I don't get your meaning."

"I mean, it seems odd to me that he would allow people to come traipsing over his fields during his busy season for nothing in return."

"He asked for nothing. Perhaps his only reward is knowledge."

"Ha, I'll bet it is. I wonder what the two of you talked about." She jingled the bag of coins in her hand. "Obviously, my family was mentioned at some point in your conversation."

Josh placed a hand over his chest where her accusation stabbed him. "Why, Miss Jacobs, surely you don't believe me an idle gossip?" For dramatic flair, he staggered back a step, as though her wound lanced deep.

"You can save your theatrics, Mr. Blake. I'm not amused that a veritable stranger is making himself familiar with our personal affairs."

He sobered his grin. "I have no wish to be strangers. I'd like very much to be friends. In fact, I wish you would call me Josh away from the classroom." If only it were possible to be more. But no, not with differing faiths. He'd probably see a locomotive float before the hard ground of religious tradition could be broken between them.

"Friends." She chewed the word as though it presented a challenge to swallow. "You want to be my friend?"

He would show her his earnestness, standing before her with his blue eyes wide and blinking. "I hope you think of me as a friend,

Miss Jacobs. I would like to prove myself helpful. Your ally. A confidant."

She drew back a pace and squared her stance as though challenged. "I'm too busy for such trifles as friendship, much less with someone like you."

The unexpected sting of her words struck his confidence. Could she possibly know who he was, what he was? A foundling whom his aunt and uncle had taken in out of pity. A woman of such a proud heritage must discern the difference between them, like a sixth sense. But earthly sonship was only a temporal measure. He had been grafted into the family tree of Abraham, the father of faith, by Jesus' redemptive work. He must remind himself that they stood before one another as equals. Jew and Gentile, slave and free, as the apostle Paul would say.

"Then allow my friendship to be your first."

Chapter 5

Gilda's heart fluttered, never having heard such a brash declaration from a handsome young man. But then she remembered Mama's warning about smooth-talking dandies who had ulterior motives and charlatans who took a girl into their confidence only to take something precious. He would *not* have her job, and therefore she must not give him her trust either.

"Why are you trying so hard, Joshua Blake? What is it you really want?"

Something in his pupils, the way they darkened with a look of longing, set her scalp tingling, and warmth swept through her. In what manner of beguiling charm did this preacher deal? Her breath staggered.

"I'd love to share what I want with you, Miss Jacobs. I want to see more everyday miracles. Like Oliver Simms making friends with the boy he bullied just last week. I want to see neighbors looking out for one another and bearing one another's burdens. I want the lonely to have friends. I want the hungry to have enough to eat and then some. I want a wave of hope to ignite hearts in this town. . . ." He stopped, looking intently at her. "What is it you want, Miss Jacobs?"

Her eyes welled with tears as the sentiments struck something tender. Something that reminded her of Papa. Surely these weren't the words of a charlatan. But oh, how could she know? She couldn't trust her own heart, grieving as it was and hopelessly naive to the ways of young men and women. Besides, what she felt—the way her stomach flipped and her cheeks flushed and her heart raced and her head swam—was all wrong. She was supposed to feel that for Abraham Herschel. One of her own kind.

But this man's words stirred her fascination more than any hoity-toity description of London or the cerebral droning of Abraham's accounts of medical school. This man's words made her vibrate with—what did he call it? Waves of hope to ignite her heart.

"I want this." Her voice came out breathless.

He took a step toward her and held out a hand. She couldn't resist placing hers in his warm palm. The hand that closed over her chilled fingers was tender, strong, and sure. But what was she doing? What rush of emotion was this that overtook her reason? It was far more than romantic twittering. She had felt this in prayer at times. In the study of the Torah with Papa. This assuring presence. *This shalom.* It assured her that nothing was missing, nothing broken. Least of all, her heart.

A charge went through her, recognizing that some force of awareness drew over her in waves at his physical contact. Mr. Blake—Joshua—radiated peace and a powerful joy that drew her like a pilgrim to a holy city.

"What is this?" she whispered.

He smiled. "You know Him. I can feel His presence in you."

Fresh tears sprang to her eyes, washing down the length of her cheeks. "Yes. *Hashem*."

"The name." He nodded. "The name I call him is *Yeshua*. Jesus."

She shook her head. "But how can this be?"

"Your heart bears witness to the Truth."

She swallowed, and the tears subsided. "So that's what you want? To convert me?"

Assurance poured through his gentle caresses as his thumbs traced over the sensitive skin on her knuckles. "I want to share the hope that I've found. God can be known, Gilda. He's personal. Not just for men, but for women too. Not just for highborn, but for commoners. Not just for Jews, but for Gentiles. Messiah has come. The Lamb slain for the sins of the world."

She trembled, her thoughts at war within her. "Mama says I mustn't trust you."

"What does your heart say?"

Her vision blurred through the glistening of emotion again. "I want to believe you, but—"

"Gilda?" Mama's voice carried down from the upper-floor window. "Come inside at once."

She released herself from his hold and withdrew, almost stumbling on the steps. She gathered the forgotten coin purse, which had fallen to the ground on her hurried way to the door, and crossed the threshold, not daring to look back before closing herself inside. She leaned back against the shuttered door, expecting relief to flood her, but instead her heart remained as tossed as a skiff on rough waters. He had unsettled something within her, and she had no clue how to set it back in place.

He should have known his task wasn't going to be that easy. Old, ingrained habits were hard to break. Stevie Beckwith came to school with a shiner as round as a tankard over his left eye. As round as Oliver's approximate fist circumference.

Disappointment compressed his innards. But then he should have been prepared for resistance, if not from unseen forces, then at least from stubborn will. Sometimes the spirit was willing but the flesh was too strong—stronger than the inclinations of the heart.

As for Miss Jacobs, she managed to maintain a perfectly benign expression all morning. It was almost maddening. She neither avoided him nor overly addressed him. She simply went on as businesslike as though none of the intimate, life-altering, soul-shaking words had been exchanged between them.

Josh sighed. Best he left God to His business while he attended to his own. It was time for the McGuffey Reader hour, and he must take his place before the class.

"Miss Beckwith, would you lead us in the first four lines?"

The young lady, who sat next to little Aggie, took her reader and nestled it between them, pointing to each word for the younger girl with her index finger as she read:

"When the stars, at set of sun,
Watch you from on high;
When the morning has begun,
Think the Lord is nigh."

Her voice carried over the room, her inflection almost theatrical, emphasizing proper diction and enunciation.

"Thank you, Elizabeth. Mr. Simms?"

The red-headed boy pushed the pages of the book flat with a heavy hand and grunted a protest.

"All you do—" He cleared his throat and started again in slow, careful cadence:

"All you do, and all you say,
He can see and hear;"

Oliver paused to sigh.

Josh raised a brow, and the boy continued:

"When you work and when you play,
Think the Lord is near."

He flipped the book closed and stretched in place as though the task had taken every ounce of strength within him.

Josh stifled a chuckle. "Master Barnes? Will you continue?"

One of the mild-mannered brothers looked at the other, and they both shrugged.

Josh clarified. "William, you do the first two lines, and Charles, finish the last."

The older brother read easily:

"All your joys and griefs He knows,
Counts each falling tear."

He slid the book over to his younger brother, who rubbed his blond bangs from his forehead and sounded out the words:

"W–whe–whe–en to Hi–im you tell you–your w–wo–woes,
"K–k–"

"Silent K," William whispered to him.

"N–know the Lord is ne–ear."

"Thank you, boys. Well done." Josh closed his book and strode a few rows back, coming to a short stop. Oliver, oblivious to his presence, proceeded to poke Elizabeth Beckwith's arm with a stick.

She whirled around on her bench and raised her hand to slap the offending object from the boy's grip, when suddenly she froze. Oliver whipped his head up, and his eyes widened, meeting Josh's gaze.

"I'll take that, Mr. Simms. And I'll see you after class."

"She was sticking her tongue out at me!" Oliver flung down the stick, and it bounced up and struck her.

Elizabeth Beckwith screamed and held her ankle, whipping up instant tears.

Josh sucked a surprised breath. The stick barely touched her. How could it inflict that much pain?

Miss Jacobs appeared at the girl's side and bent to examine her leg. Blood trickled down her stocking into her boot. "Stevie, go fetch Doc Herschel. And hurry."

Chapter 6

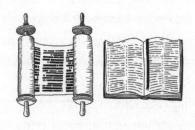

Gilda's hands trembled as she unlaced the girl's boot and gently tugged it from her foot. Such a display of contempt for order and chivalry was an outrage. This never would have happened if Papa were still here. She lifted Lizzy's ankle and held it elevated while being careful to keep the young lady's petticoats arranged modestly. Lizzy stifled hiccupping sobs, and tears streamed down her bright pink cheeks.

"My stocking is ruined now. Oh!" She held her leg above the ankle and complained.

"Dr. Herschel will be here soon, dear. Don't worry."

Mr. Blake stood over them, confusion and concern piquing his brow. "I'll go to the icehouse and fetch a chunk for a cold compress."

"Send one of the pupils. I'd prefer you stay and address that young man on his unruly behavior." She didn't care that anger flared in her voice. She just wasn't sure on whom to pin it: the ill-behaved boy or the naive assistant whom the school board would have as her replacement.

Mr. Blake tucked the offending stick under his arm and turned to seek out Oliver Simms. "I'll be right outside. Call if you need anything."

Gilda nodded and returned to comforting Lizzy. Her star pupil. Things had seriously gotten out of hand if this sweet, bright girl found herself in harm's way. Someone had better have a good talking to that boy's father. She shuddered.

Mr. Blake reappeared in the doorway. "He's gone."

"Oliver?"

He affirmed with a nod.

"Well, where has he gone off to?" She huffed an exasperated breath.

"Why don't I have the students take out their arithmetic and do sums?"

Oh, the class! All order had lapsed. She nodded. "Oh yes, please do." Gratitude and relief washed through her, lending new clarity over the waves of worry that threatened to send her thoughts racing. It was so unlike her to lose her focus. That Gentile did nothing but distract her. *In the most infernal and wonderful ways.*

The rattle of horse's harness and the pull of a brake coming from the street sounded against the foyer walls. Dr. Herschel's buggy. Gilda rose to her feet and asked Hadassah to assist Lizzy with holding her ankle up to keep it from swelling any worse. A goose egg already bulged at her ankle bone.

The reserved tread of a gentleman ascended the plank steps. "Gilda, my dear. What is this about a student being viciously attacked? What is all the turmoil?"

Gilda smoothed her skirts from where she'd been sitting beside Lizzy and smiled at Dr. Herschel's kindly concern. She had always been endeared to the man's funny ways. Too bad Abraham had none of his father's charm. "Miss Beckwith was hit in the ankle with a stick. It's bleeding and quite swollen. . ."

"A playground kerfuffle, eh?"

"Of sorts," Gilda replied.

He bent down so he could look his patient in the eye. "Is this the ankle you hurt when you fell from the tree over the summer?"

Lizzy nodded and bit her lip as the doctor's gentle hands removed her bloodstained stocking. When he pressed near the ankle, she jumped and cried out.

"Oy, I think it's a chip in the bone, young lady. It wouldn't have taken much to break that open."

Lizzy whimpered.

"Not to worry. I'll fix you up in my office, and you and your schoolmates will be back to playing in no time. As long as there are no more tricks with sticks."

"Thank you, Dr. Herschel." Gilda patted the man's sleeve. She turned and called for her assistant. "Mr. Blake, would you be so kind as to come over here?"

The doctor lingered a moment, glancing between her and the approaching teacher. "Gilda, you know my son is home now. I told him to call on you."

Mr. Blake stepped beside her. Her heart fluttered in her chest, and she placed a hand over it as though it would betray her. "Would you please assist Lizzy to the doctor's carriage?"

"Of course."

Her teaching assistant retreated, guiding the girl about the shoulders so tenderly he could have been her older brother. Gilda shook herself out of her wandering thoughts and smiled at Dr. Herschel. "It would be lovely to see Abraham. It's been ages."

"He would have paid respects to your father if he'd arrived in time."

"Yes. He sent us a letter. Very considerate."

The kindly gentleman tipped his hat to her. But his eyes followed the young teacher, giving Mr. Blake serious scrutiny. In a second, the doctor blinked and shook his head as though remembering he was not alone with his thoughts. "Good day, Miss Jacobs."

Gilda returned to her class. But what was that look Dr. Herschel gave Joshua Blake? Had Mama been talking? As though there was something to talk about! Nothing but purely professional regard existed between them. Surely.

Surely no more than that. The fluttering in her chest intensified as Joshua Blake's boots scuffed over the wood floor toward her again in his easy amble. A grin tugged at one side of his mouth.

"These are for you." He held out a cluster of roses in a sweetheart bouquet.

Her pulse sprang wildly to her throat, and she fought it down with one hard swallow. "For me?"

Gilda's eyes went wide and wondering, and her mouth gaped. Josh's own went dry, beholding the luster on her lips. His fingers brushed hers as he handed the flowers off to her. He might have touched the sun, the way her contact sent fire flashing through his blood.

He cleared his throat to make sure his voice was there before he spoke. "Dr. Herschel said they're from Abraham. Is that a custom of your people? Your forefathers send flowers down from paradise to fair maidens?"

Her round lips widened into a grin. A throaty laugh sounded, which he suspected was at his expense.

"As in Abraham, Isaac, and Jacob?" More of that intoxicating, teasing laughter.

Some of the girls around her giggled too.

"Isn't that a tradition of your people?" Josh shrugged, allowing the playful moment to linger between them. He wouldn't extinguish that shimmer in her gold-rimmed eyes for all the barges of goods on the Hudson.

"Or are you just disappointed they're not from me?" He raised one brow and let the schoolgirls titter behind their hands.

Miss Jacobs did not laugh. A blush as deep as the petals on the fragrant flowers painted her lovely cheeks. She hid the bouquet behind her back and shooed the girls back to their seats.

"If you must know, Abraham is Dr. Herschel's son. And he's going to ask me to the social next week. If I weren't in mourning, I might just agree to go with him."

Josh maintained his casual stance, his booted feet planted at an angle, though her words might have toppled him over with their unexpected blow.

"It's just as well you've made no plans, because you'll be with me for the evening."

"Is that so?" She thrust her chin up in that characteristic trait he'd admired the first time they'd met. Chutzpah.

He nodded. "Turns out you've been volunteered after all."

"I beg your pardon?" She blinked. "By whom?"

"Your mother."

He couldn't hold back a grin at her huffing breath, fists on hips, the bouquet dangling sideways.

"She said it was imperative that you attend and represent the school. And I couldn't agree more."

Miss Jacobs bustled to the front of the room and took her place beside her desk. She shoved the flowers into her tin cup. Something in the way a few ringlets had escaped the neat braids encircling her head told him that more than just her hair was ruffled. She was as affected in his presence as he was in hers. And it must vex her like a bee sting that it showed.

She clapped her hands together, drawing all eyes front and center.

"Since we have had these interruptions this late in the day, I see no point in pressing on. We'll pick up fresh tomorrow morning." The tin drinking cup tipped over, the weight of the flowers pulling it sideways, which in turn toppled her neat row of standing books. She fumbled to recover them as water dripped from the volumes. "Thanks a lot, Abraham! Now look what you've done."

A chuckle overtook Josh, but he tried to disguise it behind a cough. Nothing, however, would hide the amusement in his grin.

She cut him a glance she might have reserved for an errant schoolboy. "Class dismissed."

The students filed out, and he strolled toward her to lend a hand with the disarray on her desk, making sure to look properly contrite.

She glanced up from her straightening. "Will you drive me by the Simms on the way home? I'm going to have to speak to Oliver's father."

"Of course." He picked an apple from her basket and took a bite of it.

She released a shuddering breath. He paused chewing. Something beyond spilt flowers and wet books upset her.

"I'll go instead, if you like."

Her lashes fluttered. Was she startled and grateful he had offered? Or affronted he would presume to offer? No matter the reason. Those fluttering lashes still turned his knees to butter.

She looked down, fiddling with the bouquet. He moved in. "What is it?"

She glanced up at him. "It's nothing."

"No, you're nervous about something."

She stopped and folded her arms over her chest. "All right. I'm nervous. But I shouldn't be telling you this."

"Of course you should. We're friends."

"Friends." She tilted her head to the side, appraising the idea like a piece of goods at market. Her lips tugged into a grudging grin. "All right. So we're friends."

"What makes you nervous?"

She inclined her head toward his shoulder, as though to tell him a confidence. "They're not kosher."

"Oliver's family? Well, I didn't think they were Hebrew."

"No, not the family. The household. It's—they live—"

"They raise livestock."

"Pigs."

"Ah. I see." Josh chewed another bite of his apple. "Like I said, I'll go."

"But I'm the headmistress. It's my job. Are you offering because you wish to take my position, Joshua Blake?"

Take her job? Well, if his uncle had had his way, it was true—he would have her position. But that was just what his uncle wanted. Not him.

"Miss Jacobs. Gilda?" He took her hands and looked deep into her eyes. "I don't want to be headmaster. My aim is to preach. After this year, once I get to know the folks, I hope to start up a church. This is just a stepping-stone for me."

Her eyes shimmered with unshed tears. "Truly?"

He nodded and untucked a handkerchief from his pocket and held it out to her. She grasped it but was too stricken to pull it from his hand.

"I promise."

She swallowed, and the tears dropped from her eyes down her cheeks. "Thank you."

He glanced about to assure they were truly alone and leaned in to dab her tears from her cheeks. She didn't resist.

"You're welcome, but no thanks necessary. You're an amazing teacher, and you've clearly earned this position."

She straightened her posture and swept her shoulders back, sniffing back her momentary vulnerability. With a graceful stride that resonated with her natural dignity, she led the way to the door.

"But first, let us be clear on one thing. You mustn't call me Gilda, and I mustn't call you Joshua. Not here or in private. Not ever."

A pang shot through him. Of course she was right. What would people think? Accusations of that sort would take her job. But why did it ache to hear her say it?

Chapter 7

The acrid smell of the sty preceded the sight. Dust stirred up by his uncle's newly fixed carriage wheels obstructed Josh's view of the outbuildings and main house. He snorted the foul air out of his nostrils and drove onward to the Simms's farm.

A skinny dog ran alongside the driver's box, barking up at him before it veered off into the tall grass of a fallow field.

Sounds of working men resonated ahead of him. The groan of a wagon with a load bearing down on its frame. And squealing. Squealing so shrill he would have stopped up his ears if he hadn't needed his hands to steer the horse. Pigs at feeding time.

The dust cloud dispelled to reveal an open area between buildings, and three men at work—one pouring slop into a trough, one raking up soiled straw, and the other bringing in hay to the barn. Josh pulled up on the reins and stopped a short distance away. The last man dropped the bale of hay he had just hefted from the buckboard and turned to face him. His stocky body, broad shoulders, and red hair reminded him of an older Oliver.

"Mr. Simms?"

The man stood askance and took Josh's measure. "You Blake?"

"Yes, sir. Pleased to meet you." He tipped the brim of his hat.

"If you're here to bring my boy back to your school, you can turn back around."

Josh's ears buzzed, the tension he'd anticipated from the man rattling his nerves a bit like a hostile Sunday crowd. "Yes, I'm sure he's needed for farm chores. But that's not why I'm here."

"Ain't his chores, mister. My boy can handle both. Oliver wants no part of your classroom, with all those uppity rich folks' kids. Those spoiled brats owe my boy an apology, the way I see it."

Josh squared his stance. "I'm curious, Mr. Simms. Did he mention to you that he struck a girl and caused her injury? During class?"

"He says it was an accident. He didn't mean to hit Lizzy Beckwith. But I'm tired of that chit and her brother teasing him because of his old clothes. I'm tired of my boy trying hard to impress those folks just to be treated like he's second class."

Josh pressed his lips into a firm line. Fair enough. Hadn't he doubted Oliver had meant to hit her? The boy had thrown the stick to the floor, and it had bounced back up. But that was after he'd poked her with it. Yet could the rest be true? Josh *had* seen the boy bringing his catfish over to make amends with Stevie. He had also observed the boy studying hard. But he'd never noticed the Beckwiths or anyone else treat him unkindly. Not that he could possibly see and hear everything that went on.

"Would you mind if I talk to him? I'd like to hear his side of the story."

The man pointed to the barn. "He's in there. Help yourself."

Abraham Herschel had grown handsomer than she remembered. With a neatly trimmed goatee, matured face, and broader shoulders, he was outfitted in the haberdashery of the best tailor in Manhattan. The months away had benefited him in more ways than one. He had gotten all of his wanderlust out of the way, and he was ready to partner in his father's medical practice. Settle down. Take a wife.

Mama was positively goggle-eyed.

Gilda set her teacup on its saucer and endeavored to attune herself to her guest's conversation. But her wool skirts itched, and the sounds of her sisters playing outdoors and the ticking of someone's watch inundated her senses until she thought she would jump up and dash away. Would the man describe every arch in the Coliseum? Surely there were cobwebs that needed her immediate attention somewhere. . . .

"So you will be attending the social this evening?" Abraham's tone held the first inflection of enthusiasm, drawing her back to its sound.

"Why, uh, yes. That is, I'll be assisting with our enrollment efforts."

"Surely you can take a few moments to enjoy the spectacle. Music, dancing, food, games. It promises to be quite an evening." He lifted his hat from his lap and leaned forward in his chair.

"I'm sure that compared to Rome and Paris, our small-town amusements must seem dull." He didn't deny it. Nor did he recognize the opportunity to pay her a glib compliment. Wouldn't a man besotted say something to sweep her off her feet? Suggest that her company surpassed the charm and beauty of the ancient world, and that he couldn't wait to spend time with her? She sighed.

"Thank you for the flowers."

"Flowers?"

"The roses. Your father was called to the school for a student, and he brought them."

"Oh yes, those flowers. He's very proud of his rose garden."

She rose and took a step toward the door. So they weren't from him. Dear Dr. Herschel and her mother must have been conspiring to make the match. Poor Abraham.

Abraham stood and followed her. "I'll arrive to take you at five o'clock."

"I'm afraid I've been promised to go earlier to help set up. Mr. Blake will be by within the hour to whisk me away."

"Mr. Blake?" He firmed his grip on his hat.

"My assistant." She smiled and fluttered her lashes for effect, adding, "But if you would be so kind as to bring Hannah, Hadassah, and Mama?"

Abraham glanced between her and Mama and back at her. He bowed. "Yes, since you ask. I'll bring them gladly."

She held the door and offered a practiced smile as he departed. As soon as he left her sight, she turned and expelled her pent-up breath.

"Gilda, you weren't very encouraging."

She slumped against the closed door and took a moment to collect herself before answering Mama. "Encouraging? The man has the personality of gefilte fish. I'd have to kick up my skirts and do burlesque to get a pulse from him."

Mama gasped. "Mind what your sisters hear coming from your mouth. Gilda, I needn't remind you that the Herschels are one of the finest families in Westchester County."

"Yes, yes. I know, Mama." Gilda straightened and strode across the parlor to retrieve her wrap and hat. Remorse rose in a pang in her chest. "And I know it would make life easier if I married well and could take care of you better."

"Try to see beyond your feelings. I know he's not the most

exciting suitor. Maybe flattering words don't come easy to him. But he'll provide for you, and you'll soon understand that's more important than anything in this difficult life."

Gilda fingered the black ruffles edging her mourning bonnet and weighed Mama's words. Was money the most important thing? The way she had sold Papa's carriage for fear of running out of funds and devoted every waking hour to her teaching position at the exclusion of friendship and a normal youth, she might have believed that herself. Seeking security had driven her to a silent desperation.

But something about Mr. Blake's influence had allowed her to consider a fresh perspective. He exuded a certain quality that money couldn't buy. Though he was far from wealthy, Joshua Blake seemed like the most sincerely joyful person she had ever met.

"It will be a very busy evening for me. I'm glad you're bringing the girls. They deserve an outing. As do you, Mama."

No sooner had Abraham Herschel steered his buggy from the front of the house than the mayor's carriage appeared to replace it.

Mr. Blake had come already.

Her heart raced in anticipation of the evening's novelty. So much to do. Booths and tables to set up in the schoolyard, and decorations that the children had made to hang in the classroom.

The weather was autumn perfection, with the leaves shimmering under a golden sun. Mild warmth suffused her as she tied the ribbons of her bonnet beneath her chin. It was as though that lovely sunshine had nestled in her bosom, lending neither a searing heat nor an indifferent chill. A smile stole over her. Her escort ascended the steps.

She turned back to bid Mama goodbye and was met with a frown that darkened the shadows under her eyes.

"He's not Hebrew, Gilda."

The sunshine fled from the cloud darkening over her mother's countenance. "What makes you say this?"

"I have eyes in my head. And you had better keep yours to yourself. There will be talk."

Three raps sounded on the thick walnut door. Gilda lowered her gaze, hiding the smolder rising within her from her perceptive mother. "I am the headmistress at Papa's school, and I will not forget where I come from."

Mama's smooth hand cradled her chin and lifted her gaze to her own. "Have a care, Daughter. Men aren't books that you can study and master. Some would be the master and you their possession."

"Yes, Mama."

Released from her mother's hold and that uncomfortable moment, she proceeded to open the door. On the steps stood her teaching assistant holding an impressive assortment of flowers. Tall spires of red gladiolus surrounded by white wildflowers with lacy panicles and smatterings of petite star-like blossoms in lavender and white drew her admiring gaze, but balancing the color composition were the bright golden sunflowers. Gold, like her name. He must have picked these himself.

"These are for you, to replace the ones that got spoiled."

She gathered them carefully, cradled them in the crook of her arm. The warmth inside her returned and crept up into her cheeks. "Thank you, Mr. Blake." If only she could press them to her nose and take in the sweet essence of a gift from an admirer, but no. That was not what this was. "They'll look lovely as a centerpiece for the auction table."

Her mother's heavy sigh sounded somewhere behind her, and she took Mr. Blake's arm and hurried out the door with him before Mama could spear him with a sharp look.

Chapter 8

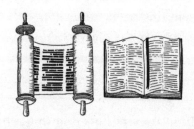

Thank you for agreeing to help me today, Gilda." Josh took his eyes from the road to gaze at her.

"Miss Jacobs," she replied.

Josh blinked at his faux pas and shook his head. "I'm sorry. I meant to say Miss Jacobs."

"And you're welcome. But no thanks necessary. It's *my* school, after all. It's only right I should help."

The wheels turned under them, filling the momentary lull in conversation as Josh processed the unmistakable way that she had—yet again—staked her claim. He'd already given her assurances he wasn't after her classroom. Why this territorial behavior, like a little terrier kicking dirt after chasing away vermin? Grinning with amusement, he realized that made him the vermin. But after a moment, the amusement gave way to a riffle of unease in his gut as he relived taunts from his childhood. Names worse than rat had labeled him. But of course, Gilda knew none of that. He would be sure she, and others in this town, never did.

"I went to see Mr. Simms. Oliver's father."

"And?"

"And I believe I discovered what's causing his behavior problems."

She turned to him, sarcasm lingering in her half frown. "Other than the fact that the boy lacks common discipline?"

His next words were snatched from his tongue. Judgment and presumption had stolen his momentum. But hadn't he made his own presumptions about the boy before he knew better? That he was a bully and a troublemaker. That his parents were neglectful. How wrong he had been to base things on appearance. He of all people should know better, so he couldn't take offense at Miss Jacobs's characterization of the boy. He would explain to her what he'd learned.

"I spoke to Oliver too. He never meant to hurt Elizabeth. He just wanted to get her to stop picking on him. I mean, sure, when he threw the stick, he was mad and frustrated, but he had no intention of it hitting her, much less causing actual harm."

"Are you telling me he claims *she's* been picking on *him*?" She scoffed.

"That's what he said. And his father verified."

"Of course they would blame someone else. They refuse to take responsibility. Well, as far as I'm concerned, if he can't confess and apologize to the class, especially to Lizzy, he needn't return."

Josh set his jaw and drove in silent contemplation. Miss Jacobs was an opinionated young lady. But she was also intelligent, rational. Surely she could see reason, especially if he presented Oliver's case more clearly. He tried again with more honey in his tone.

"You and Miss Beckwith have a special bond. I respect that.

She's bright, articulate. You've invested a great deal of time in her education."

"What does that have to do with Oliver Simms?"

"Is it possible that you're so close to the situation that you've lost objectivity? What if Elizabeth is the instigator?"

If Gilda hadn't been in a moving carriage, she would have stormed off. This man would insult her star pupil and insult her, calling her judgment into question? Her hands curled into fists so tight the blood pounded through her fingers.

"Who do you think you are, Joshua Blake?"

He had the nerve to look surprised. He cocked his head to the side and said nothing.

"You think you can swagger into the classroom that my father poured his life's breath into and presume you know better? You—you're the most arrogant, presumptuous, pigheaded man I've ever met."

The man did the most confounding thing yet. He had the audacity to laugh. Gilda shook with frustration. Astonishment. Ridiculous emotions flooded her that had no place in a respectable teacher's thoughts.

She wanted to trounce him. Or for him to retort with something more compelling than witty words or rational argument. The things the man made her feel came unbidden, the swirling mix of passions that only one thing would silence. Raging impulses drove her to distraction as the man beside her chuckled, utterly unaffected by her sputtering outrage. One gesture from him, and her fevered temper would instantly cool. She involuntarily licked her lips, imagining him pressing a kiss to her mouth and drawing the fire out of her.

No, no, no! Gilda curled her toes in her shoes. She mustn't give way to such irrational imaginings.

He looked at her with teasing in his gaze that turned her inside out. Cascades of warmth and delight threatened to drown her.

"A minute ago, you only regarded me as a nuisance, an intruder to your schoolroom. Now I'm—what was it? Pigheaded? And arrogant too?" His smile was too mischievous for a preacher. Too mirthful for a redressing. Too handsome for a business associate. She must look away before she made a fool of herself.

She took her fan out of her reticule and waved it before her flaming face. She would melt under the blue heat of those eyes.

Gilda should have been more penitent, more introspective during the Ten Days of Awe between *Rosh Hashanah* and Yom Kippur. She should have taken account of whatever transgressions had sealed her fate for the year—had brought her this. This man who rankled her and surprised her and thrilled her to her core. What manner of punishment or reward could this be from the Almighty? She bowed her head and prayed for clarity to recover her addled senses.

"I see I have offended you, Gilda—Miss Jacobs. For that I am sorry. But I'm not sorry to offer you a different perspective. Oliver is a child with feelings like anyone else. He knows he doesn't have the newest clothes or the wealthiest family. Boys can be hurt by mean or careless words just like girls."

He looked away, and his cheeks had turned ruddy.

Her heartbeat slowed to a hard thrum. Surely her exasperated words hadn't hurt his feelings. Such a confident, charming man wouldn't be affected by her harmless scolding. Unless some deep turmoil hid behind his charismatic facade. But what?

Perhaps he was right about her blind spot concerning Lizzy. Mayhap she was too fond of her brightest student to see any flaws in the girl's character. Lizzy Beckwith was so patient in helping the young ones, so generous of her time, so willing to assist Gilda and Papa in the classroom—but maybe the girl had dished a few sarcastic barbs here and there. Lord knew Gilda was possessed of a sharp wit herself. Had she overlooked it or even fostered it in Lizzy?

"I'll take your words into consideration. And just so you know, Dr. Herschel said it wouldn't have taken much to aggravate Lizzy's ankle bone. She had already hurt it at home, falling out of a tree. So I agree that Oliver wasn't the only cause, whether he intended to harm Lizzy or not."

He nodded but said little. His focus was pinned down the road, reflective, far away. Her hands folded over the bouquet, which weighed heavily on her lap. The dimming of the light in his spirits pressed on her heart with the same invisible weight.

Mr. Blake had said he wanted to be her friend. She, who had no friends. Books had been her friends. They were tame and bowed to her will and pace. But men? Aside from her genteel, quiet father, men were unpredictable. Inscrutable.

If she were to try to be his friend, she must prove herself friendly. She would reach out and learn what secret trouble he battled that had caused his light to flicker.

"When you say boys can be hurt by careless words, do you speak from experience? Were you bullied as a child?"

He laughed but flexed his jaw. "Oh, you know kids. They can say crazy things." When he turned to face her, he held that half grin. "I always won over my critics with a laugh, and if all else failed, I could run pretty fast."

He chuckled again, but his grin didn't reach his eyes. And it didn't fool her. She smiled, but inside an ache blossomed. She'd seen his kind many times. The class clown. Always dodging direct confrontation.

"So you want to be friends, Joshua?"

His eyes widened and the blue spark of teasing had returned in them. "Joshua? You just broke your own rule, Miss Jacobs."

She couldn't help an unguarded smile. "I know. I did that on purpose."

"Something tells me you have conditions to that question. Do I have to sign a contract?"

She waved his teasing words away with a soft laugh. "A contract? No. The only contract I'm interested in is the one I'll sign as headmistress." She shifted in her seat to face him fully. "But I would suggest that if you want to be friends, you'll let me in."

He cast a sidelong glance at her and nodded. As usual he seemed amused. "Let you in to where? The classroom? You hold the keys, remember?"

"I mean, let me in on your troubles. Share that burden you're carrying. It must be lonely to hold it all in."

"Oh, but I'm never alone, Miss Jacobs. The Lord is always right here." He pointed to his heart. That grin of his lingered, and his blue eyes shone sterling. "But I thank you for your kind offer."

She shrugged. "Then I guess you already have what you need."

"Wait," he stirred, his expression becoming animated. "If things go well today, with enrollment and with the fund-raisers, maybe we could draw up that contract after all. Make you permanent, official headmistress sooner, rather than later."

"Really?" She pressed her hand to her chest as excitement tumbled up from within. She wanted to jump to her feet, but the sway of the carriage made her think better of it. "You would relinquish the position so soon?"

"If it means you'll finally trust that I have no hidden agenda, that my friendship is sincere, then yes."

"Mr. Blake, that makes me happier than you know." Her smile was too familiar in the presence of a gentleman, the way she clutched his arm too forward, but she didn't care. She could kiss him, so great was her joy. But that would be—

The carriage wheel hit an obstacle and brought the conveyance down hard, and her bottom bounced up off the seat. She slid toward the open side, about to fall head first out of the carriage. Josh gathered her around her waist before she toppled out. She clutched his arm as he reeled her in to his side. The carriage righted itself with another bounce. She landed half in his lap, and she grasped his shoulders for ballast, her face and his colliding against one another.

"Oh!" She pushed back against his chest.

They must have made a cozy sight for a moment until she regained her composure and a proper distance, collecting her dignity.

He slowed the horse to a stop with one hand and reached toward her with his other. "Are you hurt?"

"No." She patted down the yards of dark brocade skirt and caught her breath. "You?"

"I've crushed your flowers."

She lifted the bouquet. A few of the gladiolas had snapped halfway down their stalks and hung limp. Other blossoms had wilted from the rough ride. But she smiled and assured him. "They're still a lovely gift, just the same."

"Nephew?" Mayor Roelantsen and his wife stepped around the corner and came to a standstill five paces away. Next to them stood a man Gilda could swear she'd seen before. His graying beard matched the charcoal color of his tailored coat. His distinguished profile held resemblance to the image of a New York City politician or figure she'd seen in the newspaper.

"Uncle Cornelius. Aunt Abigail. What an unexpected pleasure to see you here." Mr. Blake greeted, working the leads to keep the horse still.

"Mayor, Mrs. Roelantsen, good day." Gilda adjusted the hat ribbons under her chin, hoping the black bonnet still sat neatly on her head.

The mayor did not smile. He appraised them up and down, holding his walking cane forward in his hand.

"Senator Tallmadge, my nephew, Joshua Blake, and our interim teacher, Miss Jacobs."

The man tipped his hat to her and to Mr. Blake beside her, though scarcely making eye contact. "Good day." Turning to the mayor, he said, "Cornelius, I must be going. I'll reconvene with you on drafting those common school regulations at a later time. But I'll see you this evening for the speech."

Mayor Roelantsen's frown emphasized his disappointment as the senator walked out of earshot. "That's quite a way to represent our town, embracing in public. Miss Jacobs, I'm astonished. What would your father say?"

"No, Uncle," Mr. Blake protested. "It's my fault. I failed to steer around a rut, and—"

The mayor thumped his cane on the dirt path. "I'll see you both straightaway at the school." He leaned in and lowered his voice to a stern whisper. "And there had better be no more hint of this familiar behavior between you."

As the man stalked away, dragging his crimson-faced wife with him, Gilda's thoughts raced. He would accuse her of unbecoming conduct? Over a rickety carriage wheel and a misunderstanding? Mama's words came back to her.

"Have a care, Daughter. There will be talk."

Lady teachers' contracts spelled out that there must be no fraternization with the opposite gender. That was all well and fine with her. She had no intention—well, no real intention—of doing any such thing. But she had no contract at the moment. She was working on a trial basis.

She firmed a hold over her middle. Anxiety swirled, and she feared her stomach would rebel. Would they take Papa's school away from her? Others had lost their positions for less.

Chapter 9

Josh reached out to help Miss Jacobs from the carriage, but she turned aside from him. Instead, she gathered her skirts and stepped down, defiance glittering in her gaze. He paused a moment to allow her to ascend the walk to the school first. It would give him time to process what had just happened.

Uncle Cornelius's finger-pointing had pierced Miss Jacobs, that much was clear. But since there was no founding to the claim that she had—that *they* had—behaved inappropriately, Josh cast off the worry gnawing at his gut and squared his shoulders. Surely his uncle would see reason. Josh would defend Miss Jacobs with the truth and with a clear conscience. And that would be the end of it.

Before he took a step away from the carriage and toward the building, a hand fastened around his arm.

His uncle's signature bergamot scent swirled around him. He

moved aside to admit his uncle alongside him.

"Joshua, I needn't remind you what's at stake here, do I?" Uncle Cornelius's gaze bore a hardness that he'd rarely seen.

"What exactly is at stake, Uncle?" Josh replied.

"Your reputation."

The words burned like a live coal, hollowing out his soul.

Taunts and snickers and whispered words crept from the corners of his memory. Words like *foundling* crept until he shook his head to be rid of them. But they kept bombarding. *Illegitimate. Ill-begotten.* To hear the voices of past playground tormentors tell it, Josh had been the product of a tryst. At times he wondered if Cornelius and Abigail were the blood relation they claimed or if his origin was completely unknown.

"Neither of us can afford talk about you and Miss Jacobs. I have an election coming up in a month. And you—"

Josh held up a hand to silence him. He needn't be reminded what rumors of misconduct would do to a young man wishing to start out in ministry. Let alone if the truth about his past were ever to be known. To hear his uncle's disgust about the matter, he imagined the worst scenarios were true. For all he knew, he came from criminals, a fancy woman, or any manner of other undesirables.

"Then you know what you must do?" Uncle Cornelius's stern gaze locked with his.

Josh neither flinched in resignation nor answered the veiled warning with any trace of ill will. He merely held his stance. "You want me to drive the young lady out of her position."

"Mr. Simms must be livid over his son being castigated. Surely he's blaming her. It's no secret that her people loathe pig farmers. They're unclean to them. There is concern that she will foist her prejudices on others. So, you see, you're not driving her out. She's doing it to herself."

"I believe I've resolved that issue, and I'd like to—"

"Neither of us can afford notoriety." His uncle tapped the

handle of his cane into Josh's chest. "All we need is for there to be rumors of you and Miss Jacobs in an unseemly situation. It's taken years to overcome the scandal of your background."

And there it was, the age-old specter of the past rising up to haunt him. Pressure launched painful breakers against his temples with each pounding beat of his pulse. He couldn't disappoint his uncle, who had taken him in as a child, seen to his needs, put him through boarding school, and given him hope of a respectable life. What would have become of him, with no earthly accounting, born to parents who had disappeared shortly after he was born?

Josh couldn't go against his uncle's wishes. If it were just a matter of his own ruin, he would risk it, but he must not spoil his uncle's political chances.

Yet what if they could come up with a solution that satisfied everyone? His uncle need not fear scandal if the right arrangement was made. He lowered his head to say a quick prayer.

Lord Jesus, show me what to do to protect both Uncle Cornelius and Miss Jacobs. You always have a plan of redemption. Reveal Yourself.

Instantly revelation struck.

"I believe I have a plan." Josh drew a deep breath and told his uncle what he hoped would resolve the dilemma for all of them. If his uncle agreed, perhaps each of them would get what they hoped for, and no one would need to lose out on their investment. He would have a place to hold worship services in the community, Miss Jacobs could continue on as teacher and collect a better wage for her services, and his uncle would be satisfied that no untoward behavior existed between them. But would Gilda Jacobs, that impossibly beautiful, spirited, and strong-willed young lady, ever speak with civility, much less cordiality, to him again?

Gilda crossed the empty schoolroom again. Where was Mr. Blake?

Wasn't he right behind her? The small window overlooking the street revealed a sight that caught her breath in her throat. Mayor Roelantsen had caught up with Mr. Blake, and they stood together discussing something. Considering the older man's assertive gestures and tense expression, it might have been some sort of strategy session before a battle. A sinking feeling overtook her stomach. If this was a war, then the battleground was her classroom, and the spoils, her job. Swallowing her misgivings only left her with a harder lump in her throat.

Mr. Roelantsen jabbed his cane handle at his nephew and mouthed a few pointed words before turning and walking toward the door. Gilda bustled away from the window and set up a defense behind Papa's varnished desk.

The worn pine planks of the schoolroom floor echoed with the marching tread of one set of boots, followed by Mr. Blake's slower advance. As they closed in on her, the air fled the room.

"It looks to be a busy afternoon, Miss Jacobs," the mayor said. "Let's be sure to keep the enrollments flowing. I daresay we could break a record."

She drew her shoulders up to brace for the coming assault. The words the mayor would toss at her, accusing her, saying whatever it would take to dismiss her from her position.

"Nice touch, hanging your students' latest projects. Crisp penmanship. I like that."

The mayor took his nephew by the shoulder and led him to the side. "Clear these benches to the other wall and set up a table here. You can display the donated pies for the raffle and collect signatures before folks exit."

Was that it? Gilda relaxed the tension in her neck. Where was the verbal barrage she expected? Was there to be no pillory as the politician leveraged accusations against her that would oust her from her position? None came.

Curiosity flooded through her, with a suspicion that Mr. Blake had stood between her and disaster. How gallant. Surely he must have defended her against his uncle's brash conclusions about what he thought he saw as they passed in the carriage.

After a moment, she took a few steps away from the fortress of her father's desk and ventured out into the room.

"I wanted to thank Mr. Blake for organizing all of this. And for being such an extraordinary assistant. He is a true asset to the school. I see the wisdom in your decision to have two on staff instead of just one, Mr. Roelantsen. I believe it will soon pay off."

"My nephew has great plans for this building. I would save off from thanking him just yet. After tonight, gauging by the success of enrollment efforts, I believe we shall have a clearer picture of what's to be done with the position. But one thing is clear. We need not strain the budget on two salaries when one will suffice."

A lance of betrayal stabbed through her, and she struggled to breathe. She turned her gaze to Mr. Blake, who stood expressionless. Hands folded behind his back. Where was the kindness, the friendliness now? Could he truly have plotted against her all this while? Surely not. The stabbing lance twisted inside her. She'd thought he'd cared. But those blue eyes returned her stare with an inscrutable expression that chilled her to the bone.

He'd promised her that he didn't want her job. That he would give it to her. Yet there they stood, two men, a unified front just as Mama had warned her. She wanted to scream.

Her knees shook beneath her skirts. But she commanded strength and resolve to her posture. She would not go down without a fight. Let them try to destroy the tradition her father had built. Everyone loved Papa and trusted him to educate their children in the classic disciplines. If people understood that these men intended to change the fundamentals of Papa's curriculum, perhaps they would rise to her defense and save her papa's legacy. And perhaps her livelihood too.

Chapter 10

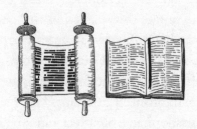

Thank you, Mrs. Beckwith. That's a fine apple pie you've donated. It should fetch a generous bid." Josh held the dessert dish handed to him by Elizabeth and Steven's mother, a handsome woman of middling years.

"Apple kuchen," she corrected.

"Ah." Josh nodded. "And how is Miss Elizabeth faring?"

"She's much better since the good doctor bandaged her up and gave her crutches. She'll be here this evening as long as she doesn't wear herself out."

"I'm glad to hear it. I look forward to seeing her well again."

"Thank you, Mr. Blake. We do too." She tipped her head down until the brim of her bonnet concealed her face, and she took her younger children by the hand, leading them through the bustling crowd.

The social had gathered such attendance already that the town's population had swollen to twice its normal size. Joshua carried the dish into the building and crossed the floor toward Miss Jacobs. A game of horseshoes commenced in the schoolyard, just outside the open window, and men were lined up waiting to pitch for a prize. A three-legged race brought laughter and cheers from the far field. An apple bobbing contest drew many of the children waving halfpennies for their chance to find the lucky apple floating in the barrel.

Mrs. Jacobs, Gilda's mother, chaperoned the pin-the-tail-on-Balaam's-donkey competition. He had to chuckle at the unique twist she had given the childhood game. Her smile and kindly ways with the children endeared her to him. Gilda was fortunate to have a mother like her.

Meanwhile her sisters, Hannah and Hadassah, flitted between tables and passersby, distributing handbills for the keynote speaker—Senator Tallmadge—who would expound on the importance of a common school to prepare future good citizens of New York.

Josh had to wait in line behind a cluster of families before delivering the confection, all while keeping a surreptitious eye on Miss Jacobs at the pie table. When she caught his gaze, she immediately turned away. Her anger toward him was palpable. She clearly suspected him of betrayal. But she didn't know the half of it.

If he could just get her alone for a few minutes, he could explain his plan before his uncle announced it. Maybe if she heard it first from him. . .

Yes, it was true, he would be headmaster to appease his uncle. But he would donate every penny of his salary to her if she would remain on as his co-instructor. How would he hope to find anyone better suited? He couldn't do without her. Neither professionally, nor in the way that a man considers a future with a helpmeet. But how could that be possible?

With God, all things are possible.

The words came unbidden, coursing hope through his veins.

He couldn't help looking her way through the milling crowd, hoping she would return his glance. If only she knew he meant her no harm. That he cared. He truly did. Surely she had sensed it?

Just as he reached her table and set down Mrs. Beckwith's apple kuchen, another student's family drew her attention away. He turned to wait at the edge of the crowd. A handbill was pressed into his palm, interrupting his thoughts. Before he could react, the person distributing them blended with the crowd. He drew it up and read:

CONCISE ACCOUNT
OF THE
LONDON SOCIETY
FOR PROMOTING CHRISTIANITY
AMONGST THE JEWS
"For if the casting away of them be the reconciling
of the world, what shall the receiving of them be,
but life from the dead."
ROMANS XI.15.
BOSTON
PRINTED BY JOHN ELIOT.
1816

The Compiler of the History of the Jews cannot but feel peculiarly interested in the fate of this Nation. And as the Jewish Repository, and other tracts published by the London Society for promoting Christianity amongst the Jews, are, as she believes, not generally known in New England, she was induced to give a brief outline of the means adopted

> *by the Society to bring this long neglected people to a cordial acknowledgement of the grand tenet, in which all Christians unite, that "Jesus Christ is the Messiah," and she indulges the hope that the attention awakened to the welfare of the "lost sheep of the house of Israel," will be extended to America.*

Josh stopped reading there, though the text continued. He scanned the crowd and spotted a gentleman in coattails and top hat at some distance from him. A lady walked at his side, holding the man's arm. She distributed papers to those she passed.

In a few strides, he overtook them and reached out for another leaflet. He confirmed it was the same printing he had been given.

"Beg pardon, are you from the London Society?" Josh offered to shake the gentleman's hand and locked with bold blue eyes. Most remarkable. He'd never seen their like except in the shaving mirror.

The lady turned her head and tugged on the gentleman's arm, but Josh's urgency detained him. "Please, may I have a moment of your time?"

The man patted the woman's hand, which rested on his arm. His smile was tired but sincere. "Come, Sarah, surely we can spare a moment to speak with the young man." He looked at the woman with a nod of assurance that seemed to bolster her. She peeked up from the brim of her hat at Josh, and her face held an expression that arrested him. Her features. What was it about them? Curiosity mingled with something. Caution?

"Thank you, sir." Josh led the way to a quiet corner of the room. "Your ministry—I've never heard of an outreach like this. I'm intrigued."

"I joined the society when I went abroad in 1815."

The man spoke like a native New Yorker. Twenty-five years

was a long time to live away without developing a British dialect. Twenty-five years was Josh's age.

"As a Christian who married a Jewish woman, I quickly realized there was little available to us but misunderstanding from both sides—Christians felt I had forsaken my heritage, and even though she came to faith in Christ, there was no warmth in the reception for us among my people. Her people treated me as an outsider. But then we discovered the society, and they have been a network of support. A family."

When he said the word *family*, the woman gasped. The gentleman took her hand in both of his. "May I present my wife, Sarah? You may call me Simeon Kaufmann. And you are?"

Josh couldn't answer. The man's eyes. Unusual, both in the intensity of color and the way they studied him in return. But that wasn't all. It ultimately came down to the woman's features. She had blond hair. Was that unusual for a Jewess? It was a similar shade, with highlights like straw on sand, to his own.

A couple who had gone abroad the year he was born. Emotion closed his throat. If only his parents hadn't died, he could imagine them as his own, a long-lost link to legitimacy, to a real family of his own. At the very least, they might mentor him on ministry among the Jewish people he had come to know. *Know and love.*

"I'm Joshua," he replied with a tone hushed with wonder. "I'm a minister too. It seems we have a lot in common. . . ."

Now that that man had finally moved away and given her some space, Gilda could breathe and think without tangling with those mesmerizing blue eyes. She would speak to Rabbi Rothstein and see if he could exert any influence on the mayor. A significant percentage of Mr. Roelantsen's constituents attended synagogue, after all. And Jewish backing had built the schoolhouse, founded the town library, and established its thirty-year tenure with Papa being its public face. Rabbi was a man like Papa had been—soft-spoken, intelligent, and influential in the most understated ways. He would see that she retained her position if anyone could.

"Miss Jacobs, do you have a moment? I'd like a word with you about my son." Gilda smiled as she shifted her focus from the line of donated baked goods to the man whose unfamiliar voice had addressed her. The muscles in her face froze at the sight of a stocky red-haired farmer. Mr. Simms.

"H–hello. How do you do, sir?" She took his proffered hand and cringed that Mr. Blake was nowhere in sight. She could use his smooth-talking charm right now, as the farmer's furrowed brows trained his disgruntled gaze down at her.

"How is Oliver? We've missed his. . .animated presence in class."

"He's a fine help to me at the farm. Smart, hardworking boy, my Oliver."

She nodded. "I'm so glad he brings you cause to be proud, Mr. Simms."

"Let's get right to the point, ma'am. I understand he caused trouble in class, and I want to ask your forgiveness and make amends."

"Amends? I, uh. . . That's very considerate of you." She couldn't be more stunned if she were plunged into the apple barrel.

"He's been taught better than he's behaved, and I want him to show the manners his Mam has tried to work in him. Some lessons don't take at first, but we aim to stick to it."

She folded her hands at her waist, wishing she could quiet the surprise churning in her belly. It wasn't an unpleasant sensation; it just set her off balance. "Indeed, some lessons take time, even when the teacher is committed." *To all of her pupils.*

She bowed her head for a moment to reflect. She had been so invested in Lizzy that she may indeed have neglected Oliver. Gilda accepted the lesson her conscience spoke. She would give Oliver another chance. "Your son has quite an aptitude for arithmetic. I should like to help him continue his studies, with your permission."

He shifted his stance to allow a more private conference. "Is Miss Beckwith doing better?"

"I've learned she is recovering from an injury she sustained over the summer. If it hadn't been for the accident at school, it might have gone untreated and caused more damage in the long run." The longer she talked with the man, the easier it was for her smile to come from a place of sincerity. He may be a gruff-looking character, but as her wise friend Mr. Blake had taught her, even boys and men had feelings. And he may be the most considerate pig farmer in Westchester County. What could be more kosher than kindness?

"In that case, I can't wait to hear good reports when he returns Monday."

"I'm so pleased to hear it." She shook his hand and bid him a good evening at the social.

Mr. Simms departed, and Rabbi Rothstein entered the schoolroom. At his side walked an older gentleman unfamiliar to her. He veered in her direction, and she waved. As they made their way over to her table, she studied the rabbi's companion's peculiar style. He wore the long black coat of an older generation, and a prayer shawl beneath his tunic. Almost like a Hebrew Rip Van Winkle awakened from a long slumber or mayhap returning from an extended stay in the Old World. As the newcomer neared, a light glimmered in his eyes—his gold-rimmed eyes.

His smile lit a spark within her. So much like Papa's. "Uncle!"

He held out his hands to her, and she grasped them. "You must be my dear niece Gilda. You look just like your Papa, may his memory bring a blessing." He kissed each of her cheeks, and she returned the gesture. Papa's only brother even carried the aroma of hyssop and lye soap like her father. Tears burned at the rims of her eyes, but fresh joy chased them away.

"How good it is to greet family! We thought we had lost you. Oh, but come. Meet Mama and my sisters."

"I've come with news I'm eager to share with you all."

"Please, join us, Rabbi."

As Gilda led the way to Mama, Uncle Mortimer placed her hand in the crook of his arm, drawing her near to his side. "Your papa would be so proud to see you continue his life's work, Gilda. He wrote to me often and told me of your dedication."

"You and Papa corresponded?"

He shrugged in a disarming way. "He knew where to find me. And he knew I would come. I'm only sorry I didn't come in time to see him once again."

"Oh Uncle. It's bad enough we've lost Papa. Now they would take Papa's school from us as well."

"Who, Gilda? Who would do this?"

"The mayor." She stopped short of saying *and his nephew*. Part of her couldn't accept that Mr. Blake—that her friend Joshua—would plot against her this whole time. But her chest ached with the crushing weight of betrayal. If only she could speak to him privately.

Uncle Mortimer exhaled a sigh. "Let me talk to your mother, and we will come back around to this. I would not allow this to happen, not even over my own dead body."

A chill swept over her despite the heat of the room packed full of people. She hoped it wouldn't come to any more death or loss. Even the loss of new and budding relationships. But any notions of what may have been with a certain Gentile were already dead. Mama would never allow the match. And even if he slipped past Mama's defenses, there were now her uncle's wishes to be considered.

A long and boring life with the young Dr. Herschel yawned before her. Surely that is what they both would prescribe for her.

Her mother had her back to them and didn't see their approach.

She was busy handing out a small prize from a wooden crate. The child took the pouch and opened it, examining three colorful glass marbles in his palm. "Thank you, ma'am!"

"You're welcome. And remember the story of Balaam's donkey. Listen to God before He sends a messenger who makes you look like a fool!" Mama laughed softly.

Gilda placed a hand on her mother's arm and turned her about. "Mama, look who's come."

Mama's umber eyes grew wide, like bittersweet chocolate morsels. "Morty? Is it really and truly you?"

She let him take her hand and kiss it. "I'm here, Ruth. I'm sorry it has taken me this long. I should have come sooner."

"The important thing is you're here now. And you, are you well?"

"I prosper in body, soul, and spirit, though I grieve in my heart. And you? Such a brave woman. No doubt you have come out tonight to honor Eliezer's memory. He was a lucky man to have you."

Mama's cheeks assumed a youthful rosy hue at her charming brother-in-law's words. Gilda smiled. Perhaps their future need not be so fearful now that Uncle Mortimer was here.

"And where are your younger daughters?" He looked about the milling room. "Aha, I see them. Unmistakable. They are the cherubim handing out the papers."

"Yes." Gilda replied. "Hannah and Hadassah are good girls. Very helpful to our mother. But you are keeping me in suspense. You said you had good news to share."

A gentle chuckle answered her. "I did promise, yes." He turned to Mama. "Ruth, I have come to return the investment Eliezer sent to me, with interest. My delay in returning has been due to a business deal I have been developing. Your husband knew of it and gave his blessing. It was very lucrative. It should take care of you and your dear girls for some time to come. But it doesn't absolve my shame that I wasn't here to help him. If only

I had come sooner, maybe he would—"

Mama waved her hand. "What happened, happened. We mustn't question the Lord's timing, Mortimer."

He took Mama's hand and patted it with his other. "*El-Shaddai*, the Sovereign One."

"And we have you now. It is well."

Gilda shifted, the conflicting demands tugging on her. School duties still beckoned.

As though sensing her imminent departure, Uncle Mortimer reeled her back in. "You said the mayor would take the school from you, Gilda. Can you explain?"

She drew a deep breath, bolstering herself to share the day's events, when Joshua Blake emerged from the vestibule. He appeared to be scanning the room. When he met her gaze, he started directly toward her.

"No time to explain. I must speak with my colleague. Please excuse me for a moment."

Gilda dashed toward the object of her thoughts, as though wishing weren't wanting. But wait. She had a controversy with him.

"Miss Jacobs. I must speak with you right away."

She fisted her hands and marched toward him. "And I must speak with you!"

Chapter 11

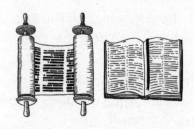

Josh's mind buzzed with thoughts he couldn't wait to share with Gilda Jacobs. Life-changing thoughts. What he'd learned gave him courage to ask what he wouldn't possibly have asked even an hour ago, but it felt so right. Kismet had smiled on him, and he was certain she would want to hear his news. Maybe, if his favor held, she'd want to share more than just his unexpected joy. Maybe, if she felt what he did, she would want to share his calling and his life with him.

She stopped in front of him, and her clenched fists and the rise and fall of her breath ignited her expression with a passion that was even more comely than he could have anticipated. Her heated stare made him all the more determined to share his ideas. "I'm telling my uncle that I want you to have the position."

Her fisted fingers opened and the tight lines in her posture gave way to surprise.

"You are? When?"

"Now. As soon as I find him. You see, my priorities have changed. Miss Jacobs, Gilda—could I possibly hope that you would consider—"

"There she is."

Dr. Herschel approached, his arms wide in a gesture of embrace. As if this interruption weren't frustrating enough, a tall young man followed. This couldn't be the doctor's son, Abraham, could it? Things were about to get interesting. Complicated, but interesting.

Dr. Herschel held her upper arms in a brief embrace and stepped aside so that the younger Herschel could occupy the space closest to Gilda.

Josh set his jaw but reminded himself that Abraham was a soul first and a competitor to his interests second.

"Gilda, would you spare us a moment of your time?" The young man, perhaps Josh's own age, stood not two paces away, sizing him up with an amused sneer. "I'm sure your assistant won't mind."

"Actually, Miss Jacobs and I were about to go and speak to the mayor together." Josh replied. He quirked a brow, issuing a subtle challenge.

"I'm sure it can wait, Blake. This is a matter of greater consequence than politics or business."

Gilda swung to face the young man. "What is it, Abraham? What's the matter?"

"The matter of our future together. It cannot be news to you that I intend to propose. But first, you must allow me to relieve you of this company"—he gave Josh a dismissive look—"and of your entanglement with this whole business."

Josh planted his feet and folded his arms over his chest.

"Entanglement?" Gilda replied. "Do you mean my classroom?"

"I know that you would serve where your father established a place in the community for our people. A noble sentiment. But I can offer you so much more in the way of influence. Surely you do not wish to remain stuck in this little town the rest of your life?"

"Stuck? What's wrong with this little town?" Gilda knitted her brows together like gathering clouds in a storm.

Josh grinned. It would appear that Abraham Herschel was unaccustomed to being disagreed with, especially by a feisty young woman.

His open amusement earned him a contemptuous look from Abraham. "This conversation is none of your business, Blake. If you had any breeding, you would take your leave. Oh, but we both know that's not the case with you, at least from what I've heard."

Dr. Herschel placed a hand on his son's arm. "The Roelantsens are our friends. Don't stir the pot, Son."

"If he were a Roelentsen, there would be no issue. But we all know he's not. He's nothing more than a bas—"

"Than a what?" a quavering female voice said from behind Josh's back. He knew the voice in an instant. *Aunt Abigail.* His stomach shrank. The poor, meek woman needn't be publicly shamed by his past. He would call Abraham Herschel out for publicly insulting the kind woman.

Abraham closed his mouth and retreated a pace. "I beg your pardon, Mrs. Roelantsen. I didn't realize you were present. I would have used more discretion."

"What, pray tell, is discreet about insulting a good man's character?" Gilda asked, abhorrence rising in her voice.

Aunt Abigail gasped. "To say things to harm my nephew is bad enough. But you would cast aspersions on my husband and me in the process as well. And the irony is, the shame was never Joshua's, nor mine, nor my husband's. It was on the family who abandoned my nephew as a baby. Because he wasn't their kind. He was born to a Jewish mother and a Gentile father. My brother's son. Joshua had fine parents, but both families refused to acknowledge their marriage. When his kind, loving parents perished, my nephew had nowhere to go and no one to love him. Except us."

Aunt Abigail bowed her head, overcome with emotion. Josh gathered her in his arms as waves of shock rippled through him. He had never known any of this. Just minutes ago, he had met a couple who might have been his parents. He had almost come out and asked if they were, because although he'd been told since childhood that his parents were dead, he'd still hoped they might be alive somewhere. But they couldn't be. Aunt Abigail had just confirmed what he'd always been told—that his parents had died.

But the knowledge that couple had left with him was the possibility of happiness between a man and a woman of diverse backgrounds if they shared common faith in Messiah and found a network of support. Surely it was the sign he had been praying for. The sign that he could pursue this beautiful woman whom he had come to admire so greatly.

Aunt Abigail's lament drew him back to the present. "We would have raised you as our own, but your uncle Cornelius's family would have disowned us. So we had to send you away to boarding school. Separate ourselves. All because your mother was Jewish." She dabbed the tear that coursed down her cheek, and embraced Josh, her face a study in sorrow and remorse.

He comforted his aunt, but the news could have toppled him like a ninepin. His mother was Hebrew? That made him. . .

Gilda gasped. "You're not a Gentile?"

Surges of shock numbed her while sensations akin to delight heated her veins. If Josh was Jewish, then all the complex emotions she felt began to make sense. The way he made her feel could only fit into the context of a proper match. *Surely my mother will approve now.*

Dr. Herschel gathered his son by the arm, shaking his head.

"Come, Abraham. Let's leave these good people alone. I believe you've said enough."

Gilda offered the doctor a sympathetic look and waited until they had distanced themselves.

"Thank you for sharing what you did, Mrs. Roelantsen. I know that took courage."

"My dear, if I could undo the past, I would. But we have much to overcome even now. My husband must walk a fine line with his constituents. It's a shame. Old prejudices die hard, I'm afraid."

Gilda poured compassion through her gaze.

"So that's why the secrecy," Joshua said. "You never wanted me to know who I was. That I am Jewish through my birth mother." His voice was solemn. But not angry. It seemed to Gilda it held a measure of wonder.

"Your uncle was afraid of the hate you would face. That we would all face. And we didn't know the first thing about raising you in any faith other than ours."

The explanations spilled out like the contents of a broken vessel. Gilda could use this revelation to her advantage, to eliminate her competition once and for all. What a scandal: the mayor's family embroiled in a marriage forbidden by their families and covering it up. But her stomach sickened at the thought of exploiting these good people, her neighbors. And Joshua. . . She would rather forsake her fondest wishes than hurt him.

As though he could read her thoughts, Joshua turned to her, and his sterling gaze held a yearning, perhaps hoping beyond hope that he would read what he most longed for in her willing expression. Was this good news to her, that he was a Jew? *Yes.* Did it create a way where there had been no way? *Oh, if only.*

She prayed with all her heart that it could.

His aunt released him. "I must find your uncle." But before she left, she grasped Gilda's hands and held them in both of hers.

"I can only ask on behalf of my community that you and your people would forgive the ways we have hurt you. We all loved your father. He was a saint, or whatever your people call good, righteous men. And if ever I have a second chance to show a loving couple my support, I won't hesitate to do so."

A twinkle lit her eye, and she included her nephew in her knowing gaze. Gilda's cheeks blossomed with heat, and a soft gasp revealed what she had been fighting to hold back. An affection for this man, which she could hide no longer.

Joshua clasped his aunt's hands, which still covered Gilda's and tilted his head toward her with tender deference. "You may have that chance soon, Aunt Abigail."

"I'll leave you two for now." Mrs. Roelantsen released them and, grinning from ear to ear, turned to find her husband.

Gilda's breath hitched. Joshua still held her hands in his. Their warmth suffused through her, imparting assurance, conviction, all the stalwart character qualities he possessed. It was as though the mere holding of hands communicated the promise of sharing all that he was to all of her. She trembled with the very idea of attachment to a man as good and as noble as her papa but so very different. Where Joshua was bold, Papa had been mild mannered. Joshua was somewhat impetuous, but Papa had been reserved. Joshua was joyful, exuberant, witty, handsome, and—

"I'll never replace your papa's place in this community, this school, or even in your heart. But I pray there is room for me in all three places so I can continue the good work he began. Gilda, do you feel the way I do? Would you consider a life with—"

"Oh no!" She broke the spellbinding moment.

Out in the square, Uncle Mortimer approached the mayor, shaking an angry fist at him. "What is this about you taking my brother's school from my niece and giving it to your nephew? If you want a war with the Jewish community Cornelius Roelantsen, you've got it!"

Chapter 12

Gilda ripped her hands away and left Josh thunderstruck. She hadn't even let the words of devotion fall from his mouth before slamming him down with an emphatic no. His heart thudded to the dusty floor as she marched straight past him out the door of the schoolhouse.

He turned to follow her retreat, disbelief piercing his heart. Outside Uncle Cornelius was being accosted in the street by a strange man in a cloak wearing a great, long beard like some figure straight out of ancient Israel. Maybe Elijah or Moses had returned, ushering in the last days. For it seemed that apocalypse had descended on the neat, tidy school social, complete with raised voices and townspeople drawing sides.

"Uncle Morty, no!" Gilda cried.

The man was her relative? That must have been what had

prompted her flight. Josh's feet couldn't carry him fast enough to Gilda's side, helping her press through the crowd to get to their embattled uncles.

"If you plan to take over the school my brother founded, you'll face my wrath, along with that of half your voters." The Moses figure shook his fist, and a cry went up from certain members of the crowd, incited by the man's words.

Uncle Cornelius retreated up a wooden platform that had been erected for the senator's speech later in the evening. Beside him stood Aunt Abigail, but her characteristic shrinking demeanor was gone. She looked out over the gathering with a serenity that seemed almost divine. Josh drew strength from her faith.

Gilda slipped away from him, weaving through the assembly toward the man she called Uncle Morty. Josh was stalled where he stood by the press of humanity that refused to give way.

Curious onlookers continued to gather, until the square became packed with both young and old, brewer and banker, cooper and cobbler, tiller and tinkerer, baker and butcher. They all drew sides until they either stood on the mayor's end of the street or crossed over to ally themselves with Gilda's uncle.

Then inspiration struck.

"Good people, hear me." Josh waved his hand above his head. "Listen, people." By degrees the crowd turned aside and made way for him. He walked, unhindered, to the podium as the clamor subsided. A sense of authority filled him with each stride. He'd always wondered about that certain shift that fell over Reverend Finney when a hush swept over the crowd. That weightless, burning passion seized him now—the anointing to preach.

"This county's forefathers put down some of the oldest roots in our young republic. Good Dutch people settled this land two centuries ago, and we continue their traditions of hard work and faith to this day. Alongside them, another ancient and revered people have come and have labored, built, and contributed to make this a truly vibrant community. For generations Christians and Jews have complemented one another here with strengths unique to each of our cultures. Why then, today, must we lay aside the foundations of grace and cooperation that have served us all so well?"

Calls from the crowd answered in phrases such as "underhanded scheming" and "hidden agenda" and "pretense of tolerance." The one that struck him with particular grief was "anti-Semitism." It hurt, because in a crowd this size, there was doubtless truth to it. Evils lurked in the heart of man that only God's love and grace could overcome. And the reverse was true as well. Good dwelled in the hearts of those who loved, and no hate could overcome it.

"It has been my privilege to become acquainted with many of you personally these last weeks since the school term began. You are raising patriotic, intelligent, civic-minded young men and women here, and I commend you all. What an example you have led. And I'm certain a goodly portion of that is due to Miss Gilda Jacobs's father. Though I did not have the honor to meet him, I have felt his legacy every day since my arrival. In the fine library collection to which many of you have since contributed. In the gathering here today, where all of you are investing in the next generation of learners and supporting the importance of education."

Whispered responses flitted through the crowd. The angry energy had shifted to a still, contemplative attention.

"I commend all of you for embracing such a learned man as Eliezer Jacobs. I urge you all to receive his daughter Gilda with the same unreserved trust you showed her father. It is my privilege to lend my most sincere endorsement to her as your next schoolmaster."

Gasps and murmurs reverberated through the public square, and movement stirred from the direction where Gilda stood alongside her mother, uncle, and sisters. They embraced her and kissed her cheek, and even from the distance that separated them, Josh could plainly see her smile directed at him. Sensation flowed from his boots up to the tingling hairs of his head. That woman could affect him like no other.

"Miss Jacobs, would you please join me at the podium?"

Josh took a deep breath and prayed a silent prayer that he would not act a fool or make a fool of anyone else. But victory came only to the bold, so he seized his opportunity.

His palms slickened, and he rubbed them together, then down his breeches. "As Miss Jacobs is making her way over, I have one more request of you good people. You have proven yourselves to be a remarkably broad-minded lot, and I wonder if I could ask you to consider one more, perhaps shocking proposal."

Gilda ascended the plank steps, guiding her dark skirts to the side as she navigated the narrow stairs.

He took her by the hand and assisted her up beside him. His uncle and aunt stood by his side quietly. Every gaze was riveted to the small platform, and the mood had shifted considerably from hostile to expectant, even amused. His uncle needn't worry about a mutiny at the polls or a tar and feathering in the public square. At least for the time being.

Gilda peered up at him with those gilded eyes of hers, and it gave him the resolve to press on, foolhardy though it might be. He gave her hand a surreptitious squeeze.

"Miss Jacobs, our paths have crossed by no other orchestration than divine providence. My ambitions never included that of a schoolteacher. Though I believe teaching and preaching are among my callings, it never occurred to me what an awesome privilege and responsibility it is to raise up the next generation of thinkers, citizens, and leaders. I have been, and continue to be, concerned with souls, but minds are not to be left to neglect. I feel we've made an effective team."

Gilda smiled and nodded her agreement to that, and the crowd applauded in agreement. But something in the way she gave him a sidelong glance as she faced the crowd again brought a chuckle to his throat. She knew he was up to something, and she was right.

He dropped to one knee, and the crowd erupted in a crescendo of gasps that quickly faded. He held her hand tight lest she faint, and spoke in his best preaching voice so everyone could hear.

"Miss Jacobs, would you agree to make our partnership complete in every sense of the word?"

The clamor in her ears went from deafening to silent in a second. The effect was so complete she thought she had slipped her mortal coil, except he still grasped her hand—his hold firm, anchoring her to her spot. She hadn't died, and she hadn't fainted either, for she was looking down into his blue gaze, which searched her from his odd, kneeling posture. What was Mr. Blake doing down there? She tugged on his hand to compel him to rise.

"If the good people of our town will allow a husband-and-wife team dedicated to their children's academic and biblical instruction, all that is left is for you to say yes. Gilda, will you marry me?"

She'd heard that. But oh, it couldn't be. This man proposing to her here, before everyone she knew. She swept the gathering with her gaze. Mama, Uncle Mortimer—what would they think? Would they understand that her heart was open to possibilities that they could not yet fathom? That this man, Joshua, had taught her something new. That Hashem had a name—Yeshua, the Messiah. And the future held a new hope she had never considered before. In time perhaps they too would embrace the newness she had found.

Her vision swam with glistening tears. Such joy filled her that she could scarcely contain it. As a tear slipped down her cheek, she shook her head. "There are conditions. A contract must be agreed upon. The *tenaim* must be discussed with my family. And I am in mourning. But Joshua Blake, I accept your proposal if you are willing to wait the customary time."

Joshua rose to his feet, gathered her in his arms, and whispered, "Let us speak to your family at once."

She allowed him to lead her down the platform stairs amid cheers and whoops from her neighbors and friends. *Friends.* She had never realized the wealth of goodwill she had possessed among these kindhearted people.

"I forbid it!" The authoritative male voice could be none other than Uncle Mortimer. Gilda's stomach shrank, and her feet became lead, stopping her dead in her tracks.

"This Gentile presumes to marry my brother's daughter? I forbid it."

Her warm, joyful wash of tears turned to ice on her cheeks. "But Uncle. . ."

Joshua patted her hand in reassurance. He gathered her to move forward again, but a figure stepped in front of them, blocking their path.

"Oh, but he is a Jew. My wife and I can attest to this." The man standing before her had come to her table earlier. She recalled his wife, who stood at his left hand. She still held a basket from which she had distributed pamphlets.

"Who are you?" Uncle Mortimer scoffed.

The man replied, "I know the rabbi who married his parents years ago. It was in this very town."

Gilda looked to Joshua. He squeezed her hand.

"His father was a Gentile, the mother, Hebrew. He converted to Judaism, but her parents would not accept him. She accepted Christ, but his family would not acknowledge her, and his father was disinherited. They sought a place where their marriage would not bring division. Their journey took them over the Atlantic, where their boat capsized. The child born to them would not have survived if not for the quick actions of a woman in a lifeboat."

"Mr. Kaufmann? Sir," Joshua reached for the man, and he turned around. "How do you know all of this? Who are you?"

The man gazed tenderly at them both. Gilda could not mistake those azure blue eyes.

"I'm your father, Joshua."

"But that's impossible. You were said to have perished."

"Only our memory. We were taken on a fishing vessel to England. We thought we had lost you until the lawyer came looking for us. He would be sure there are no other heirs to your grandfather's estate."

This day of surprises seemed unending. Gilda squeezed his hand to steady him. But Joshua did not stumble, and neither did he hesitate. He embraced the man and his wife—his mother and father—as though he had known them forever.

"Is this true?" Uncle Mortimer cried. "Who will verify this story?"

Humble head bowed, showing his *kippah*, Rabbi Rothstein raised his hand. He stepped forward, bridging the space between Gilda and her uncle. "I will attest to this truth. I was the one who married them and helped them leave in secrecy. And I will likewise stand for this young couple."

"And I." Mrs. Roelantsen's meek voice joined the rabbi's. "I swear to the truth of my brother's statement. And I too will stand for this couple."

Uncle Mortimer turned to Mama. When she raised no further objection, he shrugged.

Hannah and Hadassah ran to Gilda's side and embraced both her and her betrothed. *Her betrothed!* Could it be true?

"Is there *Aruk ha-Shalem*? A token?" the rabbi asked.

Joshua looked to her, his eyes wide with uncertainty, and Gilda giggled. "Do you have a coin in your pocket?" she whispered. "Hand it to me."

Joshua fiddled in his waistcoat and produced a small handful of coins. He poured them into her palm amid laughter as some toppled over. She scrambled to catch them before any fell to the ground. The crowd's laughter intensified. She joined in, her mirth spilling like the tinkling coins. "It's official. We are betrothed."

Her intended looked so handsome, so proud and pleased, she wished he would kiss her and end her anticipation. The way he looked at her spoke the same desire. She tingled with the realization that it was no longer a thought she must dismiss.

"I cannot argue with fate." Mayor Roelantsen said, joining his wife at Joshua's side. "Let me be the first to congratulate the couple. Best wishes, Joshua and Gilda."

"Mazel tov!"

Several of her students' parents, some neighbors, and many townspeople offered their messages of joy and felicitations. The crowd thinned. People drifted toward the next activities planned for the school social, and her view to Mama and her uncle cleared. Both moved toward her, and she met them, Joshua and his parents following.

Gilda's chest could burst with the drumming of her heart. No book or study had ever brought her pulse racing like this.

"Are you satisfied, Mama?" Gilda asked.

Mama's solemn face gave way to an exasperated sigh. And a smile. "Only you could shock me to my core. Such a strong will. Yes, Gilda. It is clear you have chosen for yourself. But Heaven help you, what will you survive on? Where will you live?"

"May I answer this?" Josh's newly revealed father held out his hand to her uncle. "Shalom aleichem. I am Simeon Kaufmann. My Gentile name is Van Deen."

"Shalom aleichem. I am Mortimer Jacobs, Gilda's uncle."

"My son stands to inherit the Van Deen house. With a few renovations, it should provide a newlywed couple a respectable place to live. Everything is now in order for the transfer of deed to him."

Uncle Morty folded his hands behind his back as Papa used to do in contemplation. "For a dowry, we will offer one-fifth of her father's investments to help you in your newlywed life."

Gilda's heart thrilled as Joshua and her uncle struck hands.

"You spared the town a calamity today, Mr. Blake. You are good with words. Let us hope they are sincere."

Joshua held Uncle Morty's arm in his clasp. "From my lips to God's ears. I speak knowing I will give an account of every word spoken. I love Gilda. It is my earnest desire to bring her joy and her people only good."

"Then you have my permission and my blessing to marry. But tell me, what are these names? Kaufmann, Blake, Van Deen. What name will my niece take to wed?"

Joshua's father bowed his head and asked permission to speak on his son's behalf. "I'm sure you are all curious on this. Kaufmann is the name Rabbi Rothstein gave us to protect our identity when we fled. Blake is from my wife's maiden name, Bloch, also chosen to protect Joshua's identity."

Mama clapped and threw her head back and laughed as heartily as Gilda had ever seen her laugh. The sudden sound startled her, but soon she was laughing also, though she didn't know why.

"Bloch? My daughter is marrying a Bloch!" Mama regained her composure. "And to think I wanted you to marry a common doctor. Do you know who the Blochs are?"

She shook her head.

"Your father's prayers have gone to the very presence of God, seeing Him face-to-face. The Bloch family teaches medicine and

Hebrew studies at university!"

"A family of teachers." Gilda gave her betrothed an admiring look. "Of course they are."

Joshua cradled her hand in his. "And so shall we continue the tradition." He pressed a kiss on the back of her hand, but his eyes smoldered like blue flames with the promise of much more.

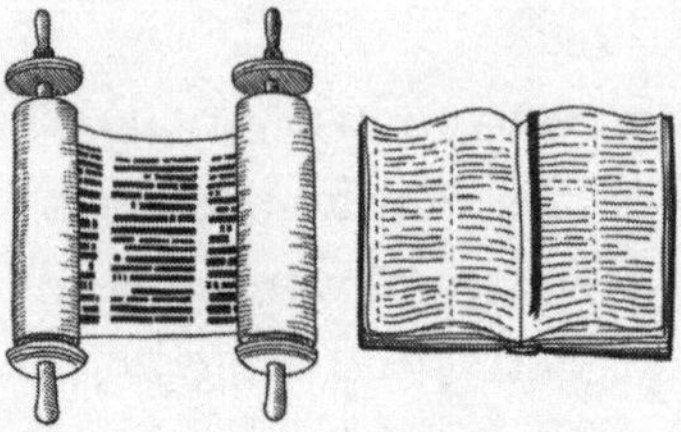

Chapter 13

September 1841

Joshua stood beneath the *chuppah*, the evening candlelight filtering through the white linen that rolled overhead in a gentle river breeze. He tugged down his waistcoat nervously, hoping his presentation matched his hopes of perfection for this long-awaited moment. His thoughts swarmed in a happy buzz, anticipating Gilda's arrival to meet him here under their wedding canopy. The procession from her house had sent his blood rushing into his ears, competing with the joyful sounds of music and celebration. She emerged along the tree-lined avenue between quaint colonial homes, brought to him by his groomsmen—Uncle Mortimer, Uncle Cornelius, and Mr. Diller.

The music quieted. The moment had come.

Gilda stepped under the canopy, close enough that her perfume skimmed his senses. Close enough that her skirts brushed his prayer shawl, but he refrained from reaching for her yet. She released Uncle Mortimer's arm and slowly circled him seven times. The radiance of his bride grew more captivating with each pass. Her flowing white mantle and veil caught reflections of the lantern light, shimmering like liquid gold over her graceful form. But her face remained hidden in the shadow of lace, and he longed to see her, partake of the passion in her eyes, the sweetness of lips that he had waited a long year to kiss.

He had vowed not to sully her bridal *mikvah* over the past year or her reputation while she ran the classroom, though it was a sacrifice he'd prayed daily he could continue to make. Many times he had almost given in to claiming her sweet lips. But the Lord had been his keeper. Soon he'd need wait no more. Every sense hummed within him with longing to receive the sweet honey of their first kiss as man and wife.

Gilda came to stand by his side, and he could almost see through the veil separating them. Her hand sought his, and their accord flowed through her touch. She grounded him as his head spun with a thousand delights.

His father's rich voice resonated with emotion as he began to speak. "Today in our presence, the wild olive tree is grafted into the natural olive tree. A man raised to a Gentile family has been grafted into the seed of Abraham, the father of faith. The root of Christianity is Judaism. We believe that Jesus is the fulfillment of the prophecies of Messiah. We believe that He will come again to gather His people to Himself in a wedding like this, the marriage supper of the Lamb."

His father held a cup and pitcher and poured. Seven blessings of the *Sheva Brachot* were recited, and Joshua partook from the glass. At last he could lift the veil and behold his bride. Gilda's eyes shimmered with joy, and she received his ring for her finger and the goblet from his hand. Josh swallowed the lump in his throat as he watched her lovely lips drink from the same cup.

Rabbi Rothstein placed the cup beside Josh's right foot, and with the pronouncement of man and wife, Josh shattered the glass.

Cheers of "Mazel tov!" and dancing broke out instantaneously, and all Josh wanted to do was kiss his Gilda. She leaned in, the scent of the spiced drink on her breath, and met him halfway.

No sooner had he made contact with her lips than the party whisked him away in celebration.

Gilda laughed as her sisters clasped her hands in theirs, raising them in jubilant dance. What a difference a year had made, from grief to rejoicing. Mama made a striking figure watching from the sidelines. Gilda whispered in Hadassah's ear, "Make Mama join us!"

Soon they encompassed her and drew her into the gaiety. Mama's face shone with a radiance that had been absent since Papa's passing. It looked beautiful on her. And Uncle Morty seemed to think so too. His gaze hadn't left her since she stepped into the moves of the dance.

Cheers and commotion erupted as Joshua, seated in a chair, was lifted up on the shoulders of several young men. She thrilled to see this man—*her man*—immersed in the customs of her people, overwhelmed by his willingness to learn her traditions and incorporate them in their wedding. Gratitude mingled with wonder that the whole community had accepted their invitation to attend and rejoice with them. And she cherished the new teachings that Joshua and his father had shared with her over the past year. A new love blossomed in her heart for a personal and intimate Savior who had made His new covenant known to her.

Something old and something new. She looked out over the schoolyard, shining in the torchlight, made festive with the efforts of the whole village with flowers, banners, fruit displays, ribbons, and bows—something borrowed. An entire town's love and goodwill.

And something blue—the lovely sapphire set in the golden ring Joshua had given her. It matched the light in her groom's eyes as he approached her, having broken away from the demands of the crowd for a stolen moment. She slipped her hand in his, and he led her under the blazing foliage of a sugar maple. His kiss—their first real kiss, encompassed her until stars fell from her spinning head and cascaded down through her, tingling all the way to her toes.

"Mr. Blake, what will the children say?" Her breath caught in her throat with an uncustomary loss for words.

"They'll say, 'There's a man who loves his wife.'" Joshua smiled and firmed his hold on her. "Now be quiet and kiss me again, Wife."

His laughter rumbled through her, his chest pressed against hers, and the thrill of the vibration was almost as intoxicating as that word.

"*Wife*. I could get used to the sound of that."

He silenced her with his affection, and she welcomed each lingering kiss.

Kathleen Maher is a twenty-first-century girl with an old soul. Her debut novella, *Bachelor Buttons*, released in 2013 through Helping Hands Press, incorporates both her Irish heritage and love of Civil War history. She won the American Christian Fiction Writers' Genesis Contest for unpublished writers, historical category, in 2012. An avid history buff, Kathleen contributes to writing-themed blogs and writes book reviews.

Kathleen and her husband share an old farmhouse in upstate New York with their family and a small zoo of rescued animals.

Love in Any Language

by Susanne Dietze

Dedication

For my favorite teacher, my mom.

To the Lord our God belong mercies and forgivenesses,
though we have rebelled against him.
DANIEL 9:9

Chapter 1

Riley County, Kansas
1870

A tin of tea, a spool of thread, and honey for our daily bread. Mary Clarence repeated the rhyme to herself as she wandered the aisles of the dry goods store, in no hurry to step up to the counter to make her purchases. Just as she'd arrived a few minutes ago, a shower of icy rain let loose over Main Street, so she'd far prefer to linger in the dry, snug store than hurry home.

There was nothing to hurry home to. Oh, her parents, of course, and her pen-and-ink project for her nephews, but Mary had all the time in the world at her disposal to see to that. She hadn't had to worry about keeping track of the time for several months now.

A tinge of bitterness crept up her throat. *If only—*

My, her thoughts had taken a turn as miserable as the winter gloom outside that gave the world the look of evening, rather than one o'clock in the afternoon. As if he shared her thoughts, the store's proprietor, Mr. Sullivan, lit another kerosene lamp by the window, making the space a little cheerier.

It took light to fight the darkness, she'd learned. As much joy as God had placed in her life—loving parents, a best friend who'd married her brother and given her two delightful nephews, a roof over her head, and food in her belly—she still had difficulty shaking off a shroud she'd only recently realized was resentment. She'd allowed herself to dwell in a bleak, cold cage formed by her unwillingness to forgive, and the worst part was that she knew she could leave it behind and enter a world of freedom and light.

But forgiveness had proven difficult, if not impossible. *Lord, help me want to forgive him at least. Maybe that would be a start.*

The shop door swung open, admitting two dripping-wet farmers along with a blast of frigid air. "That's January for you," one joked, hitching his thumb back at the cold, wet world outside.

Mary wasn't the only one with the idea of sheltering here to wait out the deluge, for Sullivan's Dry Goods was more crowded than usual for a winter Monday. A handful of farmers gathered about the squat potbellied stove; two older ladies examined notions; and a few younger men pointed to the newest wanted poster hanging behind the counter: a man with light-colored hair peeking from beneath a hat, most of his face obscured by a scarf. All you could see were his eyes and the tips of his ears.

With that vague description, Sheriff Miles would never catch the burglar.

Wanted for burglarizing two homes. Whose? Lord, I don't like this at all.

She turned away. Two little girls with blond braids trailing from beneath pink knit caps stared up at the jars on the candy counter, the taller one pointing at them while the younger one—a sister, no doubt, by their similar looks—nodded. As if aware they were being watched, the girls turned. Their blue-eyed gazes met Mary's, and the older one offered a tiny smile.

It was all the invitation Mary needed. "Which candies are your favorites? I confess to being partial to ribbon candy because it lasts longer."

The younger girl bowed her head, while her sister smiled but said nothing. Perhaps they'd been schooled not to speak to strangers.

Schooled. Curious. The girls should be in school this chill afternoon. The younger one might not be of age, but the older one certainly looked old enough, gauging by her height and the missing teeth in her smile. "Do you go to school?"

The older girl's smile slipped. "*Skola?* Nay."

Ah. The girls were among the Swedish immigrants who'd settled here in their hopeful-named town of Plenty late last spring

And the girl hadn't said *nay* but *nej*, one of only a handful of Swedish words Mary knew. They must not know English, but *school* and *skola* sounded similar enough that the girl could infer its meaning.

"*Välkommen.*" She was sure her pronunciation was faulty, but both girls smiled at her welcome anyway.

A tall, dark-blond man with a cheerful red scarf looped around his neck came up behind the girls, resting a possessive hand on each of their shoulders. While she'd never encountered the girls before, the man was familiar enough. She'd seen him about town for several months now. Each time she'd noted that ready smile of his, but today's was different, reflecting his recognition of her. "Good afternoon." His accent was strong.

"Good afternoon, sir."

His hands remained on the girls' shoulders—the capable, calloused hands of a farmer. Hands like her father's. He bent to speak quietly to the girls, with authority and affection, and Mary's smile grew. He was clearly the girls' pa, and she'd always appreciated seeing fathers lovingly interact with their children.

Even if seeing such a thing was also a reminder that she might have had her own children, around these ages, if only—

The man rose to his full height, derailing the unhappy direction of her thoughts.

"I am Kristofer Nilsson. These my *döttrar.*" He shut his eyes for a second, as if concentrating. "Daughters. Forgive me. My English is not so good."

"You're doing quite well, in fact. I am Miss Mary Clarence."

"Nice to meet you." His hands lifted to rest on the girls' caps. "Agata and Britta."

"Hello, girls," Mary said. Their response, "*Hello, ma'am*," was a splendid effort in a new language.

The littler one gathered close to her father, whispering something. Mr. Nilsson gave Mary a sheepish grin. "Britta likes your hat."

With her gloved hand, Mary patted it, a warm wool creation with cheerful fabric bluebells stitched to the brim. "It's my favorite bonnet too, Britta. Thank you."

"*Bonnet* is the word, then?" Mr. Nilsson eyed it.

"For a ladies' hat like this, yes. Like your wife wears."

His smile faded a fraction. "My wife died in Sweden."

Oh. "I'm terribly sorry."

"You could not know."

"You are kind to say so." She was about to bid them farewell when he made a noise, as if he hesitated to say something. The girls too looked at him with expectant gazes, so Mary smiled. "May I assist you in any way?"

"I don't want to trouble you."

Whatever could he want of her? Her curiosity hadn't been piqued like this in a long while. "It's no trouble."

He nodded. "Then yes, please. I am the only one of my friends to speak some English. When I ask Mr. Sullivan something, he speaks too fast for me to understand."

"Ah yes. He speaks rather fast for me too sometimes. Shall I ask him to repeat it for you?" She gestured at the proprietor.

Mr. Sullivan, a balding fellow of middle years, met them across the candy counter. "Afternoon, folks. What can I do for you?"

A tin of tea, a spool of thread, and honey for our daily bread. "Before we see to my order, Mr. Nilsson here has an inquiry."

"Jan Ivarsson's piece for his plow," Mr. Nilsson interjected.

"I already done answer about that ordered part, sir."

Mary cocked her head. "I'm afraid Mr. Nilsson didn't quite comprehend the matter in its entirety and has asked me for help. Could you explain the matter to him once more?"

"You speak Swedish now that you've got time on your hands?" Mr. Sullivan's brow quirked up.

"No." Mary's vision narrowed. "While it is nice to know you think me capable of teaching myself a Scandinavian language, Mr. Sullivan, I do not speak Swedish. But Mr. Nilsson speaks enough English that I can help relate what you say if he doesn't understand it."

Mr. Sullivan puffed out a breath and muttered something about confidentiality. But he leaned toward her with a conspiratorial look. "Miss Mary, I don't make a habit of sharing private dealings, but his friend don't speak no English a-tall, so it didn't seem so wrong, and you bein' a fine lady and all, I s'pose I could tell you."

"That would be most appreciated, Mr. Sullivan."

The proprietor took a deep breath. "Tell him I ordered it two weeks' past, but on account of that big snow we had, I'd say it's gonna be another week, maybe more before I get any shipments in. Shame too, because I'm low on lots o' goods, from crackers to shoe blacking. You don't need those, do you? Good. See, normally I'd ask the dry goods stores in Manhattan or Turtle Springs to work out a trade with me, but they're in the same condition."

"What a shame—"

"Yessir, so tell the Swedish fella here to tell his friend that he'll have plenty of time to repair his equipment before spring. Oh, and your ma's new boots'll get here eventually too. I'm sure she sent you here to ask."

Mr. Sullivan had indeed spoken in his usual rapid style, offering extraneous information. No wonder Mr. Nilsson's brow furrowed as he struggled to keep up. Mary tilted her head up to meet Mr. Nilsson's blue-eyed gaze. "It will be at least a week for the part."

"One week," he repeated.

"At least. Eight, ten days, perhaps."

"Oh. I see. Sir, thank you."

"Happy to be of service." Mr. Sullivan wandered off to assist one of the older ladies eyeing notions before Mary could request her tea, thread, and honey. Ah well. It was still sleeting out there anyway. She'd stay put until it let up.

"Thank you too, Miss Clarence." Mr. Nilsson placed his hand over his heart, drawing her attention to the fraying cuff of his coat. He could use a new one. "I understood some of his words, but not all."

"I'm happy to help. Did you study English in Sweden?"

"No, I learned on the ship here from American sailors. Speaking only. I cannot read or write English. I have a New Testament in Swedish and English to study, but I am slow."

"Languages can be difficult, especially without a teacher."

"You speak another language?"

"Bits of French and Latin. I was trained as a teacher, you see. That is, I *was* a teacher."

No you don't, Mary Clarence. Don't you go feeling sorry for yourself again. Change the subject fast. "Speaking of school, it is in session right now. Agata doesn't attend?"

His gaze followed after his daughters, who'd turned their attentions back to the candy counter. "No. She can't."

"Why ever not? Agata looks old enough to me."

"She is eight, so *ja*. I mean, yes. Britta is almost six."

"Do you teach the girls at home then?"

"Yes, but not to read or write English." His tiny smile revealed his amusement.

Mary treaded a fine line between overstepping with a parent and advocating for education, so she chose her words with care. "I commend the local school to you then. To learn English and other subjects too."

"I sent Agata the first day of school, but she and the other children from our community came straight home saying no school for them."

"No school?" There had to be a translation problem here. Children didn't get sent home from school like that. "Perhaps there's been a misunderstanding. Perhaps—"

"The schoolmaster said no English, no school. The children could understand that."

"That can't be possible." Why hadn't she heard of this happening? Surely the word of nine children being refused access to school had spread around town.

Or maybe not. Most of the affected people didn't speak English. And if this happened out of earshot of the other students, who would know?

Mary's stomach knotted. "Did the schoolmaster say anything else to the children?"

His shook his head. "I thought it must be a mistake. I went back that day, and he said I should speak to the supra—super—forgive me, I cannot remember what he is called. He is in charge of the school and also the bank."

The school superintendent and bank manager. Mary froze, but it had more to do with the superintendent, Edmund Stanley, than with the frigid weather swirling into the store through the door, which had opened again to admit an older couple. "Did you speak to him? The superintendent?"

"I try, but he is never in the bank when I go."

Or perhaps he was hiding in the back, away from confrontation. Edmund was good at that.

"Forgive me. I have said too much." Mr. Nilsson's expression was apologetic.

Oh my, his eyes were as blue as the summer sky. At once her mind filled with images of kites flying in the gentle June breeze, plucking ripe cherries from high branches and watching birds soar overhead, all against a background of cloudless azure.

Something about Kristofer Nilsson pulled her out of the winter of her surroundings, and perhaps of her mood too. She'd been cold and damp in both body and spirit not ten minutes ago, but now she burned.

"Mr. Nilsson, I realize your daughter's school attendance is a family issue. But it is also a public issue. I am a concerned citizen of Plenty, and as such, I have a sudden desire to visit the bank."

"Then we go with you." Smiling, he beckoned the girls, speaking to them in rapid Swedish.

"That's not necessary. It's still sleeting, and there's no reason for you to get damp and cold."

"I think there is every reason." His smile was warm as summer, just like his eyes.

What on earth was she doing, thinking of summer and his eyes and his smile at a time like this?

Her flushing cheeks were so hot they didn't feel the sting of winter cold on her face when Mr. Nilsson opened the door for her to leave the store.

Chapter 2

"Come, Britta, Agata." Propping open the store's door with his boot heel, Kristofer's gaze caught on Britta's bare hands. "Where are your mittens?"

She pulled them from the pocket of her new coat. "Why are we leaving? You said we could buy candy, *Pappa*."

"We'll come back, *älskling*." Once she'd tugged on her mittens, he glanced up. The dark-haired Miss Clarence waited a few yards ahead, her slender frame sheltered from the sleet beneath the barbershop canopy. "We're going with Miss Clarence."

"The lady in the *blåklocka* hat?" Agata pulled her cap down farther over her ears.

"Blåklocka *bonnet*," he corrected. "That is the word for a lady's hat in English. I don't know the word for the flowers. But ja. We will be speaking to the man in charge of the school."

Agata's eyes widened. "Can she make him let us go?"

"I don't know, but she bears the look of someone who would try, doesn't she?" Kristofer couldn't help but admire her determination. "While we are in the bank, you must be well behaved. Then we will come back for candy."

Not that he needed to remind Britta to be quiet. She was shyer than a field mouse with an owl swooping overhead. Her hand that didn't clutch his was shoved into her coat pocket, undoubtedly to cradle her favorite thing, a small red Dala horse she'd named Lilja.

But Agata? She had no such trepidations, skipping ahead to join Miss Clarence. "*Blomma*," she said, pointing to the flowers stitched on Miss Clarence's bonnet. "English word?" she asked in English.

"Blomma? Oh, that sounds like *blooms*. Yes, we call it a *flower*." She touched the blue flowers.

Kristofer and Britta had caught up by then, and they walked two by two the short but frigid distance to the bank, with Agata pointing to objects and sharing the Swedish words. Then Miss Clarence would relate them in English.

Regn. Britta looked up into the sky and winced comically when the drops hit her face.

Rain. It sounded much like the word they knew.

Pappa. Kristofer himself.

He waved, and Miss Clarence said, "Father. Papa."

Hund. A poor, skinny hound huddled under a wagon to stay dry.

Dog.

Miss Clarence craned her long neck to glance at him. "What clever girls you have, Mr. Nilsson." Her smile included Britta too, who'd remained silent throughout the exchange of vocabulary words. His little one was paying close attention, however. Little escaped her notice, even though she'd become even more reserved since her mother passed away.

He squeezed Britta's hand and said a quick prayer for guidance.

Help me be a good pappa, Gud, *and see the girls educated, as I promised Tilda before she died.*

Who'd have thought it would have been this difficult? But they couldn't receive an education in America without learning English, and while Kristofer might know how to speak passably, he still couldn't read or write. He needed help to teach his girls, and if he couldn't get it from the school, he'd see to it himself. Today they'd come to the store in hopes he could find a simple child's book, something with pictures, to help them all learn letters and words.

Instead, *Gud* sent them a lady in a blåklocka bonnet. Little did Miss Clarence know that bonnet of hers had beguiled him from the first day he saw it, because the little violet-blue harebells stitched on it resembled blåklocka, his girls' favorite wildflower from back home in Dalarna.

Thoughts of Dalarna usually included pinches of pain, and this time was no exception, but when Miss Clarence reached for the knob of the bank door, there was no time to dwell on all he'd left behind in Sweden.

He rushed ahead to open the door. Smiling her thanks, she passed him inside, leaving a subtle trail of floral soap and wet wool in her wake.

Kristofer was not a frequent visitor of the bank, but its elegance never failed to impress him. Unlike other businesses in town, it was furnished with quality woods and rich fabrics, no doubt to inspire confidence in the institution in those who visited: Walls were papered with gold-and-purple stripes, and windows were draped by heavy brocade panels tied back with purple cords. A polished oak counter divided the bank into sections, one for customers and one for employees. Behind the employees stood a tasteful wood screen, no doubt obscuring desks and private meeting areas to handle sensitive business. Numerous lamps cast a golden glow against the darkness, giving the bank the air of a cozy parlor rather than a place of business.

This man who ran the bank—the school superintendent—must be the wealthiest fellow in Plenty to afford all of this.

Not that the banker had much business to occupy himself with at the moment. The bank was empty of clients and tellers alike.

After instructing the girls to sit on a pair of padded chairs near the door, Kristofer removed his hat. "Where is everyone? Is it closed?"

"While there's money to be made? I doubt it." Miss Clarence jingled a small silver bell left on the counter.

A fair-haired, tiny-chinned youth appeared from behind the screen. He was the same fellow who had turned Kristofer away three times when he'd come asking for the superintendent. Sparing Kristofer the slightest of glances, the young man focused his small-eyed gaze on Miss Clarence. "Good afternoon, ma'am."

"And to you. Mr. Stanley, please, Ernie." Miss Clarence sounded like a schoolmarm—brisk and efficient.

"Is it something I may help with, ma'am? A deposit or—"

"No, thank you, Ernie. I require Mr. Stanley. Is he here?"

Before Ernie could respond, a dark-haired gentleman with a trimmed mustache and lean build appeared from behind the screen. "It's all right, Ernie. I'm available. What brings you out in such dreadful weather, Miss Clarence?"

His tone was as smooth as his oil-slicked, dark hair. He wore a faint smile, but it faded when his gaze took in Kristofer.

"So it's *Miss Clarence*, is it, Edmund?" Tension sparked off her like hot bacon grease spurting from the frying pan.

Interesting. She didn't like the banker, and there was more behind it than what Kristofer had told her about the schoolchildren.

"The use of surnames is a professional courtesy, Mary. Banks are formal establishments." Stanley glanced at Kristofer again as Ernie stepped back to give his employer his spot at the counter. "What's this about? Who is your, er, friend?"

Kristofer thrust out his hand. "Kristofer Nilsson. I must speak to you about school."

"Nilsson. I recall the name."

"I hope so. I've left messages for you three times."

At that, Ernie slunk back around the decorative screen, out of view.

"You speak English." Mr. Stanley blinked before taking Kristofer's still-outstretched hand for a brief, rather limp shake.

"Enough to ask you to let our children attend school."

"I don't understand." The way his blinking increased, it was clear he was lying.

"Hogwash," Miss Clarence snapped. Kristofer didn't know the word, but he comprehended her meaning well enough by the fire blazing from her eyes. She knew the banker lied too. "You are superintendent, Edmund. Your job is to see that a free education is available to any child whose parents wish for it, yet your schoolmaster forbade the new children in our community to attend. Inconceivable."

"They're not forbidden. My, what a strong word." Chuckling, Stanley brushed a speck of lint from his coat sleeve.

"What else would you call it?" Miss Clarence's hazel eyes narrowed. "They were told they cannot attend because they do not know English. That sounds as if he forbade them. *Denied*, *banned*, *barred*, *excluded*—I can think of another dozen synonyms for his act if you need more help understanding the gravity of the matter, Edmund."

Kristofer was learning a host of new words today too. Miss Clarence of the blåklocka bonnet was quite something, as strong a force as the winter storm outside.

The banker twisted his wedding ring around his finger. "I'm sure it wasn't like that."

"Then what was it like? Tell me, Edmund. You had to have known these children hadn't been in school the past four months. A parent has made an effort to see you multiple times." She gestured at Kristofer. "It is time for you to take action with Jarvis. Tell him to teach all the children in Plenty. Now."

Kristofer's arms folded. "Who is Jarvis?"

Miss Clarence glanced up. "Jarvis Leach, the new schoolmaster. Edmund's cousin."

Cousin. . . Kristofer searched his vocabulary for the unfamiliar word. Didn't that mean kinsman of some sort? "You let this man teach because he is your relative?"

"The word for this is *nepotism*, Mr. Nilsson," Miss Clarence said. "Showing favoritism or preference for a member of one's family, and that is why Jarvis was hired in the first place."

"He was qualified. That was why he was hired." Stanley paled.

Miss Clarence snorted. "No one believes that, Edmund, but I do believe you are allowing him to deny children because he's your cousin."

"So you let this man under your authority forbid my children from going to school because he is your family and he dislikes newcomers. Or because you do and this is your idea."

"That's not it." Stanley regained his color: two pink splotches on his cheeks. "It has naught to do with discrimination on either of our parts. It's—well, you must admit, Mary. Teaching children of all grades and levels in a one-room schoolhouse is a challenge."

"Indeed." Her nod was crisp. "I did it for years, as you recall."

Kristofer's curiosity piqued further. *She'd been the teacher here in Plenty?*

A vein bulged in Stanley's neck. "It's hard enough when the children speak English, but these students don't speak the language—"

"They need school so they learn to speak it." Kristofer felt like tearing his hair out at the roots.

"You are correct, Mr. Nilsson, and I think I understand now. Jarvis is too incompetent to take on any more students." Miss Clarence lifted her head. "It is clear, however, that nothing more will be gained here today, so I suggest we take our leave."

"But—" Kristofer wasn't finished.

"Thank you." Stanley exhaled.

"And I shall take the matter to the state superintendent of public instruction in Topeka."

Stanley's lips parted with a wet pop. "Not another letter, Mary."

Another letter? Interesting. But knowing there was another option that might clear the way for his children to attend school gave Kristofer a hot spark of hope in his chest. "I too will write." Even though he'd have to pay someone else to jot down his dictation.

Stanley wedged a finger between his neck and collar. "No need to bother such a busy man."

"I'm certain he's not too busy for this." She turned to leave.

"Mary, please." Stanley leaned over the counter. When she twisted back to face him, he sighed. "You're right. Jarvis is overwhelmed by the pupils he already has. If more students attend the school, whether they need to learn English or not, he'll quit. What can I do? We need him."

Kristofer rubbed his temple. "You are saying you want to employ a bad teacher?"

Miss Clarence's lips twitched. "Well said, Mr. Nilsson."

"I'll replace him," Stanley said with a sigh. "I will."

Now that he was confronted by a formidable opponent and threatened with censure, of course he would. Stanley was like one of the spiny lizards that lived among Kristofer's cornstalks, peeking out from debris to preen in the sun, proud and flexing, until he was surprised by another animal. Then the lizard would flee, leaving its tail behind as a distraction, saving what he could of himself.

At least they were getting something accomplished. Kristofer mashed his hat back on his head. "Good."

"But not yet. Jarvis must teach through the end of the school year. Summer is when teachers are hired, you know, and it's far too much trouble to replace him midyear—"

"Nonsense. You have a perfectly qualified teacher available today. Me." Miss Clarence bent her head as if explaining something obvious to a small child.

Stanley rolled his eyes. "Really, Mary, not this again."

She laughed. "I could not resist. Very well, Edmund. If you will not allow me to teach because I am female, and Jarvis is too incompetent to accept new students and you refuse to replace him, probably because he is your cousin, you leave me no choice."

"The letter?" He gulped.

"The letter. And Mr. Nilsson?" She turned to face Kristofer, her features striking in their determination. "The letters will take some time to bear fruit, I'm sorry to say. But I recall your words that Jarvis would take children once they learned English. I don't think he meant it, but I will hold him to his word. Therefore I would like to offer my services teaching your children English—your and your friends' children. If you'll have me, that is."

"You?" Stanley barked out an incredulous laugh.

"You," Kristofer agreed. She'd been a teacher. She cared enough to help him with this matter. And she was here, an answer to prayer. Gud had sent her to him today for this purpose. "I'll pay you."

"Not necessary." She turned her back on Stanley. "Mr. Nilsson, shall we discuss arrangements for the English lessons while we return to the general store? I have a few things to purchase—"

"You're doing this out of spite, Mary." The banker snapped. "Set aside your pride and concern yourself with other matters."

Kristofer had no idea what sort of matters, but it was clear by the audible gasp from Miss Clarence that the banker had overstepped.

She spun back. "Any matters with which I concern myself are none of your business, *Mister* Stanley. Do give Clarice and the children my regards."

At that she marched past Kristofer and beckoned the girls.

"Come, girls. Skola!"

"Skola!" Agata jumped up and clapped. A more subdued Britta followed, but her eyes were wide with curiosity.

Kristofer rushed ahead to get the door for Miss Clarence. Was she always in such a hurry? She certainly seemed invigorated by the prospect of teaching the children English. But much as he didn't care for Stanley, he had to make one thing clear to her. Once outside, he beckoned her to stop. "He said you had other things to be concerned with? I do not wish this to take you away from them."

Her eyes dimmed, but her smile didn't fade. "He is wrong. He has ideas of what a female should and shouldn't do, that's all, and that includes being a teacher."

"I think he is the one who stopped you from being the teacher here. So he could hire his cousin."

"Yes. It had nothing to do with my abilities, I assure you."

"I did not think that." Not at all. He thought the blame was all Stanley's.

"Edmund holds some power in this town, and sometimes power can go to a person's head—that means it makes him think he is better than everyone else. He has strong opinions. But so do I." She chuckled.

"So I see."

She rubbed her gloved hands together. "Now I have many questions for you about these students. Where will we meet? For how long? Perhaps you should come by my house tomorrow, after I've spoken to my parents and you've discussed matters with your friends. Would that do?"

"Yes. It will do." The greatest understatement of his life.

Thanks to Gud for bringing this woman across his path today, Kristofer's daughters were going to learn English.

And maybe someday they could teach him how to read it.

Chapter 3

A full week later, Mary returned the tin of tea and jar of honey to their proper places in the pantry. There. Now all of the breakfast remnants were put away before her students arrived. Which would be in—Mary glanced at the squat carriage clock ticking away on the kitchen fireplace mantel—ten minutes. "Oh."

Mother looked up from setting a pot of beans and bacon on the stove to simmer until lunchtime. "What do you mean, 'oh'?"

"I noticed the time, that's all."

This past week, Mary had introduced Kristofer Nilsson and his girls to her parents, and together they'd come up with a plan for Mary to instruct the Swedish children in English from nine to noon each morning here in her family's combined kitchen and dining area—the largest room in the house. There would be a full dozen students—the nine who'd attempted to attend school but were sent away, as well as three six-year-olds, including Britta.

Mary had shown Kristofer what each child should bring: chalk, slates, and if funds allowed, paper, pencils, and picture books. Grinning, he'd said they'd be ready.

With shaking hands, Mary set her own chalk, slate, and a clean rag atop the freshly wiped table.

Mother spied Mary's hands. "Goodness, child. Why are you nervous? You're a fine teacher."

Mary was long past being a child, but she appreciated Mother's caring tone. "I'm a teacher who doesn't speak the same language as her students."

"A hurdle you're equipped to overcome." Mother wiped her hands on her apron. "Don't fret, Mary. You'll have the children on the road to fluency in no time."

"I hope so. The state superintendent will have received our letters by now, and I imagine he'll send a new teacher soon, no matter what Edmund says."

"Edmund." Mother grumbled. "Never mind him."

"Him who? Me?" Father entered the kitchen from the hallway, rubbing his hands together to warm them.

"No." Mary didn't elaborate. There was no point discussing Edmund Stanley, because it only soured her family's dispositions. Besides, the students would be here in—*oh my, six minutes*—and it wouldn't do to greet them with long faces. "Thank you for allowing the children to meet here. Are you sure we're not going to inconvenience you?"

"Mary, we've told you a dozen times, we're delighted to host them, so long as you don't mind me coming in for coffee once in a while." Father winked and poured himself a cup of the rich, dark brew from the tin pot on the stove.

"Or for me to tend to lunch." Mother adjusted the pot of beans to a warmer spot. "And as you said, it's only for a few weeks."

Father's eyes twinkled. "Nevertheless, you need one more thing to have the look of a proper schoolroom." He set down his coffee and slipped out into the hall.

"A blackboard?" Mary teased. "An apple or a big desk for the teacher?"

He returned with a delicate silver bell in his calloused hands. "This."

"Aunt Olivia's sick bell?" Mother's invalid aunt had lived with them in her last years, using the little bell when she needed a fresh glass of water or a scratch in the middle of her back.

"Now it's a school bell. Every teacher needs one when the young'uns get rascally."

Mary kissed his cheek, then Mother's. "Thank you." Their thoughtfulness was balm to her aching anxiety. This little bell symbolized a fresh start too, because she'd been the one to purchase the bell for the school on Main Street a few years ago. Now it sat in the hands of Jarvis Leach, the incompetent new schoolmaster.

A smile stretched Mary's lips. This may not be a real classroom or a real school bell, but education would prevail anyway. She took the bell and grinned.

The muffled sounds of hoofbeats drew their attention. Mary felt her grin slip. "Someone's here."

Father gazed out the window onto the frosty yard. "The Nilssons. Looks like he's got another fellow with him too. Must be his brother." He stepped out to answer the front door before Kristofer could knock.

In a moment, she'd be teaching. Again. Her stomach swooped.

Merciful God, thank You for giving me this chance to do something I love so much. Please help me and the children understand one another. Thank You for—

"Kristofer." He entered the kitchen, his red scarf complementing his rosy, wind-cold cheeks. He slid his hat off his head, mussing his dark blond hair. "I mean, Mr. Nilsson."

"Miss Clarence." His smiling gaze met hers squarely, and her stomach swooped again.

"I think we can use Christian names. We're all friends here," Father announced. "I'm Clyde, my wife's Lorena, and we'll call you Kristofer too, if you don't mind."

"No, sir. Clyde." Kristofer smiled as he nodded a greeting to Mother. After saying hello to the adults, Agata rushed to claim a seat at the kitchen table, but Britta lingered back with her father, clutching something vibrant red to her chest.

Britta wasn't the only one wearing an uncertain expression. The man Father said must be Kristofer's brother lurked in the threshold. Although he was of similar height and build, they didn't look much alike beyond the eyes—blue as summer sky. Kristofer gestured. "My brother, Hjalmar."

Hjalmar waved, an indication he didn't know English well enough to answer. Mary nodded her understanding.

Kristofer approached Mary. The crisp scent of winter clung to his clothes, as did a few golden stalks of hay, poking into the elbow of his brown wool coat. "Britta brought her *dalahäst*. Her toy horse, Lilja. It comforts her, and she takes it everywhere, but if it is a problem, I will bring it home."

"I'm sure it won't be an issue." Mary could now see the red legs of a toy wooden horse, richly decorated with swirls of white and green paint that looked like a floral saddle and bridle. While the paint was chipped from one foot and a crack ran along the horse's underside—evidence of having been loved—the little horse was clearly well crafted. "It's beautiful."

"Thank you."

At first she thought he hadn't quite understood her remark. Then, catching the subtle tilt to his smile, she gasped. "You made it?"

He nodded. "I like painting and, er, carpentry—that is the word?"

"Yes."

"I'm making a place for books now."

"A bookshelf?"

He nodded. "Carving flowers and vines into the edging. Then I will paint it."

"If it's anything like this horse, I imagine it will be marvelous."

He shrugged and looked as if he would have replied, if a large group hadn't entered.

Her students, wide-eyed girls with their hair in braids and coronets and boys with cropped hair and fidgety fingers. Most were accompanied by parents. *Time to make a good first impression.* Mary opened her arms in greeting. "Good morning. Välkommen."

As if in response to her prayers for help, Kristofer assisted with introductions and translated ages for her so she could divide the children into groups. As she placed them around the table and at extra chairs brought in from the parlor, she made a list of their names and ages. *My, what a spread.* She placed the six-year-olds closest to her own chair, hoping her proximity would provide them extra reassurance. Then there were the oldest children, whom she placed toward the back. One of the three fifteen-year-olds was as tall as Kristofer. The lad might not attend the regular schoolhouse come spring in order to work on his parents' farm.

Each child looked at her with curiosity, except that tall boy, Oscar Blom. He stared around the kitchen as if it looked far different from his own. Perhaps it did. His gaze fixed most often on the shelf of heirlooms that her grandmother had brought from England: china teacups with pretty pink roses on them as well as porcelain figurines painted in pastels—a shepherdess, a goose girl, and a milkmaid. When Father had suggested Mother display them in the parlor, she'd insisted she liked looking at them too much to remove them from the kitchen, where she spent most of her time.

She'd teased, but she did spend a lot of time here. They all did. They rarely used the parlor except when they entertained company—and while Mary taught school, her parents would make themselves comfortable there. But the parlor had its own special items on display, heirlooms and treasures and such.

Many of the immigrants came to America with few possessions. Did Oscar's mother have something like these figurines in his own home, or had they had to leave something like them behind?

At last Mary finished her roll sheet, and it was time to begin. A thrill shot through her, part intimidation, part excitement. "Say goodbye to your parents." She waved to demonstrate what she meant, but it seemed the students knew what a goodbye was.

While the parents took their leave, Mother and Father poured cups of coffee and slipped from the room. Kristofer and Hjalmar followed, although Kristofer paused in the threshold.

Catching his eye, she smiled. "Thank you."

"It is I who thanks you, *lärarinna.* Teacher."

What a pretty word it was, and how sweet he was to say it. Their gazes held until she realized how overlong she'd looked at him, and she held up her chalk and slate. "This morning we shall work on our letters." She drew a neat capital letter *A* on her slate. "This is the first letter of the alphabet: *A.* Say it with me," she said, gesturing that they should repeat with her. "A."

He waved and slipped out.

Goodness, she must be nervous, because her heart was still thumping madly. Almost as if it wanted to follow Kristofer out of the kitchen.

Hjalmar waited on the front porch, hands shoved in the pockets of his dark gray coat. Little good that did to protect his hands from the cold: both pockets had holes in the bottoms. The coat, like Kristofer's, bore signs of repeated mending: a button not quite in line with the others, a patch in a slightly off shade beneath the arm, and brighter colored stitches here and there. "Ready?"

"Not quite." Kristofer paused at the threshold, propping the front door open with his hip.

"Why? The girls are fine. You saw Agata, eager as a pup. Britta will come around too."

He prayed so. "It's not the girls. I want to speak to Clyde Clarence for a minute. Want to come?"

"Nej. I couldn't understand a thing you two were talking about anyway."

"You would if you'd learn English."

Hjalmar grunted at the old argument. "No need. We don't need it to farm."

"What about to shop? Or to court an American girl, eh?"

"Is that why you want to learn so badly?"

"Of course not. That's the last thing on my mind. But you ought to try."

"Too much work. But you? You pick up language like a dog collects fleas. No effort at all."

Kristofer couldn't argue. He had learned English quickly, although reading it was proving to be a greater challenge. Still, Hjalmar resisted any effort to try.

It wasn't worth arguing further. "Be right back."

Clyde sat in the parlor by the window, a farm almanac in one hand and a cup of coffee in the other. His gray brows rose when Kristofer knocked on the doorjamb. "Come in, please."

Kristofer indicated that Clyde shouldn't get up. "I wanted to ask you your opinion on something. I wish to purchase hogs, and I am told a man named Richard Fuller is selling. They any good?"

From the kitchen down the hall came a chorus of "See." Mary made an encouraging noise. "*C* is for coin, like this one, and cow. Here's a cow in this picture."

"*Ko*," a young voice exclaimed, sounding a lot like his eager Agata. It was impossible not to smile.

"Fuller's a decent fellow." Clyde set down his coffee. "I wouldn't say his pigs would win any prizes, mind you, but he won't overcharge you."

"*Tack*—thank you. I will visit him then."

"If you're willing to wait though, my best sow will be farrowing sometime in the next few weeks. Her piglets are the finest I've had in all my years. I'd be more'n happy to offer you first pick for a fair price."

Even if he bought a full-grown hog from Fuller, Kristofer was more than interested in increasing his stock by adding younger ones too. "I would like that, yes. Thank you."

"Neighbors helping neighbors, I always say."

The children laughed at something. Kristofer listened to the sweet sound for a moment. "Your daughter is good with them."

"She is. She's made pen-and-inks to illustrate the letters of the alphabet and brought in a few other things to help. Listen to that."

Mary was talking about the letter *D*. "Dog. Doll. Dish." There was the clatter of a plate.

How clever to use things familiar to the children to teach them letters. The memory of his wife, Tilda, teaching the girls swirled in his head. *"Äpple begins with A."* Mary was as kind and patient as Tilda had been.

"She is a smart lady." And he could stand here all morning, learning with the children, but he'd kept Clyde long enough and Hjalmar was out in the cold, waiting. "See you at noon."

"One last thing." Clyde stood and walked him to the door. "Have you heard about the burglaries happening around these parts?"

"Some." He'd seen the poster at the dry goods store, but the illustration revealed nothing of the suspect's face but beady eyes. A hat and scarf obscured the rest of his face.

"Burglar breaks into houses during daylight hours when nobody's home. Well, they're saying it's a Swedish fellow."

Kristofer's neck prickled. "Why is that?"

"A few weeks back, the baker came home from a full day of work. He entered the kitchen door as the burglar was about to exit it. They almost collided, and both of them were startled—and the burglar barked something the baker said sounded Swedish before he bolted outta there. The baker's the only one who's had a good gander at him, and he described him for that wanted poster. Anyway, I know he might not have spoken in Swedish, and even if he did, it's unlikely you'd know who this fellow is, but if you hear anything, let Sheriff Miles know, will you?"

"Of course." Kristofer hadn't heard that the robber might be Swedish. The gossip might not be true, but then again. . .

It set a sour taste in his mouth.

Hjalmar grunted after Kristofer relayed the message on the way home. "I don't like it."

"Me neither. If it's a fellow Swede—"

"Don't tell me you believe that nonsense." Hjalmar shifted on the wagon seat. "They're making up lies about us."

"Why would the baker make up lies?"

"Because we're outsiders. They don't want the competition we bring."

"I see no evidence of that. We have good neighbors. Mary is teaching the children. This past week, Clyde has given me helpful hints for improving the land."

"Good land that isn't yielding as much as we'd hoped."

"Success takes time, and we knew that when we chose to come here. But we did get a decent yield for our first year, you must admit. We aren't starving this winter. Remember what it was like two, three years ago. Even last year."

The girls' concave bellies and hollow cheeks. Slaughtering their milk cows. Eating bread made of flour and tree bark. Tilda, bone thin, and then—

He gulped cold, clear air, Kansas air, banishing his horrifying memories. "This is *framtidslandet.*" The land of the future. "This is our life, Hjalmar."

"Ja, I know. But I'd hoped we'd have more already. Like horses that aren't so long in the tooth." He gestured at the pair of workhorses pulling their wagon home. "A thicker mattress for my weary bones. A new coat."

Kristofer understood. Visiting a fully furnished home like the Clarences' reminded him anew that they'd left a great deal behind to start over in America, and it would be awhile before they could afford to keep the house as well appointed as they wished. It took time for Kristofer to produce furnishings and trim them in the decoratively painted *kurbits* style.

Nor could they have as many things as he'd like. He and Hjalmar decided to give the girls new clothes first, but there hadn't been much money left over for the men to replenish their wardrobes. A few shirts and socks, sure, but nothing else. And while his own coat was worn, Hjalmar's gray one was almost threadbare.

"New things will come in time. Patience, Brother."

Hjalmar, never patient, snorted like one of the horses. "Ja, I hear you. But if that robber fellow really is Swedish, well, you can't blame a man for being tempted to steal when his belly's empty. Can you, Kristofer?"

Kristofer fixed his gaze on the road ahead. "We decided when we left Sweden, remember? Patience."

Despite his instruction to his brother, Kristofer struggled to focus on his tasks for the remainder of the morning. Polishing tack, inspecting the cornfields, or setting out leftover beef and corn bread for lunch—no matter the undertaking, his thoughts drifted to the makeshift school.

And Mary, who looked so eager and pretty this morning as she welcomed her students. Whose smile for him was radiant.

In the end, the tack wasn't polished well, nor could he remember much about his walk through the fields. The meat and bread were left on the counter when he glanced at the clock and realized how close it was to noon.

He hitched the wagon again.

Hjalmar met him on the drive. "I'll come along."

"Hop up."

After the short drive to the Clarence home, however, Hjalmar didn't get down from the wagon. "I'll wait."

"Suit yourself." Welcomed at the front door by Mary's mother, Lorena, a shorter, plumper version of her slender daughter, he followed the sound of singing to the kitchen. All the children sang except for Oscar Blom, who stared out the window. But he was fifteen, wasn't he? Boys that age could be easily embarrassed, or maybe he didn't enjoy singing.

Mary saw Kristofer and grinned while she sang. "Double-u, ex, wye, and zee. Next time won't you sing with me?"

"Pappa!" Agata shouted. He placed a shushing finger over his grin.

"Song more?" Elna Holmgren, one of the younger students, turned her gray eyes to Mary.

"Yes," Torkil, her twin brother, agreed.

"Nej." Oscar Blom flopped back in his chair.

"English, please, Oscar. You remember the word."

He glowered, but one of the littler children answered "no" for him.

"In any event," Mary said, ignoring Oscar's defiant posture, "it is time to go home for the day." She gestured to a small clock she'd set on the table beside her, perhaps for a lesson on time or numbers. Aside from the clock, the table was laden with slates and numerous pictures she'd drawn on paper. She'd tacked other drawings to the curtains too—pen-and-inks of animals and buildings, with large and small letters in the pages' corners.

Kristofer itched to study them.

"Remember your alphabet sheets. See you tomorrow." Mary's voice rose over the noise of chairs scraping back and children's chatter.

Britta rushed to him, holding up her little dalahäst. "Pappa. *H* is for horse."

He repeated the English. "Well done, älskling."

Manipulated by Britta, the horse poked at his elbow, over and over. He glanced down. "Do you want me to take the horse?"

Britta looked up. "No. She's eating the hay."

Kristofer's stomach dropped. There was hay stuck into his coat sleeve? It had probably been there since he worked in the barn this morning. Mary hadn't seen it, had she?

He tugged it from his sleeve and shoved it into his pocket.

"Pappa, Lilja's still hungry." Britta dropped her horse into the pocket with the hay.

Mary approached him with a grin. "Hello."

"How was it?"

"We had a good first day, I think. Well, most of us." Her gaze followed Oscar out of the kitchen. Though he was fifteen, he was tall and solidly built, his frame more like a grown man's than that of the other boys his age. Oscar's siblings, Sven and Lovisa, both bid Mary a cheerful farewell though, before hurrying to catch up to Oscar, who'd gone a far pace on his long legs.

"Was he trouble?"

"Not at all."

He didn't quite believe her. Oscar was a handful. Ensuring his daughters were out of earshot, he leaned forward. "His *moder* died on the crossing. Tripped on the ship deck and hit the back of her head. His older sister, Ebba, takes care of the house, but the family still struggles over the loss. Especially Oscar, I think. I have never seen him smile."

"How sad. Thank you for telling me. The poor boy's grieving and probably had first-day nerves too. Oh." She realized he didn't know a word. "Nerves? Anxiety. Concern."

He nodded. "Thank you for teaching me."

"I'm happy to teach you. I can do more if you'd like to practice reading."

"I'd like." Little matter that he was thirty—he'd gladly go back to school if it meant he could read English. Spending additional time with her held great appeal too.

Someone tugged at his coat hem. "Pappa, I'm hungry."

"Soon, älskling. We mustn't be rude."

"What is älskling?" Mary asked.

"A name for someone you love." He didn't know how to explain further.

"I like it," she said. "Come after supper tomorrow? The girls may come as well. In the meantime, they can teach you the ABC song."

Kristofer was still grinning when he returned to the wagon. Hjalmar eyed him askance. "What are you smiling about?"

"I'm glad the girls are learning."

"From the pretty teacher?" he whispered.

"Hjalmar—"

"It's all right if you like her, *Bror*. Tilda's been gone almost two years now. She'd want you happy. In any case, I've decided to go to town. I'll walk."

A brisk wind ruffled Hjalmar's hair. Kristofer frowned. "Where's your scarf?"

"Still in the basket. I haven't mended it yet."

"It's been three weeks, waiting for you to sew up that tear. Here, borrow this again." Kristofer loosened his red scarf from his neck and offered it to his brother. The chill snaked down his spine, but he'd be home soon. "What are you doing in town?"

His neck and throat now better bundled, Hjalmar started walking backward toward town. "Visiting."

"Who?"

Hjalmar grinned and kept walking.

His brother had a secret. Kristofer couldn't blame him for keeping it to himself. Kristofer didn't want to share the thing heaviest on his mind these days, either: his burgeoning interest in the pretty schoolteacher.

Chapter 4

The next night, Mary responded to the gentle rap at the front door at half past six. Right on time. She patted the bun at her nape and hurried to the front door. "Kristofer, come in. Where are the girls?"

"They stayed home with Hjalmar to play with Smulan."

"Smulan?" Mary held out her hands for his coat, scarf, and hat. As she hung them on a peg near the back door, she couldn't help but once again notice the frayed cuffs of his coat. Or the way the fresh-air-and-wood-smoke scent of him clung to his red woolen scarf. Had his wife knitted it for him?

"The barn *katt*. Smulan means. . ." He broke off as if searching for the word. Then he laid his calloused finger atop the table, beside a remnant of the Clarences' cleared-away supper. "This."

"Crumb?" She laughed and whisked it away with her hand.

"Crumb."

"Good thing I missed it when I wiped the table then, since it provided us an illustration to learn English." She took a seat and gestured for him to sit beside her.

"You're clever, using everyday things to teach."

Sitting this close to him did strange things to her pulse. "Using rubbish like crumbs?"

He chuckled. "Yes, if it works. Like your pictures."

She followed his gaze to the blue-flowered curtains, where her pen-and-inks were still pinned up for the children. "People learn in different ways. Some can hear things and learn it—like you, I expect. You learned English quickly by hearing others speak it. Others need to write things down in order to grasp them, and some learn best by seeing things. But everyone needs to look at the alphabet to learn it, of course, so that's why I made the illustrations."

"They're very good. You made them all yourself? This fast?" He rose and touched the edge of one of the papers: *F* for flower. "So detailed."

"I have a confession. I've been working on these every day since Christmas, when I promised my nephews, Will and Tom, I'd create a book for them. They're learning the alphabet too."

"They are blessed to have such a talented aunt." He resumed his seat, his warm, smiling eyes heating her to the core.

She had to lower her gaze. "Yes, well, I'm blessed to have them. I wish they didn't live so far away. My brother, Alva, married my best friend, Flossie, and while I love that she's an official part of the family, I've missed her since they married and moved to Kansas City. Alva runs a stationer shop. That's where all of this paper came from."

"These pictures are a work of love for them. You make it easy and meaningful for the children."

"I'll try to make it easy for you too." She took out a piece of paper. "I thought we'd study the alphabet tonight. I've written out the letters, and I'll tell you how to pronounce them. You can write down how you'd spell them in Swedish so you'll remember when you're studying them."

"No ABC song?"

"Not for you, unless you want to sing it." Her brow lifted in a challenge.

"Ah no." He laughed. "No one wants to hear me sing."

He could paint and work with wood and smile like a starburst, but apparently there was one thing he couldn't do well. She smiled and slid the paper toward him. "Then we'll do it this way, without singing. This is the capital of each letter—the capital is used at the beginning of a sentence, for proper nouns like our names, cities, things like that. This is the lower case of each letter beside it. Now here's your pencil. The first letter is pronounced—"

The back door squealed on its hinges, and Father and Mother entered the kitchen, bundled against the cold. Kristofer hopped to his feet to shake hands. "Thank you for allowing me to come tonight."

"Of course." Mother hung her coat on the peg. "We took a short walk to enjoy the night sky. Where are the girls?"

"Playing with the barn katt while Hjalmar sees to evening chores."

"Ah. Maybe they'd like to come play with the piglets once they arrive. Clyde tells me you're going to take one or two?"

"Yes. I look forward to it."

Father took his time hanging up his coat, his gaze lingering on Kristofer's coat hanging on the peg. "When I was in town today, I heard the burglar struck yet again yesterday afternoon."

"That's terrible news." A shiver ran up Mary's spine. "Who was robbed?"

"The Stanleys."

"Edmund and Clarice?" Mary gasped.

"Word is, Clarice was coming home from shopping when she saw the burglar leaving by her back door. He didn't speak this time, but Clarice got a good look at him."

"He didn't hurt her?" Kristofer leaned forward.

"No, thank the good Lord, or we'd be having a different discussion. No, the feller locked eyes with her for a second and then *ffsht*." Father brushed his hands together, gesturing something moving fast. "He took coins and toys. A ball, I think, and a spinning top that was a favorite of the Stanleys' littlest boy. Nothing too valuable, but it doesn't matter. We can't have thieving going on in Plenty."

"I agree." Kristofer sat back. "Did she recognize the burglar?"

Father's head shook. "Clarice saw his eyes but not much else of his face. He was wearin' a, well, a red scarf like Kristofer's here."

Mary dropped her pencil. "I don't like what you're implying."

Poor Kristofer didn't like it either. A muscle worked in his square jaw.

"I'm sure other men have red scarves, Clyde," Mother said.

Father shook his head. "I know and I'm sorry, but your name came up, Kristofer. You're the only fellow around here who wears a bright red scarf."

"Who?" Mary clutched her pencil. "Who said such a thing?"

Father's cheeks pinked. "Edmund Stanley."

Mary almost groaned. "Father."

"You know better than to listen to a thing that man says, Clyde." Mother set down her coffee cup. "I can't say any more about that man without spewing something uncharitable."

Kristofer glowered. "I did not steal from the banker. I was at home with my daughters yesterday afternoon."

"Of course you were." Mary's fingers and feet grew hot. "Edmund said it because he doesn't like what we did at the bank."

Mother glared at Father, who cleared his throat. "Just thought you should know there's gossip out there."

"It's not gossip. It's slander in retaliation for me writing to the state superintendent." Mary took a deep breath. "Edmund has gone too far."

"It's probably a case of mistaken identity, Mary," Father said. "Unfortunate, but I'm sure it wasn't meant as retribution."

Mary disagreed, but it wasn't worth arguing with Father in front of Kristofer. Mother must have felt the same way, because she retrieved her cup and gestured to her husband. "Come on into the parlor, Clyde, and let them study."

The light mood had fled the room the moment Father shared that ridiculous news. Mary touched Kristofer's forearm. "I'm sorry."

Kristofer stared down at her hand. "I don't like people thinking I'm a thief."

"They don't think that. *I* don't think it. I know you'd never do anything like that." Her words didn't seem to help ease the sad creases around his blue eyes. "Kristofer, you're within your rights to demand Edmund stop spreading such stories."

"I wasn't thinking of that." He let out a puff of breath. "I was thinking of Sweden."

And whatever it was, it wasn't good. Beneath her hand, his forearm grew rigid as a board.

What had he done, saying that aloud? Inviting conversation about things best left ignored?

Kristofer's fingers twitched. *Don't think about what happened in Dalarna. No going back.*

Mary's eyes narrowed. "Leaving your homeland must have been a difficult decision. Family. Land. Your wife."

"It was." Leaving her grave that last time had been the hardest thing he'd ever done, but all he needed to do now was look at the girls' rounder cheeks and know Tilda would have been glad they were here. "Sweden was—is—beautiful, with birch groves and plum trees and cold, clear streams. I miss the trees most of all."

"It sounds lovely."

"It was until the drought."

"You must have suffered terribly."

A painful lump settled in his throat. Swallowing down the pain, he forced his thoughts onto the future. The present. His hand landed atop Mary's. "You are a gentle soul. And as you see, we are well now. America is our new home. I can feed my children. Gud has blessed us."

They both looked down at their hands and at the same moment pulled away. Her hand fell to her lap. "Sometimes I'm so selfish—I think I've undergone difficulty, but I haven't, not really. Not compared to others like you."

"You cannot compare troubles." He picked up the pencil. "They come to all of us in different ways."

"But you responded to your trials with faith. I haven't."

No, he hadn't. But he couldn't tell her. She'd lose all respect for him.

"My, look at the time. We'd better get to the letters, or I fear you'll go home having learned nothing but what a goose I am," she said, shifting the pages around.

He watched her busy hands. "What does that mean, *goose*?"

"It's a bird."

"I know that, but I do not know why you are one."

Her lips twitched. "It's an expression that means I'm a silly person."

"Geese are not silly. They are—what is the word? They fight."

"Aggressive. Loud." She laughed.

"Yes, but they fight to protect their young. They are loyal birds. Nurturing. Huh, maybe you are a goose after all. A protector goose."

"Fighting for the children against Edmund Stanley?"

"Exactly like that."

"There have been a few times I've wanted to chase him down the road like an angry goose, to be sure." She rolled her eyes. "Are you a goose, Kristofer? No, more like a bear, I think. Or a horse."

"Big and—" He didn't know the word, so he puffed out his cheeks and lifted his arms.

"Fat?" She was giggling now, and he loved the lilting sound.

"Fat," he mock-scolded. "You think I am fat."

"I think you are tall."

"Like a horse. Or a fat bear."

"More like a horse, definitely." She wasn't giggling anymore, but her smile was wide. "You possess a quiet strength, Kristofer. You work hard, you are gentle with your children, and you are resilient. Oh yes, a horse."

He wanted to prolong the teasing, but he lost the ability to gather his wits. Sitting beside her, her smiling face so close to his, he couldn't summon anything intelligent or funny or remotely interesting to say. The air had thickened with something he couldn't name, something that buzzed and lulled him at the same time.

His gaze fell to her lips.

Chastising the direction of his thoughts, Kristofer shoved his gaze to focus down at his page. *A, B, C.* There, that helped his brain regain some clarity. "A workhorse though, eh? Not a fast horse."

"Racehorse?" She shifted. "Maybe. But then again, I'm a goose, not something regal like a swan."

"Better than a chicken."

She burst into laughter again. "Indeed. Now then, perhaps we should return to the alphabet. Where were we?"

"Umm, we made progress. We have come to. . . *A*."

They burst into laughter.

With Mary's help, he wrote out the pronunciation of each letter and crafted a spelling sheet of basic words he'd be sure to encounter often in his reading: *the*, *and*, *but*, and so forth. Mary had the good sense to include Bible words too, like *God*, *Jesus*, *Christ*, *faith*, *trust*, and *love*. That would be of tremendous help during his devotional times.

Footsteps on the plank floor drew their gazes. Clyde ambled into the kitchen. "Sounds too fun in here for schooling." He made a point of looking at the clock.

"It's late. I'm sorry." Kristofer gathered up his pages and hopped to his feet.

"Not that late." Mary rose with him. "The girls go to bed at eight? You have plenty of time to tuck them in."

Kristofer nodded and wrapped his scarf about his neck. Then he took his coat from the peg, laid it over his arm while he put on his hat, and—ouch. Something hard hit his foot.

Mary rushed over and picked the object up off the floor, something bright red with distinctive white and green ornamentation. "Is that Britta's horse?"

"Lilja, yes. She sent it with me tonight." He took the horse from Mary's warm fingers. "Yesterday she tucked her there, and she 'fell asleep.' She said she liked it, and she wanted to learn the letters with me tonight. It might sound silly. Not silly as a goose of course."

She burst into laughter, as he'd hoped. "Children have wonderful imaginations. And Lilja is special to her."

"The dalahäst is common in Sweden, but she took a liking to this one. She named it after a flower and has set her by her bed every night since then." He slipped the horse back into his pocket and donned his coat.

"She'll be glad to get her back by bed, I expect," Clyde noted. It almost sounded like he was rushing Kristofer home now. Did he resent Kristofer being here? He'd been so friendly up until tonight. Did he honestly think Kristofer was a burglar?

No—Kristofer shouldn't assume the worst. Perhaps the man was simply tired and ready to have his home to himself after a long day. "Thank you, sir. And you, Mary, for your time. Good night."

"There's some snow." Mary walked him out the door onto the cold porch. "Be safe."

"I will. It's only a little dusting." He struck a match to light his lantern, sending a waft of sulfur around them. The wick caught, and the lantern's warm glow settled over her, giving her hair a reddish cast and illuminating her sharp cheekbones.

His breath stuck at her beauty.

He managed to mangle another "Good night." Only then did she step back into the house and shut the door.

Hjalmar had a point about Kristofer developing feelings for the schoolteacher. The way his pulse pounded, something was going on in his heart.

Kristofer was not looking for love. He had other things to occupy him: his daughters, his land, and now this ridiculous suggestion that he might be robbing nearby homes.

Nevertheless, there was something wrong with the men in this town, not to have noticed what a fine woman Mary was. Why had no one married her yet?

Then again, Kristofer was grateful none of them had. The very idea of her courting another stabbed him in the side with a pain that even he had to admit was nothing other than jealousy.

Chapter 5

The week passed in a blur of busyness for Mary as she spent each morning teaching and each afternoon planning lessons. Then most evenings after supper, Kristofer called—eager and smiling, but always with the girls now. They served as a buffer of sorts, limiting Mary and Kristofer's conversation to the alphabet and words and spelling, so there was no more talk of geese or horses or of Edmund Stanley implying Kristofer was a thief, for that matter.

Perhaps the latter was because there was nothing new to say on the subject, and the gossip dried up like an old apple.

Nevertheless, Father's attitude toward Kristofer had changed since that first night of tutoring. Every quarter hour, he slipped into the kitchen with the excuse of needing more coffee. Surely he didn't believe Edmund. Did he expect Kristofer to nip something whilst they studied? Clear out the china or filch the figurines? Yet when she asked him about it last night after the Nilssons left for home, Father denied he was behaving unusually. "Can't a man need coffee once in a while?"

"Every fifteen minutes?" she'd countered.

Mother smiled. "Bear with your father, dear."

It made no sense.

She chose to focus instead on teaching. She offered Kristofer an almanac, and they discussed words about farming, weather, and such.

Kristofer was a quick learner. And his smile warmed her on a winter's eve better than the stove.

But no matter how many times their gazes met over their books and slates, he didn't look at her mouth again—not the way he had that first night.

She hadn't forgotten it. Even now, late on a Tuesday morning as Mary picked up a stick of chalk to write *Favorite Toys* on her slate, her lips burned as if she could feel Kristofer's kiss.

Goodness, this was folly. She knew better than to let her imagination scurry away from her like this. She was practically thirty, and as Edmund had reminded her a few years ago, far too sensible acting to attract a man and far too insensible to do anything about it.

Did Kristofer think of her that way? As a schoolmarm and nothing else? She pushed down so hard on the chalk that it snapped in two.

"Miss Clarence?" Little Tyra Eklund's eyes were wide.

"Oops, I pressed too hard." She motioned what she'd done to illustrate her words. It was probably a good thing Kristofer and the girls wouldn't be here to study tonight. Her parents had a church meeting, and it wasn't proper for Mary to entertain the Nilssons alone.

She should use the time to talk herself out of this inane infatuation she was forming for Kristofer.

As if brushing away her fascination as well as chalk dust, Mary swiped her hands. "Boys and girls, I have an assignment for you tonight."

"Homework?" Anders Gustavsson's shoulders slumped.

"Homework. I'd like you to bring your favorite toy tomorrow. *Leksack*, toy. A *docka*—a doll, a top, any toy. Yes, Britta, you may bring Lilja, even though she is here every day with you. Oscar, put all four of the chair legs down on the floor, please." His rocking was distracting, not to mention discourteous, ill-suited when visiting another's home or attending school. And this was both.

He ignored her of course, but she couldn't swear it was on purpose. He was learning the language after all, although she'd taught the children half the words she'd used. "Oscar, chair. Floor. Please."

The tall boy didn't look at her but shoved a lank tendril of his dark-blond hair from his brow and grinned.

She had enough experience with smug expressions on boys to know he understood. She strode behind him. "Oscar, I do not wish to push the chair and hurt you, but I will if you do not stop." Even if she could push it—he outweighed her by at least fifty pounds. "You could fall backward and hurt yourself or another—"

He turned to Klas Ivarsson and prattled in rapid Swedish. Klas muttered something back, probably a warning to put down his chair, judging by his anxious look at Mary.

"Oscar." Her voice was firmer now. Louder. Her blood pumped hard and fast in her ears.

He kept going, louder too, with his story.

"Oscar," his brother Sven warned.

"It's all right, Sven—"

Oscar shoved his chair backward. Into her. Oh, but it hurt. Clutching the pain in her stomach and side where the chair hit her, she leveled a glare at him. "You will stay after school. I know you understand me."

Everyone else did. The room was silent as falling snow.

"Now, we were discussing toys." Mary's tone was not as light as it should be, considering the topic, but her midsection hurt like—like she'd been struck with a heavy chair. "Bring something small with you, and we will write about it."

The children looked pleased by the assignment, while sliding glances at Oscar at the same time. Mary rang the little bell her parents had given her. "Class dismissed, except for you, Oscar."

He didn't leave with the others, which was a good start. Once the kitchen had emptied, Mary pulled out the chair beside his, sat, and rested her hands on her knees. "Oscar, we have a problem. I see you do not enjoy school. Your work is shoddy if you do it at all. You speak to others while I am speaking, which is discourteous. What is the matter?"

He met her gaze squarely then, his blue eyes the color of a lake in summer—but there was nothing warm in his expression. "No English."

"That's right. That's why we're here, to learn English."

"No English." He pointed at himself and snarled, "No."

Ah. So he'd meant he *refused* to learn English. "You don't wish to learn?"

He turned away and folded his arms.

Mary rubbed her forehead. He might not be able to comprehend all of her words, but she had to say something. *God, let something translate well to him.* "I understand you have endured some difficulties, Oscar. Coming to America must be a frightening change, and with the loss of your mother, you have suffered greatly. I wish to help you."

Meeting her gaze, he rocked back on his chair as he'd done when she'd scolded him. It was an act of sheer defiance.

"Mary?" Kristofer's voice drew her attention. He stood in the threshold, his stance protective. The girls peeked around him, eyes wide. "Agata told me there is a problem. Are you hurt?"

The pain was fading. She shook her head. "He is refusing to learn English."

Nodding, Kristofer asked the girls to wait outside. Britta clung to him, and he whispered softly to her. She slipped her horse, Lilja, into his coat pocket and dashed out. Kristofer entered and spoke to Oscar, their conversation one-sided for a full minute as Oscar sat glum and tight-jawed.

Oscar shoved his chair back and stood toe to toe with Kristofer, almost yelling. He was not the least bit intimidated by his elder. In fact, he laughed before stomping out of the kitchen.

"Sorry." Kristofer rubbed his forehead. "I didn't help matters."

"What did he say to you?"

He looked out the window, where the girls chased one another on the lawn's dead grass. "It doesn't matter."

"It does to me."

Kristofer raked a hand through his thick hair. "He said I shouldn't talk, because my own brother doesn't think it's important to learn English. Nor does he have to listen to me, because I'm a thief. Everyone says so." He tugged at his scarf and shrugged.

"That ridiculous bit of gossip is still going around? I'd hoped that no one believed that nonsense, much less repeated it."

"I chose to ignore it."

"But now?" Something had changed.

"The bank doesn't close for lunch until one. I think it's time I speak to Edmund Stanley myself."

"Not without me, you don't." Mary rushed to gather her coat.

Kristofer drove into town, slowing the horses as they approached the bank. Although Mary had grabbed her coat and the blåklocka bonnet quickly, they hadn't left immediately. First they'd had to inform her mother of their plans, and Lorena insisted the girls stay for a lunch of the savory-smelling soup simmering on the stove. He'd appreciated Lorena's gesture, relieved the girls wouldn't have to witness this confrontation, civil as Kristofer hoped it would be.

He drew the horses to a halt.

"Kristofer." Mary's gloved hand was soft on his coat sleeve, but he felt the touch to his bones. "Do you want me to wait out here? I inserted myself in this without asking you. I'm sorry, and I won't go in with you if you don't want me to."

"I want you to." He appreciated her support, but more than that, he wanted to prolong his time with her. He couldn't exactly tell her that though, so instead he decided to tease. "Stanley may use fancy words I don't know. I'll need you to translate."

She smiled, as he'd hoped. "I doubt you shall need that today, Kristofer, as well as your English is coming along. But I will be glad to be of assistance if necessary."

She removed her hand from his arm, and he hopped down. Before he could stride around the wagon and assist her onto the boardwalk, however, she'd clambered down herself.

"Always in a hurry," he teased.

"Am I?" Her eyes widened. Then narrowed. "Clarice, how good it is to see you."

A spare woman with blond tendrils escaping a deep green bonnet halted outside the bank. Her dainty features blanched with apprehension. "Mary."

Ah, so she was Stanley's wife. Mary seemed to have no quarrel with this woman, however. "Are you visiting Edmund?"

"I have his lunch." Darting glances at Kristofer, Clarice lifted a small basket. "Do you have business with him?"

"Yes, with both of you, now that you're here."

Kristofer held the door open. Clarice glanced at him as she passed him inside, her eyes curious, but at least she didn't bear the expression of a woman who was certain she was in the presence of the man who had robbed her house. *Thank You for that, Gud.*

Stanley stood at the oak counter of his otherwise empty bank, pen in hand. His head lifted and he broke into a wide smile for his wife, but the smile soured when he spied Kristofer and Mary. "What do you two want?"

"I want you to know I did not rob your house." Kristofer removed his hat. "And ask you to stop saying I did."

"I never said you did, per se." But Edmund beckoned Clarice around the counter, as if to protect her. She obeyed, but in no great hurry.

"You said enough."

Stanley's chest puffed out. "You cannot possibly know what I have said outside of your hearing, Mr. Nilsson."

Mary tutted. "Clarice, is this the man you saw?" She gestured at Kristofer.

"Now wait a minute." Edmund shoved his wife behind him. "Leave my wife out of it, and frankly, Mary, you shouldn't be involved either. This is none of your affair."

"Justice is my affair, Edmund."

Kristofer loved the way she held her head high.

Stanley seemed less impressed. "If you mean to intimidate my wife like this, I'll summon the sheriff."

Kristofer held up his hands in a gesture of peace. "No. I only wish to tell you I was with my children that day you were robbed. I do not even know where you live, sir. I would not—did not—visit your house."

"No, you didn't." Clarice stepped around her husband and set down the basket. "Your eyes are different. His were hard, cold. And the build isn't quite right either. But he's tall like you, and the scarf is identical. Such a vibrant hue. It must be from the same skein of yarn."

"There. Thank you, Clarice." Mary nodded, the matter clearly settled in her mind.

But Kristofer didn't feel much relief. Oh, Clarice was right. Anyone could have a red scarf. But Kristofer's scarf was made three years ago by Tilda. In Sweden. This particular yarn was not from Kansas.

His gut clenched tight.

Nevertheless, he nodded. "My thanks, ma'am. And I'll ask you to spread no more talk about me stealing, Mr. Stanley. I want to live in peace with my neighbors."

The banker squared his shoulders. "I've nothing to apologize for."

Kristofer forgave him anyway. "You want to keep your family safe. I understand that. But accusing me won't catch the real thief."

"Well." Stanley apparently couldn't think of anything more articulate to say.

"Before we go," Mary said. "As superintendent, you should know the children are learning English quickly. Your new teacher will be delighted to have them as students, and Clarice, a few of them are the same ages as your boys. Perhaps they'll be friends. Good day."

Mary allowed Kristofer to assist her into the wagon, grinning at him all the while. "That went well, didn't it? He should be of no bother to you anymore."

"Will he bother you?"

"What do you mean?"

"Edmund hurt you. Not just by giving your job to his cousin." Kristofer turned the horses to the road toward her house. "There is something more between you."

She snorted. "I assure you, I feel nothing romantic for that man."

"But you did once. I can tell—the way Clarice looked pickled."

"Pickled?"

"Like Smulan when another katt comes by the barn. Pickled.

Isn't that the word?"

"Oh, *prickly*, as in uncomfortable? Territorial? That's the word I think you want." She sighed, her breath swirling in the cold air. "And you're right about my having feelings for Edmund. Once. Long ago. We were young and almost engaged. He had a better disposition back then, of course."

"Of course." He grinned.

"But one Sunday after services, we had a pie auction. Do you know what that is?"

At his shake of the head, she took a deep breath. "Women of the church bake pies. The men bid money on them, and the highest bid buys the pie. It's to raise money for a cause—missions or new Bibles or something like that."

"I've bid on livestock. Never on a pie."

"Well, one of Edmund's friends bought my pie plant pie. Pie plant is tart as can be, but I added sugar. Far too much." She rolled her eyes. "I'd never baked a pie on my own before, but I was determined to impress Edmund. After his friend spat out my pie, however, no one was impressed, Edmund least of all. He was embarrassed enough to put a stop to our engagement plans the next day."

"He did not marry you because of one pie?"

"I was surprised, to say the least. He'd never minded my cooking abilities before then, but apparently that pie was enough for him to find them lacking. So much so that when he broke off our relationship, he encouraged me to spend more time in the kitchen so I could better develop the skills required to find a husband."

Kristofer's fingers tightened on the reins. "He said that?"

"He did. And within six weeks he'd married Clarice, who, it should be noted, is an excellent cook."

"I'm sorry, Mary." Kristofer's heart ached and pounded fury at the same time. Stanley was a bigger fool than he'd thought.

"I determined to move past it, and I did. I realized I had a calling to teach, so I took education courses and was hired here when the previous schoolmaster left to serve in the war. I was happy again, and I believed I'd found my life's calling. Marriage wouldn't be part of it. After all, since Edmund's friends spread the word about me, the men my age are still under the impression I don't know how to make a pie." Her laugh was hollow. "But before this school year began, he became superintendent and announced it was scandalous our town didn't have a male teacher. He said I should be grateful to have more time at home so I could focus on bettering myself so I could marry before I get any older."

It was all Kristofer could do not to turn the horses around and give Stanley a piece of his mind. Little matter that most of the words would be in Swedish, since he didn't know the English ones for *idiot* and *monster*. His fingers fisted on the reins. "He's wrong."

"You're right." Her gaze fixed on her gloves. "And it's good, Kristofer. It is a good thing I didn't marry a man like that. I'm grateful God spared me that life. So you mustn't pity me."

"Pity you? I admire you." It came out like an argument. *Gud, help me calm down.*

"You shouldn't. Despite my gratitude, I—well, I struggle to forgive him. Especially for taking my job and giving it to an incompetent fellow like his cousin Jarvis."

"I can understand that. I admit I don't want to forgive him much."

"That's been my prayer, to want to forgive him. Maybe it would be easier if he was actually sorry for how he's hurt me and the things he's said to me, but I know that his desire to be forgiven isn't the issue. And if I don't forgive him, it's, well it's like I'm drinking poison every time I think about it. It's corroding me inside, and the hurt grows. I keep dwelling on that pain rather than the blessings before me, not least of which is God's forgiveness of me."

Kristofer's gaze softened over the horizon. That was true, wasn't it? Lack of forgiveness hurt the heart as well as grieved the Lord. Perhaps it was time Kristofer forgave too. Forgave himself for things he'd done in Sweden.

"Easier said than done sometimes." Kristofer turned the wagon up the road to her house. "But I will pray for you to want to forgive. And that I will forgive him too. Right now I'd prefer to say a few choice words to him—in Swedish. I'm glad I don't know how to say them in English, or I'd fall into sin to be sure."

Her laugh was genuine this time. "Thank you for understanding, Kristofer."

"Thank you for trusting me."

Their gazes met before hers skittered away. "Admitting my failings to you has helped. I feel like I can discuss the matter with God again. I feel. . .better."

He felt a little better too, and on the ride home after dropping her off and picking up his daughters, half of him listened to the girls' chatter about making cookies with Lorena while the other half of him pondered his past. . .and his future.

Thank You for the encouragement Mary was to me today. Thank You that she trusted me. Help us both to let go of our past hurts and live in peace with You and one another. And Lord, about what happened in Sweden—

As he pulled into the yard, Hjalmar strode out of the barn, leading Elin, their long-in-the-tooth riding mare. "Home at last. Where have you been?"

"The bank." After the girls ran into the barn to visit the cat, Kristofer explained what had happened after school. "Where are you going?"

"Town. Say, can I borrow your coat now that you're home? My mending isn't holding up." Hjalmar lifted his sleeve, revealing another tear under the arm.

"We'll get you a new one soon. The next purchase after the pigs."

Kristofer shucked his coat. "Why are you going to town, then?"

"To visit my friend."

Such mystery. "Who is. . . ?"

Hjalmar toed his boot into the dirt. "Ebba Blom."

Oscar's elder sister, the one raising the younger siblings now that their mother had died. Hjalmar was interested in her, eh? Kristofer resisted the urge to tease. "See if you can talk to Oscar about his behavior at school."

"What do you mean?"

"For one thing, he refuses to learn English."

"I don't blame him, Brother. We don't need English to farm."

Maybe, but to Kristofer, life was not all about farming. He was settling in a new land with new people, and everything was different now for him and for the girls.

He was even starting to read at a far better pace, thanks to Mary.

Tonight, he'd miss visiting her for tutoring, but with her parents gone for the evening, he wouldn't dare put her in a compromising position. Even with the girls with them, he had no business being in her home without her parents' supervision.

But he would be thinking of her.

Hjalmar returned in time for supper and hung Kristofer's coat on a hook by the front door. Kristofer really should make a better tree for their coats and hats. And get new coats and hats, for that matter. Especially for Hjalmar.

Soon.

Once the girls went to bed and Hjalmar had settled by the fire with a book, Kristopher donned his coat and jogged to the barn, lighting the lamp at his carpentry workspace. Here he felt most himself, a man and his thoughts surrounded by the odors of kerosene and sawdust, hay and beast, the only sounds the animals' shuffling and snorts and the *swish swish* of sandpaper.

Mary was on his mind, as surely as if he had been in her kitchen this evening reading aloud with her. He wanted to do something for her. She wasn't being paid to teach the children, after all.

"You are a fool if you believe you are making this only to repay her," he muttered in Swedish.

Nevertheless, he took his time with the Dala horse he was crafting for her. Something for her to remember him by when she stopped teaching his daughters. Something to let her know she was far more than Edmund Stanley said she was. Something to let her know they were friends.

Even if his heart was pounding so hard when he thought of her that he recognized he wanted them to be more than friends.

Chapter 6

When Oscar strode into the kitchen with his younger siblings the next morning, Mary had to turn her back to hide her surprise. She'd half expected never to see him again after yesterday's confrontation.

She smoothed the folds of her berry-red wool shawl and schooled her expression. Oscar was a child, albeit a huge one, on the cusp of manhood. Nevertheless, he was her student. If he was willing to start afresh today, of course she would too.

"Good morning," she greeted, staring right at him. The other students responded with smiles, but Oscar didn't look up or speak.

A sense of excitement permeated the kitchen as the students arrived clutching toys of various sizes. A top, a few dolls, balls, and a tiny carved wooden flute. Then Kristofer came in with the girls, smiling over their heads at Mary. Her chest grew warm.

Agata dashed to her usual seat, waving a rag doll, but Britta's hands were empty.

This was unusual. "Britta, where is your horse?"

Her face scrunched up, and she pointed at Kristofer's pocket. "Lilja sleeping."

Kristofer slid his hand into his coat pocket. His brows knit, and he checked the other pocket. Using both hands, he searched each pocket again and patted his breast pockets. His look for Mary said it all. No horse.

Britta paled. "Where is Lilja, Pappa?"

"She's not here, älskling. Did you leave her in your room this morning?"

"I never took her out last night. I wanted to be sure she would get here safe today."

"It's true, Pappa," Agata added. "She wanted Lilja cozy in your pocket for school today, so she never took her out last night."

"Lilja." Britta sounded panicked.

Oh dear. Mary withdrew a clean hanky from her sleeve and patted the tears starting to stream down Britta's round cheeks. "Lilja probably fell out of Pappa's pocket when he took his coat off last night, and landed on the floor. She is waiting there now, I expect."

Kristofer's hand cupped Britta's shoulder. "I imagine so. Lilja is having an adventure at home."

He didn't look convinced though. He looked as if he'd have noticed a bright red wooden horse on the floor when he donned his coat. "I will look."

"And bring her back with you?"

"Not until after school, but yes."

"But I need a toy today. Everyone has toys but me." Britta's tears intensified.

Mary tapped Britta's damp nose. "I have an idea. It is something I was making." She hurried to the corner hutch where Mother displayed her heirlooms from England, and reached for a paper set between the teacups and the shepherdess figurine. "This is for your pappa, but I know he won't mind if you borrow it."

It was a pen-and-ink of Britta's little horse—sort of. The foot wasn't damaged, and she was sure she hadn't captured the swirls of decorative paint correctly. But she'd even shaded the horse as if it bore the marks of the whittling knife. It might not be Lilja, but it was a generic Dala horse that she hoped look satisfactory.

Britta's eyes widened. "It's Lilja!"

"It's silly," Mary said to Kristofer. "But I wanted to thank you for helping me yesterday, so I sketched something you made. I hope it reminds you of Dalarna."

"I don't know what to say." Kristofer took the page from Britta, marveling in the artwork. "The detail is fine indeed. You did this yesterday?"

"Last night. I was working on illustrations for my nephews' alphabet book."

He handed the paper back to Britta, who seemed happy with the temporary replacement for Lilja. "You should make copies of your pictures and send them to a publisher."

"You mean a book?" At his nod, she shook her head. "It's only a project for my nephews. I don't think anyone would wish to buy this."

"I would buy it to help us learn English, but also because your illustrations are wonderful. You are talented, Mary." He gestured to where her illustrations were pinned to the curtains. "These could go in frames on walls."

She was blushing, hot to her scalp. "Well you're quite talented yourself, carving the horse in the first place."

Suddenly he looked like a man with a secret, smug and smiling.

"What is it, Kristofer?"

"Nothing. I should go. You have a class to teach, and I have a

Dala horse to find. Ah, Clyde. Good morning."

"Morning, Kristofer." Father nodded, but his lips pulled down. He watched Kristofer until the front door clacked shut.

"Need some coffee, Father?" Mary knew that was not why her father had come to the kitchen. It had everything to do with seeing Kristofer on his way.

"Uh, no. My cup is full. Have a good class."

Why did Father seem to think the worst of Kristofer since Edmund started that ridiculous rumor? Mary had even told her parents at supper last night how Clarice confirmed that the man she'd seen leaving her house was not Kristofer, and despite that, Father's behavior bordered on rudeness.

The mantel clock struck nine. She'd have to speak to Father about it after class. She rang the silver bell and smiled at the class. "Now, let's see these toys. Anders, let's start with yours."

Grinning, the towheaded boy held up a leather ball.

Mary nodded. "Ball. Let's describe the ball, shall we? Its shape is round." She drew a circle on her slate.

Over the next hour, she had the students write down the proper spelling of each toy as it was presented, as well as descriptive words: size, color, shape, texture. She set the older children to writing short paragraphs or stories about their toys.

Oscar, of course, had brought nothing. The other older boys had brought balls, jacks, or in Klas's case, a sketchbook. Oscar's siblings brought items: Sven had a striped top and Lovisa a doll. But Oscar shared nothing, wrote nothing, and said nothing, except to subvert her lessons. Things couldn't continue like this. During class hours, Oscar was distracting at the very least, and at worst, disrespectful. He was certainly disruptive. It was time—past time, perhaps—to speak to his father.

In the meantime, however, she would try yet again to encourage him to participate in class.

"Oscar, what is your favorite pastime? What do you like to do when you are not in school?"

"Play dolls," muttered Greger Ivarsson, to snickers.

"Doubtful, Greger. Oscar, do you like to read?" She held up a book. "Ride a horse?"

"We don't have enough money for a riding horse," Oscar's brother Sven whispered.

"Nor us." Greger shrugged. "But Pappa says soon."

"That's what Pappa always says too. Soon, soon, soon." Agata swung a braid over her shoulder. "*Soon* we get chickens. *Soon* we get more fruit trees. *Soon* he and Uncle Hjalmar will get new coats. Uncle Hjalmar's ripped again, right here." She shoved her hand into her armpit.

Mary ignored the eruptions of giggles and tried to remember Hjalmar's coat. She'd noticed Kristofer's jacket had seen better days, but she'd never noticed Hjalmar's. *Lord, help the Nilssons and all of these families to make ends meet.*

Enough of the giggling. Mary quieted it with a look and then returned her gaze to Oscar. "What about fishing, Oscar? Many men and boys fish, like my father."

"I like to fish," Anders said.

"I fish too." Sven's chest puffed out.

"Do you fish, Oscar?" Mary kept her gaze on the unhappy boy.

Oscar met her gaze at last and blurted something in Swedish.

"He says he's a man and doesn't need a pastime." Ever eager to help, Agata translated.

"Fishing isn't just a pastime. It feeds a family," Mary said.

Agata wasn't finished. "Oscar also says you're a stick and an old maid—"

"Thank you, Agata. I don't need to know the rest."

Mary wasn't wounded by the derogatory term. Nor was she surprised by Oscar's words. The boy was lashing out, inflicting pain on another because he couldn't bear the pain inside him.

Her heart ached for him.

That wasn't all that ached. An ugly purple bruise had blossomed on her tender side thanks to Oscar's antics with the chair.

But she didn't hold her injury against him. Oh, he'd hurt her, no question. She didn't dismiss the severity of the act. But she couldn't forget that he was an angry, motherless boy in a new land.

Edmund's face flashed in her mind—of all the people, of all the times! She rushed to banish it, as usual, but it persisted, that face of his, one that she'd thought appealing once upon a time. But now when she saw that face, all the resentment in her chest stirred into a frenzy and—

Oh.

Perhaps. . .perhaps she should think of Edmund as she did Oscar. Not that Edmund was a motherless child, but he was broken in his own way. Everyone was broken, according to Pastor Gavell. Everyone sinned and was a sheep in need of a Shepherd. She could recognize Oscar's brokenness and forgive him for hurting her. Why, then, couldn't she recognize that Edmund was a broken man and forgive Edmund?

Oscar didn't promise to marry you. Oscar didn't take both of your dreams and—

She'd set aside those dreams long ago. She had new ones now.

Like helping these children, not just with English, but with attending regular school. Yesterday she'd received a letter from the state superintendent, assuring her that a new schoolmaster would arrive to replace Jarvis within two weeks, and the children would be welcome at the schoolhouse at the end of Main Street where they could study alongside all the other children in town. They'd be able to hold their own quite well—Mary was sure of it.

And when that time came, she had a project to occupy her: finishing her pen-and-ink project for her nephews, Will and Tom.

Kristofer's idea that a book publisher might want her pen-and-inks for a primer was exciting, to be sure. If she pursued it, she could continue teaching children in new ways, like creating educational texts.

Is this my new dream, Lord?

A cough drew her back to the present. Several pairs of eyes watched her expectantly.

Oh my, she was as bad about daydreaming as her students. "Pick a partner and take turns talking about your toy in English."

When Oscar didn't move, Mary let him be and grouped three boys together. Perhaps a few minutes apart from the others would motivate him to join in.

Alas, he examined his fingernails instead.

Just before the mantel clock struck noon, Mary rang her little silver bell. "Tomorrow we will talk about animals. Class dismissed."

"Animals?" Agata was suddenly two inches from Mary's face. "Like rhinosipests?"

"A rhinoceros?" Mary bit back a laugh. "I was thinking of farm animals."

"Boring animals. We have them at home."

"But does everyone know their English names? Once we learn them all, we can talk about rhinoceroses. And giraffes and lions too."

Agata's disappointment didn't last long. "Can I bring Smulan to share tomorrow? She's a good katt."

Oh yes, the barn cat named for a crumb. "I'm sure she is, but she has a job to do, chasing mice in the barn." Mary's gaze followed Britta, who stared out the kitchen window, her breath fogging the glass. "Waiting for your pappa?"

"I want Lilja."

"Ah yes. Lilja will be glad to see you too, I expect."

Kristofer arrived just then, and Britta ran to him the moment he entered the kitchen. She shook off his hug and thrust her hand into his coat pocket. "Lilja?"

"Britta, I'm sorry. She's not there." Kristofer sent Mary a pleading glance. "I cannot find her."

Britta stared up at him, scowling. "Do not tease."

"I wish I were, älskling, but she is not there. I searched the house and the barn."

Silent tears streaked Britta's cheeks. Kristofer gathered her close. "I will make you another."

Britta wailed something unintelligible—Swedish, but then her words were unintelligible in any language, for she was crying in earnest, making more noise than Mary had ever heard from the quiet girl. Poor thing. Poor Kristofer too. Mary withdrew a clean hanky from her sleeve and offered it to them.

A deep voice intruded into the wailing, startling Mary. "Father, you scared me."

"Sorry, Mary."

But he didn't tease her like he usually did after she was startled—because he wasn't alone. Behind him were Sheriff Miles, a potbellied man with a hook to his long nose, and—oh, not Edmund. Mary stiffened. He'd been in her thoughts, and now he was here, acting like he'd been here a thousand times. Well, he had been here back in the day, but he had no right to look so at home here anymore.

I can't help it, God. I don't want to forgive him. The queasiness in her stomach was too strong to ignore.

She pressed her roiling belly. "What's this about?"

Father eyed Britta. "I was about to ask you the same thing."

At the sight of the strange men filling the kitchen, Britta quieted, burying her wet face into Kristofer's midsection. Kristofer glanced at Mary. "Perhaps the girls and I should go now."

"Actually, Kristofer, Edmund and Sheriff Miles are here to see you," Father said.

Kristofer reached to enfold Agata as well as Britta in his arms. "I don't understand."

"Mr. Stanley here says you speak English?" Sheriff Miles approached Kristofer, his right hand subtly moving to rest over his gun belt. *What on earth?*

"Some English, yes."

"Mr. Nilsson, you were at the bank yesterday, according to Edmund Stanley here."

"Ja."

He'd spoken Swedish, the only indication he was upset by the sudden interrogation. Mary glared at Edmund. "I was there too, as Edmund well knows."

Nodding, Sheriff Miles glanced at her. "Yup, he mentioned it. Now Mr. Nilsson, after visiting the bank, what did you do?"

"I brought Mary here, gathered my daughters, and went home."

"And did what, exactly?"

"I did chores and cooked supper."

"Your wife didn't put supper on yesterday?"

Mary'd had enough of this nonsense. "Mrs. Nilsson passed away in Sweden, Sheriff. What is the meaning of this?"

The sheriff ignored her. "Did you return to town later in the day, Mr. Nilsson? After starting supper?"

"No, why would I do that? I worked in my barn, but that is as far from the house as I went until this morning when I brought the girls to school."

Sheriff Miles rubbed the bridge of his hooked nose, a casual gesture that didn't fool Mary a bit. "See, Mr. Nilsson, the blacksmith was robbed yesterday. The culprit took some tools and spare change from the desk."

"That's terrible news, but I am afraid I don't know what that has to do with Kristofer. Unless—" Mary's already queasy stomach lurched. "Are you suggesting Kristofer did that? Because he didn't, and Edmund Stanley, you know it."

Father gave her arm a gentle squeeze. "Was it by the man in the red scarf, Sheriff?"

"Nobody saw the burglar this time to say a word on the scarf—in fact, it could be a different thief altogether, I s'pose, but the culprit left somethin' behind when he broke the rear window and crawled through it to snatch those tools." He nodded at Edmund, who pulled something from a pouch. Something bright red. With legs.

"Lilja!" Britta exclaimed.

"Lilja?" Kristofer's voice was rough.

"Nonsense. Just because it's a Dala horse doesn't mean it's Britta's." Then Mary's stomach swooped. One of the horse's forefeet lacked paint.

Britta snatched Lilja from Edmund's hand, an uncharacteristic show of assertion from the shy girl. "Oh Lilja."

"So it *is* her horse?" Edmund smirked. "See, I told you so, Sheriff."

Britta kissed the little red snout. The sheriff's brow rose. "Guess that answers that."

Kristofer nodded his agreement, but he didn't look nearly as pleased as Britta.

Mother appeared in the doorway. "Girls, why don't you come into the parlor with me? Tell me more about your cat."

"An excellent idea." Mary took their shoulders and guided them into the hall.

"You too, Mary," Father suggested.

"Oh no, I think not." Mary spun back once Mother had the girls in hand.

The instant the parlor door shut, Kristofer's shoulders squared. "I cannot guess how Britta's horse came to be there. I have not visited the blacksmith in weeks. Britta's horse has been missing since yesterday though, as Mary can tell you."

"*Mary*, is it? So informal." Edmund's brow quirked at Father. "How do you feel about their familiarity, Clyde?"

Mary couldn't hold her lips together. "What are you doing here, Edmund? Last I heard, you're not deputized."

His sigh was the most patronizing thing she'd ever heard. "I happened to be passing the smithy when Sheriff Miles found the dolly horse—"

"Dala," she corrected. "Because it is from Dalarna."

"And he kindly let me inspect the evidence. Good thing he did, because I remembered Nilsson's girl playing with it during your visit to the bank."

"*Pfft.* I don't recall you paying any note to the girls that day."

"Well I—er, did. Fleeting glance. But I remembered her holding something red."

Her brow quirked. "It could have been an apple, for all you knew."

Sheriff Miles rubbed the back of his neck. "That feller Ivarsson was there by the blacksmith and said Mr. Nilsson's girl had one like it. That's when you said you recognized it, Stanley."

Mary's well of patience had run dry. "Sheriff, I don't know how the burglar got his hands on Britta's horse, but I strongly suggest that individual is framing Kristofer. Why, you have an eyewitness to back up Kristofer's claim of innocence. Clarice Stanley already confirmed Kristofer is not the thief she encountered at her house. She looked right at Kristofer and said so."

Brows furrowed, the sheriff eyed Edmund. "Your wife got a gander at Mr. Nilsson here and said he's not the one she saw?"

Edmund flushed. "Well, yes."

"Wish you'd a-told me that earlier instead o' wastin' my time."

"Nilsson could be in league with the burglar, and that's how the horse came to be at the scene of the crime." Edmund's lips pinched.

"Or Miss Mary's right, and he's bein' framed. Either way, there's someone else out there according to your wife's word. Might not be too smart of you to let on you didn't believe her." Sheriff Miles stroked the gray stubble on his chin. "All righty, Mr. Nilsson, you're free to go about your business, but don't leave Plenty, all right? This ain't over, and I may have more questions for you."

"But Sheriff, you can't let him walk out of here," Edmund spluttered. "That's his horse."

Mary made a sweeping gesture at the door. "Father will show you two out. Good day." She sent her father a silent message with her eyes.

Father didn't look pleased, but he left her alone with Kristofer, as she'd wanted. The moment the men were out the door, Mary expelled a huge breath. "Oh Kristofer, I'm so sorry. I know you'd never steal."

"But Mary," he said, his voice low. Soft, for her ears alone. "I may not have done these crimes, but I'm a thief all the same. No better than the man they're seeking."

"You—"

Kristofer could have completed her sentence for her—*You are a thief, crook*—but he clamped his lips shut instead, allowing her time to gather her thoughts. His confession had caught her unawares, and his timing was terrible, considering they only had a moment of privacy.

But when she said he'd never steal, well, he couldn't lie. Not to her.

She deserved the truth from him. Even if she no longer wanted to have anything to do with him afterward. Even if the shocked look on her face hit him like a kick to the gut.

She took a deep breath, and when she next looked at him, the expression in her eyes was inscrutable, almost cold. "I have a million questions."

He didn't understand "a million," but there was no mistaking the fiery resolution in her eyes. "I'll tell you anything you want."

"You stole something."

"More than one something."

"From a house?"

"A store."

"Like the burglar is doing now? With the scarf disguising your face?"

He shook his head. "I took one small thing at a time so the shopkeeper wouldn't catch me."

"Was. Took—past tense. Does that mean it's over, or do you still do it, here at the stores in Plenty?"

"In Sweden."

"Why did you take things?" She was so composed, so detached, it was almost as if she felt nothing.

He wished he could say the same. "Three years ago the summer was wet. Too wet for a good harvest. The following summer we had a drought. Seed died in the dry soil. Our crops were bad for two years. Not just our crops, but all of Dalarna's."

When she didn't say anything, he cleared his thickening throat. "We had to eat our dairy cattle, and we baked bread made with tree bark—not enough flour. Then one day Hjalmar brought home a tin of fish. He said he gambled for it. We didn't approve of course, and I chastised him, but we ate the fish anyway. When he brought home another tin, I knew he hadn't gambled for it, not again. He'd stolen it. But the girls were so hungry, I said nothing. It tasted like mud, for all the pleasure I took from partaking in ill-gotten food, but I ate."

He paused, listening to Clyde and Lorena chatter with the girls in the parlor. The girls' laughter was his favorite sound in all creation.

He could listen to it for days on end, but right now it signaled that he had a little more time with Mary, who stood watching him, eyes wide, her hands clasped at her stomach.

"Hjalmar left to look for work in another village, saying it was one less mouth to feed, but we had so little it didn't matter. Tilda, my wife, snuck her portions to the girls. When she got sick, she had no strength left. I don't think she wanted to fight, because living meant taking bites from her daughters' mouths. But when the hour of her death was close, I grew desperate. I used the little coin I had to buy a half-rotten onion at the store, something to boil with water to bolster her. But when I went home, I had a box of meal hidden inside my coat pocket."

Her hands went to her mouth.

"I knew it was wrong. Hated myself. Still do. I sinned against the shopkeeper and God, willingly so, first by saying nothing when Hjalmar stole, then by stealing it myself. Even so, it was too late for Tilda. She died that night."

"Kristofer." The whisper came out from between her fingers.

"We did not need to think twice about coming to America after that. Hjalmar didn't find work of course, and we heard great stories about the land of plenty. And when we found a town by that name, we knew, along with our neighbors, this would be our home. Hjalmar and I made promises to each other. No more stealing. We would start again and trust God here."

Her hand lowered to her throat, where her fingers played with her high lace collar. "I'd heard of the drought. I knew you all had suffered, but I didn't know how much."

"I know it doesn't make up for it, but once the corn harvest came in, I mailed money back to that shopkeeper from my old village. I don't know if he received it though. He might have left Dalarna as we did. Regardless, I hope he can forgive me. I have asked God's forgiveness, not just for stealing but for not trusting Him. I am not sure He has, or will."

Her father's voice grew louder, as if it emanated from the hall. He'd no doubt be in the kitchen momentarily, putting an end to this conversation. Kristofer tried to smile, but it didn't feel like it worked well, the way his lips wavered. "Perhaps I should not have burdened you with such an ugly story, but I wanted you to know who I am."

Her hand left her throat. "I don't judge you. The Lord knows I have no business doing so. But I also know He is quick to forgive. It's His character. Who you are is His child, Kristofer."

"You are far too kind to me, Mary."

Clyde entered the kitchen, hands at his chest, gripping his red suspenders. "The girls are looking at needlepoint patterns with Lorena, and while they're occupied, well, I've got some questions for you, Kristofer."

"Of course." Kristofer expected no less.

"You really don't know how that horse of Britta's came to be at the smithy?"

"No, I truly do not." Kristofer went back through the sequence of events in his mind. "Britta put Lilja in my pocket yesterday, right here in the kitchen. I wasn't paying close attention though, with all that happened with Oscar."

"Oscar?" Clyde looked to Mary. "He giving you trouble?"

"A little. I'll tell you later, Father." Mary's gaze was fierce on Kristofer. "Could it have slipped out of your pocket when we visited the bank? Maybe Edmund scooped it up, and when he saw the blacksmith's had been robbed, he left it there to make you look guilty."

Clyde's brows knit. "That's quite an accusation, Mary. Edmund's a lot of things, but I doubt he'd go that far."

"Of course. And I'm sorry for suggesting Edmund could have done something like that." Mary looked down, her cheeks pinked.

"I tend to think the worst of Edmund."

"He's a scoundrel, Mary, but we shouldn't assume he's guilty of perverting the law," Clyde said.

She flushed a deeper hue.

"I admit I wondered the same thing for a moment, Mary." Kristofer offered a small smile, hoping to ease her self-reproach. "But I noted Lilja after we finished at the bank, when I assisted you into the wagon. My side pressed the wagon box, and I felt her in my pocket."

"Do you remember anything about the horse after that? Maybe it fell out in the wagon." Clyde rubbed the back of his neck.

"I looked, but it wasn't there. Nor was it in the hay when I returned, or the yard. Truly, I looked everywhere. I have no idea how it came to be at the scene of the robbery."

But then he remembered.

Yesterday, while Britta's horse, Lilja, was still secure in Kristofer's coat pocket, Hjalmar had borrowed his coat.

Chapter 7

The way Kristofer paled made Mary's heart jump to her throat. Something was wrong. "Kristofer, what's happened? Are you ill? Are you—"

"I know who the robber is, after all." Kristofer's eyes shut. "I don't wish to believe it though."

"Who?" Father and Mary blurted at the same time.

Kristofer's Adam's apple worked, as if he had trouble swallowing. "Hjalmar. He wore my coat to visit his friend yesterday after the girls and I got home."

"Are you sure?" Father's voice was low.

"Ja." Kristofer didn't seem to have noticed he'd slipped into Swedish. "The wind picked up, and his coat is threadbare. I gave him mine outside the house."

Mary's pounding heart slipped down to her stomach. Hjalmar

had promised Kristofer he wouldn't steal again, hadn't he? They'd come for fresh starts in America, but if Hjalmar was stealing from their new community, well, it would hurt Kristofer to the core. Feel like betrayal. Cast a pall on their family's reputation.

He looked so stricken, Mary scrambled for alternative explanations. There had to be some innocent way Britta's little horse could have ended up at the blacksmith's the day it was burglarized. "Does your pocket have a hole in it?"

Kristofer punched both hands into the pockets and pulled them out to scrub at his face. "No. The stitches are good."

"Did he, oh, I don't know, take it off to help the blacksmith with a task?"

"I don't know, Mary, he said he was visiting a young woman, but—"

Kristofer didn't need to finish. She could read the words in the sad turn of his eyes.

Mary touched his shoulder. She didn't care if Father disapproved, but she had to show Kristofer she cared and wouldn't abandon him now. "Have you seen any evidence of Hjalmar being the burglar? Has he brought anything home lately that is beyond his means to buy?"

"No, but—"

"Wouldn't he have replaced his coat if he had money?"

"Not if he's hiding the loot until suspicion passes." Sighing, Father leaned against the kitchen counter. "Has he stolen anything before, Kristofer?"

Oh but Mary wished Kristofer didn't have to tell Father his story under these circumstances, but Kristofer patted her hand, which still rested on his shoulder, and gave her a small smile. She lowered her hand, and he began his tale again, not excusing his or Hjalmar's behavior when they stole food.

"My whole life I tried to be a good man," he continued. "I followed God's commandments, helped my neighbors. A few years ago, when my crops were ripening in the fields and my wife and daughters were healthy and strong, I would have insisted I would never steal from another. A churchgoer like me, steal? Of course not."

Father looked down.

Kristofer shook his head. "Yet I stole. I hated it then and I still hate it, but as much as I would like to tell you I will never steal again, I can't, Clyde. Now I know I am weak, capable of committing any sin. I am not as good a man as I thought I was, and I need God's help."

I'm capable too. Mary's fingers went to her mouth. *Just because I haven't stolen, how do I know I wouldn't fail? I've failed in so many other ways. The grudges I've held, the darkness I've allowed in. Thinking the worst of Edmund time and time again, refusing to forgive him.*

Her thoughts melded into prayer. *I haven't wanted to forgive him, Lord, and I've used it as an excuse to hold fast to my resentment. Yet You sent me students and Kristofer and—oh God, I'm sorry. Sorry for closing my heart off to You. Sorry for fighting what You've ordained for my life and not trusting You with it.*

Something let loose inside her chest, like a dam yielding to a wall of water. Wave after wave crashed through her, warm and cleansing. Did it show on her face? Her eyes stung as if she'd been crying, but her cheeks were dry.

Father's jaw was set; Kristofer stood at attention, as if he was ready for anything Father said or did. They hadn't noted her moment with the Lord, and that was for the best. It was private, a work He'd done in her. And would continue to do in her, undoubtedly.

Thank You, Lord.

She licked her dry lips. "We all need God's help, Kristofer. I trust He has forgiven you, but I don't think you've quite forgiven yourself."

"I cannot forget it, no."

"Well, forgiveness is a complicated thing. You're not the only one with work to do in that area. Maybe it's time I take my own medicine."

"Medicine. You're sick." His face paled again.

"No, sorry." She chuckled. "It's an expression. It means I need to listen to my own advice. I suggested you forgive yourself. Well, I need to forgive Edmund and keep going to God with my struggle with him. When he came here with the sheriff today, insinuating you were the thief even after Clarice said you weren't, inserting himself like that—oh, it made me madder than a wet hen."

"A wet chicken is not a cheery chicken—that expression makes sense." He smiled, but his mouth tightened. "I am a wet chicken too, thinking Hjalmar might be responsible for these thefts."

"Wet hen," Father corrected. "And I admit my dander's up too."

Mary looked up into Kristofer's face. "*Dander* means pretty much the same thing."

"I thought so."

Mary's chin lifted. "I think it's time we go talk to Hjalmar."

"I think we need to talk to the sheriff," Father countered. "I'm not going to say it was all right for you fellas to steal when you were hungry, but I understand it. But you aren't hungry now. And stealing is a crime."

Kristofer nodded. "We will go together."

Mary understood the determined look in his light eyes. He wanted to be there when his brother was confronted with the evidence—not to warn Hjalmar, but to show him he stood on the side of the law yet loved his brother.

Mary reached for her coat and flowered bonnet. "I'm coming too."

Father threw up his hands. "I should've expected as much."

"But the girls." Kristofer was shaking his head. "I must get them home. It's mealtime."

"Lorena will feed them." Father waved his hands. "More than enough ham in the larder."

"She won't mind keeping the girls two days in a row?" Kristofer looked relieved even as uncertainty flickered over his features. "I hate to be a burden."

"A burden? Ha. She loves them. Our only grandchildren are boys, so she's enjoyed having little girls around. Wants to get them started on a needlepoint project."

Mary paused tying her bonnet under her chin. Not only had Father said Mother loved the girls and compared them to grandchildren, but he'd grinned when he said it. Now that he knew Kristofer wasn't the burglar, was he thawing toward him?

That was all well and good, but now wasn't the time to allow her thoughts down that road. Kristofer set his hat square on his unruly waves and tugged on his gloves. He glanced at her, his expression grim.

He would need her friendship and support, because by the end of the day, Hjalmar might well be in jail.

Every time Kristofer turned off the main road and passed the wild plum trees at the boundary of his homestead, he gained an excellent vantage of the property he and Hjalmar shared, followed by a surge of gratitude. God had given him so much: the cozy house with a spire of smoke escaping the chimney; the snug barn housing a dairy cow, horses, and his woodworking tools; and the farm itself, which provided honest labor and food for his family.

Today, however, with Mary on the wagon seat beside him, Sheriff Miles and Clyde Clarence riding alongside, only the gnawing ache of grief filled his chest.

"This your place?" Sheriff Miles's tone indicated he already knew the answer.

"Yes."

"It's lovely," Mary said as she gazed out over the fields. A small smile played on her lips as if she could envision them green with unripe corn.

Even under such gloomy circumstances, she looked for the best, the spring that would follow the winter.

And spring will come, won't it, Lord? For the land and for our hearts. Give us courage to do what's right.

Hjalmar exited the barn, bundled against the cold. Spying them, he lifted a hand in greeting. Then his arm froze, perhaps when Hjalmar recognized the sheriff in the group or the forbidding looks on their faces. Or maybe because Kristofer didn't wave back.

At least he didn't run.

Kristofer pulled into the yard. What was the scripture? *"To the Lord our God belong mercies and forgiveness, though we have rebelled against him."*

God was here with them in this difficult time. And despite their past mistakes and transgressions, He wasn't going anywhere now.

"What's wrong? Where are the girls?" Hjalmar met the horses' heads as Kristofer set the brake.

"They're eating lunch at the Clarences'. The sheriff has questions for you."

"They won't be good questions, I don't think." Hjalmar patted one of the horse's necks. "Everyone's looking at me like I stole their favorite sheep."

While they tethered the horses and Clyde assisted Mary down from the wagon, Kristofer regarded Sheriff Miles. "I'll translate, if you trust me."

"I don't know you to trust you, Mr. Nilsson, but I figger I can tell by lookin' at your brother whether or not he's lyin', no matter the language."

A gust of wind sent a chill down Kristofer's back. "Why don't we go inside?"

The sheriff nodded. "While we're walking, go ahead and ask

him what he did yesterday when he wore your coat. But don't tell him why or what happened. I wanna see his face."

Kristofer asked the question.

"Visited a friend."

"Ebba Blom," Kristofer confirmed.

"Yes."

"Did you go anywhere else?"

"Nej. Why?" Hjalmar stomped his boots on the front porch and led them into the house, which was thankfully tidy. It smelled of the lunch Kristofer had left warming on the stove: fried *köttbullar* and pan gravy, rich with cream. The girls loved the little meatballs seasoned with pepper, but they would have them for supper now. If this mess was settled by then.

Kristofer ushered everyone into the small parlor and offered them seats. He'd long wondered if Mary would ever see the inside of his house, imagining it under far better circumstances of course. When his brother wasn't being interrogated for burglary, and when he had completed more furnishings. Did Mary find his home too simple? Too lacking?

What a time to think of such nonsense. Once the guests had been seated, he lowered himself into a chair across from Mary. "Hjalmar, at the Bloms', who else did you see?"

Hjalmar sat slowly, watching the sheriff. "Her family of course. Herr Blom and her siblings. Kristofer, what's going on?"

"One moment, Hjalmar, and I can tell you." He turned to the sheriff. "Hjalmar is sweet on Ebba Blom. He says he was at her house yesterday afternoon with her family." When the sheriff rattled off more questions, Kristofer again faced his brother. "The sheriff wants to know what you did you when you visited."

"Did?"

"With Ebba. Did you drive into town? Take a walk?"

"It was too cold for that. We stayed in. Played a board game.

Then I came home for supper. Who cares what I did? Nothing untoward, if that's what he's suggesting."

"No, Hjalmar, he's not—that's not it. Did anyone else come or go?"

"Why?" Then his eyes widened. "Is Ebba sick? Hurt? What's happened, Kristofer?"

"No, Ebba's fine." Kristofer glanced at the sheriff. "I'm telling him now."

"Go ahead." Sheriff Miles's eyes fixed on Hjalmar.

The sheriff wasn't the only one watching his brother closely. *Don't lie to me, Hjalmar. Please.* "The robber struck the blacksmith yesterday afternoon. But this time he left evidence behind: Lilja."

It took a moment for Hjalmar to react. "Britta's horse?"

Kristofer nodded. "It's Lilja, for sure. The paint is missing off her foreleg. The thing is, last time Lilja was seen, she was in the pocket of my coat. Which you borrowed."

Hjalmar stood. Everyone else did too, and Kristofer didn't miss the sheriff's hand going to his belt. Kristofer put up his hands. "Hjalmar, don't do anything rash."

"Stupid, stupid." Hjalmar's face reddened. "I could wring his neck."

"What's he saying?" The sheriff stepped closer, and Clyde pushed Mary behind him.

Kristofer moved between the sheriff and his brother. "He's the sheriff, Hjalmar. You can't threaten such a thing without consequences. Think!"

"The sheriff? What are you talking about?" Hjalmar shoved past Kristofer.

"Wringing his neck? You can't—"

"Not him. That *pojke*. What was he thinking?"

"What boy?"

"I said, Mr. Nilsson, what's he saying?" The sheriff's voice was louder.

Kristofer could hardly hear himself think, the way his heart pounded in his ears. "He means no harm," he said in English, then returned his focus onto his brother. "Hjalmar, you're scaring everyone. They think you're the robber and you're going to hurt someone. What's this about a boy? What boy?"

Hjalmar startled, as if a bucket of cold water had been splashed on his head. "I need to see Ebba."

"No, you need to tell us what's going on."

Hjalmar's hands fell. "Oscar. He must be the robber."

Mary gasped, clearly having understood a word amid the Swedish. "Oscar."

Sheriff Miles's eyes narrowed. "Who's this Oscar fella?"

"Ebba's brother. He's fifteen," Mary answered. "One of my students."

"That one who's caused you trouble," Clyde added, his arm going around her shoulders.

All the anxiety pooling in Kristofer's chest drained, replaced by relief that Hjalmar hadn't stolen after all. But an ache formed alongside it, a gnawing concern for Oscar and the Blom family. Oscar was so young. Why would he do something like this?

The sheriff folded his arms. "I sure hope your brother ain't makin' up a story, castin' blame on a boy, Mr. Nilsson."

"I don't think he is."

Mary shook her head. "Oscar is grieving his mother's sudden death on the crossing from Sweden. It's been a year, but he is still angry and hurting. He, well, he lashes out on occasion."

"Anything serious?"

Her hand went to her side. "Not. . .really."

Sheriff Miles tipped his chin at Kristofer. "Tell your brother to start talking."

"Let's sit down again," Kristofer said, hand on his brother's shoulder.

Hjalmar left his hands visible on the armrests of his chair, as if wishing to communicate he had no intention to harm anyone. Once he started talking, Kristofer had to stop him so he could inform the Clarences and Sheriff Miles what his brother related.

"When Hjalmar arrived at the Bloms', he hung the coat on the rack by the front door. The only one to leave the house was Oscar. He said he would be in the barn, but he was gone a long time. And when Hjalmar left the Blom house, the coat hung from a different hook on the rack. A similar thing happened when Hjalmar borrowed my red scarf. He hung it on one hook at the Bloms', and it didn't look quite right when Hjalmar retrieved it, but he thought one of Ebba's younger siblings was teasing him somehow. Now he thinks Oscar took them and wore them."

The sheriff whistled. "A veritable masquerade."

Mary leaned toward Kristofer. "That means he disguised himself."

Count on his favorite teacher to help Kristofer with his new language. He smiled at her, and when she smiled back, his ears got hot.

Rubbing one fiery lobe, he turned to Hjalmar, whose smirk indicated his red ears hadn't gone entirely unnoticed.

"Keep your thoughts to yourself, Brother."

"I didn't say anything." Hjalmar's smirk didn't lessen.

"Then let's return to the topic at hand. Have you seen any of the missing items at the Blom house?"

"Nej." Hjalmar's forehead scrunched. "There hasn't been anything new that I've seen. Not since Sven's birthday presents."

"Like what?"

"New mittens, knit by Ebba and Lovisa. Suspenders from Herr Blom. Oscar gave Sven a striped spinning top. It looked quality but used. I assumed he'd scrounged to buy it secondhand."

When Kristofer finished translating, Mary gasped. "The thief stole toys from the Stanleys' little boys. Their youngest lost a top, remember?"

Now that she mentioned it, he did.

Sheriff Miles stood. "Oscar could be our man, then. Er, boy. We'd better visit the Bloms. Do they speak any English?"

"Only the little ones who've attended Mary's classes." His heart heavy, Kristofer stood once more. "I'll show you the way to their farm, and I will help translate."

The sheriff nodded. "Let's get this done. It's starting to snow."

"We'd best hurry then," Mary said.

Clyde forestalled her with his hand on her elbow. "I think we'd be of better service if we went home and helped your mother with Agata and Britta, don't you?"

Gaze fixed on Kristofer, she sighed. "Very well. We'll keep the girls until the matter is settled. Don't worry about them."

"I won't. Not if they're with you." But he would worry about Mary as well as the girls. All of their hearts hurt for the young man who had made such poor decisions with grave consequences.

Lord, give us wisdom with this child You love.

Before he left, Kristofer removed the warm meatballs and gravy from the stove, storing them in the icebox. Then he stepped out into a gently falling snow with Hjalmar and the sheriff to confront Oscar and, God willing, end this debacle once and for all.

Chapter 8

A trickle of icy air seeped beneath the parlor window, chilling Mary to her bones, but she didn't step away to avail herself of the cheery blaze crackling in the hearth. Not when Kristofer was out there helping with Oscar.

"The snow is thickening." The soft snow that had started while they were at the Nilsson homestead was now falling in earnest.

"Don't fret." Father didn't look up from the newspaper. "Kristofer's Swedish. He can handle a little snow."

"It's not a little."

"It's not a blizzard either, Mary."

"And it's not just Kristofer out there. I'm worried about the others too."

"Mm-hmm."

He had her there. She hadn't particularly given Hjalmar much thought this afternoon. But he knew what she meant. Oscar, Sven, and Lovisa were her students. That poor family.

Mary's finger tapped the frigid pane. "It's been three hours. Do you think something prolonged them at the Bloms'? I hope there wasn't violence or—"

"Don't go borrowing trouble, Mary dear. Trust the Lord."

Her lips fell silent and still. She didn't trust Him much at the moment, did she? In fact, she'd hardly prayed.

As the wind swept swirls of snow through the bare trees outside and chorused into a high-pitched *whoosh*, she resolved to let God handle the weather. And Kristofer's safety. Everyone's safety, she amended, even though it was Kristofer's face on her mind.

At last she stepped away from the window. "I'll be in the kitchen, though Mother and the girls don't need me. They have the stew well in hand."

Father chuckled but stopped at the noise suddenly competing with the wind—horse hooves on gravel. "They're here."

But it was only Kristofer who entered the small foyer, divesting his snow-dusted hat, coat, and red scarf. Mother patted his gold-stubbled cheek. "Cold as ice. Come into the kitchen, where it's warmest. I have coffee for you."

He grinned. "Coffee sounds good."

Mary's stomach lurched. Mercy, was she jealous of her own mother touching Kristofer's cheek? It was a maternal gesture. If Mary did it though, it would be a brazen act. Yet she wanted to do it anyway, to take his cold hands and warm them with her own.

What was wrong with her, wanting to be such a. . .a forward hoyden? She'd never felt such a compulsion around Edmund.

Kristofer sat close to the kitchen hearth. Mother handed him a mug of fresh coffee—which would do far better at warming his hands than Mary's cold hands would do—and both of his daughters snuggled on his lap. He kissed their heads, and they patted his cold nose. At that moment, Mary realized what was wrong with her.

It wasn't exactly wrong, but it wasn't good either.

She was falling in love with him. Mary—the prissy spinster who couldn't bake a pie, according to Edmund. Mary, the woman who had determined she'd never marry because God had given her other things to do with her life. Mary, who would be devastated when the new teacher arrived and Kristofer, whose heart surely still belonged with his first wife, politely thanked her for teaching his family English and went on his way, out of her life.

Stretching behind Britta, Kristofer set down his mug on the hearth, safely out of harm's way. "I'm afraid Oscar is gone."

"What do you mean, 'gone'?" Father sat opposite Kristofer.

"He was in the barn when we arrived, but when Herr Blom took us there, he was gone. He must have overheard us and ran away. There were some tracks to follow, but the trail ended."

"Did his family know what he was doing?" Mother hung his damp scarf from a hook by the fireplace mantel so it would dry faster.

"None. They are bereft. Hjalmar stayed with Ebba to be a comfort, but the sheriff and a few of the Bloms' neighbors and I have continued looking. I came back to see about the girls, but if I may leave them with you a short while longer, I will return to the search." As Agata hopped from his lap, Kristofer adjusted his position, stretching his leg toward the fire.

Mary held his gaze over Britta's head. "You shouldn't go out in this snow."

"Oscar is out in it too, but he isn't wearing a coat."

He was right. Oscar could well freeze to death, and Mary's chest ached with worry for him. "Lord have mercy. Will you stay for a warm bowl of stew first?"

He shook his head, brushing the top of Britta's head with his chin. His stubble pulled some of her fine blond hairs out of their braids. "I need to get back."

"Of course, and the girls are fine with us," Mother insisted.

"I'll go with you." Father stood.

"I'll send some provisions." Mother bustled to the stove.

"I'll help." Agata ran behind her.

Britta didn't move. Neither did Mary. For several seconds, Mary and Kristofer held gazes as the fire crackled, and the only movement was Britta making her little horse, Lilja, climb Kristofer's chest.

"Pappa, you're cold." Her words broke whatever was tethering his gaze to Mary's.

"Am I?" He blinked.

"You forgot? Silly Pappa."

Silly Mary too, to be staring at him like a moon-eyed schoolgirl. Could he tell by looking at her that she had feelings for him?

Her hands went to her warm cheeks. "I'd best help my mother. You stay here and thaw."

She cut chunks of crusty bread while Mother filled two canteens with water and Agata counted out three strips of jerky for each man. "One, twoooo, tree."

Mother glanced at Mary as if waiting for her to say something. Then she smiled at Agata. "Th," she said, offering the correction Mary usually gave. "Three."

Mary didn't care about proper pronunciation at the moment. Her hands shook as if she were the one out in the snow.

Father returned, bundled up, rolling a blanket into a tight cylinder—probably for Oscar, once they found him. "We'll be back by dark for that stew."

"You'd better be, Clyde." Mother glanced out the window at the snow.

"We will take care." Kristofer rose, carrying Britta in his arms.

"Nej." She clung harder to his neck.

Kristofer jiggled her in his arms. "What is it, älskling? You have

Lilja back. You are warm and safe. I know you like it here."

"But I like you here too. All of us together. You stay with us."

Much as Mary wanted him to stay too, she knew that out in this weather, Oscar could be in even more trouble than he already was. She held out her arms. "Shall we have a story, Britta?"

"The one about the girl and doll?"

"Oh yes, that would be perfect for today."

Britta reluctantly nodded. Kristofer handed the little girl into Mary's arms, and their hands brushed.

Kristofer didn't step back. "Is she too heavy for you?"

"No." But Britta was far heavier than any child she'd held before. Her nephews stopped wanting her to carry them when they were four. She adjusted Britta onto her hip, and Britta's arms went around her. Lilja pressed cold and wooden into the side of Mary's neck.

It felt strange and wonderful, a comfort in this time of worry.

"Be safe."

"We will," Father answered for Kristofer. "Come on."

The house seemed colder and quieter when they'd gone. But Mary couldn't stand at the window watching and wishing, not with Britta in her arms. She forced a smile. "Why don't we read that story now, Britta? Agata, would you like to join us?"

She could read aloud and pray silently at the same time, couldn't she?

She was about to find out.

Mary's prayers were answered no more than an hour later, when Father and Kristofer entered the house, accompanied by a flurry of snow. "Didn't find Oscar. Getting too thick out there to keep looking," Father explained, his voice muffled beneath the scarf he'd wrapped around his mouth and nose.

Mary didn't hesitate this time. She touched Kristofer's chapped red cheek. So cold! To cover her bold act, she tugged at his scarf, as if that had been her intention all along. "Come get warm."

"Thank you, Mary, but I can't. I'm taking the girls home while I still can. We have animals to tend, and Hjalmar is still at the Bloms."

Oh. "Of course."

Kristofer's eyes were soft. "We will continue looking for Oscar in the morning when I bring the girls for school."

Father nodded. "In the meantime, the sheriff's got a few fellas out looking for a little longer, but hopefully Oscar's smart enough to take shelter in someone's barn."

Mary prayed so. "I'll prepare the girls."

Mother took Agata while Mary assisted Britta into her knit cap, scarf, mittens, and coat, before securing Lilja in the pocket. Without thinking, she kissed the girls atop their caps. Oh, she'd grown so fond of them, their smiles and laughter and little-girl smell. "Good night, Agata, Britta."

"Is there school tomorrow if there's still snow?"

"Not if it's too heavy to get through." She glanced at Kristofer. "But you girls can still stay with me while your pappa looks for Oscar."

He nodded his thanks, shook Father's hand, and then reached for hers. His frozen-stiff glove scraped her wrist. "Good night, Mary."

Then they were gone.

"Lord, give the Nilssons safe passage home, and protect Oscar." She hadn't realized she'd prayed aloud until Mother responded with "Amen."

Strange how quickly she'd grown accustomed to the Nilsson family being around. The girls at school, evenings tutoring Kristofer—they'd filled her life so completely that she'd almost forgotten how it used to be when her kerosene lamp was the only thing chasing away the gloom of a long winter's evening. After supper Mary returned to her old pattern, setting up her sketchbook and ink at the kitchen table.

"Working on your alphabet book for the boys?" Mother asked, untying her apron strings.

Mary nodded, beginning the first lines of an owl. "Kristofer thinks I could publish it."

"Land sakes, but he's right. I was thinking too small, knowing how much your nephews would like a book like this from you, but I imagine other families would love it too. I never had anything like that when I taught you the alphabet. Just a stick of chalk and a slate and my terrible drawings."

"I don't remember them, but I'm sure they weren't terrible."

Mother laughed. "I don't know where you got your talent, Mary. Not from me. Straight from God I s'pose, and look at how you're using it."

It didn't take long, however, for her fingers and feet to sting from cold, so she went up to bed. To her surprise, she slept and woke to weak but nevertheless present sunshine. Here and there, the snow looked slushy, like it would be mud tomorrow. A warmer day ahead, to be sure. *Thank You that it's not as cold, Lord. May Oscar be all right and quickly found.*

She dressed for school in her blue plaid dress, brushed and pinned her hair, and rushed downstairs to get breakfast on and prepare for school.

And to see Kristofer. Now that she knew she had feelings for him, what should she do?

Don't touch his cheek again, you goose.

No, Mary would be on her best behavior. Normal. Proper. His children's teacher. His tutor. His friend. A specimen of ladylike gentility—

Oh! There was his wagon, pulling into the yard!

She patted her hair and forced herself to count to ten before she went to meet the Nilssons at the door.

Before she got to seven, Mother had opened the door. "Look at you two, rosy-cheeked and smiling today. How is your kitty, Smulan?"

"I love her." Agata gave a high-pitched mew as Mother laughed and helped her with her coat.

Mary rushed to help Britta, but first the little girl had to free Lilja from her pocket. "You know, we will have baby pigs any day now."

"Baby animals are my favorites, but don't tell Smulan," Agata said.

"They're all adorable, aren't they?" Mary gathered both coats to hang in the kitchen. "Except maybe spiders."

The girls giggled.

"Pappa says we are staying here after school." Britta hopped into the kitchen on one foot. "Maybe until supper."

"Yes, that's right. Where is your pappa now?" Mary was quite proud she'd managed to keep her tone even and light. Why, no one would be able to tell from her voice that her heart was skittering like a bird's.

Britta shrugged. "He told us goodbye."

"And to behave," Agata said with a sigh.

Mary peeked out the window. The wagon was gone. Father appeared from the barn with two riding horses, along with canteens and extra blankets. Kristofer followed after—he must have stabled his wagon and horses in the barn. He didn't glance at the house as he mounted the horse Father indicated, and they set off to rejoin the search for Oscar.

Watching them go, she breathed a prayer for the boy's safe return.

Only half her students attended today. The Blom children stayed home, and Inga Ivarsson said her brother, Klas, and the other older boys were helping in the search for Oscar.

"Why did Oscar go outside in the snow?" Agata asked.

Mary chewed her lip. Did the children know Oscar was accused of burglarizing several townsfolk?

"My pappa said he took a walk and got lost," Malin Lindvquist said, sparing Mary from answering. "But everyone knows Oscar is smart enough to find shelter."

"I hope so." Britta's voice was small as ever but clear, and it drew every eye.

They were frightened for him, all of them. They might not all like him, but they cared for him and wished him well.

Sometimes teaching wasn't just about letters and numbers and grammar. It was about caring and comforting and modeling behavior. Washing hands. Showing good manners. And seeking the Lord.

Mary set down her chalk. "Why don't we pray together?"

"That is a good idea." Britta set Lilja atop the table and took her hand.

Everyone stood and joined hands. Mary prayed for Oscar and the searchers. Then she began the Lord's Prayer in English, which they'd been working on for a few days. Every child recited it and ended with a loud "Amen."

Mary hugged each one when they left for the day, and after a quick lunch with Mother and the girls, she started a pan of apple cider and cinnamon sticks simmering on the stove. "So, girls, Mother said you've started needlepoint projects. Will you show me what you've done?"

The girls rushed to Mother's sewing basket to retrieve their samplers.

"It's going to be the alphabet." Agata shoved hers an inch from Mary's eyes.

"Oh yes, I see."

"Mine too." Britta set hers on the table.

The girls' stitches were imperfect but wonderful. Mary grinned. "I love them already."

Agata nodded. "Our samplers look good, don't they, Mrs. Clarence?"

"They do, indeed." Mother smiled. "Let's sit close to the fire and work, girls. Before I join you though, I need to look in on the sow. She might need more water. She's seemed thirstier the closer she gets to farrowing."

"Maybe she'll have the piglets today." Mary hoped so, for the sow's sake. Poor thing looked more than ready.

Britta clapped. "May I come too?"

"And me!" Agata was already running to the coat rack for her hat.

Mother laughed. "Of course."

"I'll stay here, if you don't mind." Mary smiled at her mother. "I'll set up to work on my pen-and-inks, and in a while I can make popcorn."

"What's that?" Agata scrunched her nose.

"Corn that gets hot and—" Mary's hands mimed an explosion. "Mmm."

"Sounds like a wonderful treat." Mother reached for her coat. "Girls, do you have on your mittens? Very well, let's go."

After one last check of the heat level under the pan of cider, Mary went upstairs to fetch her supplies. Last night she'd noted the ink bottle had run low. Best get a fresh one now. The top drawer of her desk drawer had none, however. Were they out of ink? She'd thought Father had brought a few bottles home from Sullivan's a week or so ago. What had he done with them?

Oh yes. Mother had been writing letters. Mary crossed the hall to her parents' room and sat at Mother's escritoire. Out the window, she could see Mother and the girls tromping across the path to the barn through the melting snow. Agata was dancing, and oh, Britta was too, a sort of hop-dance.

She loved those girls, through and through.

Her heart warm, Mary opened the top drawer and found a fresh bottle of ink. She returned to her room, gathered a thicker shawl and her pen and paper, and started downstairs. The screech of the kitchen door opening met her in the stairwell.

That was fast. Maybe one of the girls had come to tell her there were piglets! She hurried down the rest of the stairs. "Are they here? How many—"

Her words stuck on her tongue as she entered the kitchen. It wasn't one of the girls. Or Mother. It was a boy, his panic-stricken face turned toward her, his hand closed around Mother's shepherdess figurine.

Kristofer, Father, Sheriff Miles, every man she knew was out looking for Oscar. But he was right here in her kitchen. What should she say? Do? She swallowed hard and prayed.

"Hello, Oscar."

He panted hard. Stared at her.

Maybe he'd bolt like a wild horse. Part of her hoped he would so the girls wouldn't see this when they returned from the barn, wouldn't be scared.

The other part of her feared for Oscar and what awaited him for the rest of his life. He needed help. Needed it now.

Clutching her papers and ink to her chest, she stepped toward him. "Why don't you put that down, Oscar?"

A horse whinnied outside. Whose? She couldn't see it from her position. Father could be back or—

It wouldn't be Father, not this early. That could only mean one thing. "Did you steal a horse? A *häst*?" Horse thieving was considered more serious than stealing coins or tools or toys—to most people, anyway. "Let me help you."

Did he comprehend her words? *Lord, may he at least understand my tone. My outstretched hand.*

His gaze fixed on it. His hand still grasped her mother's heirloom figurine.

"Your family is worried, Oscar. Why don't we talk to the sheriff? In peace."

What was the Swedish word for peace? She hadn't a clue, so she mimed what she hoped was a contented expression and forced a soft exhalation. It didn't correspond with the rapid thumping of her heart, which was hidden beneath the feeble shield of paper she clasped to her chest. "Peace."

He took a ragged breath. She'd never seen Oscar look like this, maintaining eye contact, like he was listening to her. He understood something, thank God.

She stepped closer. Stretched out her hand again. "Put it down, Oscar, and we'll talk."

The horse outside whickered again. Oscar jumped back from her. "Nej!"

Oh no, he couldn't run again. He'd freeze and steal, and she was not about to let that happen.

She reached out. Gripped his sleeve.

Spinning into her, he shoved. Hard, his hands at her chest. She fell back.

The impact at the base of her skull didn't hurt. Instead, a buzzing filled her ears. Her body hummed, like she was out in the air before a lightning strike. And then the room went dark.

Kristofer paused, hand midair, ready to knock on the Clarences' kitchen door. The door was ajar, however, the barest fraction of an inch, a foolish mistake that let out precious heat and allowed winter cold to creep into the house. Mary and her mother wouldn't leave the door unlatched on purpose.

Riding in, he and Clyde had gone first to the barn, where Lorena, Britta, and Agata patted the heavy sow. Mary was still in the house, and Clyde suggested Kristofer go tell her they returned empty-handed once again. He had some news to share though. The sheriff planned to send a wire to the neighboring towns asking for help to catch Oscar.

"Mary?" He stomped slush from his boots and pushed the door all the way open. "Are you here?"

She didn't answer. He'd wait outside then, as was proper, but then he heard it, sizzling, like something on the stove had boiled over. He went on in, heading for the stove, and as he rounded the table, a figure rose by the hearth, nearly startling Kristofer out of his skin.

Oscar, his bloodshot blue eyes full with tears. "I didn't mean to." The boy gripped his hair, as if about to tear it from his scalp. "She's dead, like *Mamma.*"

"Who's dead?" Kristofer's stomach rippled. Then he saw papers strewn over the ground. Mary's pen-and-inks.

He shoved past Oscar to find Mary, supine on the floor, her head propped against the hearth. *Dear Gud.* "Mary, älskling, look at me."

Oscar started to sob.

Pushing aside Mary's high lace collar, Kristofer pressed two fingers into her neck. *Thank Gud, a steady pulse.* Then his fingers gently walked around her skull, to the hot lump at the back of her head. He was no doctor, but when he touched it and she winced and let out a moan, he trusted she'd awaken.

"Mary, älskling, I'm here. You're safe." He pressed a swift kiss at her temple.

Her eyes didn't open, but her wince intensified. "Oscar."

"I know." He looked up at the sobbing boy. "She's going to live."

Oscar's mouth worked, but no sound came out. Then he spun on his heel and fled the kitchen, knocking into the table as he went.

Kristofer had made difficult choices before back in Sweden. He made another now, leaving Mary's side to chase Oscar. This had to end now.

Oscar was already halfway across a fallow field, but fury and determination flooded Kristofer's veins. He would pursue Oscar until he had no more breath.

But he also had to ensure Mary was cared for. He smacked the side of the barn with his palm as he ran past it. "Clyde! Get to the house! Mary!"

Oscar looked over his shoulder at him, but if the boy expected Kristofer to stop, he was mistaken.

"What's— Go, Kristofer!" Clyde's shout came from behind. "I'll get her!"

Kristofer didn't turn around. Not when a pang pinched his side. Not when the cold air burned his lungs or the uneven ground caused his ankle to roll.

Oscar was far younger, but he probably hadn't eaten in a day or more. He was not even off the Clarence property when Kristofer lunged, grabbing Oscar around the waist and tackling him to the mud-slushed earth.

Kristofer squeezed Oscar's arms, but the boy didn't fight. Shuddering, he cried. "I'm sorry. I didn't mean to hurt her."

"I know." Kristofer wasn't Oscar's *foder*. He barely knew the boy, but right now Oscar was a frightened child. He unpinned Oscar's arms and lifted him to sit. There in the soggy field, he wrapped one arm about the boy's quaking shoulders. "I know, Son."

Clyde found them that way, sitting side by side, wet and muddy. He carried rope but let it go slack in his hands. "Don't think we'll be needing this."

"Not anymore." Kristofer shook his head. "Come, Oscar. Let's get you warm, and then we'll talk."

He didn't need to say anything about the sheriff. The panicked look on Oscar's face said it all, but he nevertheless nodded and rose.

Kristofer kept a steadying hand on Oscar, but his gaze fixed on Clyde. "Mary?"

"Awake, with a towel of snow to her head to keep down the swelling. She's gonna want to talk to you. And frankly, I will too. Stay a spell, will you?"

Kristofer nodded. After he'd seen Mary unconscious on the kitchen floor, fearing for a horrible moment that she was dead, well, he had a few things to say to Clyde too.

Chapter 9

Mary's kitchen had never been so full of people except for the first day of the makeshift English school when all of her students and their parents gathered around the dining table. But that had been for five minutes, maybe less, and this crowd had been crammed in here for more than an hour.

The sheriff came. So did Oscar's father, Hjalmar, and Ebba, each with stricken faces and a million questions fired off in rapid Swedish. Behind them were members of the search party, including Edmund.

He met her gaze while she slumped on the hearth with a dish towel packed with snow against the back of her head. For a moment, she thought she glimpsed a softening in his eyes, a flash she hadn't seen in years.

"Hello, Edmund."

His nod was stiff. "I received a telegram. The new teacher arrives next Monday. Cousin Jarvis will be out of a job, but your precious students will be welcome in class per the state superintendent's orders. Hope you're satisfied now."

Did she look it, ice to her head, throbbing pain in her temples? Probably not. "I am, Edmund."

"You're welcome."

"I didn't thank you."

"I'm the superintendent, and I remedied an error."

"No, Kristofer and I wrote to the state superintendent because you failed to ensure you'd employed a proficient schoolmaster. Goodbye, Edmund."

His lips popped apart. "I have no intention of leaving. I'm a victim here. My house was burglarized. This matter involves me too."

"You don't have to leave of course. But I'm finished here."

Finished allowing his words and deeds to wound, shape, or affect her.

He blinked, uncomprehending. Instead of resentment clawing up her throat, she felt nothing. Except maybe pity. That's when she knew something had changed. "I forgive you."

"Me? For what? Hiring Jarvis?"

"For that, and for telling me I wasn't marriageable. For telling your friends I wasn't marriageable. Oh, you didn't know that I heard that, did you?"

The red splotches forming over his cheeks, the twitching of his fingers, the way he opened his mouth but no sound came out—it was almost comical, but it was also pitiable. *Thank You, Lord, for sparing me marriage to a man who cannot ever admit he's wrong. And thank You for helping me now. Thank You for working this change in me and helping me want to forgive him.* "I hope you'll forgive me too. I've resented you for a long time, Edmund, held things against you, grumbled about you, even reviled you. But I'm done now. I wish you well. Goodbye, Edmund," she repeated.

He snorted and pushed his way to the other side of the crowded room.

The kitchen door swung open again, letting in an almost refreshing wave of cold air. Mother wove her way between the men to beckon the newest guest. "Thank the good Lord you're here, Doc. Mary's here by the fire."

The middle-aged doctor felt her pulse and examined her pupils and poked around the lump on the back of her head. "Swelling seems to have stopped, but keep ice on it until supper. If you'd hit a few inches lower, well, we might not be having this conversation."

That made Mother cry.

Mary gripped her hand. "All I got was a bump and a story to tell."

Mother kissed her temple. Which reminded her—

Kristofer had kissed her, hadn't he? Just like Mother had. Nothing romantic about it, but heat suffused her cheeks.

"Are you feverish?" Mother's hand flipped over to gauge her temperature with the back of her fingers. "No fever. You've been by the fire for a while. And there are too many bodies packed in here."

"Where's Kristofer?" Mary clasped Mother's fingers again.

"He took the girls home. They didn't need to see this, and frankly, he was soaked to the skin after tackling Oscar to the ground like he did. Your father offered to loan him a clean pair of pants, but all of us knew nothing in his closet would fit your long-legged fella."

"He's not my fella."

"You know what I mean." Mother sighed. "Oh bother, Edmund looks like he wants more coffee. I'd better start a fresh pot."

Kristofer was a good father. That was one of the things she'd admired about him right from the first. It was good he'd taken the girls out of this mess.

Perhaps she should get out of here too. Mary snuck up the

stairs to her bedroom.

She didn't want to sleep and, with the noise downstairs, probably couldn't even if she wanted to. But at least up here it was slightly more peaceful. Propping the snowpack behind her head, she lounged atop her bed and folded the quilt over her legs, looking out the window at the pale sunlight.

She listened to the voices fade downstairs, the front door unlatching and latching, the oven door screeching open and thumping shut. She tried to pray, starting each effort with a petition for Oscar or a note of gratitude to God for helping her forgive Edmund, but then those specific prayers would dissolve as thoughts of Kristofer permeated her brain. *He kissed me, Lord. I didn't imagine it. What am I supposed to do with that?*

"Mary," Mother whispered, poking her head into the doorway. "You asleep?"

She pushed the quilt aside. "No. I'll help with supper."

"No need, the chicken's in the pot. Besides, you have a guest. Kristofer's back."

Mary leaped up so fast, her pulse thumped in the lump at the back of her head, but she didn't care. She abandoned the snowpack and shook the wrinkles from her dress. She must look a fright.

Downstairs she started to turn left into the kitchen, but Mother cleared her throat and pointed at the parlor. Why there? It wasn't as warm as the kitchen, and they really only used it when the kitchen was otherwise occupied, like when she was teaching. Or when they entertained important visitors.

Kristofer stood in the center of the room, wearing Sunday clothes, ears red, the ends of his hair damp, and his jaw freshly shaven. He didn't smile but stared at her like he was about to impart some horrible news.

Her hand went to her quivering stomach. "Are you all right?"

"Are *you* all right?" Kristofer's serious gaze searched her face.

"When I saw you on the floor, I thought—" He swallowed. "Do you pain?"

"I'm not hurt." Oh my, he smelled like shaving soap. "I'm fine."

Although the way her heart was pumping, hard and fast, she was probably in danger of apoplexy.

Father cleared his throat. Oh—there he was in the chair. She hadn't seen him. "Guess what happened in all the fuss today, Mary? The piglets came. Ten!"

Quite a number. "How's the sow?"

"Strong and content, a good mama. Kristofer gets first pick of 'em. He'll tell me which, and I'll make sure they go to him once they're weaned."

Was that why he was here? Dressed in his Sunday clothes to pick out piglets? "Now?"

"Thank you, Clyde. Maybe later?" Kristofer fidgeted.

"Oh, of course." Father seemed mighty jovial. "I've got something to say anyway. Why don't you all sit down?"

Mother perched beside Father in the only remaining chair. Mary lowered herself onto one end of the horsehair-stuffed sofa. Kristofer sat at the edge of the other end, leaving a wide, cold gap between them, probably big enough to accommodate the sow and her ten piglets.

Father leveled Kristofer with his gaze. "I owe you an apology."

Kristofer blinked. "I do not understand. You are nothing but kind to me."

"That's not quite true. See, I could tell— Well, Mary was tutoring you, and I admit I wasn't quite convinced you didn't know who the thief was. I thought you protected him with your silence."

"Oh Father." Mary's heart ached. "I could tell you didn't trust Kristofer."

"I didn't want you hurt, pumpkin, spending time with someone who wasn't good enough for you. Not again."

He'd seen her feelings for Kristofer and wanted to protect her from being heartbroken as she'd been by Edmund? "This situation isn't remotely the same," she countered. "I'm the girls' teacher. I tutor Kristofer. I—"

I am not the reason he comes here. She couldn't say it aloud, but she hoped Father understood.

Kristofer stood and shook Father's outstretched hand. "I understand. But I want to make sure it is well with both of you that I continue tutoring with Mary. If Mary is willing, that is."

"Of course I am." Mary didn't have to think twice.

"You're a fine man, Kristofer. A fine, er, student for Mary. We couldn't be happier." Father's voice had turned so grave, Mary looked to Mother, who was grinning and clasping her hands to her heaving bosom.

Kristofer was serious too. "I will do my best by her."

What on earth was happening? "So we can still study English?"

Father grinned. "Fine by me."

"Oh yes, Kristofer should keep coming by in the evenings. To *read*. Reading is important, and here you are in a new land, doing all you can to improve yourself. Mary is such a good teacher too." Mother nodded. "Bring the girls with you. Now that they can start attending the regular school— You heard that, didn't you? Edmund said the teacher arrives next Monday— Anyway, I'll miss seeing Agata and Britta's bright little faces every day. We're working on a project, the three of us, samplers, and— Oh." She stopped when Father nudged her arm. "Yes, well, perhaps I should look in on that chicken."

Mary recalled the oven door opening not fifteen minutes ago. "Didn't you just put it in?"

Father took Mother's elbow. "I'll help judge how it's progressing."

"But the chicken will still be raw," Mary said to no one in particular.

Then she realized she and Kristofer were alone. He resumed his seat across the sofa from her and took a deep breath.

"So," Mary began.

"I brought you something," he blurted. Digging into his coat pocket, he withdrew Britta's Dala horse, but the red paint on the foreleg had been repaired.

"Lilja?"

"No, this is new. For you. To thank you for teaching us, the girls and me. I've been working on it for a few days."

She turned the figure in her hand, admiring the craftsmanship, the swirls of paint. Ah, the crack wasn't there. This was, indeed, not Lilja. "I love it. It means so much to me that you made me a Dala horse. It'll remind me of teaching the girls—and you. But it sounds like we'll still be studying English in the evenings."

He shifted closer to her on the sofa so their knees were touching. "About that. I must warn you, Mary, when I come for schooling, I won't want to be studying."

"You won't? But you just said you wanted to continue our tutoring sessions."

"I do. And I want to read, but I won't want to then, when we're studying together. I will be sitting with you at the kitchen table, and I'll be directed."

"Directed?" It was hard to think, the way he was looking at her. "You mean directed by your desire to read? It's a good thing to be focused on studying."

"No. I'll be focused on something *else*. Not the books."

"Your farm?" Her voice was a whisper.

His head shook a fraction. "I'll be thinking how much I want to hold your hand and take a long walk under the night sky. I'll be looking at your lips and your hair and your eyes and won't care about reading. I'll be directed by you."

"Oh." She licked her smiling lips as understanding dawned. "I think you mean *distracted*."

"Distracted." He shrugged as if, for the first time, he didn't care if he learned the right word or not. "I don't want you to just tutor me, Mary. I want you to court with me."

"You want to court me," she corrected, her voice teasing.

"Doesn't it take a *with*? Two people to court?"

"I suppose it does."

"Your father and mother approve."

"You asked them?"

His brow quirked. "We weren't really discussing tutoring just now, Mary."

She replayed the conversation in her head. *"You're a fine man. . . . Couldn't be happier." "I will do my best by her."* "Oh!"

His eyes were as serious as a tombstone. "When I saw you down on the floor, I was so scared, Mary. Everything changed. I knew you were more than my friend. I understood why I am always so anxious to see you. Why I want to be with you. Why I want the best for you. I want to court you."

Her breath was ragged. "Are you sure? What about Agata and Britta? Would they mind if we—"

"*Jag är kär i dig.*" He inched closer. "I'm in love with you. They love you too, but not the way I do. Not the way I hope you love me."

Oh! "I love them too. But not the way I—I love you."

"That is one of many things I love about you, how you love my daughters."

"I love the way you love them too. You're a good father, Kristofer."

"So do you want to court with me, älskling? Ja or nej?"

He was so close that when she nodded, the tips of their noses touched. One breath. Then two. His hand reached behind her neck, gentle so as not to hurt the goose egg still throbbing behind her head. Then his lips met hers, soft and sweet as apple butter, and it was a good thing she was sitting down, because her knees might give out.

Sometime later a pan banged on the stove, loud as a shotgun blast. Mary jumped from Kristofer's arms.

"Say, I reckon Kristofer's itching to select his pigs," Father announced from the kitchen. "I'm gonna go fetch him right now, Lorena."

"You do that," Mother yelled.

Not so subtle, those folks of hers.

Kristofer's smiling eyes radiated warmth the sun couldn't match. "Will you help me pick out pigs?"

"I'm not an expert, but I don't want to be anywhere else."

"Perhaps I can sneak another kiss when we are in the barn. If you do not mind."

"Mr. Nilsson." Mary grinned. "I insist."

Epilogue

Summer

"Ready?" Mary Nilsson asked her husband of five minutes.

"Ready." Kristofer adjusted a wayward laurel leaf from his wife's bridal crown. Then he placed a soft kiss against Mary's temple that she felt to her toes.

"Then let's take our seats. I imagine everyone is hungry." He assisted her into one of the chairs set at the small table beneath the wildflower arch set up behind the church and took his seat beside her.

Mary might have been the teacher, but she'd learned a bit about Swedish customs during the last few months, and she was delighted to incorporate several into her wedding, like the floral arch. Instead of a bonnet or veil, she wore a circlet of laurel leaves atop her dark hair, and she'd placed coins in each of her shoes. Their friends and family all brought dishes for a festive smorgasbord lunch reception. And—

"Don't forget, everyone gets to kiss you." Agata pressed her lips against their cheeks in rapid succession. "It's tradition at a *bröllop* to kiss the bride and groom."

Mary's nephew Tom, who was five, scowled. "I'm not kissing nobody."

"Me neither." Tom's seven-year-old brother, Will, covered his lips with his hands.

"Nobody's kissing you two anyway," Agata said. "You're not the groom."

Britta made her little horse, Lilja, kiss Mary's hand.

"All right, you four, time to eat." Flossie, Mary's sister-in-law and matron of honor, gathered the children.

"The food smells wonderful." Mary's brother, Alva, rubbed his stomach.

Mary's growled in response. "Where's the preacher to say grace?"

Ah, there he was, talking with Hjalmar, Kristofer's best man. Though Hjalmar had helped with the corn, he'd spent a lot of time helping Oscar Blom's family too.

Oscar had gone willingly to the sheriff. He'd had quite a turnaround after pushing Mary that day in her kitchen. Seeing her on the floor like that—the way his mother had died—had broken something in him, and he was determined to repay what he'd stolen and receive whatever punishment was meted to him.

Since the items were returned and Oscar was so young, the lenient judge counted time served as his sentence but suggested that the Blom family leave town, which was not an uncommon practice when doling out punishment, Mary had learned. The Bloms hadn't moved far, just to Turtle Springs, but Hjalmar would soon be joining them permanently, once Kristofer bought out Hjalmar's share of their farm and Hjalmar married Ebba.

Kristofer now watched his brother. Mary nestled against his shoulder. "We'll see him often, I'm sure."

"You're right, Wife. And today is certainly not a day to be sad, eh? Not when we have so much to thank God for. Our corn crop is ripening for harvest, the sky is blue, the piglets from your father are growing fat, the girls are happy, and I am married to you." He looked as if he might kiss her, but something caught his eye. "Ah, Sheriff Miles. Thank you for coming."

The lawman rested his fists on his hips. "I hear we're supposed to buss the happy couple or there's trouble."

"Big trouble." Mary laughed.

"I don't want to have to arrest m'self then." The sheriff pecked Mary's cheekbone.

Her parents waited behind him. Mary exchanged kisses with both of them, and while Mother kissed Kristofer on the lips, Father settled for a handshake.

There were more kisses—from her students and their parents, her friends and Kristofer's friends, and several rounds from Britta and Agata.

Pastor Gavell waved his arm. "All right, there'll be more time for kissing later. Let's bow our heads."

After grace, they dined on fish and cold dishes—the hot dishes came afterward, then cheese, according to Kristofer. At some point, Kristofer's hand reached beneath the table to take Mary's. His hot, calloused fingers linked through hers. She didn't ever want to let go, but then Britta ran up and patted Mary's cheek.

"When is cake, Mamma?"

Little Britta, shy and sweet, had called her Mamma.

Mary's eyes stung with tears. "Soon, little one."

Kristofer swiped her cheeks with his thumb. "No tears now."

"They're happy tears." Joyful ones, birthed from the blessings God had given her these past several months. A changed heart. Kristofer. The girls. Mercy for Oscar.

"Because it's finally time for cake?" Britta looked confused.

"Yes, that too." Mary gathered her in a hug.

Then Agata, who had come running, asked, "Cake now?"

When Kristofer could retake Mary's hand, he smiled down at her, that smile that warmed her more than the summer sun overhead.

She smiled up at him. "*Jag älskar dig.*"

"I love you too." He grinned.

It didn't matter the language. The meaning was, and ever would be, perfectly clear.

Susanne Dietze began writing love stories in high school, casting her friends in the starring roles. Today she is the award-winning author of a dozen new and upcoming historical romances who's seen her work on the ECPA and *Publishers Weekly* bestseller lists for inspirational fiction. Married to a pastor and the mom of two, Susanne lives in California and enjoys fancy-schmancy tea parties, the beach, and curling up on the couch with a costume drama and a plate of nachos. You can visit her online at www.susannedietze.com and subscribe to her newsletters at http://eepurl.com/bieza5.

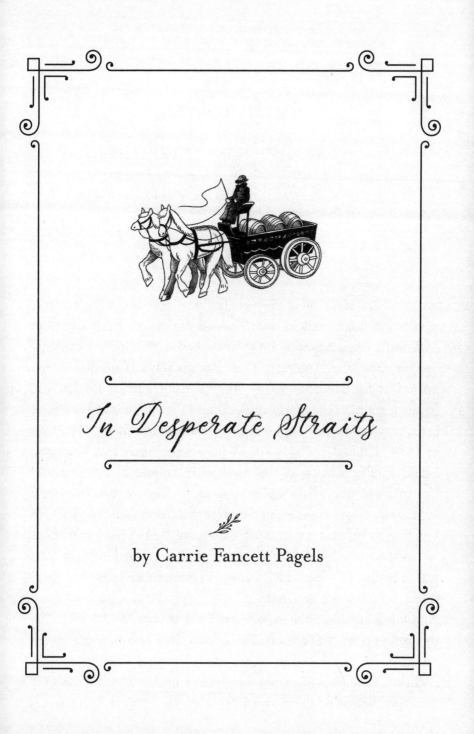

In Desperate Straits

by Carrie Fancett Pagels

Dedication

To Mary Jane Barnwell and Tamara Tomac, for sharing and encouraging the love of Mackinac Island books at the Island Bookstore and for their many kindnesses toward me.

Author's Notes

Students in rural areas, especially in one-room schools, were reported to attend school from November through April and from May until August before 1900 (www.heritageall.org/wp-content/uploads/2013/03/Americas-One-Room-Schools-of-the-1890s.pdf). But the students in my story are not needed for harvest. Instead, many of the island students and their families would have been busy the entire "high season" of summer. So for this story set in 1894, I have school begin in mid-September. The Mackinac Island Public Schools at that time were housed in the beautiful Indian Dormitory. This was no tiny one-room schoolhouse but a large, imposing building not far from the fort. You can visit this building today, as it is part of the Mackinac State Historic Parks.

In this novella I refer to the devastating Great Hinckley Fire, which really did occur in Minnesota in September 1894. My characters, however, are fictional.

Only a small number of soldiers lived at Fort Mackinac during this time period. In fact, I had to stretch their occupation a bit for my story. As mentioned in the wonderful book *A Desirable Station: Soldier Life at Fort Mackinac 1867–1895* by Dr. Phil Porter, only eleven soldiers lived there after 1892. I borrowed the real-life names of Captain Witherell, Lieutenant Geary, and Lieutenant Vance, but the rest of the characters are fictional, as are the captain's daughter and Miss Dearing (named for a special York High schoolteacher).

There really is a large Percheron farm in Pickford, Michigan, in the Eastern Upper Peninsula of Michigan, which supplies most of the dray horses on Mackinac Island today and has for the past several decades. Sweet Grass Farms Percherons is real; the Hadley Percheron Farm, however, is fictional. I've always loved Percherons. These gentle giant horses do the hard work on Mackinac Island, where no cars are allowed. So, to visit, you must take a boat or ship and then travel by foot, carriage, horseback, or bicycle.

Part of the inspiration for this novel came during a hay wagon ride up to the Cannonball Express on Mackinac Island for barbecue. I was in an orthopedic boot for my foot (I could barely walk for about five years), and I couldn't manage to get up onto the wagon bed. The wonderful driver, Judy Bishop, allowed me to sit up with her as she drove, and she shared about her vocation with me.

You'll revisit a number of my characters from these previous books: *My Heart Belongs on Mackinac Island: Maude's Mooring*; *His Anchor* in *First Love Forever*; and the Christy Lumber Camp Series.

Acknowledgments

To Abba Father—my hope is in You alone. Thank you to my son, Clark, for brainstorming a really fun Victorian twist on a chapter. *Merci* to my amazing critique partner, Kathleen L. Maher, who also has a novella in this collection. Much gratitude to Susie Dietze and Rita Gerlach, who are kind ladies and fantastic to work with.

Thank you to Erika Bishop of Sweet Grass Farms Percherons for all your help, and to your sister-in-law, Judy, for inspiration for this story. Very much appreciated.

God bless my Pagels Pals group members who support my writing ministry.

Thank you to Glenye and Christopher Oakford and "Moo," who loaned their names to the story, and to the many others from whom I "borrowed" names.

Much appreciation to Becky Germany, who suggested a schoolteacher's collection to us. Thank you to my erstwhile agent, Joyce Hart, who is a true blessing. We couldn't get our story out without our wonderful editor Becky Fish. And thank you to all the folks at Barbour Publishing who get our book babies out into the world and who answer questions, especially Laura Young. Thank you to the readers who continue to buy our stories and keep us working!

Prologue

Hadley Percheron Farm
Pickford, Michigan
May 1893

Gathering breakfast plates, Maggie Hadley peered over her father's shoulder at the front-page headline of *Soo Evening News*: Country Heading toward Economic Crisis.

Pa jabbed a stout finger at the paper. "The country might be in a crisis, but people will always need horses to pull their wagons."

Maggie's gut clenched as her two youngest brothers exchanged a quick glance and pushed away from the long oak table.

John brushed back a lock of auburn hair from his hazel eyes. "You haven't forgotten about those auto mobiles they are starting to build, have you, Pa?"

Pa snorted. "Only a fool would think they'd ever be able to pull heavy drayage down the streets." He kept his gaze fixed on the newspaper, but her brothers rolled their eyes heavenward. Maggie shot them what she hoped was a quelling look.

"We're going out to feed the horses, Pa," John called over his shoulder as the boys headed toward the front door.

Pa grunted in agreement.

Ma, seated to Pa's left, set her napkin on the table. "Our bank is out in that barn. All that horseflesh. No need worryin' about rich people's problems."

Pa turned and looked up at Maggie. "Your ma is right. Go on and get those dishes started, Maggie girl, in case our company shows up early."

Ma tucked a stray blond curl behind her ear as she rose from the table. "The Huntingtons will be here in a bit."

Pa's lips worked into a thin worry line before he turned his attention back to the paper. Maggie strode away to the nearby kitchen and glanced out the window into the yard. She had been warned to mind her p's and q's while the wealthy railroad owner and his son visited. And that didn't sit well with her. At twenty-one-years-old, why should she have to be treated like a child?

Maggie set the dirty dishes on the wood counter. She pushed scraps for the dogs off into one bowl and the rest into a covered tin receptacle that they used for garbage. She removed the hot water from the stove and poured it over the dishes. Maggie carefully set the heavy pot back on the stove and then returned to the sink and added baking soda to the water, then swished it around with her scrub brush. Out the window, she could see their two hounds chasing one another in the yard.

Ma moved alongside her. "Those two sure love to chase each other, don't they?"

"Yes, they sure do." Beyond the dogs, her two brothers shoved each other playfully. "As do your two youngest."

Chuckling, her mother dipped her blue-and-white-speckled coffee mug into the dishwater. "They better not engage in such behavior when that prim-and-proper college boy shows up with his father.

Scowling, Maggie began scrubbing the dishes. "Just because his father owns half the national railroads, it doesn't give them a right to prance in here and try to buy Pa's horse stock."

Ma elbowed her gently. "I think you mean *our* not *your pa's* horse stock. This is a family business, after all." Ma, raised in Michigan's Eastern Upper Peninsula, had learned to fend for herself and perform many "men's" chores her entire life. And she obviously considered herself an equal with Pa.

"So you think Pa means it when he says all of us have a crack at running this farm? Me included?"

"Of course. And if he didn't. . ." Ma snatched a wooden spoon from the dishwater and waved it around, spattering the counter with droplets. "I'd have to make my point with a rap on his noggin."

Maggie laughed. "You wouldn't."

"He won't try me." Ma tapped the spoon against her work-roughened palm.

Pa joined them. "What's that?"

"Our daughter could help run the farm one day, when you can't."

"She can try, dumpling. Doesn't mean she will." Pa winked before Ma playfully attempted to hit him with the spoon. He ducked away.

"Now wouldn't that be a good sight for Maggie's potential beau to see once he arrives?"

"What?" Both Ma and Maggie spit out the word in unison.

"Sure thing." Pa stroked his short salt-and-pepper beard. "Instead of selling that young college fella and his pa any of our horses, I'll pull an old switcheroo and have him married off to Maggie in a trice."

Maggie stared at her father. Her mother's eyes were wide as saucers.

"You've plum lost your mind, Mr. Hadley." Ma shook her head and sighed.

Chuckling the whole way, Pa headed toward the heavy oak front door and closed it securely behind him.

"Well, I never." Ma huffed a breath.

"As if." Maggie plunged her hands into the hot dishwater and swished the dishes around. "I suppose if they needed a maid, they could consider me." But a wife? Never.

"Still, it wouldn't hurt for you to purty yourself up a bit."

Maggie ceased stirring the water. "Ma? Do I need to drive both you and Pa over to the new asylum in Newberry?"

"I don't think it's in operation yet." Ma smirked. "Besides which, if you drove us over there, then those town folks might think you're more than a little odd yourself."

"If I were a man. . ."

"Yes, I know. If you were a man, you'd be the best dray driver around. All of Pickford knows that, and they understand. But town people—"

"Another matter entirely." As Ma had said numerous times. So this was to be Maggie's life. Washing up and doing housework instead of working outside all day long.

"I'll finish up the dishes, and you go fix yourself up." Ma laughed. "At least practice some of your womanly ways on this city fella. It can't hurt."

If it got her outside and near her beloved horses, then Maggie was all for it. "Yes, ma'am."

Jesse Huntington surveyed the large white, wood-clad farmhouse set amid rolling fields of grass. Hardwood trees bordered the property. He blew out an exasperated breath. With this depressed economy, what was his father doing trying to purchase some of the

Hadleys' draft horses? And since they were so busy already with railroad company business, why bother with this odd venture?

Father's anxious laughter, while conversing with the owner, frayed the edges of Jesse's own nerves.

"Mr. Hadley, do you enjoy the rustic life here?" Father's jovial tone, directed at the Percheron farm owner, didn't imply condescension, but still Jesse cringed.

The bearded man, who stood a head shorter than Father, grinned—apparently taking no offense. "Love it. Love my life. Very blessed. Love all these critters." He gestured around to the massive draft horses that were getting their fill of grass in the nearby field.

"Exactly. The simple life." Father drew in a deep gulp of air. "Away from all the stench of the city."

Jesse suppressed a laugh. The air smelled strongly of horse manure emanating from the nearby open barn. But a gentle breeze did carry a tinge of fresh evergreens and hay. Jesse would go mad if he lived in a place like this. Now that he'd finally graduated college, he would much rather be back in Father's office in the city.

Mr. Hadley shrugged. "With five sons and a daughter, it's never been a simple life."

In the distance, a drayman slapped the reins on the back of two stout draft horses and turned them onto the Hadleys' property. With a straight back, a large slouch hat pulled low over his brow, and a navy bandanna wrapped around his neck and mouth, the rider looked more an outlaw than a delivery man. Jesse glanced at Mr. Hadley, who removed a handkerchief from the pocket of his overalls and wiped his brow.

He raised a suntanned hand. "Excuse me for a moment." Mr. Hadley loped over to the drayman, who'd stopped about two stones' throws from the barn.

Jesse squinted, removed his eyeglasses, wiped them with his monogrammed linen handkerchief, then put them back on. A white-and-blue-checked shirt peeked from beneath the driver's jacket sleeves. That and his somewhat small-looking scuffed brown boots struck Jesse as odd.

Father scowled. "There's nothing on that dray. Wonder what he wants."

"Maybe he's picking up something from the Hadleys." Throughout his life, Jesse had been warned that others might try to harm them because of their prominent social position, but it seem that the drayman was well known to Mr. Hadley.

As they watched, the driver, with an alacrity Jesse rarely observed, maneuvered the horses and dray around and back out onto the dirt road.

"Those must be some of Hadleys' horses. Strong and sure-footed. Did you see that turn they did? Exceptional." Father's mood was downright jovial today, something Jesse hadn't observed at the office.

"Yes, an exceptional turn." Was it the horses who were responsible or the driver? That took some skill to execute the tight turn.

Mr. Hadley rejoined them, his pleasant features tense. "Sorry about that."

Father tapped his walking stick into the mud. "Were those your horses, Hadley?"

"Yes." The man's terse tone would have dissuaded Jesse from more questions, but not Rutherford Huntington III.

"Your driver? I've never seen anything quite like it." Father leaned in, as if expecting a reply.

Striding forward toward the barn, Mr. Hadley ignored the question and waved toward the stalls, filled with the Percherons they bred and cared for.

Two young men attired in work clothes and floppy hats mucked out the stalls. They grinned at Jesse, and he smiled and tipped his hat back at them, suddenly feeling ridiculous in his suit. "Beautiful horses." Unneeded beauties though, too far from the Huntingtons' Charleston home, and an unnecessary purchase in the current difficult economy. Where he and Father needed to be was in Charleston, at work.

For the next hour, they looked over the various horses. Mr. Hadley was willing to discuss selling only four. Jesse ambled out of the barn and into the sunlight. He pulled his gold pocket watch, a graduation gift, from his vest and flipped open the cover. It was getting late, and they'd need to leave soon.

The farmhouse's front door opened. A slim young woman dressed in a simple brown work skirt topped by a white apron and covered in a dark navy shawl tightly wrapped around her trod toward them. She looked to be nearly as tall as he was, with wide shoulders. As she neared, his breath caught. If someone had merged a Nordic warrior woman's strong face with that of a gentle English rose, it would have resulted in this young woman's beautiful features. Her focus was pinned on the back of Mr. Hadley. But then she cast Jesse a quick glance. He waited for a second and longer look that was sure to come despite his spectacles. Most young women he met made sure they fixed him with an appreciative sustained appraisal. Some were coyer than others about it, but this young woman took about as much notice of him as a fence post. A niggle of irritation worked through him. Hadn't he complained that the only thing that drew attention to him was his money, or rather his father's money? She was likely the farmer's daughter. Perhaps she didn't feel he would give her the time of day.

Since she was taking no notice of him, Jesse surreptitiously watched as she crossed her arms and paced behind her father and his own. With that cross look on her face, she didn't seem any happier about this purchase than he was.

Jesse took several long strides to join the small group.

The young woman tapped Father on his shoulder. "If you live in

South Carolina, like you're saying, then why would you want to buy Goldy and Silver way up here?"

Mr. Hadley wrapped an arm around the young woman. "He'd like them for his Mackinac Island home."

"Why? You can't possibly require two Percherons to pull your carriage, sir."

Father laughed. "But I want them. They're spectacular. I love quality, my dear."

"We do have quality Percherons here, Mr. Huntington." Hadley gave his daughter what was probably supposed to be a stern look, but the young woman glared right back.

She cocked her head. "Will you stable them here with us then, out of season?"

Father's jowls shook as he laughed. "I like you, young lady. You'd have made a good businesswoman."

Miss Hadley jutted out her jaw. "I'm the best—"

Her father waved his hand, and she ceased speaking, which surprised Jesse. She seemed like the type who'd keep on talking over anyone else who got in her way. Vivienne, his younger sister, could do that with such southern charm that almost no one else realized she was doing it.

"Maggie, go run and have your mother bring one of the contracts from my desk in the house."

She bobbed her head once, and then actually ran like a man would, across the yard to the house.

So, would Jesse ever know what this Maggie thought she was the best at? Perhaps they'd have an invitation in for a hearty lunch.

Father pulled out his pocket watch and checked it. "I'll need to sign that form, pay you, and we'll need to be on our way, Mr. Hadley."

Now Jesse would never know. Unless he asked. "Excuse me, Mr. Hadley, what was your daughter trying to say she was the best at?"

Both older men fixed him with a penetrating gaze that bespoke volumes. He raised his hands. "Sorry, I was curious."

"Curiosity killed the cat, Son." Father shook his head in disapproval.

"I'm not a cat."

Mr. Hadley guffawed. "You got your pa on that one. So I'll let you in on a little secret."

Jesse leaned in. "Yes?"

"She's the county fair winner three seasons running for best jam."

"Jam?"

"Yes, sir, she is." Mr. Hadley beamed.

Jesse had been sure she'd been about to disclose something fascinating. Something different. But somehow the disappointment he felt should have made it easier to leave. He didn't believe Miss Hadley was about to say anything about winning blue ribbons for making jam.

"Here it is!" Maggie jogged into the barn, her shawl flapping open to reveal a white-and-blue-checked shirt. Like the breakneck speed dray driver was wearing earlier. And on her feet were similar, if not the same, brown work boots worn by the expert driver.

Jesse smiled and chuckled to himself. Miss Hadley shot him a quizzical look, and he rubbed his jaw, trying to stifle his delight with his discovery. Too bad he'd never see her again.

Chapter 1

Charleston, South Carolina
January 1894

Jesse Huntington settled in at his home office's massive mahogany desk, which had been cleared except for one tray piled high with letters from creditors. Father's grave had barely been dug, months earlier, before Jesse had discovered the desperate financial straits they were in. He reached for the silver personal correspondence tray, and his heart lurched when he spied Mr. Reynolds's name and address on it. He slit the envelope open and pulled out the single page and scanned it. He crumpled the cryptic rejection letter from Mr. Reynolds in his hand and tossed it into Father's black leather–covered wastebasket. Still no job for him. *One of my last hopes.* His jaw muscle spasmed.

The eight-paneled office door creaked open. Mother, attired in her expensive and frivolous black mourning gown, peeked in, the wide puffed sleeves, satin fabric, and ornate lace speaking volumes about her opinion of his announcement that they must cut expenses. She clutched a newspaper in her hand as she eyed the stack of bills. "How long do you think we have?"

The sum of what was left in the accounts and in the cash he'd kept for emergencies would be gone in a trice if she kept up her spending. Not long at all if he couldn't procure a job. "Enough time to get us up to the island and back to the. . ." He'd almost said *summer home*, but now the West Bluff cottage on Mackinac Island would be their only home.

"Back to our new home. We'll still be among our own kind there—even if they're mostly Yankees."

Mother sniffed. "As was your dear father."

She'd loved Father. No doubt about that. Who else would put up with his long absences and cantankerous moods? Some of Mother's devotion no doubt stemmed from having been pulled up from being an impoverished southern belle and to being married to a wealthy man. Father had saved her family's estate and plantation, but now both were about to be sold to pay off their creditors. "Your least favorite northerner just sent me a one-line rejection."

"Mr. Reynolds also refused you?" Her lips compressed in anger. "Wait until I see him on the island. I'll give him a piece of my mind."

Jesse couldn't help but laugh. "Mother, your genteel calling out would likely be perceived as a compliment by him."

She likely had no idea that her soft reprimands, in her southern belle style, would be completely lost on the northern iron mine magnate who was possessed of an imaginative assortment of profanities. Mother blinked up at him, her right hand clutching the newspaper so tightly that it began to crumple. "The advertisement has been published."

Jesse extended his hand and accepted the paper. He opened to the appropriate section. *A Large House on the Battery.* That had to be it. He scanned the notice, his chest muscles tightening as though battery was being committed upon him. He refolded the *Charleston Gazette* and passed it back to his mother. A house was not a home. Home would be wherever he and his family landed on their feet.

"If anyone asks, you did take that tour of Europe your father promised you."

"I'm not going to lie." He'd worked the summer after his graduation from Harvard alongside his father. Then the horrendous hurricane had hit Charleston in late August. As Jesse and the entire family were en route to evacuate to Summerville, his father's heart had failed him. "At least the house survived the hurricane relatively unscathed." Unlike Father.

Mother's eyes widened, and she blinked back tears. "I never knew. . ."

Jesse handed her his handkerchief and pointed to the nearby settee.

She shook her head. "I had no idea how much our so-called friends despised your father."

Jesse ducked his chin and stared down at the wool Persian rug at his feet, one of Father's favorites. "He was a Yankee." As were the Huntington children, by default. But more than that, his father had turned out to be a ruthless businessman, something that Jesse hadn't realized until he'd worked directly with the man. The only time he'd seen Father relaxed and generous in a business deal was when he'd bought the Percherons in Michigan. The image of a strawberry-blond young woman stamping her booted toe in the dirt came to mind.

"Well, I will always remember that first and foremost I am Camille Calhoun. Papa always told me no one could take that from me." Mother's countenance altered oddly. She laughed. "We'll enjoy our summer resort home, and by fall we'll be back here and the world will be set aright." She beamed up at him, a southern belle at her most charming.

Jesse stiffened. Mother's moods had been somewhat unpredictable before Father's death, but now she was becoming irrational. Short of a miracle, their world as they knew it would never be the same.

Hadley Percheron Farm
March 1894

Maggie sat, her heavy skirts arranged around her, on a wood bench made from two stumps topped by a wide slat of wood. She rubbed a flannel rag sopped in saddle soap into harness leather while Pa and the veterinarian from Mackinac Island looked over their Percherons. Soon it would be time to transfer the horses back to the island.

Dr. Howerter, as usual, took his time examining each draft horse. "They're all looking pretty good to me, Buck."

Pa nodded. "Wish I knew how many they're gonna contract for this year though."

"Hard to say with the economy being what it is right now."

"It's got to turn around soon." Pa patted Bear's rump. Bear was his favorite. And he was also the horse Maggie normally used when driving the dray into town for her family's business.

"I heard your boys had to take positions elsewhere. Will they be coming back at least for the season?"

"Winter got so slow they had to take up jobs in the logging camps and over in the Soo at the new locks being built. But my two youngest will be back soon, and we stipulate in our contracts that at least one Hadley will be driving dray for Danner's dray service."

"I see. I thought you had an arrangement like that with Danner."

Maggie turned away and rolled her eyes in irritation. She was a much better driver than any of her brothers. Too bad the islanders couldn't simply look the other way, like the folks in Pickford did, when she made deliveries. At five feet eight inches tall, she might not compare to her brothers at more than six feet and with well-muscled arms, but she was strong enough to load and unload moderately heavy supplies.

From the open barn door, she saw their neighbor Phillip Crist ride in. The families took turns picking up mail when it was delivered to town. Normally Mr. Crist would be on horseback, but today he was driving the mercantile owner's light carriage. As the carriage moved forward, the passenger with Mr. Crist, wrapped in a navy wool blanket, slumped forward.

It was her brother Russell.

"Russ!" Maggie ran out of the barn and into the yard. Ma came out of the front door, and the two of them moved toward the carriage, where Mr. Crist was assisting Russell down. Pa and Doc ran up and each wrapped an arm around her brother, who looked as pale as death.

"What happened?"

"A tree came down on him." Mr. Crist removed his hat. "A widow-maker."

Doc gave him a sharp glance. "Then he's lucky to be alive."

"Let's get him to his room."

Hours later they'd gotten Russell settled in his own bed, and he was sleeping comfortably. They'd also sent word to Newberry for a physician to ride out. Ma and Pa sipped tea and rocked in their matching ash wood rockers. "Ought to look at the mail, I reckon."

Maggie got up from the table, where she'd been peeling potatoes, and brought them the twine-wrapped stack that Mr. Crist had brought from town. She returned to her task when she heard Ma gasp.

"This is from John's landlady, Mrs. Scholtus. It says he's been badly injured at the Soo Locks site. Oh my poor boys!" Ma began to cry.

What would they do without her brother's incomes to help? Maggie grabbed her work coat and headed out to the barn and to her beloved horses. She had to do something to help. She passed Goldy and Silver's stall but then turned back around. Mr. Huntington, their owner, had died, and they'd received no payment for stabling them that winter. Pa didn't want to bother Mrs. Huntington because he'd read they'd lost their fortune. What if they wanted to sell Goldy and Silver to someone who abused them? She stepped into the stall and patted Goldy on her side and then pressed her cheek against her neck. What would the Huntingtons do? They had a contract showing that the horses were theirs.

A contract.

Mr. Danner.

The Mackinac Island businessman would have to honor his contract this season. She could put her horse skills to good use. She could drive dray, posing as one of the Hadley boys. Because it wouldn't be only Goldy and Silver being sold by the Huntingtons—if her family couldn't take care of taxes and business expenses, the whole stable was threatened.

Maggie straightened and then leaned back, peering up at the barn rafters as if some other answer would come to her there. But those softly whispered words in her heart of a contract with Mr. Danner swirled around in her soul, urging her to take action.

Could she?

On board a train headed north

Jesse's sister Florence lay with her head on his shoulder as they rode north on what had once been one of his father's train lines. Her soft snores were no rival for the noise of the train tracks and the sounds of conversations around them. What a strange sensation to be in a regular passenger car. Mother, seated across from him, kept her eyes closed, but he knew she wasn't sleeping by the way she kept shifting in her seat. He'd covered her with a wool blanket that he'd also draped across Vivienne. His youngest sister was busy taking notes on the passengers, which she'd explained was for her theatrical pursuits. He didn't bother arguing with her. Father had forbidden her aspirations, and Mother was too distraught at present to discuss what Vivienne could and could not do.

He glanced down at his copy of the *Detroit Free Press* which included several articles about the May Day riots. He'd hoped to pursue some of Father's lesser contacts in the North for possible work, but with all this discord, would it be safe to bring his family to any of those cities? He could leave the women on Mackinac Island if he procured a job in Chicago or Cleveland and bring them down when things calmed. But no one had yet even replied to his inquiries, much less outright rejected him. He glanced at the classified section, which along with the usual search for lumberjacks and laborers, also contained several teaching positions posted for hire.

Vivienne waggled a finger at him. "A penny for your thoughts."

He exhaled sharply. "They aren't worth that much, so hang on to your money."

Her lips formed into a pout. "That's all you ever think about."

"I was talking about selling those Percheron horses, not only because we could use the funds. . ." He rubbed his forehead. He must be more tired than he realized, because he'd almost blurted out that he'd been discussing selling the horses so that he could go to Hadley Farms once more.

"But what?"

"Hmm?" He blinked at his sister as she twirled a long strawberry-blond ringlet around her index finger.

"If it's not about the money, then what's that about?"

He gaped at her. *Because I want to see Maggie Hadley again. I want to challenge her to race her dray back into the yard again so I can tell her I know it was her.* "Because I don't like leaving things unsettled." That was true enough.

"Oh. Pooh." Vivienne blew out an exasperated breath, which puffed up her bangs. "Florence said that bill was not of much account."

He was about to correct her but thought it was better to change the topic. "I recall that several professional theatrical companies come to the island."

"I imagine they'll continue to come. People still want to be entertained to distract themselves from their difficulties."

"And they have a local theatrical group you might be able to investigate now that you'll be staying on the island year-round."

Her blue eyes widened. "When you say it like that, it sounds so real, doesn't it?"

"I'm afraid it is true. We've at least got this home though." For how long he couldn't be sure. What would happen if he couldn't find some kind of work?

Chapter 2

Danner's Stables
Mackinac Island

Maggie sat across from Mr. Stan Danner, her brother Russell's floppy workman's hat firmly atop her head, covering her hair. The way the dray company owner kept glancing at her head, he no doubt thought she ought to remove her hat out of respect during this interview. Why hadn't she thought about all the places where she'd be expected to take off her head covering? How was she to attend church services while she was on the island? She'd have to buck up and cut her hair short—maybe to her shoulders. She glanced up at the businessman from beneath her hat brim.

Mr. Danner heaved a sigh. "You're pretty much a lightweight, which concerns me."

The stable owner was, himself, a compact but wiry man. Maggie bit back a retort and forced out her newly acquired baritone voice,

"I'm a hard worker."

"So your Pa says." Danner tapped the letter in front of him on his pine desktop.

Maggie nodded.

He cocked his head at her. "With the May Day riots, I'm short of dray drivers right now, Mickey."

"Yessir, I'd heard about that." Workers were fed up with their ill treatment and had rioted to protest. "The dock boys commented upon it when I told them where I was going."

A muscle in the older man's jaw twitched. "Without your brothers, we're having trouble keeping up with orders."

"My brothers told me how much they enjoyed working here."

"Hmm, yes." He rose and turned away from her, rubbing his jaw.

"The Hadleys have always tried to honor their contracts." Granted, the contract as written was decidedly one-way, with Mr. Danner being required to offer a position but the Hadleys not required to fulfill it.

The man paced by the back wall and seemed to be stalling. "Yes, and your Pa surely told you how that contract is written."

"Yessir." Hadley men. Not Hadley women. Why had Pa included that one word? One simple word that could prevent her from keeping her family from sinking. They were in desperate straits for sure. She ran her tongue over her lower lip. Surely he couldn't tell she was a young woman. And Pa said he'd never told him. Her two youngest brothers swore they'd said nothing about their sister.

"Your eldest brother by far was one of the chattiest draymen I've ever had." Danner fixed her with his deep brown eyes.

Her heart sank down to her scuffed boots. "He loves to tell a good story. Sometimes makes up all manner of things."

The man's lips pulled together. "Like that he had a younger sister who'd make the best dray driver of all if only she weren't a woman?"

Maggie clamped her eyes shut, cringing.

Danner laughed. "Mickey is a fine name for a young lad. Has a nice ring."

His words jolted through her.

"I believe I'll give you a try." He extended his hand.

He knew. Mr. Danner knew she was Pa's youngest—a daughter—and yet. . .

"You're still gonna hire me?" Maggie swallowed hard.

"That's right. You might be too young to even shave yet, but I'm desperate for drivers. I guess your pa must be too, eh?"

Maggie exhaled the breath she hadn't realized she'd been holding. "Yes, sir."

"I value the Hadley horses, and I need more drivers. I'm willing to overlook your, um"—he gestured to her and frowned—"youth, on one condition."

Oh no. "Yes, sir?"

"Need to see your driving skills for myself. See if that eldest brother of yours is right about your skills."

She usually drove alone, but Pa and her brothers had accompanied her after she'd learned to drive. "Sure thing, Mr. Danner."

"All right, then. Let's go down to the docks and pick us up some luggage."

Luggage? Pa had said there would be a worker with Maggie to unload the bags and she'd only drive. Would Mr. Danner expect her to load and unload? Might as well find out right now if this was going to be an issue. Maggie sent up a quick prayer. "Sir, I need to let you know I'm only fit for driving and dealing with light to moderate weights, not for loading and unloading heavy goods."

"We'll tell my other customers that maybe in a few years when you've picked up another fifty pounds or so of muscle, then I'll let you deal with their cargo and baggage."

Except there wouldn't be all that muscle on her ever, which made her chuckle. "Thank you, sir."

He stood and grabbed his soft, floppy cap. "We'll figure something out. In the meanwhile, I'll do the loading and unloading today, and you just handle my horses." He gave her a hard stare. "Come to think of it, they're likely your own Percherons anyway."

"Yessir." Pa said that more than eighty percent of the dray horses in Danner's stable were from their farm.

"Come on, follow me."

Inside the huge stable, Maggie's eyes widened when she spotted Bear and Moo, from home, feeding at a trough. Bear's ears twitched, and he raised his head and fixed Maggie with his big brown eyes. Moo lifted his head too and flicked his tail back and forth before leaving the trough and heading toward Maggie. He stopped a foot away and bent her head and nudged Maggie's barn coat pocket. She pulled out a carrot, palmed it, and offered it to the majestic Percheron.

"Looks like you'll get along well."

"They're my favorites." She stroked Moo's neck.

"Ah, we're not supposed to have favorites among our children or our horses." Danner winked as he too reached into his pocket and held out a chunk of apple for Moo. "But he's a sweetheart, and there are no two ways about it."

"They both are."

"Well, let's get these two beauties ready to go."

Soon they'd hitched up Bear and Moo, and Maggie and Mr. Danner had mounted the dray. This was different than driving into town at home. Even though the island was only about six miles square, in summer the population increased to thousands of occupants, many of whom congregated downtown not far from the stables. "*Be alert at all times*," Russell had warned her. "*This isn't a country drive.*"

As she directed the horses from the stables onto the street, a stout woman clutching a blond boy's hand stepped out into traffic.

Maggie brought the pair of horses to an abrupt stop. The way the woman glared at her from beneath her wide-brimmed hat, a person would think Maggie had done something wrong, not the other way around.

"This will be regular behavior around here." Danner sighed. "But you handled that well."

They'd turned onto Cadotte Street and had traveled only a block when a pair of bicyclists, two young men wearing matching red-and-white-striped shirts and khaki riding pants zipped in front of the dray. Maggie was ready to rein them in, but the horses acted as though nothing had happened. She'd experienced this kind of reckless behavior during summers at home in town too. Some people sure didn't think much about their lives.

"Turn up there and then pull over by Doud's Market."

Her brothers had emphasized where different stores and specific businesses were located to help Maggie get her bearings; otherwise she might not have seen the sign, because on the side of the business was painted an advertisement for Foley's Photography Studio. A line of carriages was parked alongside the main street as far as she could see. Bear and Moo acted as happy as could be. She set the brake.

The sun broke through the cloud banks and illuminated a ship that had pulled into the harbor.

"The last of the summer crowd, I'm thinkin'." Danner scratched his cheek. "But I'm expectin' a family coming in with a full load."

"Oh." Why hadn't he said so back at the stables?

"I keep watchin' for them, but this is the last ship expected into Haldimand Harbor today, so maybe this time."

"But if they don't arrive, we'll help someone else?"

"No. If they don't arrive, then we'll head up to the fort." His mouth pulled as though he was chewing on his lip. He didn't say why they'd go to the fort, but Russell had told her that a big part of his drayage job was hauling to and from the fort.

Bear's ears flicked as though he heard something that worried him. Maggie sat up straighter. Moo stomped his foot. Maggie surveyed all her surroundings. The fort's garden lay to her left. Although not many soldiers were still stationed there, they continued to grow fresh vegetables. Baby cornstalks tufted at the ground, and lacy green carrot tops populated a long row.

Danner motioned to the garden's end where melon vines grew. "With our milder climate here on the island, we can grow a few more things than on the mainland."

Maggie kept her focus on her surroundings. A heavyset man standing on the sidewalk nearby lit a cigar. Bear lifted his head and tugged, but she held fast. "He doesn't like smoke." Bear had narrowly escaped a barn fire at his previous owner's home. He could ignore chimney smoke, but they kept him from open fires at home and no one smoked at Hadley Farms—it wasn't allowed.

Whistling, Danner pointed to Bear's ears. "On the island, we distract Bear by whistling or talking to him if we've got him around smokers, of which we've many."

"Good idea." Maggie watched as Bear settled right back down into his sturdy Percheron dispositional ways. He shook, jingling the metal hardware on his harness. "Do you think he's reacting more like he would at home with me here now?"

"That could be it, Mickey." Danner grasped his hat as a gust of wind threatened to carry it off.

Maggie continued to scan the street for other vehicles and pedestrians. The ship, now moored, began to disembark passengers. "I'm watching for a young, dark-haired man with his mother and two sisters. All the womenfolk have reddish hair." Danner cast a look at her. "Like all you Hadley men have."

It was true. The Hadleys all had some red in their hair, from strawberry blond like hers to a flaming red like Russell's.

Maggie's hip muscles began to cramp. Truth be told, she wasn't used to waiting anywhere this long. How would she handle the position if she had to sit for hours on end. Just when she thought she couldn't stand another moment, Mr. Danner pointed to the last cluster of people leaving the boat docks. "That's the family I was speaking of. I'll hop down and let the Huntingtons know we're here. You pull in behind that last carriage that's fixin' to leave."

"The Huntingtons?" Did that include the one man who could expose her secret? They'd lost their fortune, businesses, and home in Charleston and hadn't even paid the winter boarding fees for their horses, yet they were here on the island now? Perhaps it was a different family by the same name. But as she stared, gape-mouthed at the handsome dark-haired young man whose spectacles covered what she knew were beautiful hazel eyes, she swallowed hard. She needed this job. And she wouldn't let him ruin things for her.

What a different kind of journey this had been to Mackinac Island compared to years past. Jesse held tight to his boater hat as a Straits of Mackinac breeze gusted. Around him, other men did the same. Even his sisters, whose befeathered and lace-encrusted hats were secured with many hat pins, gripped their wide brims. The ship's horn startled him, and his ears rang.

Mother lifted an eyebrow at him. "I should think you'd be used to that sound after all these years."

He shrugged. His nerves were as taut as a high wire strung over a precipice. The island school hadn't sent him a reply as to when his interview would be scheduled. No interview, no job. No job, no money. And very little money left. . .

"Look!" His sister Florence pointed to the dock where a queue of workers awaited to direct passengers and to carry luggage to the hotels.

This year, compared to last, there were at least twenty percent fewer porters holding wheeled luggage carts. Which wasn't bad, considering the economy. Perhaps Jesse could find something up here. Or several positions.

"First-class baggage?" The heavyset porter approaching them was one Jesse didn't recognize from previous years.

"No, it's in storage below."

"Oh." The man's ruddy face altered from smiling to slight condescension, something Jesse had never experienced before their fall in society but which he experienced now all too often.

"At least we'll get to enjoy the season." Mother sniffed.

"How we'll do that on the allowance Jesse gave us will be a miracle." His sister Vivienne fished around in her reticule and pulled out some Dr. Fisher's Cure-All Mints, opened the tin, and offered one to each of them.

Jesse raised his hand to decline. The porter seemed to be taking his time, perhaps not expecting much of a tip.

A trim man in dungarees, a navy vest, plaid shirt, and floppy cap jogged toward them.

Mother straightened. "Why it's Mr. Danner. He's the owner of the stables, you know. He's come out to greet us." She beamed as though one of her aristocratic former friends from New York had taken it upon themselves to come down to the wharf. The strange gleam in her eyes, which he'd witnessed now for months, since father's death, intensified.

Jesse didn't recognize the man. Not that he'd noticed many of the workers on the small island. When they'd come north, he'd been too preoccupied with his studies and riding roughshod over his younger sisters, who were prone to getting themselves into scrapes.

As he approached, Danner slowed to a quick stride, finally stopping a few steps away from them.

"Mr. Danner!" Mother called out and extended her gloved hands as though welcoming him to her court. "How lovely to see you."

The stable owner removed his cap and dipped his chin. "Ma'am." He nodded in turn at Jesse, Florence, and Vivienne.

A tiny muscle in Mother's cheek twitched as she lowered her hands to her sides. "Thank you for coming to see to our needs in person."

Danner offered a shy smile. "Happy to oblige."

In the distance, Jesse spied their baggage being removed from the ship.

Danner followed his gaze. "We'll get that picked up shortly from the porter, and we'll haul it up to your. . .um, your. . ."

Mother waved her hand airily. "Our summer residence."

The stable owner frowned. "Thought you were taking up year-round residence now. Ain't that right?"

Jesse nodded slowly, locking gazes with the older man, hoping to convey that they were.

Grabbing his arm, Mother glanced between Mr. Danner and himself. "We're expecting Jesse to set things aright soon. He'll probably be taking us to New York in the fall once he's landed a proper position there."

Mother had always embellished the truth. She claimed such exaggeration was her birthright as a southern belle. But lately she seemed to believe her lies. He'd have a chat with her later. He patted her hand. "For now, we are indeed taking up life on the island, Mr. Danner. And thank you for your assistance in getting us settled."

If Jesse didn't find a position soon, they would indeed be leaving the island, or at least he would to go wherever he could procure employment. A pang of regret cinched his chest. Father was gone, and many of his cronies had also lost their fortunes. The ones who hadn't gone bust were circling the wagons and hiring their own family members. Many had indicated that Father's brutality in business dealings was now being returned to his son. Sins of the father and all that.

After the porter joined them and Jesse had tipped him, Mr. Danner took their belongings and pointed toward his dray, parked across the street near the market. The driver tugged a scarf up around his face despite the warm day and shifted in his seat. Strange behavior, but he needed to focus on getting his family settled.

Mother leaned in. "Dear, it's over a mile to the cottage."

Jesse fingered the coins in his pocket that had been saved in case they required a taxi. Although he'd warned Mother and his sisters repeatedly that they'd have to walk up to their home to save money, he couldn't bring himself to make them travel the distance on foot. A year ago, one of their servants would have directed their driver to bring their private carriage down to retrieve them. But their driver hadn't been rehired, and their carriage sat gathering dust in the carriage house. The stables were empty. That thought triggered the recollection that he'd not paid the Percherons' boarding fee. Somehow, some way, he would travel to the Hadleys' farm and take care of the matter. How, he didn't know. Why he felt compelled to do so, he wasn't quite sure. If he were honest with himself, he knew the answer, but. . .

Florence nudged him from behind with her reticule. "What are you waiting for?"

Jesse removed his arm from Vivienne's, shoved his glasses up his nose, and waved at a taxi driver.

Vivienne's eyes widened. "Do you mean we can take the taxi?"

"Of course." Florence moved alongside them and tugged at her short cape.

Vivienne slipped her arm back through his. "I knew you'd come around."

Mother patted his arm. "Dear, we can't be treated like peasants. It simply won't do." Her patronizing smile skewered his heart. She still couldn't accept how dire their straits were.

The driver, a tousle-haired man in his early forties, named his fee, and Jesse swallowed. It was a pittance compared to his old allowance but expensive considering his now limited means. He handed over the coins and then assisted the women up into the coach.

As they traveled on the back streets and then up the incline to the lane past the Grand Hotel and on toward the West Bluff cottages, Jesse's spirits sank. He'd expected to be relieved to be here. But with no job and their assets quickly dwindling, their remaining home might soon have to be sold. Heat prickled his forehead, and he wiped his brow.

"Are you well, dear?" Mother patted his hand. "It's rather chilly out for you to look so feverish."

Florence cast him a quick glance. "He's likely sweating out how he'll feed all of us, Mother."

"Florence!" Vivienne's pixy face contorted into shock. "Don't even tease about such things."

Jesse met his youngest sister's pleading gaze. "Florence is what you might call a humbug."

"Ha!" Florence glared at him. "Humbug, I say."

Vivienne giggled. "She is, isn't she?"

"I didn't raise you girls to behave in such a manner." Mother lifted one genteel eyebrow, and both sisters laughed.

"Father did." Florence tugged at the fingers of her gloves, as though straightening them, a nervous habit of hers. "He always told me to face facts squarely and unafraid."

But when her cheeks reddened, and Florence turned to look out the window, Jesse spied a tear trailing down her face. He closed his eyes. *God, if You're out there, I could use some help.*

The carriage abruptly stopped, and Jesse reached across his mother to prevent her from propelling forward and across the aisle toward his sisters, both of whom clutched the edge of their seat with one hand and their hats with the other.

"Jack Welling, I near to killed you!" The driver called out as a slim boy drove by on a too-large blue bicycle. With a pinched pale face and sad eyes, Jack reminded Jesse of his own reflection in the mirror that morning. Jack's family owned a beautiful yellow home on the cliff, not far from their own. His parents owned and operated the Winds of Mackinac in town.

The carriage once again moved on, and soon they'd arrived at their cottage. Heady scents greeted them from the blooming lilac bushes and trees that dotted the entire property. Soon their spectacular roses would bloom, as would the hydrangeas that banked around their wide front porch. The two-story, Queen Anne–style home sat back from the street with maple trees affording it some privacy from passersby.

Jesse climbed out of the carriage and helped his family down. Although he could ill-afford to tip the driver, the man had well earned it by stopping quickly and sparing the lad in the street. What if he'd hit young Welling? Could Mother hold up under any further trauma? She stood now, as she always did upon their arrival, hands clasped at her waist, inspecting the gardens and exclaiming over the loveliness she found there. Vivienne cavorted around like a spring lamb while Florence crossed her arms over her chest and tapped her booted foot as she stood by the door, waiting for it to be unlocked. Jesse slipped coins into the driver's hand and heaved a sigh.

Almost as soon as the carriage departed, the dray arrived. Mr. Danner sat alongside the driver, smiling. The driver's eyes appeared stricken. What could possibly be so terrifying? When the youth looked up directly at Jesse and his scarf slipped down his face, instant recognition jolted through Jesse. He took two steps back and almost tripped over one of the planters beside the walkway. He continued to watch the dray driver. What was Miss Hadley doing driving a dray on the island? She pulled her neck scarf up again, and Jesse retreated.

Jesse fumbled in his pocket for the house key, finally retrieving it and then dropping it onto the damp ground.

Florence whirled around on the porch. "Aren't you going to unlock this door?"

Mother's shocked expression and her retrieval of another house key from her reticule must have quelled Florence's ire, because she now wore a contrite expression. "Florence, I am yet the head of the household, not your brother. I shan't have you shrieking at either of us like a fishmonger. . . ."

Jesse didn't catch the end of the sentence. Purposefully, he turned and followed the dray around to the back, where they'd unload. Maybe he'd made a mistake. Maybe she had a brother who'd possessed a face too pretty for a man's. Jesse had seen such things before.

He watched as the dray driver climbed down from the dray rather than jumping down as most men would do. An image came to mind of Vivienne at day school in Charleston, engaged in one of her many theatrical productions. Vivienne playing the part of a boy. These were difficult times. Desperate times for many. The May Day riots had shown that. If Vivienne and Florence were on their own and couldn't get work as women, what might they resort to? He didn't want to allow his mind to go there.

What would Miss Hadley need to pass as a young man? She'd need some dirt or theatrical makeup to hide the lack of any facial hair and to conceal the feminine contours of her high cheekbones. And while she wore two layers of shirts, they'd be too heavy if the sun burst from behind the clouds again. But she'd need one shirt to cover and another atop that to disguise. Something lighter for warmer days that were sure to come. Jesse rubbed a hand over his aching brow. He had enough females to concern himself with. Why was he seeking out trouble? Better to accept that Miss Hadley wished to portray herself as a lad and go along with "his" act and maybe even applaud it. But assist? He could barely manage his own family. Still, his natural inclination was to help. If he could. And right now he could assist with the baggage. He rolled up his shirt sleeves.

"If you and I unload, Mr. Danner, then I should be able to bring these belongings into the house on my own." Jesse jerked a thumb toward the back of the dray.

"Sure thing, young man." Danner grinned. "My new driver only handles the smaller bags. He's young and has some filling out to do, but he's a fine driver."

Jesse blinked rapidly as he resisted the urge to raise his eyebrows in disbelief. Meanwhile, the driver turned his back to them, fists on slim hips, apparently surveying the load. Inhaling deeply, Jesse joined in, pulling the heavier baggage forward.

Soon the three of them had the luggage unloaded. Mother had brought a wardrobe trunk, a coat trunk, and several others with Heaven only knew what inside. Jesse packed five crates of his books, his basic clothing needs, and a typewriter. Vivienne surprisingly had conveyed only one trunk of clothing and another trunk of costuming and fabric needs and her sewing machine. Florence took along one small box of clothes and hats plus a large portfolio of father's business papers, which the family hadn't yet finished reading. Then there were sundry boxes whose contents were a mystery to him, most of which the driver carried to the back entryway.

When the dray driver remounted up onto the seat, Jesse resisted the urge to assist her. What he should have been doing was carrying some items into the back of the house. Instead, he gaped up at her, and she turned and caught him staring. Her mouth parted, revealing even, pearly white teeth. Her face was striking, despite a scarf pulled up to her chin and her cloud of hair hidden beneath a hat. He looked hard at her, trying to imagine if someone who'd not previously met her would immediately know she was a female.

He fisted and unfisted his hands at the injustice of a young woman having to put herself into what could be a dangerous situation. He'd have to look out for her. Somehow. Some way. Her face reddened, and she averted her gaze.

"What's your name, lad?"

She ducked her chin and mumbled, "Hadley. Mickey Hadley."

"Nice to meet you, Mickey."

She didn't look up.

Mr. Danner waved. "He's the brother of the usual fellas who drive for me. And he drives just as good as them too! First day on the job, and I'd say Mickey is a keeper."

"Congratulations, Mickey. Thanks for bringing our belongings up for us."

She nodded, then whistled and moved the huge Percherons around in a tight circle, directing them back down the drive alongside the house.

As they went, Jesse couldn't help the concern growing in his heart. He'd make sure he paid off the horses' board to her family as soon as he could.

Chapter 3

Maggie stewed in her own juices as she drove the dray back. The very handsome Jesse Huntington wasn't supposed to be anywhere near Mackinac Island this summer. What was he doing here? And he knew. Mr. Huntington knew that Maggie was a Hadley daughter passing herself off as a son. If he knew, then who else would figure it out? Not something she wanted to contemplate.

Mr. Danner nodded in approval as she had the pair of horses navigate a tricky turn. "Good job. Like a seasoned driver."

Her cheeks heated at the unexpected compliment. "Thank you."

"One of the biggest challenges to the dray drivers is managing these wide turns while watching for tourists walking, bikes darting in and out, and other carriage riders."

Not to mention those riding their horses as though they were on an outing in the woods when they were in fact in downtown traffic. Her brothers had shared their experiences with her, but it was her own trips to Pickford, which could be a busy small town on market day, that had honed her skills. "It can be tricky, but I do love driving." Maggie couldn't help but grin as she directed Bear and Moo to make the wide left turn into the stable.

"Fine job today, Mickey." Mr. Danner patted her shoulder.

When they came to a stop, she prepared herself for the rest of the work that would come. Mr. Danner hopped down. Maggie touched the brim of her hat. "Sir, since this is my team, would you need me to go ahead and take care of Bear and Moo?" That would normally be expected.

He rubbed his chin. "Seems to me that this being your first day, we'll have Leonard and Jerry help you out." He waved two tall dark-haired young men forward.

She exited the dray and moved forward to rub Moo's side. Later she'd spend some time with them in their stalls. They had a special connection, and she was awfully glad to be with them again.

The first of the men extended his hand to her. "I'm Len, and that's my little brother, Jerry."

Maggie hoped her handshake was firm enough, but the man's large hand dwarfed hers. If he noticed, nothing showed on his even features.

Jerry wiped his hands on his red handkerchief and didn't offer his hands. "Heard you were from Pickford. We're from down the road a piece in Newberry."

"Nice to meet you." She kept her voice low like she'd been practicing.

The two men set about unharnessing the team.

"First-timers." Danner leaned in. "But they've been taking good care of Moo and Bear, and I'd prefer to allow them to continue to do so."

"Yes, sir."

Something in the man's dark eyes told her these brothers needed the work. "If you're as good a driver as I sense you are, you might be able to help me train them to drive the dray. I can't spare the time myself right now, nor can any of the other drivers."

Maggie dipped her chin in acknowledgment. "And if you need someone to clean tack, any extra work, I can do that too." She hoped she didn't sound too eager.

"Sure thing." Danner scratched his cheek. "Follow me, and I'll show you where you can bunk down until the cold weather sets in."

Maggie had heard from her brothers that bathing could be a problem for her but that since Mr. Danner gave the Hadleys a private space, she might be able to manage. She followed her employer to a small rectangular room at the far right of the barn behind the office area. He opened the door and waved her past. The room wasn't much better than a stall, with a narrow bed on one wall.

"We'll move you up to one of the servants' rooms at Winds of Mackinac once the season ends. Tends to get a might chilly at night in August." A shadow passed over his face. "We've had a spell of illnesses this past year."

He opened the trunk at the base of the bed and pulled out a pillow and three blankets. "This should keep you plenty warm, but you let me know if not."

She nodded. The room was already cool and damp in the daytime.

"When it's time for a bath, you go over to the back of Winds of Mackinac and let them know, and they'll fix you one up that night when their laundry time is over."

"Yes, sir."

"You'll take your meals at Rosie's."

That café was a good twenty minutes by foot. If she spent forty minutes to and from, that didn't leave much extra time. She had a routine of prayer and Bible study at night. It would be awfully nice to explore the island too.

"They'll give you a box lunch to take with you and a good discount on your dinners if you take them there."

"I plan to pick up something at the market for supper. Might I be able to eat in my"—she bit off the word *stall*—"in my room?"

"Sure thing. But you might enjoy eating out by the water a might better. That's where your brothers liked to eat. Down at Fairy Beach is a popular spot."

"Thank you. They made up a little map for me."

"We'll get you an official stable map too." Danner inclined his head toward the exterior wall. "We're right next door if you need anything at all. Night or day."

Although he surely meant to reassure her, Danner's fatherly tone of concern had the opposite effect.

Jesse rose from his desk and stretched. He'd given his typewriter a good workout with more employment queries to companies in the Midwest. Two nights with a cool breeze ruffling the curtains had done him a world of good. He'd not realized how much the southern climate had sapped his energy when heat and humidity encompassed Charleston. In the past, he'd always looked forward to the relaxing season on the island. Now, though, he needed that extra stamina to track down a job.

A light rap on the door sounded, recalling days when one of their former servants would be announcing breakfast. Instead, Florence stood there, an apron covering her drab skirt, her shirt sleeves rolled up. "Egg, cheese, and ham casserole."

"Any toast?"

Florence snorted and turned on her heel before heading back into the hall. Yesterday's attempt at toasted bread resulted in black briquettes being tossed out into the garbage, and the house had filled with the scent of Florence's failure. Mother had demanded that they send to Mrs. Christy's Tea Shoppe and Bakery for baked goods, but Jesse had quashed that habit before it got a chance to form.

At least they had a loaf of bread left from Doud's. Jesse had never considered how much he personally consumed until Florence's hand had slapped his away from the bread plate at dinner the previous night. "You have a two-piece-per-day allowance," she'd warned him.

Maybe he should get Florence to dress up like one of the soldiers at the fort. It wouldn't take much for her to fit in up there, and they'd feed her. He laughed as he imagined his take-charge sister having to submit to her superior officers' orders.

As he headed down the hall, someone knocked at their front door. He cringed. There was no butler, nor would there be one. Not now. Maybe not ever again. That was a hard reality to accept. He opened the door, trying to remove the scowl from his face.

Jack Welling stood on the porch, hat in hand and wringing it as though it was full of water. He rocked side to side.

"May I help you, Jack?"

The boy peered past him into the house. "Where's all your help?"

Jesse exhaled loudly. "I've locked the servants all in the carriage house. They're quite annoying this year for some reason."

The boy's eyes widened. "That ain't nice."

"No, it isn't nice, but it is what was needed." He winked at him. "Do you hear them yelling back there?"

Jack stood stock-still for a moment. Then he bolted from the porch and around the back of the house. Jesse stepped onto the porch, ruing that his eggs would soon be cold. Possibly inedible. In the distance, a ship steamed toward the harbor. How many of their fellow West Bluff residents would arrive today?

The boy sped back around the corner, panting.

"Jack, how long have you known me?" Jesse made a comical face. "Would I ever make up a silly story?"

The boy scowled but then laughed. "That's a good one. But what did you really do with them?"

Jesse coughed, covering his mouth with his fist.

"I betcha got 'em down in one of the caves, right?"

He and Jack had made up some incredible stories over the years when the boy had visited them, often showing up unannounced at the Huntingtons' home requesting "stories with Jesse."

"That's right. Our entire staff is chained on the back side of the island."

"What did they do?"

Jesse leaned in and whispered, "They woke me too early on my first day back."

The boy made a face of disbelief. "That ain't good enough."

"Well, indeed it isn't enough trouble to chain them up, but I was in a terrible mood." And that part of his story might be true. He was fast becoming a curmudgeon.

"No, no." Jack swiped at the air. "That ain't enough of a good reason for your story."

"Ah. It's the story you complain about."

The door opened, and they both turned to see Florence. She glared at them. "Either come in here and eat or have it out here before the eggs turn stone cold."

Jack took a step forward. "Not yet, Flo. I need to know a good reason why your servants ain't here. And why they've been chained in a cave on the back of the island."

Florence's mouth dropped open. Then she squared her shoulders. "Every single one of them had bet in town at the tavern that you, Jack Welling, wouldn't win the race next weekend."

"Are you serious? I'm gonna win!" He slapped his hat against his thigh.

"Well, of course you will." Jesse patted the boy's shoulder.

Florence crossed her arms. "My sister and I and Jesse corralled all of those foul people, and we had Mr. Danner's new driver take them all to the cave."

"Until they come to their senses." Jesse winked at the boy, whose serious expression suggested he almost believed the story. "We had to avenge their slur on your abilities."

"Oh. Well, that makes sense." Jack turned as if to go. "Wait, I gotta ask something."

Jesse closed his eyes for a moment. Jack could turn story telling into an all-day venture if he was allowed. "What's that?"

"My dad wants you to tutor me." Jack wriggled his nose in disdain.

Digesting that request and grateful that Mr. Welling obviously hadn't shared the Huntingtons' plight with his son, Jesse nodded.

"So you will?"

"Yes, he will." Florence tugged at Jesse's arm, pulling him toward the door. "Come back later, Jack, and give us the specifics."

As soon as Jesse was inside, he fixed his sister with a long gaze, but she simply rolled her eyes at him and stalked off toward the dining room. Mother would have fainted had she observed Florence's demeanor on the porch. When Jesse joined his sisters and mother at the long, rosewood dining table, Florence glared at him before pointing to his plate, which she'd put at Father's spot. Jesse slid the plate and silverware over to his own seat. He wasn't his father. And he'd have to find his own way. But how did he do that when every path seemed blocked?

Chapter 4

Maggie opened her bleary eyes to soft sunrise light filtering through the square window over her narrow bed. Elsewhere, tourists and summer residents were no doubt still sleeping in their comfortable lodgings. She threw off the itchy gray wool blanket and lowered her feet to the hay-strewn wood floor. Maggie drew in a breath and immediately began sneezing. How nice it would be to have indoor plumbing like Pa had installed at home this past year. She'd thought her days of outhouses were over. But that was not to be. First she'd wash up before she headed to the necessary.

Every morning for the past three days, Maggie's face had literally been a sight for sore eyes. She stood and took two steps toward the small wall mirror. Today was no exception—red, swollen eyes reflected back at her. Beneath the mirror sat a square walnut table on which her pitcher and bowl stood. She poured water into the basin, dipped her washcloth into it, then patted her eyes. She'd never had swollen eyes like this at home. It must be from sleeping in a barn.

"Oh no," she groaned. This would not do. Not at all.

Between the noises from the nearby hotel boarding house and the horses in their stalls, and from sneezing much of the night, Maggie hadn't gotten much sleep her first few days. When she did slumber, Jesse Huntington kept showing up trying to help her—and he treated her like a lady, which she really couldn't have happen. So that resulted in nightmares she sure didn't need.

She dressed quickly, pulled her brother's jacket from a hook, and headed off.

When she returned to the stables, she found Mr. Danner speaking with a tall, strapping young man who was stroking Bear's neck. As she approached them, the stranger smiled at her, his light eyes sparkling with good humor. He stepped away from Bear and extended his broad hand as she reached them. "Eli Mitchell, nice to meet you, Mickey."

Mickey gave his hand a firm shake back. "Good to meet you too, Eli."

"Eli will be your partner on the days you're not delivering to the fort." Mr. Danner patted Eli's shoulder. "You're ready for solo outings, but I'm keeping you on the easy routes for now, as we discussed."

"Yes, sir." Today she'd deliver her first drayload to the large, limestone-walled fort atop the hillside.

"Since you're new, that's a fairly direct route. And you'll encounter no trouble with those soldiers unloading the goods. They unload them mighty quick. It's part of the contract with me that they do all the lifting, so you stay right in your seat and let them do their work."

Eli nodded. "They'll pull off everything lickety-split." He brushed his hands quickly together to illustrate.

That was what she needed. But how was she going to manage

on the days Eli rode with her? Would he guess her secret?

Danner winked at her. "Best get on your way, Mickey."

Hours later, Maggie pulled the team to a halt outside the fort's gates, high on the hill at the back entrance. A scrawny, blond-haired soldier who couldn't be much more than eighteen held up his hand.

"Stadte yur bizihnez!" Blue eyes flashed in his narrow ruddy face. From his accent, she'd guess he hailed from an eastern European nation. Mr. Danner said over a third of the men were born outside the United States.

Spitting to the left of the dray, Maggie hoped she gave the impression of an irritated male dray owner. "What's it look like, soldier?"

The private stomped forward. "Vant you I report for dizreespeck?"

"No, sir, I wanta get this stuff in here and out so I can come back up with another load."

Apparently she'd spoken too fast, because the young man blinked up at her, his cheeks reddening further.

She leaned forward and spoke in a slow, deep voice. "I got more loads to bring back."

"Goot." He rubbed his face, which looked almost as smooth as her own. "Know yur way?"

"All the way back around to the left." The quartermaster's building was located there.

"Goot. You go." He waved her through.

Maggie exhaled a long, slow breath as she clucked her tongue at Moo and Bear. Soon they were inside the gates. She glimpsed a handful of uniformed soldiers carrying rifles. They marched in formation on the green lawn at the center of the square of buildings inside the fort. A chestnut-haired young woman watched the men. Attired in a filmy white dress tied with a pink bow at the waist, the beauty stood at the edge of the field and clutched her wide-brimmed pink hat to her head. As the dray moved closer, its wheels crunched over crushed white limestone rock. The young lady turned and faced Maggie. She waved languidly and smiled. The soldier directing the others, with stripes on his sleeve, frowned. He stroked his handlebar mustache and shot Maggie a glare. She flinched. The young woman turned back around and appeared to be giggling. The mustachioed man's cheeks reddened.

Ahead of her, a soldier carrying a wooden tray filled with papers glanced between her and where the men were marching. When he reached the dray, he laughed. "Best not even think of breathing the air that the captain's daughter does."

Maggie puffed out a breath. "I sure won't."

"You're new here, right?"

Maggie nodded.

"I'm the captain's clerk, Private Abernathy. I can tell you right now Dora Witherell is a whole lot of trouble."

Keeping her chin ducked low, Maggie prayed she was believable as a young man. "She looks a might long in the tooth for me, sir."

"Only twenty." Abernathy pointed back toward the gate. "Didn't stop her from flirting with Private Belsky, and he's only sixteen."

"Sixteen?"

"He lied about his age to get in. His folks need the money. And I tell you what, with all the men out in the streets trying to find work, I think you and I can count ourselves lucky, can't we?"

Abernathy raised his eyebrows high.

Maggie dipped her chin.

Movement in the distance caught her eye. The brunette strode purposefully toward them.

The soldier's eyes widened. "You best get on to where you're going unless you want a shiner from Sergeant Mauvais."

"No, sir. I mean, yes, I best move on. Thank you, Private Abernathy."

"You can call me Abernathy, everyone does." With a gap-toothed grin, he turned and called out to the approaching woman as Maggie directed the team on, her heart beating rapidly.

Great, exactly what Maggie didn't want to happen—she'd been noticed. She was supposed to be well in the background. And now not only had she been spotted by a flirtatious female, a perturbation if there was one, but the mean-looking sergeant apparently thought Dora was his domain.

What had happened to *"Steer clear of situations and keep your head down,"* which had been the advice Pa and Mr. Danner had given her? First Jesse Huntington showed up, and now this young lady. What next? Her hair, tightly wound around her head and hidden under her large hat began to irritate her. That long hair had to go. What if her hat blew off? She couldn't chance yet another problem. She'd already procured a pair of shears from the town mercantile. She chewed her lower lip. Why was she worried about what Jesse might think?

Maggie directed Moo and Bear to move forward. She kept her attention focused on the trail that led behind the main buildings and away from the parade grounds. But somehow she felt Sergeant Mauvais's gaze burning through her until she rounded the corner and he could no longer see her. She exhaled a long breath. What happened to Mr. Danner's assertion that this would be an easy assignment?

The soda shop on the main street, a favorite of Jesse's, hadn't seemed so far from the bluff when he was brought by carriage. But today he'd had to walk past the Grand Hotel, keeping his hat low on his brow, not that the wealthy therein would stoop to recognize one of their fallen. Then he'd traversed down the hill and to the sidewalk on the road that circled the island, which eventually became Main Street in town. At this pace, his shoe leather would wear out before summer was over.

He neared the Winds of Mackinac and looked around the front

yard for signs of Jack, who was supposed to meet him soon. No sign of the boy or his pretty sister, Maude, but their gardener, bent over a rosebush, shot him a scowl. "If ya ain't stayin' here, keep movin' on by."

Had Jesse stooped so low in station that even a laborer thought he could chastise him? He'd have a word with Mr. Welling about the gardener when he got a chance.

Continuing on, he wove between tourists on the sidewalk. He passed an "Indian Relics" shop and May's Fudge Shop, and his bearings began to shift and settle into place. Same old Mackinac Island that he knew and enjoyed. He spied Al's Soda Shoppe ahead, a great place to treat his sisters and experience some of the local charm, since many islanders frequented the place. When the family had other social activities solely for his sisters, Jesse had been free to visit Al's on his own. He'd enjoyed sitting in the back corner, where he could read his books and enjoy a phosphate or two. Today, though, he'd donned dress slacks, a shirt and tie, and a vest. He left his jacket behind. He didn't want to seem too formal for his tutoring session with Jack.

When he opened the door, the bells jingled. Inside, only two customers, a pretty buxom blond woman and one of the officers from the nearby fort, sat at a small table the furthest from the door. Soon, once the fort closed, there would be no soldiers on active duty on the island.

The owner looked up from folding dark green napkins into a neat pile. "Mr. Huntington, welcome back."

"Thank you, sir."

The shop owner arched a silver eyebrow at him. "I hear you're tutoring my great-nephew."

"I am."

The man chuckled. "Good luck with that one. He'd rather run or ride his bike than sit in a chair."

"What about a booth? Would he stay put there?" Jesse gestured toward a booth adjacent the wall and took his seat.

"I'm not a bettin' kind of man, but odds aren't good that he'll show up here no matter what he told you."

Jesse exhaled a quick breath. Jack Welling had always seemed to like him a great deal. At least he enjoyed Jesse's stories. "I'll have a soda water please." He plunked down the cost indicated on the small chalkboard sign.

"Have a seat, I'll bring it to you. As you can see, we're mighty slow today."

Was the economy having that kind of impact, or was it because the season wasn't fully in swing? The town had seemed scantily occupied with vacationers this morning, but the family didn't usually arrive so early in the season. Jesse slid into the booth.

Al brought him his drink as Jesse was glancing at his pocket watch. "What'd I tell you, Mr. Huntington? Jack will leave you high and dry and then laugh when he finds out you waited for him."

Jesse arched an eyebrow at the older man.

When the bell jingled again, Jesse couldn't help but grin. Al stared, gape-mouthed, as Jack ran into the shop, the door slamming behind him.

"I ain't late, am I?" The boy slid into his seat, across from Jesse.

Jesse shrugged. "No, you're right on time."

"Whew, good." Jack beamed. "Maude's boyfriend, Grayson, bet my dad that I wouldn't make it."

Al shook his head as he walked to the counter, lifted a hinged section, and stepped back behind.

"Really? He made a wager?" Jesse waggled his eyebrows at the boy, who laughed.

"Only because I wouldn't let him—that old Grayson—tutor me."

"Why not?"

Jack's nose twitched. "He's boring."

Jesse leaned back against the booth's wooden back, his shoulders connecting with the cool wood. "I can't guarantee I won't be the same."

"Ha. It ain't your nature, as my teacher says." Jack's expression morphed into a scowl. "But what does he know? He says it isn't in my nature to learn to write a decent paper."

"He said that?" Jesse scowled, wanting to adjust that teacher's attitude.

"My dad helped get rid of him after Maude told him about it."

"That's good you have a sister who speaks up for you."

"Yeah, when she's not busy helping everyone else." Jack sniffed.

"Well, young sir, I am here for you now." Jesse sipped his drink.

Al returned and slid a napkin onto the table and then placed a cherry phosphate atop it. Then he reached into his heavy green apron pocket and pulled out another napkin and made a display of unfolding it and laying it atop Jack's lap. "In case of spillage."

"Thank you, Uncle Al." But as soon as the man turned his back, Jack pulled a face. He leaned in to whisper, "He thinks I'm a clumsy oaf ever since I tipped over a full glass of cider during the Autumn Festival."

"How long ago was that?" Jesse sipped his soda water.

Jack swiped his sleeve back and forth across his nose, as if scratching it. "A long time ago."

"How long?"

"Last fall." Jack dropped his arm and crinkled his nose. "And I wouldn't have knocked it over if Bea Duvall hadn't tried to grab the last doughnut right when I had already reached my hand out for it."

A conversation about "ladies first" would have to ensue another day. Today they were going to review their summer plan. "Is this Autumn Festival a regular event?"

"Yup." Jack leaned over his phosphate and sucked up a prodigious amount of the fizzy red beverage.

If he remained on the island, Jesse would find out a lot more about what went on year round. "All right then. I'd better get started. I have a lot I wanted to ask you today."

An hour later, after much review, Jesse had a much better idea of where they'd need to focus their scholarly attentions.

Jack stood and stretched. "What'cha doin' this afternoon?"

Hopefully today the school superintendent might finally send a note to him for an interview. Jesse slid from the booth as the front door to the shop opened and a group of five men entered, all in dark suits. He recognized Mr. Welling and smiled and nodded at him.

Jack ran toward his father and threw himself into his arms. Welling patted his son on his tawny head.

"Jesse and I have big plans, and I'm gonna be readin' and writin' well before school starts back."

Jesse coughed into his fist.

"Is that so?" One of the men, who appeared to be in his fifties, with a wide girth, moved away from the group and toward him. "Might you be Jesse Huntington then?"

Jesse extended his hand to the man, whose firm grip belied his apparent soft life. "Yes, sir."

"I've been meaning to contact you. I'm Beckett Nouri, the superintendent of schools." His dark gaze pierced Jesse's. "I'm glad you really made it to the island."

How should Jesse reply to that strange comment? "Yes, sir." He was there. Obviously Nouri didn't think he'd show up.

"Well good then. Come by the office later this afternoon, and we'll chat."

Did that mean an interview? "Yes, sir. Thank you."

"Glad to run into you." Nouri turned to rejoin the others, who'd edged up to the counter and placed orders.

Island life. Was that how things would work then? Something inside reminded him of the peace he'd felt when he'd approached the shop earlier. Something bigger than himself was at work. Something he'd not given a lot of thought to before.

Chapter 5

After a week of sleeping in the stable's "bedroom," Maggie's eyes were swollen nearly shut. And breathing was difficult until she was halfway through the day and outside away from the barn. Today would be her third outing with Eli Mitchell, for a dray job up on the East Bluff. She strode up to her team and patted Moo's head. He gave her a nudge, and she laughed. "Moo, I don't know what I'd do without you." Every night she visited the two horses and shared all her woes. They were good listeners.

She climbed up into her seat.

"I'm here," Eli called as he jogged toward them.

He bounced up onto the bench seat of the dray, beside her. "You look like you fought with a Michigan bobcat."

Maggie grunted. "And the bobcat won."

The young man laughed. His banter during their drives had

made it easier to endure the long days. "If Abigail ever saw me lookin' like that, I think she might run."

"Ha. Your wife would know you anywhere." The newlyweds were so preoccupied with one another that Maggie was grateful. Eli's thoughts were mostly on his wife, and he loved to speak about the dark-haired beauty who'd captured his heart.

"That might be." He rubbed his square jaw. "But seriously, Mickey, you better see Doc Cadotte about your eyes."

Maggie urged Moo and Bear to move forward out of the barn and onto the street. "Can't afford a doctor."

The wagon wheels creaked as they rolled out into an opening in traffic. "Maybe you better find someplace else to lay your head at night."

Free was free. She had to keep this job. "I need to find something to fix my symptoms."

Eli slapped his hand against his forehead. "The Huntingtons."

Maggie's hands jerked against the lines, and the horses slowed. Then she forced her hands to a relaxed hold. "What about them?"

"My Abigail is friends with the youngest girl. They're gonna be in a stage production together next month." Eli gushed as though this was the first time she'd heard about this event.

In fact, Maggie had heard about Abigail's role repeatedly since the first time Eli had ridden with her. "Thank you again for that ticket to the play, but what does that have to do with me?"

"Vivienne, that's Miss Huntington's given name, and she told Abigail to call her that—she said she desperately needs a driver." Eli guffawed. "I love how Abigail says that word, *desperately*."

Maggie resisted the urge to roll her eyes. "The Huntingtons don't have horses, do they?" As well she knew.

"Vivienne says her older sister is working out a way to get them back on the island, if they can find a driver."

Which meant the Huntingtons would have to pay off the

winter fees. Ma and Pa would be able to put some aside for taxes. Then Maggie's wages could go toward the feed for the horses for the coming winter. "I still don't see what that has to do with me." She'd not told Eli how desperate things had gotten for her family.

"Here's the thing—Vivienne wants to find a part-time driver who will receive room and board."

"Is the room in a barn?" Maggie turned her head to the side and sneezed.

"In a carriage house, so not quite as bad. And it's upstairs and enclosed. One of them fancy two-story deals like Abigail and I live in."

"I'll talk to Mr. Danner about it." Would he allow her?

"Your free time is your own. You tell Miss. . .Vivienne what hours you're available. Negotiate the deal."

"Thanks, Eli."

Eli jabbed a sturdy elbow in Maggie's side, and she tried not to wince. "We fellas got to stick together, Mickey, right?"

"Yup. Gotta watch each other's backs." And thank God Eli had a strong enough back to help with the jobs outside the fort, of which there had been more than Danner had anticipated, since they'd still not fully filled their need for drivers.

That night, after walking the forty-minute round trip to Rosie's diner, Maggie headed up to the Huntingtons' grand home, which they called a cottage. She stood on the front step for a moment, then decided she should go to the back door. But they had no servants to answer back there, not unless they'd hired someone. The front door opened. Jesse Huntington's broad smile quickly vanished as he surveyed her from head to toe. He stepped outside and closed the door behind him.

"What are you doing here?" He crossed his arms. "And why are you dressing up and passing yourself as one of your brothers?"

Ire rose up in her. "You owe my family money," she blurted out.

His face registered shock at her words and then shame. "But

you needn't come up here. You could have sent another bill."

"Yet another bill?" She scowled at him. "I sent you plenty last winter that went unanswered."

A muscle in his jaw twitched. "We'll take care of that soon."

She nodded, looking down at her scuffed brown boots. Why did the man have to look so blasted handsome even when he was being difficult? "That's not why I'm here. I'm here about the driver position." About the housing that went with it.

"What on earth do you mean?"

She raised her head and returned his steady gaze. "Your sister, Vivienne, said you need a driver."

"Vivienne?"

"Yes." Since he apparently didn't know about what was going on, Maggie wasn't about to discuss this further with him. "Can you please get her?"

"A driver," he muttered under his breath, "is just what we don't need." He whirled around and opened the door. The scent of burnt ham carried out. If that was the type of food Maggie would be eating here, maybe she'd not save much money after all on her meals.

The door reopened, and both the blond and red-tinged brunette sisters appeared.

"Oh, this is just delicious. We'll have a driver again." The younger girl extended a dainty hand. "I'm Vivienne."

The other young woman nodded gravely and then thrust out her hand. "Florence Huntington."

"Pleased to meet ya both. I'm Mickey Hadley."

"You were our driver when we arrived." Vivienne squinted up at her, and Maggie averted her gaze.

"Yes'm."

"Vivie needs rides to and from town at night, as may our mother, and we'll need a driver once our horses arrive on the island." Florence's clipped voice was as different from her mother's genteel southern drawl as was possible.

Maggie turned toward the elder sister but kept her head lowered slightly. "And when will that be? For the horses?"

"In fact, your father, Mr. Hadley, sent us a letter saying they were being shipped this weekend and Mr. Danner would help send them up." Florence tapped her black boot to emphasize her words.

Vivienne edged slightly forward. "Your father actually suggested we contact you, Mickey, to see if you might be interested in our arrangement. But I'd hoped my dear bosom friend Abigail would have her husband drive for us at night."

Florence huffed a laugh. "But we can't afford to pay him, and the Mitchells already have lodging and meals with the Wellings." Florence's no-nonsense tone continued to perplex Maggie. Weren't southern women more docile?

"Yes, you're quite right, Florence." The pretty blond girl's dulcet tones clashed with those of her sister.

"If you're interested, Mr. Hadley, follow me and I'll show you the carriage house." Florence bustled past her, and Maggie turned and followed.

Vivienne linked her arm through Maggie's and leaned in. "Now I don't mind telling you that none of us Huntingtons is much of a cook, but we're trying our best. And Florence has become a proficient fisherwoman."

She couldn't keep her eyebrows from shooting up. "Really? Because I'm pretty handy with a skillet."

Vivienne leaned in. "I'm quite sure you are, *Miss* Hadley."

Maggie turned and stared at the girl beside her, who had raised a finger to her pursed lips. "How did you know?" She'd have to fix it. Work harder.

"Oh pooh." Vivienne tossed a blond curl over her slim shoulder. "I got to thinking about what your brother Russell used to tell me."

Florence turned and scowled. "You had no business running

around with him last summer."

Vivienne giggled. "But we had so much fun, and it was invigorating to be free of Jesse's tyranny."

"A slight exaggeration. Our brother isn't a tyrant. He's more of a—"

"Bully." Vivienne pouted.

Florence made a guttural sound. "He's no more a bully than I am."

When Vivienne rolled her eyes upward, Maggie couldn't restrain her giggle. She liked these two Huntington women.

"All right, he's not a bully or a tyrant, but he always thinks he knows best."

"Because he's usually right, when it comes to you." Florence pulled a set of keys from her reticule.

Shrugging, Vivienne withdrew her arm from Maggie's. She pointed to the two-carriage-wide and two-story-tall carriage house. "What would interest you in driving for us?"

Maggie rubbed her eyes. "Being able to sleep at night, and breathe, might be good reasons."

"What do you mean?" Vivienne cocked her head.

"My room is in the barn. And even though I am in our Percherons' barn plenty at home, I don't sleep there."

"Of course you do not." Florence nodded firmly. "This will work out perfectly for all of us."

"I'll help you look a little more manly." Vivienne placed her tiny hands on either side of Maggie's face. "And I can help you with a bit of theatrical makeup."

"All right."

The girl dropped her hands and clapped. "This could be so much fun having Russell's sister right here with us."

Florence caught Maggie's eye. "You cook up the fish I catch and teach me some more basic cooking skills, and I'll be very grateful.

The books I've read don't adequately explain the techniques."

Vivienne shrugged. "We eat a lot of burnt food."

This seemed too good an opportunity to be true. "What's the catch?"

"If our brother figures out that you're a woman, he'll likely ensure that you have absolutely no opportunity for fun." Vivienne's perfect lips formed a pout.

"Absolutely no fun?" Florence's droll repetition was followed by her leading them up the stairs to the second-floor entrance. "If one would like to put oneself at constant risk and consider that fun, then Vivienne is correct. Some of us, however, can find joy in the simple things."

Vivienne sighed as Florence unlocked the door. "Jesse always makes sure we don't get into what he calls mischief."

"Until he was working with Father last summer." Florence turned and wagged a finger at her sister. "And now I have to say I don't blame Jesse for watching us, or rather you, so closely."

Cheeks pink, Vivienne ducked past Florence into the long, spacious room.

"Your brother already knows I'm Maggie Hadley." She removed her hat, her now-short hair brushing her shoulders.

"He knows?" Vivienne gaped at her.

Florence pulled a white sheet from a blue upholstered chair that looked far too pretty for a carriage house. "How?"

"I met your father and brother at our home last year, when he purchased two of our horses."

"Aha." Florence and Vivienne exchanged a knowing look.

"Aha, what?"

"Did he speak with you?" Florence's tone was judge-like solemn.

"Briefly."

Vivienne giggled. "No wonder he wanted to personally go to your parents' farm when we got up here."

Had he truly wanted to come to Pickford? "To settle the bill, I'm sure."

Florence crossed her arms. "Humph."

Was that footfall Maggie heard on the stairs?

"No wonder he's always asking us if we've seen our driver around town." Vivienne practically bounced in her cream-colored pumps. "Oh, romance is in the air. It surely must be."

Flummoxed, Maggie could only stare, open-mouthed. This kind of thinking had to be stopped. "As long as there's no hay dust floating around up here, I think that's what will matter."

Jesse popped his head around the doorframe. "What's in the air?"

Sun pierced the Irish lace curtains in Jesse's east-facing window. Although he had a beautiful view of the harbor, this room also afforded the earliest sunlight in the morning. He tossed back the brocade coverings on his bed and rose. His bare feet connected with the wool, latch-hook rug, and he smiled at the soft touch of it. Florence had already started going through the house, cataloging all the items. At least his rug would stay, for she felt it couldn't bring much if sold.

He put on his robe and tied the belt at his waist, then slid his feet into his expensive leather slippers—another item Flo couldn't sell off.

At least he was sleeping better at night, knowing that Maggie Hadley was safely ensconced in the carriage house. One less worry for him. Although having her so near had prompted him to spend more time in the evenings checking on her. She, his sisters, and even his mother had also enjoyed a rousing game of pinochle and had taken tea together after church on Sunday.

He descended the stairs and stopped at the landing when he caught a view of his mother in the mirror on the wide oak hall tree.

She was draping a silky-looking black shawl over her crisp, white pintucked blouse. A hideous cameo, one he recognized as one of his grandmother's, perched at the top of Mother's blouse. When she wrapped the shawl around her narrow shoulders, she looked almost. . .frightening. With her pale skin, ebony hair streaked with silver, and lips lightly rouged, she resembled a ghoul. Jesse shivered.

"Mother, where did you get that ghastly shawl?" He completed his descent down the stairs.

She whirled away from the mirror and arched one dark brow. "You should thank me to wear this."

He shoved his hands into his robe's deep pockets. "And that would be why?"

Florence peeked around the corner, clutching a biscuit in her hand. "She's cozying up to Mrs. Nouri."

"Ah." Poor mother. "You're willing to dress like the superintendent's mother if it helps my cause?" He'd still not heard anything back following his interview.

She wagged her index finger at him. "You'll see. I've found a way to get you that job."

Not one word from the school board yet, after a week. But connections could be everything, as he well knew. "And how will that be?"

Florence guffawed, then covered her mouth with her free hand.

Mother glared at his sister. "Remember what you promised me, Florence Catherine."

His sister gestured as though she was locking her lips tight and then throwing away the key. She spun on her heel and headed toward the back of the house, presumably for breakfast.

"Did you already eat, Mother?"

"I'm not hungry." She turned away from him and back toward the mirror.

He was grateful she hadn't caught his disapproving glare. He schooled his features back into a placid expression. Mother wasn't eating still, here on the island. His younger sister had been taking in her garments. Vivienne was accustomed to working on costumes for theatrical productions, and those skills came in handy now.

"I'm going out," Mother announced.

"But we don't have a driver until Mickey returns."

She sniffed. "I have a friend coming for me on the half hour."

"Who is this friend?" Was his mother already being courted, despite being in mourning?

"A lady friend, if it is any of your business, which it is not." Apparently Flo's demeanor was rubbing off a little on Mother.

Jesse pressed a hand to his chest. "My apologies."

She nodded curtly. "Accepted." Lips pinched tightly together, she went to the door and stared out the glass panes. Then she swiveled toward him. "I'll also be going out this evening. On my own. So the carriage will be in use, and I'll have Mickey wait on me."

What was she up to?

Chapter 6

If Jesse knew what Vivienne had asked her to do, would he be angry? Maggie watched from the driver's seat of the Huntingtons' carriage as the young woman exited onto the walkway. She clutched her reticule to her chest as she hurried away from the Christy Tea Shoppe. Earlier that day, Maggie had spied Florence toting a tin pail of goods into town and down a narrow lane. What had Florence traded now in order to procure some baked goods for her family?

The Huntingtons' horses were a bit twitchier than Moo and Bear. Still, the pair didn't react when a group of four boys raced down the main street, hooting and hollering as they went. Passersby on the walkway by Lake Huron gawked at the boys.

Vivienne soon returned to the curb, hoisting up a small but bulging bag. "My mother will love these almond buttercream cookies. They're her favorites." Moisture gleamed in her eyes.

Trying to conceal her concern, Maggie dipped her chin and lowered her voice. "Best get in the carriage, miss, and let's be on our way."

"Oh Mickey, I'm so worried about my mother. She's not been herself since we've been here." Vivienne burst into tears and then swooped into the carriage.

The carriage rocked only slightly as Vivienne settled herself. After checking traffic, Maggie directed the Percherons onto the road again. When they reached the Huntingtons' home, she was surprised to see Jesse's mother, attired in black from head to toe, standing beneath a tall oak tree that edged the drive. She waved to Maggie.

"Don't unhitch the horse, I'd like to be taken out to a social engagement."

Vivienne disembarked and went to her mother and gave her a quick hug. "Mother, I brought your favorite cookies. See?" She opened the bag to display the baked goods.

"Soon we won't have to live on a pittance." Mrs. Huntington's pointy chin tipped upward, and she squared her shoulders beneath what had to have been the most hideous black silk shawl ever made. Even a country woman such as Maggie's mother wouldn't have been seen in such a covering. And what had happened that the woman believed their finances were about to improve? Had Jesse landed a job in the city? He'd continued to send out applications, he'd said, but without success.

The woman, looking like an apparition with all her black clothing floating around her, approached the front of the carriage. "Young man, I'd like to go to Mrs. Nouri's home in town."

Maggie stiffened. Mr. Danner had specifically instructed her to stay away from the woman and her home. But she wasn't driving his dray; she was driving the Huntingtons' carriage. "Are you sure, ma'am?"

She cringed as the woman shot her a scathing glance. "Did I not just say?" Then she appeared to draw in a slow breath. "My deah young mahn, I will not issue you an order that I am unsure of." Her heavy southern accent was back in full force.

"Yes, ma'am. Do you need help into the carriage, ma'am?"

"No, thank you. I can manage." Mrs. Huntington sniffed and then climbed into the carriage, slamming the door behind her in a fashion that could not possibly be construed as evidence of a southern belle's presence.

Maggie exhaled a long, low breath and directed the team to circle out of the drive and back down toward the road.

As they approached the small clapboard house, which sat a street back off Market Street, Maggie spied elderly women wrapped in similar black lacy crocheted silk or wool shawls. All wore black or dark skirts. Some had black arm bands. Unease worked its way through her hands, and the horses must have noticed, because they wandered a bit and she had to bring them back under control. A sharp thump from within the carriage alerted her as they neared the small house, her employer's sign to stop and let her out. She pulled next to the curb.

Mrs. Huntington exited the carriage and stepped onto the sidewalk. She turned and pointed her finger at Maggie. "Now, not a word. . ."

A stout woman, the butcher's wife, if Maggie recollected correctly, hurried alongside Jesse's mother. "Mrs. Huntington, it's so wonderful that you could come out."

Mrs. Huntington, cheeks flushed, turned from Maggie toward the other woman before finishing her warning.

The unease she'd been feeling built as the two women strolled off, arm in arm down the street toward Mrs. Nouri's house. Moments later, barely thinking of where she was going, Maggie found herself at Reverend McWithey's manse near the church. If ever she needed some spiritual advice, it was now.

Why me, Lord? Jesse's first conversation with God in a long while seemed so short. And since he'd lost his father and almost everything of worldly value in his life, it seemed strange he'd not asked the question earlier. Maybe that was because he wasn't sure if God could be trusted with things that men could fix by putting their will into something. Father had taught him that. But his father was wrong. Given that he was about to yank his mother from the home of the school superintendent's mother—the same man who controlled whether Jesse would get the one actual possibility of a job on this island—he needed some help from a power greater than himself. Jesse sighed and exited the carriage.

Maggie had dropped his mother off earlier and then spoken with their preacher. She'd returned to the house and shared what Reverend McWithey had told her. Although Jesse would not make a scene, he had no intention of allowing his mother to sit in on a séance at Mrs. Nouri's home. Father would be rolling over in his grave if he had a notion of such behavior.

Jesse waved at Maggie as he headed toward the place where numerous wealthy ladies, many from fine families and all sharing some tragic loss, were gathered. Ahead, although the sun was only now setting and twilight cast a golden glow, the Nourises' heavy curtains were fully shut, which shouldn't have surprised Jesse. Although Vivienne had argued with him and Maggie that perhaps Mother was simply researching for a play that the community would be doing in the autumn, a theatrical production in which someone died during a phony séance, Jesse was pretty sure that wasn't her goal. Especially not when Florence finally admitted to them that Mother wouldn't allow her to box up Father's personal jewelry for keeping because she intended to "use it" herself. Flo had learned that Mother was bringing them to Mrs. Nouri's home with the intention of conjuring up a connection with Father.

What if Mrs. Nouri's servants wouldn't let him in? Jesse scanned the street. Most of the tourists were in for the night or heading toward their hotels. Workers were already in bed, getting the rest they needed to wake at the crack of dawn, for they were still in high season and grateful for a job. Carefully Jesse crossed the street and approached the two-story home. Even in this light, he could see that the building could use a coat of paint. And weeds had sprung up all over the front yard. Why did the superintendent not help her maintain the property? Furthermore, why did he allow his mother to run séances in her home? Candlelight or lamps flickered behind the dark curtains as Jesse walked around to the side of the home. Scruffy shrubs hugged the home as he approached the back. A narrow, covered entryway door was at the center of the back of the structure. He continued around the side. Strangely, on the west side of the home there was yet another narrow doorway. He sensed movement from the detached one-deep carriage house in the back and hurried around to the front. He mounted the three stairs to the oak door and brought the brass knocker down once, twice, three times.

An ebony-skinned manservant attired in a gold-embroidered satin vest and dark breeches opened the door. "No men admitted tonight, sir."

When he went to close the door on him, Jesse put his foot inside the door and moved forward into the entryway. The servant, more slightly built, stepped back, eyes wide.

"I'm looking for my mother, Mrs. Huntington."

The man waved his white-gloved hands. "No names here, sir."

No names. Well, that figured. Because even though such behavior might be considered in vogue among the Victorian elite, among many other conservative churchgoing folks, such as those who primarily populated this island, trying to contact the dead would be frowned upon.

"Where are they?" Jesse practically growled. Not only was he unwilling to have his mother engage in this behavior, but neither would he have her squander what funds they did have. Fully half of the cash he'd hidden in Father's cigar box was gone, and he believed his sisters when they denied taking it. And sure and for certain Maggie hadn't. He'd not even asked her. Didn't need to. When she'd come to him and shared about what his mother was about to do, a little part of his heart went to her in payment.

"Please, sir, I can't lose my job."

Jesse understood the pleading in the man's voice. "Help me get in there then, and get her out of there."

"Wait here, sir. Let me tell her there be an emergency at her home."

"All right. But make it quick." Jesse fingered the gold watch in his vest. How much longer would he be able to keep his timepiece?

In a few moments, his mother joined him in the entryway, the scent of incense clinging to her clothing. "What's wrong, Jesse?"

"Come along, Mother." He frowned at her in warning. "I'll tell you later."

Once outside the building, he intended to give her a piece of his mind. But she was his mother. On the other hand. . .

She reached into her burgundy velvet reticule and pulled out an envelope full of cash. "I'm sorry. I should have asked. But I was so desperate to ask your Papa about what we should do that—"

Nearby a door creaked open. Jesse placed a finger on his lips to indicate for Mother to be quiet. He pointed to the side of the house. He took her hand and led her to the corner. He ducked his head around in time to see a slim man, attired all in black, enter. Mother looked too, just as the door closed. This must be the human who would project a spectral voice to answer attendee's questions from the great beyond.

"Oh," she breathed the word on a disappointed sigh. "I can guess what that's all about. I'm not so daft as to not know I was about to be duped."

"It's all right, Mother." Jesse patted her hand. "But please don't do that again."

"I promise. But, oh Jesse, what now about the job?"

"What about it?"

"The superintendent's mother was going to put in a good word for you, but with me leaving the meeting, I wonder if she'll do so." Mother pushed a strand of hair back from her brow. "I wonder if my payment for reaching your father was supposed to be akin to buying a favor from her with her son."

Jesse shook his head. "If the superintendent is in on this nonsense, then I don't want anything to do with him." But with few choices left on the island for work, what could he do?

Having been summoned by the superintendent for an interview that very next afternoon, Jesse spent some time with his grooming. He'd need a haircut and a shave. But why was he bothering? This entire situation with the man's mother had almost put Jesse off the notion of trying his hand at teaching.

Soon Jesse was settled in the barber's chair. He'd need to go home to change into his suit afterward. He removed his spectacles and tucked them into his pocket. The barber sharpened his razor on the long strop alongside the chair. "I hear you're interviewing for the teacher's job, is that right?"

"Yes, sir."

"Shame that James Baker had to cancel his contract at the last minute."

"Oh?"

"Good thing you're here."

The scent of lime hung thick in the air. A boy of not more than twelve swept up the hair clippings from the floor.

"But aren't you the Huntingtons' son?"

Oh no, here started the fishing expedition wherein the locals would try to learn Jesse's personal business. "Could be. What if I am?"

"Oh, no need to get worried. You wouldn't be the first boy from those cliffs to have to join those of us down in the village, if you know what I mean."

How low the high and mighty could become. Was that what he meant? "Please simply cut my hair and give me a good shave, and I'll be happy." And he'd give him a good tip if he stopped with his questions.

Later, as he sat in the interview chair, a hard black Windsor with spindle back that dug into his spine, Jesse wished he'd allowed the barber to practice his interrogation skills on him. With his terse manner and narrow, beady eyes, Mr. Nouri continued to ask Jesse about his schooling, his work history, and why he wanted the job.

About to lose his patience, Jesse shoved his glasses to the bridge of his nose. "Sir, it seems to me that perhaps you don't wish to hire me."

Nouri's dark brows knit together. "I may have reason."

Reason? What reason could he possibly have? Jesse sat at the edge of his seat and cocked his head. "Sir?"

"You were seen coming from my mother's home last night."

Jesse's lips involuntarily pursed. "Yes, sir. I was taking my mother home from there."

"Oh?" Nouri's shoulders flexed beneath his tightly cut dark wool suit. "My mother felt you'd been discourteous to her manservant."

"Sir, you've asked me a great many questions. May I ask you one?"

He shrugged. "Why not?"

Leaning forward, he fixed his gaze on the older man, as his father would often do in a business deal. "Do you condone your mother's behavior?"

"Her behavior? What do you mean?"

"These séances she holds in her home. That's what I mean. Wherein older women, widows like my mother, pay exorbitant fees to contact their loved ones."

"What?" The man shot to his feet so fast that a small crystal paperweight globe on his wide walnut desk rolled off toward Jesse, who scooped it up in his hands. "How dare you make such accusations, young man."

Face hot, Jesse slowly rose. "It's true."

The man sputtered but then turned away from Jesse to face the windows behind him.

Should he go or stay? Something pinned Jesse to the spot. If Mr. Nouri didn't know about his mother, perhaps it was high time he did. When the man still said nothing, Jesse cleared his throat. "Sir, I know what I had to do with my own mother, and if you feel the same as I do about such things, you'll surely speak to yours and set her straight. In a respectful way, of course, sir."

Nouri said nothing.

"I'll see myself out, sir."

"Wait." The man swiveled around and fixed Jesse with a surprisingly understanding look. "I'll get my mother in hand, and you keep yours above reproach as well, and we'll get along fine."

"Yes, sir."

"Sit down. Let me tell you about your duties and the pay and whatnot." Nouri ran a hand back through his dark hair and lowered himself to his seat again.

Really? He had the job? And he'd gotten it by speaking honestly. Memories of his father jumped to mind. Father had been frank and clear in his business dealings. He'd never cheated anyone, and he'd regretted terribly all those who'd been affected when his businesses failed. But could the same be said of his cronies? Did his fellow businessmen speak honestly when they denied that they owed his father any debt of obligation? Maybe Florence was right. Let the books speak for themselves.

Chapter 7

If Jesse's two sisters hadn't been with them on this picnic, Maggie would have found the outing almost romantic. On her free day, after church, they'd ridden bikes out to Arch Rock. Mr. Welling had loaned them the bikes and had cautioned Jack that he couldn't join them.

Florence spread out a moth-eaten pink wool blanket on the ground. They had excellent views both of Lake Huron and of the limestone arch formation high on the hillside. Jesse plopped down and spread himself out on the blanket. He pulled his straw boater hat over his face and feigned snoring. Vivienne laughed and plucked the hat off his handsome face.

Maggie shook her head and pulled the picnic basket free from the front of the bike. "If you don't work, you don't eat is what my ma always says."

Florence huffed. "Jesse will starve then, because he didn't buy, prepare, or transport any of these items."

He jumped up and strode to Maggie. "I believe you ladies will have to eat your words."

Vivienne rolled her eyes. "Why is that?"

His warm fingers brushed against Maggie's, sending a thrill through her. He took the woven-wood basket and opened the left hinged lid. "What do you see in there?"

Maggie peered inside and lifted the wax paper covering a deep square tin. Thick sandwiches were stacked high. She removed the top piece of bread. "Tomatoes even? And is that ham?"

She looked up.

He was beaming. "Yes, indeed."

Vivienne rushed forward and opened the other side and peeked in. "Apple salad? Oh, is that German salad too?"

Florence joined them and reached into the middle section. She pulled out a bag and opened it and looked inside. She sniffed appreciatively. "Those are Mrs. Christy's chocolate pecan bars, if I'm not mistaken."

"You aren't mistaken." Jesse waggled his eyebrows. "And your friend Abigail can keep a secret, Vivie."

"From me?" Vivienne feigned a pout.

Florence poked him. "You must have gotten an early paycheck."

"I did. Although it's only the beginning of September and school won't begin until later in the month, Mr. Nouri surprised me with an advance."

"Hurrah." Florence pretended to wave a flag.

Jesse pushed her hand down. "And although you mock me for *not* working to make this picnic happen, I did all I could to make it a fun surprise."

Maggie wanted to hug his neck. He'd even kept the secret from her. Their eyes met, her cheeks heating when they'd held the gaze a bit too long.

"Well"—Florence brushed her hands together—what did you do with the picnic that we had put together?"

With Maggie working all week and driving Vivienne back and forth to theater practice each night, she'd not had much chance to help the sisters with cooking. Florence had learned to make a passable chicken salad sandwich from tinned meat and mayonnaise. The soldiers had given Maggie a few items from the fort's garden. And Vivienne had baked two loaves of wheat bread that had not quite fully risen. That was to have been their picnic.

Jesse brought the picnic basket to the blanket's edge and set it down. "Abigail was going to pick ours up and deliver it to the Oakford family, who took in those orphans."

"That was awful news about the horrid fire in Minnesota." Vivienne's eyes misted over.

Maggie blinked back her own tears. She'd read about the devastation in one of the papers left at the stables. "I don't think Hinckley will ever recover from that devastation."

"The Oakfords' nieces will be in my classroom when we start, but Mrs. Oakford says they barely speak." Jesse sat down on the blanket. "I think I'm in for more than I bargained for."

"Things happen though." Maggie didn't mean to blurt out her comment. Surely these three Huntingtons knew how quickly life could change.

As if in agreement, a breeze stirred the leaves on the ground, some already golden. They whirled around them for a moment before settling again. All were quiet, and a pensive solemnity cloaked them as Maggie settled on the blanket.

Florence kicked off her sturdy black shoes and sat beside Maggie, tucking her skirts around her. "We won't be able to do this much longer." The way she said the words, as if she wasn't really speaking about the autumn weather, stirred Maggie's curiosity, but Jesse and Vivienne looked nonplussed.

Vivienne slowly lowered herself onto the blanket, arranging her skirts around her.

Jesse passed out tin plates, napkins, and utensils. "I'll say the blessing."

Maggie couldn't keep her eyes from widening. She'd been praying that Jesse might show more interest in God's direction, as he never voiced any. Maggie had been the one to say prayers at meals at the Huntingtons' long cherry table.

"Lord, for all You have given us, may we truly be thankful. For the work You have offered and that which You have prepared for us to do, may You enable us. May we be thankful for this food You have provided. In Jesus' name, amen."

When Maggie opened her eyes, Jesse opened his and looked directly at her. A thrill skipped through her heart. Even if nothing ever became of their friendship—and how could it—still she would treasure the progress he was making with God in his life.

If Maggie Hadley had been attired in a gauzy teatime gown and glittering with jewels, as the young ladies at the Grand Hotel often were, she couldn't have looked more appealing. Although she wore a broad-brimmed hat, summer had brought a glow to her complexion and freckled her pert nose. Her bright eyes and perfectly shaped lips urged him to move closer to her on the blanket. But with two sisters watching and Maggie passing as a lad, any such movement would be unthinkable.

He reached over, grabbed a cluster of grapes, and popped one in his mouth, then leaned back. "Guess who I am, Vivienne."

"That's easy." Vivienne grabbed the grapes from him. "You're Julius Caesar from our play."

"No, I'm Christopher Oakford who plays the part of Caesar." He winked at Maggie, and she blushed.

Vivienne swatted at him, and he leaned away. "That makes no sense. Christopher is acting as Caesar, and therefore you were acting as if you were Caesar not as Mr. Oakford."

"Nope." He reached for more grapes, and Maggie leaned in, broke off a cluster, and handed them to him, smiling.

Florence gave him one of her imperious looks. She'd pull off a better teacher face than he'd manage. "Don't expect Jesse to make sense. His arguments are often circular."

All three women laughed.

"I don't argue. I persuade."

"How about when I told you I wished to take a ferry to St. Ignace?" Vivienne arched a brow.

"That's different. You never would specify exactly why you needed to go." In fact, she'd not even made up a reason that he might have approved.

"I wanted to see a friend. And I'm almost eighteen. I ought to be able to keep some things to myself, like Flo does."

Florence gave her a quelling look, her features flashing a warning. "If your friend was a respectable person, you'd have no hesitation in telling Jesse."

Maggie waved her hand. "Please, let's enjoy our lunch. I only have the one free day."

"Sorry, Maggie." And he was. He didn't wish to upset her. "Let's take a walk after we eat."

If he had his way, he'd take her hand and walk with her. But how would that look? They'd both be run off the island. Either that, or Maggie would have to reveal her true identity and give up her job.

"I brought my harmonica." Maggie beamed.

"Did Eli finally teach you that last Stephen Foster song?" Vivienne took a bite of salad.

"He did."

They finished their lunch and strolled along Lake Huron. Each

Huntington shared a little bit more about themselves than Maggie had previously known. Florence had completed a bookkeeping course over the summer by correspondence. Vivienne was asked to join a traveling theatrical troupe but had refused. And Jesse had purchased some books on best education practices and had read through most of them.

"I can't say that I agree with some of the methods that our modern teachers use." Jesse bent and picked up a maple leaf tinged with yellow, red, and orange. "This one's a beauty, isn't it?"

He passed the leaf to Maggie, and she accepted it, painfully aware of his sisters' wide eyes.

"We're fortunate we've got each other." Vivienne touched Jesse's shoulder.

Florence clutched her hands at her waist. "Since we've been sharing, I have something to tell you all."

Jesse cocked his head at Florence. "What is it?"

"I've secured a good position for myself, and I plan to leave for Detroit within the week."

"What?" Jesse stared at her.

Vivienne hugged her sister. "That's so exciting."

"Where? What are you doing?" Jesse rubbed his forehead.

"Many years ago, Father took me to a railroad investors' meeting in New York."

"I remember."

"I met a lady there who said if I ever wished to learn more about business to contact her."

"I thought the men actually shut you out of the meeting and you only spoke to the cleaning lady." Frankly, he'd thought Florence had made the thing up.

Flo grinned. "Yes. Except she was no ordinary cleaning lady. She's a wealthy businesswoman. And my new boss."

He arched an eyebrow. He couldn't have her living in Detroit without protection. "You'll live where?"

"In one of her homes. She's currently residing elsewhere, but she has several servants who will be there to help." As the breeze kicked up again, Florence clutched her hat. "And I'll work diligently to procure you a placement in her business, Jesse. Have no worries."

He heard Maggie's almost inaudible gasp and resisted the urge to reach and squeeze her hand. When he turned to look at her, he caught her stricken look. Why did Florence's offer not stir something within him other than anxiety?

Chapter 8

The steep steps of the Indian Dormitory building, which housed the Mackinac Public School, loomed imposing before Jesse. *First day of school.* He'd never stepped inside a public education building in his life.

"Good morning, Mr. Huntington." Miss Dearing, an attractive brunette with a willowy figure, taught the younger students.

"Good day." Would it be?

She laughed. "You look petrified."

He rubbed his chin. "Maybe merely terrified."

"Ah." She smiled and stepped toward the stairway. "I've sometimes wondered if these stairs were built on a steep incline to impress the Indian families whose children were brought here."

"Or to deter the parents from running in to take their children back home." Jesse blinked back a memory of facing similar steps, albeit brick not wood, at the boarding school he'd attended in Richmond, Virginia. Maybe what he was feeling right now wasn't concern over his lack of public school experience but the unease he'd felt every year when Father had unceremoniously deposited him on the school steps. At least Rutherford Huntington had escorted his son there, unlike many other parents.

"Why would they want to prevent their children from receiving a proper education?" Miss Dearing held her skirts aside with her left hand and clutched the rail with her right hand as she began to climb the stairs.

"I don't know much about the values of the local natives."

She cast him a sideways glance. "You'll find that we have many Indian students among our classes. And Métis children as well."

"Truly?" He caught up to her on the stairs, stepping alongside her.

"It would behoove you to learn more of their culture." She definitely was sounding like a commanding schoolmarm.

"Agreed." He offered what he hoped was a charming smile.

They reached the landing at the top. "If you need help, please feel free to call on me after school." She placed her hand gently on his.

When he looked into her eyes, a soft lavender, he didn't see the spark that always loomed in Maggie's. He searched her gaze for a moment, not wanting to see any attraction there. Such a situation could be disastrous for him as a first-year teacher. Nothing there but a sweet, clear, kind look. "Thank you, Miss Dearing."

She released his hand and drew in a deep breath. She turned toward the street. Jesse followed her gaze. A breeze threatened to lift his hat, and he grabbed it. Despite the thick ribbon that secured her bonnet, his fellow teacher grasped the brim of her bonnet.

"Who is that young man down at the street, Mr. Huntington?"

At first Jesse didn't see anyone walking. Then he spied a dray moving at no more than a snail's crawl by the school. *Maggie.* Even from this distance, he could spy her red cheeks. Had she seen the two of them talking? He cleared his throat. "Oh, that's Mickey. He drives for Mr. Danner and also drives for my family at night."

"How strange that he'd lurk there at the street."

"Perhaps he's come to bid me a good start to the school year. We've become good friends." Why then did he wish it was more? But when Jesse waved at Maggie, she didn't wave back.

Miss Dearing quirked a dark eyebrow at him. "Perhaps the superintendent tipped him to ensure you'd actually showed up."

"What?"

"There's a betting pool going on down at Foster's Tavern as to how long you'll last."

"Is that so?"

"Yes. One fellow bet you'd not show up at all. And the longest bet is that you'll be gone by Christmas."

By Christmas? Wasn't that what his sister Florence had implied when she'd departed the previous week? That she'd find him a spot by then so that all of them could come to Detroit. He'd never thought he'd have to rely on his sister to help him find work as a businessman. But if he did, then he'd be leaving behind. . . His gaze fixed on the best friend he'd ever had.

With a flick of the reins, Maggie sent her team forward.

First day of school and the pretty schoolteacher was already putting the moves on Jesse. Steam seemed to boil up inside of Maggie as she directed Moo and Bear around a corner and over to Eli's house. He'd not shown up this morning, and Mr. Danner had asked her to check on her dray partner. He'd given her a route to do if Eli accompanied her and an alternate plan if he was unable to work.

They soon pulled down the carriage house drive to the mint-green home of Eli and his bride. The door at the exterior stairway flew open and Abigail emerged.

"I thought I saw you, Mickey!" Wrapped in a too-large robe, Abigail looked even younger than her twenty years. More like a girl.

"Where's your husband? Sleepin' off your good cooking?" Maggie tried to ask the other woman questions like her brothers might have done.

"He's sick."

Maggie's first inclination was to gush over how sorry she was. But her brothers wouldn't have. "Sorry to hear that. Tell him to get on the mend soon."

"Pray for him, Mickey."

Maggie touched her hat brim, like Russell would have, but didn't reply. Of course she'd pray for him, but a man wouldn't necessarily shout that back. Playing this role was getting harder and harder. Bits of herself were being chipped away every time she acted this part. She directed the horses around and back to the street. Since she didn't have Eli, she'd need to run up to the fort. Which meant she had to drive back in front of the school again.

Why did she have these strong feelings for Jesse? She'd been courted before, not that Jesse Huntington was courting her, but never had her heart's yearnings overcome her like they did when she was with him. But there would never be a romantic relationship between them. At least not one that would lead to what she really desired—a husband, home, children, and a future together. They had become fast friends. But that was as far as things would go. One day his future and finances would alter dramatically, and he'd be back in the good graces of high society. Wealthy people always seemed to pull out of these things in the end. Florence's departure illustrated that truth. Maggie chewed on her lip.

She directed the horses to the wharf and picked up the cargo destined for the fort. Then she continued on her route. Every time she went to the fort by herself, she was on pins and needles. Sergeant Mauvais always seemed to show up wherever she was, which was usually at the quartermaster's. And even though he had no business there, the man snooped about as the soldiers unloaded boxes. Thankfully, Dora had never crossed Maggie's path again, but maybe the sergeant was simply ensuring that if she did show up, she'd not have an opportunity to converse with the dray driver.

Maggie approached the fort. The greens were empty save for the private at the gate, a handsome tall blond of about twenty. "*Ole nopea, on pian juhla.*"

Maggie frowned at him. "Speak English." She recognized one of the Finnish words as "hurry." She'd heard a lot of Finnish lumberjacks around Pickford but hadn't picked up much of the language.

"Sorry." The man lifted a hand in apology. "You need hurry with these things—there is party."

"The horses only go so fast, soldier." Maggie spit in the dirt.

"Go then!" He waved her forward. "You get trouble with sergeant if his lady doesn't get her t'ings."

Shoulders stiffening, Maggie flicked the reins.

When she pulled in behind the quartermaster's building, Sergeant Mauvais ran toward her, his face mottled red. "Where have you been?"

When it looked like he might try to climb up beside her, Maggie instinctively grabbed the whip, as Pa had taught her and which Danner had sanctioned in such instances. "Get back!"

"Dora Witherell has returned this morning, and the comestibles we ordered aren't here."

Don't think like a woman; think like a man. Maggie's hands shook, so she pressed them down on her thighs. "First of all, Mister—"

"That's Sergeant—"

Maggie waved her hand dismissively. "First of all, Sergeant." She leaned forward, whip still in hand. "I'm not responsible for your orders coming or not. That's whoever you're doing business with."

He scowled at her. "Still, you could have gotten this up here quicker."

Maggie couldn't have the sergeant thinking he could bully her. "You're lucky you even got these supplies today."

He narrowed his eyes at her. "Why's that?"

"My boss didn't mention anything about a rush on this order, nor did the dockmaster."

Mauvais fisted his hands. "They were told."

"Mr. Danner would have instructed me if he'd heard."

"Well, that"—he burst into a string of profanities so foul that Maggie fought the urge to wince—"dockmaster was told."

Although she was quaking inside, Maggie shrugged. "In fact, sir"—she let derision drip off that word—"if my dray partner, Eli, had been with me today, these items might not have been delivered until tomorrow."

"Now you see here." Spittle flung out with each word he slung. "We might be leaving this"—more profanity ensued—"island soon, when the state takes over, but the army must remain a priority."

She couldn't help herself. "You're speaking of a beautiful young lady's party, not of the needs of the military." And an army outpost that was mighty small.

The man's lips drew together so tightly that they almost disappeared. He stared at her for the longest time, and Maggie met his furious gaze. He took two steps closer to the dray and peered up at her, his features beginning to soften.

Oh no, she'd overplayed her hand. He was looking at her too intently, and the steam had gone out of him. Did he know?

What had she done?

Chapter 9

"Can I put up the October calendar?" Opal Duvall stood in front of Jesse's desk and rocked back and forth.

"May I?" He hoped his gentle reminder wouldn't frighten the skittish child.

Her lips formed an O. "You want to do it, Mr. Huntington?"

He chuckled. "No, but since you are asking permission, you're asking if you *may* change the calendar." The previous afternoon, the children had made their own classroom calendar during art time.

"It's too heavy for her." Benjy, a tall Chippewa boy whose real name was Bemidii, waved his hand over the heavy canvas calendar.

Tristan, who possessed the most serious expression Jesse had ever seen on a child, unfolded his lanky fourteen-year-old frame from his too-small desk. "I'm the oldest student. I should put it up."

Tears gathered in Opal's light eyes. "I can stand on a chair."

As classroom chatter increased, Jesse raised his hand. "That's enough." Thankfully his class stopped talking. A month earlier he'd have had to bring his ruler down hard on the desk to silence them. Surprisingly, when they'd learned that he'd never bring that same ruler down on any of their hands, much less a rod on their backs, the students had become more compliant. He'd found that the carrot motivated them much better than the stick.

"The calendar needs to be where all the pupils can reach it, because we plan to continue decorating it." He picked up a felt cutout of a dray and another of a hammer, and displayed them. "If we reach all of our math and English goals for this week, then Mr. Christy, the master craftsman at the Grand Hotel, will invite us over for a visit and demonstrate some basic woodworking skills."

Bea raised her hand. "*May* I sit up front with the dray driver on our way to the Grand?"

He arched an eyebrow at her. "No, Miss Duvall, you will have the very important job of watching over our youngest students." He'd be enjoying the ride sitting next to Maggie, and none of his students would be any the wiser that he was sitting next to a young woman who'd become very dear to him.

The girl sighed.

Jesse continued, "In return for your assistance, you'll be able to sit with Mickey on the drive back."

Bea whooped. Jack rolled his eyes.

Jesse cleared his throat. "I am sure you will not display such behaviors inside the Grand Hotel."

Bea nodded primly.

Waving wildly, Jack Welling looked like he might burst. "What about the Harvest Festival?"

Jesse pressed his eyes closed for a moment. He simply couldn't reprimand the boy, whose mother was terribly ill. He nodded and met Jack's gaze. "If all of you are well behaved, then the Grand will host us at the close of their season for the festival."

The entire classroom erupted in pandemonium until Jesse waved his arms overhead. "I only told you what the Grand Hotel required. Let me explain what I'm expecting in order for us to have our Harvest Festival during schooltime."

He reviewed their agenda, detailing expectations of each grade level. Then he gestured to Opal and to Tristan. "Our oldest student shall assist our youngest in affixing the calendar to the wall." He pointed to the spot where he'd hammered in two nails earlier that morning. Soon the two had the cloth calendar hanging from its top loops, which they'd wrapped around the nails.

Looking out at his very own class of students, warmth flowed through Jesse. Pleasure at forging relationships, at accomplishing the task of settling uprooted children into a safe and secure environment, and at teaching them skills that could last a lifetime all combined to bring him a joy he'd never known.

"I can't believe festival day is already here." Maggie leaned her head against Moo's neck and stroked his side. "I feel guilty that I'm glad Miss Dearing's class won't be coming too." The younger class had too many children who were sick.

The brown-and-white Percheron nickered.

"I'll pray for the sick students, their parents, and that none of the staff takes ill." She patted Moo's neck and then headed to the other side of the dray. "Bear, I think you're ready to go home, aren't you?"

Strong winds in the straits had prevented the pair from being transported back to the mainland the previous week. "I'm relieved you and Moo got to stay here with me awhile longer too." She stroked Bear's black neck. "You're such handsome and good boys. What would I do without you here?"

"Ahem." Mr. Danner came alongside her. "You ready to head

down to the school?"

"Eli's getting the last few bales of hay for the kids to sit on." He'd not be coming with her though.

"He's becoming a fine driver under your tutelage."

"Thank you."

"And I imagine you've heard. . ."

She nodded. "A baby on the way." Abigail had told Vivienne, who in turn had told her family and Maggie. So Maggie had known even before Eli had shyly shared his happy news with her. Would Maggie too one day become a mother? And why did her imaginings include little babies with dark hair like Jesse's?

"There's Eli now. He has another surprise for you later."

"What?"

Mr. Danner grinned enigmatically but didn't respond. He pointed to the driver's seat. "Hop on up and get those children up to the Grand. I've heard they've been barely able to contain themselves all week."

"Yes, sir." She offered a mock salute and soon was heading out with Moo and Bear and off to the school.

Brisk air swirled falling maple leaves around the wagon wheels as she drove. A street sweeper waved to her as she passed, and she nodded. Ahead, two older women stepped into the road, and Maggie eased her Percherons to a halt. She didn't need the hay all tumbling off the dray bed. Hopefully the rest of the way she'd have no bicyclists darting in front of her. Unlikely to happen since the tourists had now returned home except for a stray few. She'd learned not to worry herself about islanders on bicycles, for most handled themselves expertly around the carriages and drays.

Within a few minutes, she pulled up by the school. Jesse, dressed in cream-colored dress pants, a navy vest, and a navy-and-cream-striped jacket looked the epitome of elegance. He wore a bowler hat and carried a large box.

Jack Welling, a frequent visitor at the Huntingtons' home, led the group of students down to the dray. "Girls first." Although he waved to the back of the dray and smiled, when he turned his face toward her, she caught him wrinkling his nose. He mouthed to her, *Should be boys first*, and she couldn't quell a laugh that escaped.

Once the girls had settled, the boys jumped in, making enough noise to wake the occupants of St. Anne's graveyard on the hill far away. Maggie put her fingers between her teeth and whistled.

It actually worked. They quieted down. She smirked in satisfaction. How did Jesse manage these imps every day? Although the idea of having her own children seemed a good one, she couldn't fathom trying to teach someone else's offspring. Unless they were learning about horses—that she could manage.

Jesse got up and slid next to her on the bench. "Good day, Mickey. Or should I say, good morning, loser?"

She jabbed her elbow into his side. "If you hadn't cheated, I'd have won that last round of rummy." More likely he'd won because she'd been too busy gazing across the table at him. At least Vivienne didn't catch her making eyes at her brother, like she had the previous game.

He raised his palms and splayed his fingers. "I never cheat."

"Ha!" She looked back. "All set, Jack?"

He gave her a thumbs-up. She turned back around.

Jesse leaned toward her. "Mrs. Welling isn't improving."

"The ladies at the steam laundry said Mrs. Duvall is also very ill. Bedbound I heard."

Jesse frowned. "Bea hasn't said anything. But Opal has been very quiet the past few days."

"Keep praying for all of them." She looked at him. "You do pray for your students, don't you?"

"I didn't used to pray much at all." He sighed.

"No?"

"But something about this island. Something about being here. . ." His voice trailed off. Although she was looking ahead, she caught him staring at her out of the corner of her eye.

Jesse cleared his throat. "I find myself getting reacquainted with God after a long time of silence."

What did she say to that? "That's good. That's very good." That was all she could manage?

"Say, would you help me rehearse my lines for Vivienne's play?"

"Sure." Vivienne was putting on a little production of children searching for, and finding, a treasure and being grateful for their good fortune. That was part of the Harvest Festival later in the afternoon.

As they rolled along toward the hotel, the children sang "The Farmer in the Dell," while Jesse murmured his lines.

"Jesse, you're so good with your voices for the different characters."

"I'd better be." He laughed. "Vivienne will scold me if I don't perform the way she wishes."

"Yup. Vivie is a demanding taskmaster." Maggie shook her head. "That's why I don't volunteer to do anything but drive for her."

"Because you're perfect at that?"

"Well, if you say so."

"Vivienne says so, as does Mr. Danner."

She smiled in satisfaction. As they rounded the tight corner, Jesse's shoulder and thigh pressed in against her, stirring an awareness of his masculine presence that she didn't need showing on her face. She didn't mind, but if anyone saw her rosy cheeks. . . He pulled away, grabbing the side of the bench.

"Sorry."

They pulled in front of the beautiful white building that dominated the cliffside. With the largest porch in the world, the huge painted pine structure commanded the attention of anyone who'd visited the island. Normally Maggie would bring the dray to the back for unloading by employees. But today they were met in front under the high arches by Mr. Christy, who had helped set up all manner of Harvest Festival activities for the children. His wife, who owned the tea shop and bakery, was supplying cider and doughnuts and cookies.

Once the children and Jesse had exited the dray, someone on bicycle moved alongside Maggie on the driver's side. She looked down into Eli's beaming face. "What are you doing here, Eli?"

"Mr. Danner said you get to attend."

She frowned in disbelief. "Why didn't he say so to me?"

"That's his surprise for you." Eli moved his bike to the rack on the side.

I'm getting to stay. What a day this could be.

Jesse turned and looked at her, his handsome face wearing a quizzical expression.

Eli hopped up. "Danner said it's high time I did the dray run on my own, and it's also time for you to get an extra day off."

"Really?" She'd loved their autumn fairs in Pickford.

"Get down, man, and I'll be on my way." Eli beamed up at her.

Now, an hour later, Maggie threw her third-in-a-row ringer of horseshoes around the pole. Every one of her tosses had hit perfectly.

Beside her, Jesse groaned. "That's embarrassing."

Jack handed Maggie a sugar-dusted doughnut. "Congratulations, Mickey." He turned to face Jesse. "Ain't nothin' embarrassing about having a drayman beat you, Jesse."

Jesse cleared his throat.

"Mr. Huntington, that is." Jack made a face. "It ain't like some dumb old girl beat you, like Bea beat me in the potato sack race."

Maggie stifled a laugh.

Opal ran toward them, crying, crimson streaking her hands. "I got cut!" Her heartrending shriek made Maggie want to cover her ears, but Jesse bent and wrapped an arm around the girl.

"Let me see." He pulled out his creamy linen handkerchief and wiped at her palms.

Bea ran toward them, face contorting in disgust. "She's only got a bit of raspberry jam on her hands, that's all."

"I got cut." Opal glared up at her sister.

But when Jesse kept wiping, the child's hands showed nothing but a thin bloodless scratch. He held the handkerchief out to Maggie. "Smells like raspberry to me, Mickey. What do you think?"

Maggie bent and sniffed the fruity scent. "You have raspberry jam for blood! You're one lucky girl, Opal." She patted the girl on the head. "No wonder you seem so sweet." She winked at the child.

Bea rolled her eyes. "You're only encouraging her, Mr. Hadley."

Maggie shrugged and pulled a coin out of her pocket and handed it to the younger girl. "Go buy a trinket at that booth over yonder for your ma. Somethin' to cheer her up."

Opal blinked up at her through wet eyes. "Thank you, sir." She skipped off, clutching the coin in her fist. Bea followed slowly behind.

"Nice of you." Jesse inclined his head so close to her that she could feel his warm breath on her wind-chilled cheeks.

Heartbeat ratcheting upward, Maggie stayed stock-still. If they were alone, if he leaned in closer, she could bend toward him and kiss him. But they weren't alone. Yet how she longed for that possibility. And for more time together.

October's nip had necessitated Jesse moving Maggie from the carriage house into the Huntingtons' larger home and into an upstairs bedroom, but with November fast approaching, Jesse had to ensure they'd all be warm. To that effect he'd asked Mr. Christy to help them obtain more wood to burn. Jesse rode one of the Wellings's bicycles home from work, expecting to meet the man at the house. Maggie was supposed to have driven the loaded dray up to the bluffs. But as he arrived, he saw that the dray parked in their drive stood empty. Perhaps Mr. Christy had helpers who unloaded the wood with him. One could hope.

He strode up the drive, which could use more crushed stone, and to the brick walkway. Light snow dusted the holly bushes edging the house. Laughter carried from inside as he opened the door.

"I'm home, Mother." He removed his hat and scarf and hung them on the hall tree and then did the same with his wool coat.

"We're in the parlor," Vivienne called out.

Jesse entered the room, which would soon be blessedly warmer after the supply of wood.

Garrett Christy nodded at Jesse as he accepted a cup of tea from Mother. "Thank you, ma'am. And good to see you again, Jesse."

"Thank you for bringing the wood up to us."

Christy's teacup clinked as he set it down hard in its china saucer. "I was only making a social call today, Mr. Huntington."

Mother blinked up at him, that strange absent gleam still in her eyes that had been there since Father's death. "Son, Mr. Christy says he needs to speak with you privately about a matter."

Jesse's gut clenched. *No wood. A private matter.* This could not be good. He'd paid the man before he'd departed for the mainland. It couldn't be money. Or had the price gone up?

Mother rose and then brushed at her skirts to straighten them. "I'll leave you gentlemen to your business." She offered Jesse a charming, southern belle half smile before bestowing the same upon Garrett and departing the room.

"Best sit down." Garrett's dark eyebrows drew together. "I have a few questions for you."

"All right." Jesse lowered to the divan and poured himself some tea, his hands shaking enough to rattle the teapot's lid.

"Mr. Welling has educated me on the construction of many of these homes up on the bluff."

"Sir?"

"You see, most are built for summer-only living. And with the hard winter we may get, you may not be able to keep this house warm even if you fill the fireplaces ten times a day."

"What?" But somewhere in the back of his memory, Jesse recalled his father saying something to that effect.

"I didn't want to discuss this problem with your mother, as she seems rather. . ." Christy rubbed his dark beard.

Jesse cleared his throat. "My mother hasn't recovered from the many losses she's suffered."

"I understand. All that loss can make a person feel like goin' away to their own little world. My wife got like that for a while after her ordeal."

Mrs. Christy had nearly been killed by a deranged man when she was younger. She'd been a great encouragement to the Huntingtons.

"I appreciate you not asking Mother." What was he to do? Jesse's sips of tepid tea only exacerbated his chill. "You didn't bring us back any wood then?"

"I did. It's down at the docks. But, Mr. Welling, he sat me down and explained that only a few homes up here can be occupied year-round."

"I can't afford to rent someone else's home." Where would they go?

"He has his hands full with his wife so sick, but not so much that he didn't realize you couldn't stay up here all winter. So let me talk with him again and see what he has in mind."

Jesse covered his eyes with his hands and rubbed his face briskly against the headache that was building, then he dropped his arms.

"I'm counting my blessings every day, but I can't see the blessing here."

"The way I see it, you got a few choices. You can try to suffer through the winter, maybe move your family down to the first floor. We can ask some of the old-timers on the island for advice. We can look for rentals for you."

"I couldn't pay."

Christy raised his broad hands. "I don't rightly know what we'll find, but we won't know unless we ask around. Maybe someone's got a winter-worthy warm house they'll let you use if you'll simply maintain it."

Pride leaped up and grabbed Jesse by the throat. He couldn't manage a word. His family wouldn't take charity. But how long would it be before all the windows in the house iced over?

The craftsman rose. "I'll check on things for you. And Maggie and I will bring some of the wood up tomorrow after school."

Jesse nodded and stood. Mr. Christy had figured out early on that Maggie was not a young man, and he'd not betrayed her confidence.

"I'll let myself out, no need." And the broad-shouldered man, whom Jesse realized was still wearing his Mackinaw coat, headed out.

Stay and freeze? Or swallow his pride if a warm home was offered?

His sister entered the parlor, holding a small tray of cookies. "Goodness, I know his wife is an amazing baker, like his sister, but that shouldn't have caused Mr. Christy to run off."

She set down the tray then turned to warm her hands by the fire. "When does that next load of wood get delivered? I feel like I am parsing out logs like in that *Little Match Girl* story."

Jesse laughed. "Things are not quite that extreme."

"My lips are turning blue."

"Not quite."

"It feels like it when the wind rattles the windows and seeps in the cracks."

"I thought you and Mother were going to add some more of those heavy draperies you found in the closet."

"We did, but there were only enough for the bedrooms."

He could convert the parlor to a sleeping room, and the office as well. But where would they all fit? *Lord give me wisdom. Give us provision.*

Chapter 10

November already. Maggie sat at the Huntingtons' kitchen table, the scent of rising dough and cinnamon wafting from the covered bowls she'd set nearby. She and Vivienne had received starter dough from Mrs. Christy and had gotten their own loaves started that evening. She'd washed up and sat down to copy Mrs. Christy's recipe onto a card for her own files. Jesse sat at his small desk in the adjacent parlor, grading papers. He looked up and smiled at her, then gave her a cheeky wink. She blushed and returned her focus to the bread's ingredients.

Mrs. Huntington carried the silver mail salver to the table. "I'm afraid the butler didn't bring this to you earlier, my dear."

Maggie searched the woman's placid face to see if she was jesting. She looked serious. There was no butler nor any other type of servant in the household. "Thank you, ma'am."

"You're welcome." She swiveled and silently exited the room. Jesse's sad eyes followed her. He must have heard their exchange.

Maggie turned the envelope over, and her heart leaped when she recognized Pa's scrawl. Chicken scratching was what Ma called it. Maggie chewed on her lower lip. Pa never wrote letters unless he wanted a point to be made or if some bad news had to be conveyed. Ma handled all the letter writing even to his kin, with Pa giving ideas of what to tell folks. Would Pa be telling her to come back home? He said he'd write if her brothers got work or if things changed for the better on the farm. She unsealed the envelope and unfolded the letter:

Dear Margaret,

I have news. Some good, some bad. No fears—God is good. First, your Ma has been real sick. But our neighbor, Mrs. Crist, has been tending to her, as have I. Ma's on the mend now.

Maggie exhaled a breath. Several women Ma's age on the island had died recently from a vicious illness. She continued reading:

John got work in Newberry, building that new asylum. Russell is fully recovered. And here's the best news of all, my girl—you can come home soon. Russ wants his job back with Mr. Danner, and he wants to get over to the island before the hard freeze so that you can get a boat back home before then.

So we'll be able to have a family Christmas together. I know how you love all the celebrations. And Ma would be cheered by your return home.

Home? Why did her heart sink at the thought? She ought to be excited. Thrilled. The place she loved to be and was fully loved and known. But as she glanced across the dining room at Jesse in the parlor, she had to face the truth. She was in love. In love with a schoolteacher with a one-year contract who could be gone at any time. Who came from a social status so far above her level that she couldn't even fathom it. And whether Jesse would admit it or not, at some point his family's connections would have to result in more lucrative employment. A business position far from here. Far from her. She dropped the letter into her lap and exhaled loudly.

One day soon she'd have to return home. How many days from now until her brother would arrive? She'd pack her bag, wave goodbye to Jesse and hug his sister and mother, and head back to Pickford. And she'd return to the same home, same family, but her heart would be heavier from that day on. A tear escaped down her cheek, and she swiped at it.

"What's wrong?" Jesse's eyes flashed concern.

She shook her head. "My mother's been ill."

He rose and came to her side. "Will she be all right?" He gently touched her shoulder.

Maggie nodded as her tears overflowed, not because of her mother, whom she was sure would recover, but because she'd be leaving him. "Yes, she'll be fine."

"I'm glad." He wrapped an arm around her shoulder and squeezed.

She's seen him perform this affectionate gesture a hundred times with his sisters and mother, but when Maggie looked up at him, she saw something more than the concern that would normally be there. In his eyes was a longing that she recognized, one simmering in her own heart. His eyes widened, and he brushed the hair back from her forehead and leaned toward her. Her heartbeat hitched in her chest.

Footsteps sounded in the parlor, and Jesse released her. Both turned to see Vivienne carrying a large box into the room.

"Mind if I join you? I've got to get these theater props finished."

Guilt must have shown on their faces, because Vivienne glanced back and forth between them a few times.

Jesse gestured toward the letter. "Maggie's mom has been very sick, but she's on the mend now."

"Oh. Well good." Vivienne set the crate of fabrics on the table. She removed lace and ribbon spools and then pushed them around the table like she did when she was nervous. Vivienne had expressed a desire to have a complete room dedicated to her creations.

Maggie looked up. "I think you'll have more room soon for your projects."

"Oh?" The girl's fair eyebrows drew together. "Why is that?"

Trying to keep her tone even, Maggie squared her shoulders, feeling the cotton fabric of her work shirt bunch between her shoulder blades. "My pa says my brother Russell will be coming soon to take his position back. So I'll need to leave."

"Leave?" Jesse seemed to suck in a breath. His handsome features tugged in concern. Did he care as much as she did? He must. And even with this bad news, the thought that Jesse Huntington, who had one year earlier been the son of one of the wealthiest men in America, cared for her, buoyed her spirits.

"I'm afraid so."

"When?"

"By Christmas."

"And Russell is returning?" Vivienne's voice came out almost shyly.

Maggie cocked her head at the younger woman, who was chewing her lip.

Vivienne moved closer to her brother. "Didn't Flo say she'll know by Christmas if they can offer you a position in Detroit?"

"Oh." Maggie couldn't help her surprise. Why hadn't he said anything?

Jesse's cheeks turned a warm shade of red, and he patted his coat pocket. "We've been passing around her latest letter. Would you like to see it?"

No, I wouldn't. "Certainly."

He passed the missive to her, and Maggie forced herself to touch the warm paper that had been tucked so close to Jesse's heart. Where she wanted to be. But that would not be happening now. Nor had it ever been a possibility.

"Before you leave us, Miss Hadley, I'd like to share some business advice with you to pass on to your father."

Miss Hadley? Now she was Miss Hadley again?

"Certainly, I'm sure he'd appreciate it, as would I." Not as much as she'd have appreciated other things though.

"Good, then we'll begin as soon as you're finished penning your response to your family and I am done grading my papers."

"What type of advice do you have?"

"Some suggestions about collecting debts and about putting some teeth in his contracts."

She stifled a bitter laugh. How ironic coming from someone who had delayed repaying her hardworking father until the last moment possible. She'd been a fool. Jesse would be going on his way. And so would she.

She rose from the table. "I'm going up to stoke my fireplace before I go to bed." Even doing so would barely take the chill from the room—and certainly not from her heart.

Jesse surveyed his classroom, satisfaction surging through him more rampantly than in any of his previous endeavors. "Class, since it's the month of Thanksgiving, I'd like you to write down three things you're thankful for this year. Then fold that slip of paper up and bring it to the front for our cornucopia." He patted the wicker basket that Mrs. Christy had sent in early that month, full of cookies for the children.

Soon Opal Duvall joined him at his desk. She handed her folded paper to him, then slipped her tiny hand into Jesse's. "You're the bestest teacher ever, Mr. Huntington."

"Best." Jesse adjusted his tie.

"That's not humble to agree with her." Ephraim scowled at Jesse from his seat in the front row.

"I'm not agreeing with Opal; I'm correcting her." Though he ought not do so, given everything the poor child was going through at home. Still, this was his job.

"You shouldn't look a gift horse in the mouth, my ma says." Bea crossed her arms over her chest.

Jesse frowned and was about to explain that the expression didn't apply to the situation, but Jack elbowed forward. "Yeah!" Obviously Jack didn't understand the gift horse analogy either. Jesse sighed.

Jesse squeezed the little girl's hand. "First of all, Opal, instead of 'bestest,' you should have said 'best,' as in 'best teacher ever,' when you spoke."

When Jack opened his mouth to protest, Jesse pointed at him. "Not one word until I have finished."

The boy tucked his chin against his flannel-covered chest.

"Next, Ephraim, I did not agree with Opal's assessment of my capabilities." He met the child's gaze. "In all humility, I can say I am a novice at teaching." He did love the children far more than his novice's heart would admit.

"What's a novice?" Jack, despite insisting on maintaining *improper* grammar, did like to increase his vocabulary.

"Oh, I know!" Mary Elizabeth, seated adjacent to Ephraim, waved her hand. "It's in the Catholic church when—"

Jesse shook his head. "No, you mean *novitiate*. That's not the same as *novice*."

"Oh." A tear spilled onto her cheek.

"It's all right, Mary Elizabeth. That was an excellent attempt."

Bea brought her folded paper to the front and smirked. "She was wrong."

Jesse fixed the older girl with what he hoped was a piercing gaze. But when she rolled her eyes and walked away, he figured he must have failed.

Opal patted his arm. "You are my favorite teacher. Does that make you the best?"

"No, not really." Jesse pointed out the window to where snow was gently filtering down. "I could choose a favorite child in the infamous January snowman contest, but that would not make their execution of a frozen man to be of an excellent quality."

"Do you have a favorite student?" Opal's hopeful gaze stung his heart.

He leaned in. "I have favorites." He winked at her.

"Who are they?" Ephraim lifted one dark eyebrow.

"Do you really want to know?" He stood.

"Yes."

"All right, students, stand in a line here." He gestured to the left side of the blackboard.

His pupils rose from their desks, creating a commotion, and formed a queue. When they'd all settled down, he pointed to Marcus, who stood in the front. "Write Ben's full name down on the board please, then take your seat."

"Middle name too?"

"No."

Marcus scowled but wrote out Benjamin's first and last name. He stomped off to his seat. Jesse gestured for Opal to move forward. "Write Mary Elizabeth's name on the board."

"But she's not up here in line."

"She will be in a moment." Jesse caught the older girl's gaze and quirked his index finger at her, to come forward. "And please help

Opal with the spelling."

They continued on until the last child, Benjamin, grinned at Jesse. "I reckon you want me to write Ephraim's name up here, don'tcha?"

"You're a smart boy, Benjamin."

The children all returned to their desks, smiling.

Opal raised her hand and glanced around at her classmates. "So we're all your favorites?"

He pointed to the board. "That's my list, so yes, you're all my favorites."

Was it his imagination, or did the children in his classroom hold their chins a smidge higher now? He grinned, sure that they did.

"Now, class, next we're going to expand on our writing task for the day. So I want you to write one paragraph on something you hope to be grateful for in the upcoming year."

Would 1895 be a good year for him if it didn't include Maggie?

Chapter 11

The white limestone walls of Fort Mackinac gleamed in the sun on the hillside, taunting Maggie as December's frigid breezes gusted in off the Straits of Mackinac. Maggie directed her Percherons to pull the fully loaded dray away from the docks. She puffed out breaths above the heavy blue scarf that Rebecca Christy had knit for her as an early Christmas gift. She tugged on the matching knit cap. With both items on, she'd startled herself earlier when she'd looked into a mirror and could have been glimpsing a reflection of her eldest brother, whose eye color and slightly almond shape matched hers perfectly.

She'd directed the team onto the snow-covered streets as soft, clumpy flakes of snow whirled down. The world was quieter with the filmy white cover. Smoke rose upward from occupied homes' chimneys. It was easy to tell which houses were empty for the off-season.

Moo and Bear navigated the turns and headed up the steep incline to the back of the fort. Which soldiers would off-load their supplies and bring them in? With the fort closing soon, she prayed Sergeant Mauvais would be gone, but Eli had said the man had been thrown out of Foster's Saloon the previous weekend for disorderly behavior. Maggie heaved a sigh.

Eli and Mr. Danner had earlier in the day brought the Mackinac Island students up for an early Christmas party at the commander's residence. It would have been nice to have Jesse be there now, as she arrived. But that wasn't to be. She chewed on her lower lip as she approached the gate.

A lone soldier huddled inside the wooden guard shack. Private Abernathy stepped out and waved to her. "Good morning, Hadley."

"What are you doin' out here, Abernathy?"

The clerk wiped at his beet-red nose. "We're short-staffed with all the departures."

"Was Mauvais one of those?" A girl could hope. And pray.

Abernathy grunted. "You'd think so, after that episode in town, but no, he's still here."

Her heart sank. So not only was the horrible man still there, but the beautiful teacher, Miss Dearing, presided over the commander's party where she could demonstrate how she was so much more suitable for Jesse than Maggie could ever be. *I shouldn't be so uncharitable.* Miss Dearing had never been anything but kind to Maggie. And she'd never done anything to suggest she was setting her cap for Jesse. Still, with Maggie about to depart for the mainland, she couldn't help her wild imaginings.

A gust of wind penetrated her heavy wool coat and swirled snow up around the private's legs. Moo and Bear shifted in their braces.

"It's an ill wind that brings no good." Abernathy laughed at his own pronouncement of the saying. "I'm off to Lieutenant Geary's home in a moment to grab some hot cider. Stop back by here on your way out, and I'll bring you a mug too."

"They're holding the party there?"

"Yes, special announcement coming, I heard."

"Oh?"

"Yes, I believe the captain's daughter will finally receive a ring from the lieutenant."

"Which won't make Mauvais too happy." Maybe that's why he'd gotten into trouble at the saloon.

Abernathy laughed. "Yeah, you can bet he's not invited to the party."

A burly man with sergeant's stripes, the only man in the lightly occupied fort to possess such a rank, swiveled toward her as she neared the quartermaster's building. She cringed. *Mauvais*. She unconsciously jerked the horses to a halt, startling herself when they stopped. The man scowled at her, but was that also a leer beneath his whiskers as he waved to move behind the quartermaster's building instead of into the courtyard? She hesitated.

He bellowed out, "Forward," resting his hand on his hip.

Swallowing hard, she directed Moo and Bear into position.

One of the privates strode into the space between the quartermaster's building and the adjacent one. Before he turned his back to her, he gave her a wicked grin.

Fear prickled her skin.

"It's *Miss* Hadley, isn't it?"

When Sergeant Mauvais jumped onto the back of the dray and began laughing, Maggie looked for her escape. Where could she run?

The occupant of the beautiful two-story officer's quarters, Lieutenant Woodbridge Geary, offered the children a tour of the rooms, all of which had been decorated beautifully for Christmas. "Welcome to my home. Since this is Company C, Nineteenth Regiment of Infantry's last Christmas here, Captain Witherell has graciously given us leave to celebrate together."

Miss Dearing, attired in a splendid pink-and-cream skirt with a matching jacket, seemed to be blushing. "Thank you so much, Lieutenant Geary."

When Geary lifted Miss Dearing's hand to his lips, even the tiniest of Jesse's pupils could have knocked him over with a feather. Miss Dearing and Lieutenant Geary?

Then their host, with Miss Dearing on his arm, led both classes into the parlor. Although spacious, the children did need to spill out into the hallway. Jesse remained behind in the kitchen, surveying the spread of desserts that Mrs. Christy had sent up from her shop. Fruitcake, scones, and several types of cookies covered almost every surface.

Moving into the kitchen entryway, Opal Duvall clutched her sister Bea's hand, eyes wide. "Is that awful Lieutenant Elliott here somewhere, Teacher?"

The girls' beautiful sister, Sadie, had once been courted by the lieutenant. "He's on leave to visit his family, so no he's not here." Thank goodness, for the girls were still upset by the man's bad treatment of their beloved older sister. With their mother so ill, he'd not been sure they'd even attend the party.

"Good." Bea stamped her booted foot then swung Opal back around and headed down the hallway toward the parlor.

Jack Welling, dark rings under his eyes, shuffled into the kitchen with Ephraim. "We're ready for the decorating contest."

Jesse pointed to a pile of sugar cookies stacked on the oak counter with three bowls of colored frosting and shakers full of what looked like crushed peppermints. "I think those are what Miss Dearing wanted."

"We'll bring 'em to the dining room, sir." Normally, Jack would be off like a shot. His mother's pneumonia had worsened, and instead the child ambled back behind Ephraim.

Whispering a prayer for both Mrs. Welling and Mrs. Duvall, Jesse turned in a slow half circle to take in the spacious kitchen. Beyond the square space was a small room for a cook. But with only a dozen or so men left at the fort, Geary used the room as a study. He'd left a bowlful of walnuts atop his desk and several nutcrackers for the children to use later for yet another contest. Jesse stepped into the hallway that connected the kitchen to the study. A good-sized window to his right afforded a view of the roadway into the fort. Movement caught his eye. That was Maggie sitting atop the dray, stacked high with supplies. She was on her own today. His heart ached to think that soon she'd be leaving. But what could he do? He had nothing to offer her.

Captain Witherell's daughter, a notorious flirt whom he'd been warned to avoid, sashayed into the small space. "Hello. I'm Dora Witherell, the captain's daughter." Unease riffled through him as she smiled up at him in what most would consider a charming fashion.

"Jesse Huntington. Pleased to meet you."

A minx-like expression flittered over her even features.

Miss Dearing strode back into the kitchen, her pink-striped skirts swishing. With her dark hair all piled in what his sisters called an updo, she was indeed a pretty woman. "Mr. Huntington, the children are ready for the cookie contest."

He gave her a mock salute. "Yes, ma'am."

Miss Witherell flipped her palms opened. "Well, Miss Dearing has her lieutenant here, but mine has not yet arrived."

His fellow teacher adjusted her lace collar. "Your father said he'd be here soon."

"Until then, may I borrow your associate, Miss Dearing?"

Borrow him? "It's only a few steps to the dining room, Miss Witherell." He gestured down the hallway.

With the tilt of her head, she reminded him of his mother and her expression when she was about to launch into full southern belle mode. "But with a handsome gentleman here to escort me, why would I want to be alone?"

Alone? She was in a house bustling with children. It was pointless to resist. Jesse extended his arm and walked the willful woman to the well-appointed dining room. Unfortunately, she didn't release his arm when he attempted to drop her hand.

Miss Witherell leaned in. "When Zebulon sees me with you, he'll think twice about being late the next time."

So she was hoping to make the lieutenant jealous. Jesse exhaled a slow, deep breath. If it were Vivienne behaving in this manner, wouldn't he go along? Would it cause harm? He patted the woman's hand. Jesse bent and whispered in her ear. "My dear Miss Witherell, I have two younger sisters. I'm not totally ignorant of the ways of young ladies. But I assure you, I'm also aware of how perturbed Lieutenant Vance would be to see me standing so close to you—especially since it's rumored he's to propose today."

"Propose?" Cheeks reddening, she blinked up at him.

Yes, he'd ruined the surprise, but by golly someone needed to wake this young lady out of her flirtations for a day, which should be memorable for the right reasons.

"Excuse me." She whirled around and then strode off more quickly than he'd imagined her heavy skirts could possibly allow.

The children set about decorating their cookies, laughing and elbowing one another as they did so. Today, in contrast to earlier in the school year, the orphaned children were smiling and joking, while Jack and the Duvall sisters kept to themselves, worry tugging at their features.

Private Abernathy, who'd ushered them in at the gate earlier, carried a mug of hot cider down the hallway. He stopped at the dining room and held the mug aloft. "Just bringing the dray driver something to warm him on his way back."

"I'll come with you." He checked in with Miss Dearing and grabbed a handful of cookies that he wrapped in a napkin. "Let me grab my coat."

He and Abernathy stepped out onto the broad porch. He shivered as a cold gust shot through him.

Movement behind the quartermaster's building, viewed in the space between that building and the adjacent one caught his attention. What were the men doing back there? And why was someone standing in the bed of the dray, with Maggie?

"Stop!" Someone's faint cry for help surged him into action. He raced down the wood walkway and through the snowy field toward the commotion.

Maggie had hinted to him that she believed the soldiers suspected she was a woman. He'd dismissed his niggling fears by rationalizing that the men wouldn't dare touch her with their superiors there because such behavior would carry grave consequences. No, that couldn't be it. They wouldn't. They couldn't do anything to harm the young woman who had come to mean so much to him. But as he neared the buildings, he heard the Percherons' sounds of distress. And then Sergeant Mauvais's distinct voice. "You're getting what's coming to you."

A knit cap and scarf, blue like the ones Mrs. Christy had given Maggie, flew through the air and onto a nearby low snow bank.

Jesse ran on, gaping as one of the privates climbed up into the dray and tugged at Maggie's overcoat.

His heart hammering and vision blurring in his angry charge, Jesse still couldn't miss as Sergeant Mauvais ran a finger under Maggie's chin, then bent and tried to kiss her. Quick as a flash, she wielded a horse whip up in her hand and brought it down hard on his head.

Jesse finally reached them, Abernathy on his heels, as the

sergeant staggered backward but then lunged toward Maggie, who was busy slapping the whip at the private, who tried to grab it.

"Stop this at once!" Jesse rushed toward Maggie. Knowing that he might be assaulted, he grabbed a thick branch from the ground in one hand and waved it at the men. "Don't make this any worse for yourselves."

Abernathy shook his head at the two men. "You'll face repercussions for your behavior today."

Sergeant Mauvais rubbed his head. "This little. . ." He let out a string of profanities. "She's been passin' herself off as a man for a long time, and she needed to learn a lesson."

"I think you're the one who needs to learn a lesson, Sergeant." Jesse narrowed his eyes at the man, rushed at him, and commenced his instruction.

Epilogue

Pickford, Michigan
May 1895

Maggie patted her shoulder-length curls in approval. "Thank you, Ma."

The reflection she saw in the mirror looked much different from Mickey.

Ma pointed to Maggie's image in the oval mirror. "You do look right pretty."

Sighing, Maggie swiveled around and took her mother's hands. "I don't think that's what caused Jesse to fall in love with me."

"I'd agree." Ma's face grew red.

"Have you been reading his letters?" Maggie searched her mother's face and found confirmation. "Ma!"

She crossed her arms. "Your pa snuck a peek too."

Maggie stared, gape-mouthed.

Her bedroom door opened, and her father ducked his head inside. "Look at my beautiful Hadley girls."

"I'm hardly a girl." But Ma went to him and kissed his cheek.

"And neither am I."

"You look like one again." Pa made a swirly motion near his hair.

Maggie turned toward her vanity table and retrieved the pink crystal *vaporizateur* of French rosewater perfume that Vivienne had sent her. She squeezed the bulb several times. "There. Now I definitely smell like a lady too. And not like a lady dray driver."

Ma laughed. "You're willing to give that up?"

"You've wanted to prove yourself for a long time, Daughter." Pa's tone held a hint of secrecy. Or was he trying to make sure she'd be happy to be the wife of a Mackinac Island schoolteacher?

Outside her window, a rider attired in a stylish coat, dark buffed boots, and a top hat entered their yard atop a black gelding. *Jesse.* Her heart leaped.

"He's here," she whispered.

"We'll go greet him." Her parents left her, closing her bedroom door gently behind them.

Maggie's heartbeat skittered into a rhythm of its own. Ever since Jesse had rescued her from Mauvais, they'd been honest with each other about everything. He'd shared that he loved teaching too much to accept the offer from Florence's employer to move to Detroit. She'd told him of her desire, had she been a man, to run her own stable or dray business. And she'd confessed that she'd missed Hadley Farms so much that she sometimes felt ill on the island.

"Maggie?" Ma opened her door. "Someone's bursting to see you."

When Maggie entered the living room, Jesse's eyes lit up. If he had opened his arms to her, she'd have swept into them as she had after the attack. His arms were home, no matter where they lived.

Tears pricked her eyes. She loved him so much.

"I have news." Jesse's smile faltered.

"Have a seat." Pa gestured to their two facing divans by the fireplace. Jesse waited for Maggie to sit and then settled beside her at a respectable distance.

"Thank you, Mr. Hadley, for putting a word in for me with the Pickford school board." Jesse brushed his dark hair back from his forehead.

Maggie felt her eyes widen. "Pickford Schools?" Jesse loved his island school.

"I have a contract offer." Jesse patted his pocket.

"Then Maggie and you would be nearby?" Ma clasped her hands together and beamed at Pa. But Maggie's father's eyebrows drew together.

"Maggie has some offers too." Pa patted his own jacket pocket and then withdrew several envelopes.

"What?" Maggie reached for Jesse's hand.

"Let's hear them, sir." Jesse squeezed her fingers in reassurance.

"Danner, your sister Florence, and your mother." Pa dropped the opened letters down on the small oak table that sat between them.

"You opened my letters?" *Again?* At least if she were married, she'd open her own correspondence.

"You'll find they're all addressed to me." Pa smirked. "With an additional unopened letter to you inside each one."

"Which leads me to believe you're somehow involved in these offers, sir."

"I did listen to and read all your business advice, young man, and perhaps I do have a stake in these offers. I do, after all, own a thriving Percheron business."

Maggie swiped the letters from the table and scanned the first one from Mr. Danner. "He'd like me to train his drivers either here in Pickford or on the island. Depending on where we end up living, he says." Maggie peered at Jesse, who hadn't officially asked her to marry him yet.

He opened the second one. "Mind if I look at Flo's?"

She waved her hand. "No, go ahead. Everyone else seems to enjoy reading my mail."

Jesse chuckled as he read his sister's note. "Her employer asked Florence if there was something else she could do to help me, since I turned down the job in Detroit."

"And?" Maggie reached for the letter.

"She's bought the stables and dray businesses I suggested."

Maggie scanned to the bottom of the letter. "And she says you and I could run the businesses together, as they're all primarily in-season, when you won't be teaching."

"Oh Maggie, we'd love to have you here, but that's a dream for you." Ma's eyes filled with tears.

"Of course we'll expect you to enter agreements with Hadley Farms, upon suggestion from Mr. Huntington."

This was too much to take in. And what did Jesse's mother have to say? The envelope to Pa was addressed from Atlanta, where Mrs. Huntington had gone after Christmas. Jesse's aunt had sent for her and, faced with winter in a small rental apartment over a store, his mother had quickly accepted.

"You read it, Jesse." Maggie sniffed and handed him the pale pink note.

He rolled his eyes. "If this says what I think it does, then she'll ask that you discuss her situation with me privately. She'd never put it in writing."

"Her situation?" Pa shifted in his seat.

"Ah, she's being courted by one of her old beaus and won't be leaving Atlanta until her own wedding date is firmly set." Jesse glanced at the note, waggling his head back and forth in impatience.

"Yes, she wrote a note about nothing, and I'm to tell you."

"But your sisters, they'll be able to come for a June wedding?" Ma leaned forward.

"Vivienne and her theatrical troupe will be returning to the island next week."

Jesse's youngest sister had been performing throughout the Midwest, despite Jesse's and his mother's objections. She'd simply left when Jesse moved into the apartment near his school and sent him a telegram from Detroit.

"Russell will be happy she's back." Ma pressed her fingertips to her lips.

Pa cleared his throat. "Yes, they're quite good friends, I understand." His stern glance suggested that no one comment further on that topic.

Maggie stood and held her hands at her waist. "There seems to be a difficulty in making all these decisions, given that the offers assume I'm getting married."

"Oh." Jesse reached into his vest pocket and then dropped down on one knee. "It took being in desperate straits to open my eyes. If a lady dray driver will marry an island teacher, I believe God will bless us both."

Maggie stared at the ring in his outstretched hand.

Pa scratched his chin. "That sounds suspiciously like you're making up her mind for her. You take the Mackinac teaching contract renewal, and she then helps run the island carriage businesses."

Ma shoved Pa's arm. "You should know Maggie won't let anyone make up her mind for her."

"Yes." She laughed.

Jesse rose and embraced her.

When he released her, she schooled her face into a grave expression. "What makes you think I was agreeing to your proposal and not affirming my father's observation?"

"Because I'm a teacher, and this year I've learned some lessons on love."

As he slid the ring onto her hand, she knew that was one sentiment she couldn't argue with.

ECPA-bestselling author **Carrie Fancett Pagels, PhD**, is the award-winning author of more than a dozen Christian historical romances. Twenty-five years as a psychologist didn't "cure" her overactive imagination! A self-professed history geek, she resides with her family in the Historic Triangle of Virginia but grew up as a "Yooper" in Michigan's Upper Peninsula. Carrie loves to read, bake, bead, and travel—but not all at the same time! You can connect with her at www.CarrieFancettPagels.com.

A Song in the Night

by Rita Gerlach

I call to remembrance my song in the night;
I meditate within my heart,
And my spirit makes diligent search.
PSALM 77:6 NKJV

Chapter 1

Baltimore, Maryland
January 21, 1904

Karien Wiles brushed away the frost from the windows beside the front door. Although she disliked the cold and the gusts of wind that blew through the city from the harbor, she loved how softly and silently the snowflakes fell.

A childlike feeling came over her, an anxious sensation to pull on her boots and head out. The branches of the dogwood tree in the yard glistened with a coating of snow. The street looked like a patchwork quilt of brown and white, and the wheels of carriages and wagons crushed the snow into puddles that sparkled in the sunlight.

An envelope had been pushed through the brass mail slot, and she bent to pick it up. She pushed open the flap and read the insert. Her mother came down the staircase, perfectly dressed as always in a lilac skirt and white high-collar blouse, her hair loosely pulled into a chignon. "Who's it from, Karien?"

"Oh, nothing to worry about."

"Usually when a person says that, it means there is."

Karien tucked the note into her sleeve. "Honestly, I don't know one way or another, Mother. Mr. Stein has called for a staff meeting."

Her mother's eyebrows arched. "You're not going out in this weather, are you? I'm thinking of Liza as well. She's not accustomed to the cold weather."

"It's only a dusting, Mother. Look out the window. You'll see."

Her mother walked over to the parlor window. She drew back the curtain and peeked outside. "I suppose it isn't too bad."

"I think it's beautiful. Everything looks so clean and bright, like in the story of *The Snow Queen*. You read it to me when I was little, remember?"

Her mother glanced at her. "You're such a romanticist."

Karien smiled. "Yes, I suppose I am."

"I'd think snow makes you miss your father, the way he used to play with you in it."

"It doesn't take snow to make me miss Papa. I think about him every day." There was a hill in the park one block over, and her father would take her there to sled ride. She'd come home soaking wet, shivering cold, her cheeks red as apples, and her father carrying her on his shoulder. To Karien, he was the first man she had ever loved, and no one could ever match his strength and goodness or the wisdom he possessed.

Putting the curtains back in place, her mother picked up a ball of yarn and her knitting needles. "Karien?"

"Yes?"

"Does the cold affect your hands?"

Karien shook her head. "You worry so. My hands will be fine."

"Wear your gloves, dear. Otherwise, your hands will be frozen by the time you reach the academy. The cold could affect your playing."

"They'll warm up, and I never go out without my gloves."

Her mother sighed. "I wish you and Liza had a gentleman to escort you."

"I know you do. You remind me daily."

"If you did, I wouldn't worry."

"You'd find something." Karien kissed her mother's cheek. "I do love you for it, you know. Poor Liza has no one to worry over her."

"Surely you understand why I grow concerned when it gets dark."

"We'll be home before dark." Karien walked over to their old family piano and opened the lid. "I'm perfectly safe."

"Even so, it would set my mind at ease to know a gentleman escorts you home. Why can't Mr. Stein or Mr. Peaks?"

"Mr. Stein has a flat above the school, and Mr. Peaks walks home to his wife in a different direction. Mother, you know female teachers can't step out with a man, except he be a relative. I cannot be courted or married if I want my position."

"It's a silly rule. Men can but women can't."

"All the thinking in the world won't make it happen." Karien played a scale.

"Well. . .I'll stop thinking about it if that's what you want, but I won't stop praying. The Lord hears the prayers of mothers and will provide."

"I have no doubt He will. But for now, Liza and I have a meeting to go to." She closed the piano lid without making a sound. She always treated it gently.

"What could be so important?" her mother asked.

"I'm not sure. Most likely something to do with the curriculum."

"Surely he makes allowances on a day like today."

"I doubt it."

"How can you know for certain?"

"Two weeks ago, Liza and I stood outside Mr. Stein's door and listened to him shout at poor Miss Smith."

"You mean the teacher who has been there for who knows how many years?"

"Yes, Shirley Smith. She missed the morning staff meeting for the second time and. . ."

"And what, dear?"

"I shouldn't say, Mother. It's gossip."

Her mother pursed her lips. "I don't want the details, Karien. I only want to know if Mr. Stein is such a fiend to fire a teacher for being late, that's all."

"There was more to it."

Her mother leaned forward. "I bet it had to do with that rule I dislike."

"You are good at figuring things out, Mother."

"Then I'm right. It was a man, wasn't it?"

"It was. One afternoon I ran into Miss Smith at the Tea Room, and a gentleman was seated with her. I promised I wouldn't say anything, and she swore he was her cousin, a distant one but nonetheless her cousin. I had no reason to doubt her. I felt so sorry for her when she rushed out of Mr. Stein's office in tears. He had let her go. Liza and I tried to explain to him that she told him the truth. He did not believe us. Then he warned us to let it be an example to us of what would happen if we did not abide by the rules of our contracts."

"So sad if he did not believe her. Besides, if a teacher wishes to marry, she can leave her position. The school can hire someone to take her place. A woman should take care of her home and family. Children need their mother at home."

"I agree, Mother. If I should ever meet someone I want to marry, that is what I'll do when we have little ones."

"You did read the terms of your contract, didn't you?"

"Every word."

"Well, Karien. You know what I always say. There is a silver lining to every dark cloud. Dress warm, dear. I don't want you falling ill."

"I'll wear the new scarf you knitted." Karien picked it up from the chair where she had left it. "You make the prettiest scarves."

Her mother set her knitting aside and stood. "I'll fill a thermos with hot soup for you to share with Liza. What a grand invention the thermos is."

On the next-to-the-bottom step of the staircase, Karien slipped on her leather boots. She wondered when she'd be able to afford a new pair. Money had been tight on a music teacher's salary. She tugged at the laces and tied them. She imagined wearing a new pair of black, button-up boots with wool inserts to keep her feet warm.

She sighed, stood, and drew on her wool duster. At the hall mirror, she fastened the top button. The light from the foyer window turned the color of the coat from camel to muted pink. Karien liked the color, grateful she had been able to afford it on sale.

To match the fashionable motor scarves ladies were wearing, Karien had set a sheer scarf over her cartwheel hat and looped it beneath her chin. It would keep it on her head if the wind blew. She slipped on the white wool gloves her mother had knitted.

Liza Gable came down the staircase bundled from head to toe, only her eyes showing above her scarf and below her wide-brimmed hat. She had been lodging in the Wiles home for a year, and Karien loved her like a sister. Gifted with a sense of humor, friendly, and extremely well versed in poetry and classical literature, Liza made the evenings something to look forward to for Karien. They had long discussions on books and would read to each other long into the night.

Liza's brown eyes glanced at the front door. Then she drew

down her scarf. "How cold is it out there, Karien?"

"Freezing." Smiling, Karien wiggled as if cold. "Come on or we'll be late."

Liza went down a step. "I wanted to stay wrapped up in the blankets and sleep. Mr. Stein has nerve making us come in for a staff meeting on a weekend."

Karien checked the top button on her duster. "It is unusual. As long as I've been teaching at the academy, we've never been called in on a Saturday."

"Where did you buy that lovely duster?" Liza sighed and touched the fabric. "I love the color, and the fabric is very fine."

"I bought it at O'Neill's Department Store on sale after Christmas. It still cost me a good amount of my paycheck. But I needed a new coat."

"I like the Glass Palace store. Just thinking of it makes me want to go shopping instead of going to a meeting. I wonder if Mr. Stein will even think of stoking the stove in the teachers' lounge."

Karien opened the front door. Freezing air bit her cheeks. Drawing her collar close, she stepped out onto the porch. "Come on, Liza. We'll only be out in it a few minutes, and we can have something hot to drink at the academy."

"I do hope so. I can't go without hot coffee or tea in the morning." Liza stepped over the threshold onto the porch.

The roof blocked much of the sunlight, and the breeze caused the hanging lamp to sway. Holding on to the railing, Karien headed down the brownstone's steps. Liza followed her with a buff of her rosy cheeks. The men in the neighborhood had cleared the steps and part of the sidewalk. Across the street, a group of boys threw snowballs.

Karien carried on down the street to the corner with Liza behind her. "I'm afraid of slipping," Liza said. "I'm not used to this kind of weather. It's warm in Louisiana." She kept pace with Karien.

"I won't go back there, Karien. Too many mosquitos in summer and oh so hot. We have hurricanes too. I'm deathly afraid of those. This is unpleasant too. I feel like I'm always cold, except in summer of course."

"We're almost there." Karien stopped and looped chatty Liza's arm through hers. "Take a moment to admire the snow. The dusting on the trees is lovely. See how pure it looks and how it settles on the branches." She looked at her friend. "You have written poetry. Can you see it in this?"

"Yes, and I do like it. I don't like the cold."

"I love the evergreens most, don't you? I've only seen some in the park. Let's hope we see a cardinal today."

Liza heaved a breath. "I wish I could be like you. You're always so optimistic."

Out in the street, people dodged wagons, carriages, and the occasional novel automobile. The bell to the corner grocery jingled as people stepped inside. The happy sound reminded Karien of snowy outings. Papa would pull her on a sled along the street. He would take her inside the store and buy a newspaper and the latest monthly copy of *McCall's* magazine for Mother. He'd treat Karien to a peppermint stick or a box of Cracker Jack.

The Margaret Brent Academy for young ladies ages eight through fifteen stood on the corner of Liberty Street, tall and imposing. Karien paused with Liza and looked up at the lofty windows.

"Why hasn't Mr. Stein gotten the building owners to paint the trim around the windows? I see peeling paint from here."

"Expense, I suppose." Karien stared at the old building. Thin layers of snow lay over the windowsills and the niches in the bricks. "Maybe they are waiting for spring when it is warm enough to paint."

After looking both ways, she and Liza stepped out onto the street. A streetcar, pulled by two draft horses, sloshed through the melting snow. Icy water and street sludge splashed her coat.

"I should have known," cried Karien. "Just look at my new coat."

Liza huffed. "There's no way to avoid these mishaps, Karien, unless we wait until the street is completely clear. Don't worry. You can clean your coat."

Karien shook her head. "Well, let's see if we can make it to the other side without someone else coming along and splashing us." She clutched one side of her duster and shook the icy mix from it. Then she lifted it above her ankles and hurried on. Liza gasped and sped up beside her.

"Karien, you're showing. . .dear me. . .you're showing a bit much, don't you think?"

"*Dear me*, Liza. I think not."

"You'll ruin your stockings."

"Better them than the hem of my duster."

The sun brightened and made her blink. She hoped it would melt all the treachery before her. She fixed her eyes on her destination. A policeman in blue with a double breasting of gold buttons stood at the bottom of the academy steps twirling his baton. She hailed him, hoping he'd see her and offer aid. But with all the street sounds, she failed to capture his attention.

The wind picked up, and she set her hand on her hat. They had to hurry or they'd be late.

Before she reached the sidewalk, the rumble and sputter of an engine sent a shudder up her spine. From the corner of her eye, an auto headed right for her. A horn bellowed. She grabbed hold of Liza and rushed to the curb. Her foot sunk into a dip. She stumbled. Down she went flat on her bottom.

Liza stepped back. "Karien!"

Stars darted before Karien. Lightheaded, she shook her head. Dear oh dear, her skirts were up to her knees. Frantic, she pushed them down. Then a strong pair of arms slipped under hers.

"Miss, are you all right?" Confused at what was happening, Karien squirmed out of the man's hold and remained on the cold ground.

Another man in a cap and goggles hurried up to her. "I'm sorry, miss." He held out gloved hands to her.

Karien stared forward and set her palms flat on the ground. "You almost ran me over."

"Are you hurt?"

"What do you think?" A firm, masculine voice came from behind her. "Move back."

"Who are you to tell me what to do?" The driver stood up and clenched his fists.

Liza leaned down beside Karien. "Look at your clothes."

"I won't." She tried to get up.

"Let the gentleman help you."

Karien swallowed. "I can do it." She turned to the right, and tried to figure out how to get up without looking foolish. "I guess I do need help," she admitted.

The man behind her put his arm under Karien's and lifted her. All she could see were his hands and that he wore a brown wool overcoat. The way his arms felt around her when he pulled her back felt as if she were being wrapped in a snug blanket. They were warm and strong.

She looked down at her duster and wanted to cry. The hem was smeared with mud. She forced back the tears, and a shiver passed over her. The red clay mud of Baltimore would leave a stain. Into the rag bin would go her duster, stockings, and possibly her skirt. She hadn't the money to replace them.

Liza put her arm around Karien's shoulders.

"I'm fine, Liza. Please, don't get yourself in a tizzy."

"I can't help it." Liza frowned at the driver "You could have run into her, you. . .you crazy driver. Just look at my friend's clothes.

They're ruined all because of you, you cad."

The driver pulled his goggles down. "I said I was sorry. Besides, she should have been watching where she was going."

The man who had helped her up moved in front of the two ladies. "Before this escalates into something neither party wishes, I suggest you get back in your machine and continue on to wherever you were going."

The driver, a head shorter than Karien's knight in shining armor, squinted at him with an ashen face. He nodded. "Right. Well, I'll be going."

The policeman pointed his baton at the driver. "Hey, what do you mean by driving at that speed? You could've sent this lady to the morgue." He gave Karien a look of concern and said, "Sorry for sayin' so, miss."

Karien swallowed. *Morgue!* What an alarming thing to say. The idea this could have been her last day on earth rattled her. She straightened her toppled hat and composed her nerves. The only harm done was to her pride and the ruin of her duster. She'd forgive the man for startling her.

"It's all right, Officer. I'm fine. I made it in time, and I cannot completely blame this gentleman. There's a dip in the grass, and I stumbled."

"You mustn't make excuses for this man, miss. You were obviously caught off guard." The officer stepped up to the driver and puffed out his barreled chest. "So what do you think I should do with careless drivers such as yur-self, sir?"

The driver glowered. "There are no rules about speed here, no signs posted or anything. You can't hold me responsible for her mishap. She stepped into that dip and fell."

"Then why did you stop?"

The driver's face paled, and he refused to answer. The officer jutted out his chin. "I'd like to haul you before a judge. A few nights in jail should make you think twice about driving like a madman."

Karien, kindhearted and forgiving, knew she had to intervene. The thought of this man sitting in a cold jail cell overnight because she lost her balance could not be borne.

"Officer, as I tried to explain, the mishap is partially my fault. I should have been more careful." She touched his sleeve. "There's no reason to arrest him, is there? I'm not hurt. No real crime was committed."

The officer twisted his mouth and glared at the man. "Well, if you insist, miss."

"I do, Officer."

"Then be on your way, mister, and watch where yur goin' from now on." The officer turned to Karien. "Be more careful crossing the street, miss. There aren't a lot of those autos in town yet, but you never know when one will come barrelin' around a corner." Then he walked away with a whistle and a swing of his baton.

Karien turned to the man who had helped her. Now she saw him more clearly. His hair matched his brown coat and slouch hat. She glanced up at his eyes. His hair touched the tips of his ears, and his face had the slightest whisper of a man who worked outdoors. She thought it of interest that he did not wear the fashionable mustache of the day. Instead, his face was cleanly shaved and his hair cut a bit longer.

"I guess I was too dazed to thank you. My deepest appreciation."

"No need to thank me. Shaken?" he asked.

"Who wouldn't be?"

"What can I do to help?"

She gave him a sidelong glance. "Not a thing."

He looked at the ground. "You landed hard. Someone needs to fix that dip."

Liza tugged on Karien's sleeve. "Come on, Karien. We don't want to be late."

"I'm coming, Liza." She glanced at the gentleman standing before her. "I have to go."

"How about lunch? It'll make you feel better."

They reached the stairs in front of the academy. "Sorry, I can't."

Liza went through the doors, turned and frowned. He lifted his hat to her. Then he slipped it back on. "I understand. It was presumptuous of me to ask. You're Mrs. . . ."

"Miss Karien Wiles."

Perhaps he did not realize it, but Karien saw relief glisten in his dark brown eyes. "Nathan Archer at your service."

He extended his hand, and she shook it. His grip did not hurt, but the strength in it surprised her. With that kind of hold, she'd not slip or fall. She smiled, knowing her mother would have been pleased. For a female teacher, handshakes were rare out of caution, a most inane rule that demeaned common courtesy.

The wind blew, and Karien held down her hat. A slip of her hair fell forward.

"I'm surprised by the wind here," he said. "I thought the tall buildings would block it."

"You're not from Baltimore, Mr. Archer?"

"No. Please, call me Nathan."

"I couldn't possibly. We don't know each other."

"True. I suppose it's expected in the city to be formal."

"You suppose correctly."

Karien felt the oddest sensation. She did not want to leave. She thought it interesting how Nathan Archer studied the placard on the building. His eyes narrowed and he looked at her. "The Margaret Brent Academy for girls. Student or teacher?"

"I teach music appreciation." She headed up the steps. It would not bode well with Mr. Stein if he saw her with a man.

Nathan hurried beside her. "Let me get the door for you. There are patches of ice on the steps, and you could slip." He held out his arm for her to take.

Karien scrutinized the glassy patches. A little smile curved her mouth. It would be quite an embarrassment if she did slip and fall—again. She gave him a quick smile of acceptance and set her hand in the crook of his elbow. Avoiding the ice, he led her up the steps to the door, a wide heavy thing with brass fixtures. Before she could push down the latch and open it, the door swung in.

"You'd better hurry, Miss Wiles." The academy's housekeeper faced her. Thick spectacles made her green eyes look twice the size, and the tight bun on top of her head looked like a small bird's nest. She'd been employed at the school long before Karien began teaching there, as long as anyone could remember. Middle-aged, Mrs. Temple was highly esteemed for her energy and kindness. Every morning, coffee and tea awaited the staff. Each child in attendance greeted her with respect as if she were descended from the famed Margaret Brent. Karien greatly admired her.

Mrs. Temple shoved her hands on her hips. "The rolls are about gone, Miss Wiles. The only thing left is tea and coffee. Who's this?"

"Oh, Mrs. Temple, this is Mr. Archer." She pulled off her gloves. "Mr. Archer, this is Mrs. Temple. She takes care of the school for us."

He inclined his head. "You do an excellent job of it, Mrs. Temple. I've never seen a school foyer as clean and bright as this one."

"You're familiar with academies such as this, Mr. Archer?"

A smile lifted the left side of his mouth. "I'm afraid not, but I'm familiar with foyers."

Mrs. Temple giggled. Ah, so he had a sense of humor. Karien hung her duster on the rack beside the door. She would know Mr. Stein's on sight, a gray great coat with a clipped fur collar. Not a sign of it. She felt a tinge of guilt to be glad for it.

"How do you know our Miss Wiles, sir?" Mrs. Temple had a knack for questioning visitors, especially gentlemanly ones.

"We just met." He stopped short when Karien shook her head.

She then drew up to Mrs. Temple. "Mr. Archer gave me his arm when he spotted the ice on the steps."

Nathan cleared his throat.

Mrs. Temple set her hands on her hips. "That's not what Miss Gable said."

Karien blushed. "Yes, well, I fell because of the uneven ground out front."

Mrs. Temple put her hands over her ample hips. "That sidewalk is treacherous. Something should be done."

"Truth is some dunce drove around the corner and startled Miss Wiles," Nathan said. "I won't let the sidewalk take all the blame."

Mrs. Temple's mouth hung open. "Poor dear. Did you help her up?"

"I did, and with pleasure."

"It would've been tragic if Miss Wiles had been injured."

Karien pulled the hat pin from her hat. "I dread to think of it, Mrs. Temple." She turned to Nathan. "Again, you have my thanks, Mr. Archer." Without a second thought, or the idea she should invite him in, Karien set her hand on the door to close it. Mrs. Temple stepped in front of her.

"You mustn't hurry Mr. Archer away, Miss Wiles. Where are your manners?"

Karien stepped back.

"We've hot tea and coffee, Mr. Archer," Mrs. Temple said. "Won't you have some?"

He smiled. "No thank you. I must be going."

"Oh, that's too bad. Perhaps another time."

"Miss Wiles tells me she's here for a staff meeting. How long do you think it might last?"

Karien looked at him and widened her eyes. Such a bold question to ask.

"Oh, not more than an hour, I should think."

"She tells me it's against the rules, but I'd like to escort her and her friend home if she'd like. There's a lot of ice and slush out there, and it will be dark soon."

Karien spoke up. "Mr. Archer, we cannot—"

"There's no harm in a gentleman walking you home when the sidewalks are dangerous." Mrs. Temple's brows arched. Then she smirked at Karien. "I'll not breathe a word, Miss Wiles. Let the gentleman take you home."

Karien glanced at Mr. Stein's office door. "But if Mr. Stein should find out."

"Like I said. I'll not breathe a word."

Chapter 2

Karien watched Nathan walk down the steps. His gait seemed cheered. Had he told the truth that he was happy to have met her? She had to admit she was glad he had. She did not believe in coincidence. Everything happened for a reason. Many things in life were divinely appointed.

She wondered why they had been brought together. The manner in which they met brought a smile to her lips. He too avoided an auto in order to save her. Its horn sounded like a foghorn and bellowed above the neigh of the horses that pulled wagons and carriages, the jingle of harnesses, and the cry of a street merchant hawking hot peanuts.

She watched him brush down the sleeves of his coat where the street muck had splashed. Then she covered her mouth to stifle a giggle. She must have looked ridiculous sprawled out on the sidewalk with her clothes splattered and her hat askew. It must have been a funny sight for bystanders. Liza certainly found no humor in it. Karien knew she'd been shaken and embarrassed by the whole thing.

Nathan's concern for her welfare captured her interest. Perhaps he meant to be gentlemanly and nothing more. She stood in the open doorway gripping her arms against the cold. He smiled, touched the brim of his hat with one finger as if to salute her, then walked off down the street. She leaned out and watched him tip his hat to ladies and step aside for others. She attempted to figure him out. He didn't have the accent of Baltimore men, nor of Marylanders. He didn't dress as stylishly as most, no bowler hat, cane, or fancy suit. She wondered about the boots he wore. She had seen those same boots in shop windows meant for equestrian sport. The color of his attire intrigued her as well. Most gentlemen dressed in black or deep navy blue. His clothes were earthy in color and seemed more practical than fashionable.

There was more to Mr. Nathan Archer than met her eyes.

Mrs. Temple leaned forward. "He'll come back, and when he does let him escort you home—and Miss Gable too. There's nothing in the rules says you can't."

Karien turned. "That's true, Mrs. Temple, there isn't."

"I bet your mother worries with you walking home in the dark."

"She worries no matter what time of day it is. She did tell me it would give her ease if a gentleman walked me and Liza home."

"Well, you should heed your mother's advice for your own protection. We may be in a good part of the city, but some people would take advantage of young women alone."

Karien braced her arms. "Dear me, Mrs. Temple. Why are we standing out here in the cold?" she said as she went to close the door.

"Why indeed, Miss Wiles?"

Karien stopped when Mr. Davis, the postman, called up to her from the bottom of the steps. He lifted his cap and positioned his mailbag over his shoulder. “Got a boatload of mail for Mr. Stein.” He walked up the steps and handed Karien a stack of letters. “I’ve never seen so much mail for the academy in one day.”

She struggled to take the load into her arms. Stepping back, she passed the letters over to Mrs. Temple and shut the door.

“Mercy,” said Mrs. Temple. “Look at all these letters. Whatever do you think is going on, Miss Wiles? Why would Mr. Stein be getting all these? It’s never happened before.”

“I don’t know,” Karien said. “I doubt its fan mail, unless he’s been up to something we don’t know about.”

“Maybe he’s been giving some kind of performance down at the music hall near the harbor,” Mrs. Temple laughed. “Wouldn’t that be a hoot?”

Karien smiled at the idea. “Indeed it would be. I can’t imagine Mr. Stein leaping around on a stage in front of an audience.”

“Nor can I.” Mrs. Temple slapped her hands together. “Well, we’ve lollygagged long enough. I’ll go check on the coffee and tea.”

Karien sighed. “I’m dying for some hot tea and honey.”

“I bet you are. You’ve been delayed long enough. The others have been waiting in the lounge, and I doubt any of them know how to brew.”

“I know how to make coffee,” said Karien. “My father taught me. He used to make it for himself and my mother every morning until. . .until he was taken from us.”

On the table beside the door sat a brown wicker basket for calling cards. Only one lay in it today. She took it out. *Nathan Archer, Refuge Farm, Virginia.* She smiled. He left it on purpose, and so no one else could claim it or throw it in the bin, Karien tucked it into the cuff of her blouse. To her, it was a sign he would keep his word and return for her.

A heavy blow landed on the front door, and the sound of it echoed down the hallway. Mrs. Temple gave Karien a pleading look. "Would you get it, Miss Wiles?"

She hastened back, pulled the latch, and found a gentleman in a gray overcoat and cap standing outside with one of her students. "Mr. Hollister, Mary Beth. Classes aren't in session. It's Saturday."

Hollister threw his head back and stiffened. "I want to see Mr. Stein."

"I'm sorry, he isn't here." Karien set her hand on the girl's shoulder. "He's due to arrive soon, if you'd like to wait."

"I've not got the time to wait."

The girl stared up at Karien. Eight-year-old Mary Beth's blue eyes always touched Karien's heart. She was a mild child who lit up when Karien would lead her class in a song. "Mary Beth, I'm glad to see you're feeling better. I heard you had a terrible cold, and we missed you in class."

Mary Beth curtseyed. "Yes, miss. I'm better now."

Karien wrapped the girl's scarf snug against her throat and looked up at her father. "And you have her out in this dreadful weather, Mr. Hollister?"

"My daughter is well enough. Please tell Mr. Stein that Mr. Hollister is quite put out. Quite put out indeed."

"Is there something I can help you with? If it's about Mary Beth's grade—"

"It has nothing to do with her grades." Hollister twisted his mouth. "Apparently you've been kept in the dark."

Karien frowned. "I don't know what you mean."

"Oh, you'll know soon enough."

Mary Beth shook Karien's skirt. "Papa is sending me to a school in Boston, Miss Wiles." The child's eyes watered.

"Boston?"

Hollister moved his daughter back. "That's right. My daughter won't be coming back to this school. Her mother and I are very put out."

"Why isn't she coming back, sir? She's one of my best students. She has exceptional talent that should be nurtured. Are you displeased with the education we've provided?"

Mary Beth's father huffed, clutched his daughter's hand, and swung back to the door. "No, Miss Wiles. I assure you, her talent will be nurtured. I am obligated to say nothing more on the matter to any of the staff. Good day." He stepped up to the door.

"Mr. Hollister, please won't you wait for Mr. Stein and discuss whatever it is that has caused you to remove Mary Beth? He should be here any minute."

"As I said, I haven't time to wait. Give him this." He took out a note from his breast pocket. "Tell him I expect a check by tomorrow afternoon. I want reimbursement for the tuition I paid up front." He tipped his hat. "Good day, Miss Wiles, and good luck."

Making a swift turn, the man pulled on his daughter's hand and left. The door slammed shut, and Karien winced. *What does he mean by wishing me luck?*

She glanced at the sealed note in her hands. Something disturbing had truly occurred.

Chapter 3

I can't believe it. Mary Beth seemed so happy here." Karien could not shake the ache in her heart. Had she somehow been the cause? She hoped Mr. Stein would give her the Hollisters' address so she could write to them and make further inquiry as to why they had removed Mary Beth. She knew the chances were slim he would. He'd tell her that academy business was none of hers.

Mrs. Temple set her hand over her mouth and shook her head. "Mercy, Miss Wiles. I don't know what to say. This is disturbing."

"You heard?"

"Enough to know how sad it is to lose a student."

"I wonder why he withdrew her."

"You handled the situation well. I wouldn't have known what to say."

Karien shook her head. "Something is wrong."

"I agree."

"First we get called in for a meeting. Mr. Stein is nowhere to be seen, and we are kept waiting. Then a stack of letters is delivered and Mr. Hollister arrives fit to be tied and tells me he's removed his daughter."

Mrs. Temple opened the door to Stein's office. "Perhaps we should put that note on his desk with the others."

Karien handed the envelope to Mrs. Temple. "Please do, and then we can try to put it out of our minds."

"There's a reason for everything, and things may not be as bad as we're assuming. You should be thinking about that nice young man you met today."

Karien blushed. Who was this man? The mere mention of him caused goose bumps to sweep over her. She'd just met Nathan Archer, and she hadn't stopped thinking about him—not for a minute.

The grandfather clock in the foyer chimed the hour. She tripped her fingers along the chair molding and walked with Mrs. Temple toward the teachers' lounge. The paintings of previous headmasters, their stern eyes looking down on her, seemed to scrutinize her every movement. Margaret Brent's portrait, Maryland's first female landowner, did not. The artist had captured determination and bravery in the eyes, strength in the line of her jaw. A slight smile curved her mouth, and it seemed as if she approved of Karien Wiles.

Mr. Peaks, the mathematics instructor, took out his pocket watch and glanced at it. "We've been waiting for over an hour. If Mr. Stein isn't here in fifteen minutes, I'm leaving. My wife will want me home for supper."

"It must be nice to have a spouse to go home to." Karien looked at the women in the room. "Don't you agree, ladies?"

Mr. Peaks nodded. "I agree with you, Miss Wiles, whether they do or not. You ladies should be allowed to marry and keep your positions, just as we men."

Karien touched the bridge of her nose to signal him. His specs were crooked as usual, and he made the adjustment. Liza and Miss Cora Breck were seated near the potbelly stove beside Mr. Peaks. The stove shimmered with heat. Yet the cold day seeped through the leaks in the old windows and made Karien shiver.

A book balanced on Liza's knee. Karien glanced at the title, *Jane Eyre*, and thought the binding looked familiar. Jeweled leather in blue hues and rough-cut paper made it special.

"My father gave me a first edition like the one you're holding when I was in my teens," she told Liza. "It's a favorite of mine."

Liza's cheeks reddened. "I hope it was all right. I took it from the bookshelf in your mother's sitting room. I promise to put it back when I'm finished."

"I don't mind." Karien sat down beside Liza. "Such a romantic story, don't you think?"

"Hmm. Dark and romantic. Mr. Rochester must be one of the greatest sinners in all of literature, but at least he redeems himself in the end, unlike Heathcliff."

Miss Breck, a most astute teacher of history, snugged her knitted shawl around her shoulders. She wore her hair so tight in a bun it pulled at the corners of her eyes. Karien had a notion that if she could brush it out and show her how to wear the latest trend of a loose twist on top, Miss Breck would no longer complain of headaches. But Miss Breck would have none of it. She was the epitome of an aging schoolmarm set in her ways.

"That kind of writing would never have been tolerated back in the early 1800s," said Miss Breck.

"Perhaps not, but the book was a bestseller." Karien handed the copy to her, but Miss Breck held up her hand. She did not wish it.

"I have read it."

Karien nodded in order to keep the peace in the room. "With

your knowledge of history, Miss Breck, you must be correct. But surely there were lawbreakers then as there are today."

"I only know what I've read, Miss Wiles. *Jane Eyre* gives a clear warning to lovelorn females to guard their hearts. It is a lesson we must all be aware of."

What had Miss Breck seen and heard? Had she seen from the window Nathan Archer, or heard them speaking in the foyer? She opened her mouth to ask but shut her eyes, leaned back, and decided such a conversation would be too risky.

"Miss Wiles, why didn't you ask the gentleman in?"

Karien's mouth fell open. "Gentleman, Miss Breck?"

Mrs. Temple looked at Karien and jerked her head toward the table set with coffee, tea, and a few glazed rolls. Her expression warned Karien to choose her words wisely.

"Yes, Miss Wiles. I saw you from the window coming to the door with a young man."

Karien went to the table and poured a cup of coffee. "Cream or sugar? Or would you prefer to get it yourself?"

"Black, Miss Wiles, and yes, I can help myself," Miss Breck said. "But I've had enough."

"You must excuse Miss Breck. She's not as broad-minded on the subject of *amour*," Liza said.

Karien sipped her coffee. "Oh, I'm sure that is not true. Is it Miss Breck? A person doesn't have to be married to understand love. With your knowledge of history, you would know better than any of us in the room."

"History is my subject, so I suppose so."

"Speaking of love, what is your opinion on the rule about female teachers remaining single? The times are changing, and perhaps the rule should change too."

Miss Breck drew up her shoulders and raised her chin. "I am a suffragette at heart, Miss Wiles. When it comes to the teaching profession, however, I refuse to put women on an equal footing with men."

Karien set her cup and saucer down. "About the rule, Miss Breck?"

"We all have our place. We all must obey the rules. You signed your contract, didn't you, like the rest of us?"

"You mean, did I sign the same contract as you and Miss Gable? I did."

"Well there you have it. I hope that young man does not return and cause you any problems. Mr. Stein would not like it. Unless he is a relative. Is he a relative, Miss Wiles?"

"No, Miss Breck. He is not." Karien changed the subject to the weather. "I wonder if this cold snap will ever end." Did she intend a double meaning? Getting into a debate over the rules for female teachers would lead to ill feelings. She was, after all, the low rung on the ladder.

"You're flushed. Are you feeling all right?" whispered Liza.

"It's the heat from the stove." Karien stood and set her coffee on the table. Mr. Peaks remained quiet, sitting with his legs crossed, blissfully drinking his coffee.

"I'm getting annoyed waiting." Miss Breck shifted in her seat and stared at the clock.

"To pass the time, let's have Miss Wiles tell us how she was saved from being run over," said Mrs. Temple.

Miss Breck bent her brows. "You were run over?"

Karien shook her head. "I was not, Miss Breck. Bruised perhaps, but alive."

"I'd like to hear more of the story behind your rescue, Miss Wiles," Mr. Peaks said. "Give us the details. It can't be any less exciting than sitting here all day waiting for Mr. Stein."

"There really is nothing else to tell. An auto came around the corner, and I fell getting away from it. Mr. Archer lifted me up."

Liza sighed. "He turned out to be very gallant."

Karien smiled and whispered, "I think so too."

"These men and their automobiles. They drive too fast," said Miss Breck.

Mr. Peaks settled back in his chair. "I've never liked automobiles."

"They are the future, I think." Karien picked up a newspaper and set it on her lap. "There's probably something in the paper about them, if we look."

"Should it interest us, Miss Wiles?" Miss Breck frowned.

"Probably not, but you have to admit, we should admire the transcontinental drive Horatio Jackson made last year."

Mr. Peaks pushed back his glasses. "It's all publicity to get the public to spend their hard-earned money on contraptions that break down and are worthless within a year's time."

The front door opened and slammed shut. "At last," Karien sighed.

Mrs. Temple poked her head outside the door. "It's Mr. Stein."

"It's is about time," Mr. Peaks groaned.

"It certainly is," said Mrs. Temple. "He's gone into his office and shut the door."

Mr. Peaks stood. "How much longer are we expected to sit here?"

"I don't know. Perhaps he's going over the accounts."

Karien turned. "The school certainly could use a large donation. The windows are drafty and the walls need a new coat of paint."

"Maybe he's spending money on new materials." Miss Breck glowered deeply. "I don't like book salesmen or salesmen of any kind, but we certainly could use new spellers."

Chapter 4

Mrs. Temple's shoes could be heard clunking down the hallway toward the teachers' lounge. A moment more and she paused in the doorway. The pallor of her skin had changed from wintery pink to snowy white. Her eyes were larger behind her glasses. Her hands trembled, and she gripped the doorframe.

Concerned, Karien stood. The look on Mrs. Temple's face confirmed her belief. Things at the academy had definitely gone south. She had never seen Mrs. Temple look so bleak. "Are you all right, Mrs. Temple?"

"Oh Miss Wiles!" Mrs. Temple pulled away from the door and fell into tears.

Everyone rushed to her except for Mr. Peaks. "Tears, Mrs. Temple? Must you cry in front of us?" He folded the newspaper he'd been skimming, and smirked.

Karien put her arm around the weeping housekeeper. "Must you be so unfeeling, Mr. Peaks? Can't you see how upset she is?"

"Upset, Miss Wiles? More like overly emotional."

Mrs. Temple moved back. "Don't mind me. I've been on tenterhooks lately. I get weepy at the drop of a hat these days."

Karien had never seen Mrs. Temple weep, not even when one of the girls dropped an ink bottle in the hallway and ruined the new rug.

Peaks folded his arms across his chest. "I expect we're supposed to go to the office and speak to Mr. Stein. Heaven forbid he should lower himself to join us in the lounge."

Mrs. Temple wiped her eyes and thrust her hands on her hips. "Well, you'll be put out to know Mr. Stein wishes to see you first, Mr. Peaks."

Karien glanced at Peaks, who pushed the rim of his glasses back, stood, and straightened his tie. "It sounds urgent." He smoothed back his thinning hair. Karien knew his neat appearance would do no good if Mr. Stein had made his mind up about something.

"It must be about the mathematics curriculum for next term," Peaks said. "He was most displeased at some of my scholars' marks."

"It's probably that." In an attempt to keep everyone's spirits up, Karien smiled and spoke cheerfully. "I wouldn't worry." She sensed differently. "Perhaps he wishes you to look over samples of new books and needs your opinion."

"If only it were that simple," murmured Mrs. Temple.

Peaks pulled at the edge of his vest. "Well, whatever it is, I shouldn't keep our headmaster waiting."

He inched past Mrs. Temple. She followed behind him. What went on was unclear, as Karien and the other ladies were silent, shocked. They were supposed to have a meeting together. Instead, they were being called in separately. Queasiness sank into her stomach. She stared at the open doorway. Her thoughts drifted and grew fixed on the worst a Saturday meeting meant. In all the time she had taught at the academy, one had never been called.

Liza paced the floor. "I think something is wrong."

"Me too," said Miss Breck. "I'm not going to sit here all day waiting to find out."

Karien remained calm, even though her nerves were taut. "We've no other choice, Miss Breck. Have another cup of tea."

Miss Breck tossed back her head. "I've no stomach for tea. Mine is doing backflips as it is. Mark my words. I think Mr. Stein is going to hand each of us our walking papers."

"We cannot assume anything. There is no reason to be worked up over something we know nothing about."

"You saw how upset Mrs. Temple was. The poor woman cried."

"Mrs. Temple could have been crying for many different reasons. If she wanted us to know, she would have told us why."

Miss Breck slapped her hand on the table beside her. "Mrs. Temple was in distress. I'm going to find out why."

"You can't barge in, Miss Breck."

"Stop me." Miss Breck jumped up from her chair. "I'm going to stand outside the door and listen."

"Maybe Mr. Peaks is getting a raise in salary."

Miss Breck narrowed her eyes. "He already makes more than we do."

Liza stopped pacing and looked at Karien. "It's because he's a man. We are educated as well as him and should get equal pay."

Karien shook her head. "He has a family to support. We should go lightly on Mr. Peaks." Karien smiled and hoped to change the subject. "Have you seen the newest child? She's as pretty as an angel."

"Angel or devil, I don't care," said Miss Breck. "I'm going to listen at the door. It would be better to find out and be prepared than wait and be shocked." Out the door she went, her long black skirt whipping around the corner of the door.

Liza walked over to Karien. "What do you think, Karien? Honestly, what is your heart telling you?"

"I am sorry to see Mrs. Temple in tears. I'm worried about her. But I will not assume anything until I talk with Mr. Stein."

Liza wrung her hands. "What kind of trouble could there be?"

"Perhaps none."

"For once, Karien, put your optimism aside and open your eyes. Clearly there is something wrong."

What kind of reply could Karien give her friend? She bit her bottom lip. Then she looked at Liza. "Let's follow Miss Breck. Perhaps I can get Mrs. Temple to tell us."

"You are worried, aren't you?"

"I have not said I am."

"Admit it, Karien. You are as worried as the rest of us."

"All right. I admit it, Liza. How can I help it with the way everyone is acting?" She walked out into the hallway, and at the end of it she could see the short row of chairs against the wall and the winter sun fade from the windows.

Voices could be heard behind Mr. Stein's door. Mrs. Temple looped her scarf around her neck and sniffed. Miss Breck dared to lean her ear closer to the keyhole. She held her finger to her lips when Karien and Liza entered.

"You're going home, Mrs. Temple? Would you like one of us to walk with you?" Karien set her hand on Mrs. Temple's arm.

Mrs. Temple shoved a hat pin through her hat. "I only have a half block to go, Miss Wiles. I prefer to walk alone."

"I think it would give Mr. Temple ease if you did have someone walk you home."

"Really. It is all right." Tears welled in Mrs. Temple's eyes. "I'll never forget how nice you've been to me."

"Can't you tell us what's happened?"

Mrs. Temple pulled out a hankie from her pocketbook and blew her nose. "I've been let go, Miss Wiles."

"What? He cannot do that."

"He did do it."

"But why? What reason did he give? You work so hard and are more valuable to the academy than any of us teachers."

"Thank you for saying so."

"It's true."

Liza stepped forward. "If he let Mrs. Temple go, what does it mean for the rest of us?"

"As far as the rest of you, I was not told a thing. Whatever has happened, I hope Mr. Stein has positive news for you. If not, stand up to him. . .if you can."

Karien attempted a reassuring smile. "We'll demand he reinstate you."

Liza wrung her hands. "I think Mr. Stein is cutting our salaries. Or worse, he plans to sack all of us and is hiring new teachers at lower wages."

Mrs. Temple shook her head, and the feather on her hat quivered. "Oh, don't think too bleakly, Liza dear. Most likely, he is cutting expenses. Else why would he let me go?"

Liza looked at Miss Breck. "You might be right, Miss Breck. We're getting our walking papers."

Miss Breck straightened up. "I can't tell. Their voices are muffled."

Mrs. Temple pulled on her gloves. "I must say my goodbyes to you ladies. My husband will be wanting a hot supper this evening." Then she smiled. "And I shall want a second slice of chocolate cake."

Karien's heart broke to see Mrs. Temple step out the academy door. It would be for the last time. Since the day Karien had come for her final interview, Mrs. Temple had greeted her with a warm smile and a good word. Each morning she had coffee, tea, and biscuits ready in the teachers' lounge. She had kept the school clean as a whistle, and she showed a great deal of patience when the pupils had run over her freshly polished floors.

Liza rubbed her nose. "I'm glad Mr. Temple has a job at the bank. Mrs. Temple will not want for anything."

"They'll get by," said Miss Breck. "Still, it is an outrage, and I want an explanation from Mr. Stein about why he has done this to a faithful employee."

Liza tapped Karien's arm and in an alarmed voice said, "I know I keep saying it, but do you think it's true we might be let go?"

A tinge of worry welled up within Karien. It would be devastating to be let go. Her salary paid the bills. Her mother had a small account left to her by Karien's father. It would not be enough to keep them comfortable.

A smile struggled over her lips as she looked at her distressed friend. "Forgive my outlook on this, Liza. I know it's bothering you that I'm trying to look on the bright side. I cannot think of a single reason why."

"We'll soon find out, won't we?"

"Yes, and when he calls one of us in, we will go in together."

Chapter 5

The office door opened. Miss Breck jumped back, and Mr. Stein and Mr. Peaks stepped out. Peak's face looked as stiff as his starched white collar. He kept his eyes forward, his lips pressed. He took his coat from the rack, dragged it on, and pushed on his hat.

Karien approached him. "Is everything all right, Mr. Peaks?"

"I'm appalled, Miss Wiles. It's unfair. . .unconscionable. A man of my qualifications should not—"

"Good day, Mr. Peaks." Mr. Stein stepped forward and held out his hand. Mr. Peaks glanced down at it, sneered, and left without saying a word.

Mr. Stein opened the door wider. "Miss Breck, since you are first in line at my door, you may come in. We need to have a chat."

Karien thrust her hands to her sides. "Wait. Why did Mr. Peaks say those things? Did you give him notice, sir?"

Mr. Stein hesitated. "I should've known this would happen. Yes, I let him go."

"And Mrs. Temple?"

Stein raised his hand. "She will not be returning. None of us will."

Karien drew in a breath. "None of us?"

"Yes, Miss Wiles. Before any of you object, I need to see each of you individually."

"Why? We three ladies know what's coming." Karien stepped beside Miss Breck and put her arm through hers. "We need to support each other in our time of trouble. Don't you think that is fair?"

Mr. Stein drew in a breath, faltered.

"I agree." Liza abruptly stood. "I want to be with my fellow teachers when you throw down the gauntlet. It's only fair."

Mr. Stein's face flushed, and he put his hand on the doorknob. "As headmaster, I—"

Karien walked past him into the office. She turned. "We won't have it any other way. You'll have to put up with us, Mr. Stein."

The others followed Karien's lead. Mr. Stein shrugged and made his way around his desk to his chair. A chill flowed through the old window frame that faced the street.

"No use in closing the door, ladies." He sat down and drew off his spectacles.

Karien, Miss Breck, and Liza remained standing. Karien drew in silent deep breaths to shore up her spirits for what was coming. The atmosphere thickened. The radiator under the window rattled.

Stein arranged three envelopes on his blotter. A snowball hit the window, and Miss Breck jumped. Stein leaped up and threw open the sash. "Get away from this window, you rapscallions." He stuck his head out farther. "Officer! Officer Mahoney. Stop those kids from throwing snowballs."

Karien heard Mahoney shout up at the window. "They're just

boys having a bit of fun. Keep your window closed before they throw one and hit you in the face, sir." His warning made Karien smile, a tight smile under the circumstances.

Stein slammed the window shut, latched it, and sat back down. "Let's hope there are no more distractions."

"We are listening, Mr. Stein." Karien crossed her hands over her waist. She kept her composure even though she had an overwhelming desire to rush out of the room.

"I'll get right to the point. Funds have been low. Rising costs have made upkeep difficult without tuition increases. The board of directors made the decision to close the academy and sell the building. I'm terribly sorry, ladies, but your time here is at an end. Each of you," and he handed out the envelopes, "are given a severance. I wish you all the best in finding other positions. I realize this is short notice, but I've no other choice. I'm also out of a job and can sympathize."

Liza was a dear soul, and it bothered Karien to hear her cry. Miss Breck's normally passive expression was replaced by gloom. The curve of her lips and the downturn of her forehead surprised Karien. She'd never seen her look so glum.

"We'll be all right, ladies."

"Oh, Miss Wiles. It is a black day. A very black day." Miss Breck put her hand on Karien's shoulder. "Even the sun has passed behind the clouds."

Tears welled in Karien's eyes. Heartbroken to lose her job and to see her friends crushed by the blow, she pushed them back. "There is a silver lining to every dark cloud. Let's find ours and not lose hope."

"Clouds are still clouds and carry rain, Miss Wiles."

"True." Karien bit her lower lip. "God causes the rain to fall on the just and the unjust. All I know to do is trust Him."

Pale, Liza stepped out of the room. Karien followed. The hall tree, once heavy laden with coats, hats, scarves, and sweaters, toppled against the wall as Liza grabbed her coat. "What are we going to do, Karien? How am I going to afford to pay your mother rent?"

Karien reached her friend. "Let's not worry about it now."

Weepy, Liza tied her scarf around her neck. "What am I going to do?"

Karien helped her when her fingers fumbled to tie a knot. "We are going to go home and have a hot supper. We're going to treat ourselves to an extra helping of pie, then sit in the other room and play backgammon. At bedtime, we will kneel together and pray. In the morning, we'll look in the newspaper to see if there are any teaching jobs."

Liza's glassy eyes stared forward. "I don't know what I would do without our friendship, Karien."

"Nor I without yours. Dry your eyes."

"I will miss our girls. They must be sad as well."

Karien drew on her coat. "I'm sure they are. This explains what happened earlier with Mary Beth."

"I was going to read *Jane Eyre* to my girls. Now. . .I can't." Liza sniffed and wiped her nose with her handkerchief. "I'll go to my classroom and get my books."

Karien nodded. "Of course."

"Will you stay behind to pack your things?"

"Yes, then we'll head home. It will take me some time though, and I would like to have a private word with Mr. Stein."

"If you don't mind, Karien. I'd like to go. I'm too upset to linger here. Your mother worries about us walking alone, but I'll be fine."

"Don't say anything to Mother. I'll talk to her."

Miss Breck hurried over to Karien. She put her arms around her and embraced her, then kissed Liza's cheek. "You are both excellent in your fields. I've no doubt you'll find other positions. Goodbye."

"What will you do, Miss Breck?" Karien asked.

"Retire. I was planning to anyway. I'll go to my cousin in Bethany Beach."

Karien tucked her scarf into her coat. "I'm so glad. The salt air is so pleasant."

"I'll savor every moment, Miss Wiles. Write to me when you both are settled. Simply address your letters to me at Bethany Beach."

Karien stood beside Liza and watched Miss Breck march over to the front door, throw her coat over her shoulders, and walk out with her head held high.

Seated behind a large mahogany desk intricately carved along the borders and legs, Mr. Stein was encircled by foggy light caused by the drawn curtains behind him. Usually such light would have made Karien see a divine kind of haze, but not when it illuminated Mr. Stein. He wore a black suit. The only color on him besides his white starched collar was a gold watch chain attached to a buttonhole. A thin man, he had never married, and lived in solitude in a room at the top of the building, where he kept his treasured first editions. No one except Mrs. Temple had been permitted to enter his living quarters.

Stein peeked over his spectacles. "Miss Wiles. Is there something else?"

"Can I talk to you for a moment?"

He set down his fountain pen. "There's nothing else I can do about the situation. Talking about it would be a waste of time."

Karien glanced around the room and stood in front of the desk. Its size engulfed the man. She pulled her gloves out of her pocket and gripped them.

"It's cold in here, Mr. Stein. How do you stand it?"

"I'm accustomed to all kinds of temperatures, Miss Wiles."

"Are you sure? I can get you some hot tea from the teachers' lounge."

He feigned a smile. "No thank you. What is it you want?"

"I was wondering if you've had a chance to read Mr. Hollister's note." She glanced at the stack of papers and whatnots on his desk. "Mrs. Temple set it there, on your blotter, with the other mail."

He searched through the pile. "How do you know about it?"

"It was I he spoke to." Karien stepped closer. "He was upset. I didn't know about the academy closing and had no indication he did either. I hope there's nothing I did to cause him to remove his daughter. He would not say either way, and it has caused me worry."

Mr. Stein leaned back. "You were not the only teacher Mary Beth Hollister had. It is arrogant of you to think you were at the center of her withdrawal."

Karien set her hand on the desk. "I was concerned about my pupil."

Stein put on his glasses and looked at the note. "Please, sit down."

Gripping the edges of her scarf, Karien lowered herself into the swivel chair.

"Mr. Hollister does not mention you. The rest is business you have no right to know."

"But I do know something. He told me he expects a refund of the tuition he paid."

Mr. Stein sighed. "That is not your concern."

Karien nodded. "You're right. I apologize. I'm glad it is the fact the academy has closed and nothing else. We've had a good reputation up until now."

"We've had an excellent reputation. Now it is history, and we must all move on. You understand of course."

"Of course I do. Still, I will never forget my time here."

Karien's heart raced. It always did when she got bad news. This time it hurt. More than losing her position, the knowledge that she would not see her students again caused her chest to tighten.

"Oh, do not look so bleak, Miss Wiles. I'm truly sorry, but closing the academy could not be helped. We've lost students over the last year to the more prestigious New England schools, and that had an enormous impact on our income. Moreover, the repairs needed are too costly. I'm afraid the building will be sold."

"To start another school?" Karien hoped it to be true.

"I've been told an investor purchased it and plans to make the rooms into offices."

"That is deplorable. He should be stopped."

"I'm afraid that is impossible."

Karien drew in a breath and stopped the tears from falling. "Well, I will leave with good memories."

"And I leave you with some advice, if you are willing to hear it."

Indeed she hoped he would. Perhaps he could guide her in the direction of another position. He did know many of the headmasters of other private institutions.

Karien scooted forward. "I'm listening, Mr. Stein."

He stood, straightened his vest, and proceeded. "When you decided to become a teacher, you shouldn't have had any reservations as to your duties."

"I was not aware I had. You never said—"

"A teacher must be stern, Miss Wiles, immovable."

"Of course, but also patient and kind in order to bring out the best in students."

"Yes, and you've been both. You have not, however, been firm." Stein looked her straight in the eyes. "Miss Wiles, you are too soft with your students."

"In what way, sir?" she said.

"How do you discipline insubordination?"

"They must apologize and perform some kind of task."

"Such as?"

"A variety of things."

"For instance?"

"Writing something out several times. Cleaning the blackboard, or in extreme cases sitting apart from the others."

"Not the birch rod?"

She balked. "No sir."

"Mr. Peaks had success with it. Why not you?"

"Because I never needed to use it, Mr. Stein. What good does it do to inflict pain in order to—"

"Miss Wiles. Have you considered your methods might prevent you from being hired elsewhere?"

"My methods have worked."

"I cannot give you a good recommendation when it comes to disciplining children, if I am asked to give it."

Karien gripped her hands. "But my classes are not academic. Music appreciation is to mold character. I've had no serious problems with pupils misbehaving. In fact, music has improved their willingness to learn."

"I've no doubt what you say is true. But I must be honest. As I recall, we had this conversation before when one of the girls threw her books onto the floor in a fit of temper."

"She was frustrated."

"It was unacceptable."

Lowering her eyes, Karien contemplated his objections to her way of thinking. She hadn't had his years of experience. But she could not bring herself to inflict punishments that went beyond the pale. "If I cannot teach, Mr. Stein, I don't know what I will do."

"Advertise for piano lessons or find another profession that would be more suited for you. Truth be told, marriage would be your best option."

"Easier said than done, sir. You should know."

He glared. "I've lost nothing by remaining a bachelor, Miss Wiles. My burdens are lighter. My days are quiet, and my money is my own."

"Even so, companionship is—"

"Unimportant to me, Miss Wiles." He slipped his finger inside his starched collar and stretched his neck. "These topics are not appropriate for us to discuss. I didn't allow you back in here for that."

"Your advice I marry caused a diversion, Mr. Stein."

He sighed and sat down. "It is a closed subject between us. Now, if there is nothing else, and I hope there isn't, I've work to finish."

"I have some music sheets in the music room I'd like to collect. I paid for them myself. And Miss Gable asked if I would collect her books for her."

Mr. Stein turned his attention to a ledger and began writing in it. "You may collect them, Miss Wiles. Good day."

She turned to leave, then turned back. "What will you do, Mr. Stein? Where will you go?"

"Back to my family's country home in Vermont. It is high time I retire, and it is as good a place as any."

"It sounds ideal. Baltimore has grown too crowded." She tucked her gloves back into her pocket. "I fear for its future."

"As do many others." Still, he did not look at her. "I wish you all the best, Miss Wiles. Please close the door behind you."

Karien did as he asked and headed for the music room. The door stood open. Its polished brass knob made her think how many times she had turned it. A glass window set in the door had been clean and sparkling, but today she saw fingerprints made by her students on it. She thought of each of her girls. Where would they be going now that the academy had closed? She remembered each face, each name, and a bit of grief over being parted from them washed over her.

Upon entering, she realized she had to face the sudden change with dignity and not allow herself to fall apart. "Gather yourself together, Karien Wiles. You don't want anyone to see how broken up you are." She whispered those words as she went inside the classroom, reminded how Liza told her she was the most optimistic person she'd known. Yet optimism often refused to see reality in its true light. Nevertheless, it was much better than walking around with a pouty face and teary eyes. She could—and would—grieve in private.

Chapter 6

For the first time during her tenure at the academy, Karien could hear the classroom clock tick away. It hung on the wall above the blackboard. She stared at it and watched the second hand move. Then she stepped over to her desk and ran her finger along the edge. Upon it lay her music sheets and books. The windows came alive with sunshine, and she gazed outside. The dreary winter clouds parted, but the wind remained high.

It was not unusual on days like this for the sky to be thickened with gray clouds one moment and then be blue the next as the clouds were whisked away. Fan-like, the sunlight spread over the baby grand piano in the front of the room. The usual seemed unusual on a day like today. Silver light framed the windowpanes and sparkled.

She walked over to the piano and sat down on the wooden seat.

Her fingers brushed over the aged ivory keys that had turned from white to mellow beige. Then she closed the top and turned to face the door—hoping Nathan would walk through it.

He had promised to return for her within the hour. He was late. Ah, if he did not show, then he'd not see that her eyes were slightly red nor hear the news—the sad, awful news. She could not expect a knight in shining armor to come rescue her from trouble and despair, could she?

Thinking he had forgotten her, she gathered her books and music sheets, placed them in a box, and headed out the door. It could not be helped. Distressed, she turned and glanced back into the room for the last time. The desks were set in a neat circle. Pictures of Mozart, Vivaldi, Chopin, and her favorite composer, George Frideric Handel, hung on the wall. The furnishings must be left behind. The music she'd take with her.

She heard the front door open and Mr. Stein's voice. "Miss Wiles is in her classroom down the hall. Could you hurry her along? I need to lock up."

A shiver passed through her, and Karien stepped over the classroom threshold holding her belongings. Nathan came down the hallway and removed his hat. When she realized she stared at him, she felt a flush cover her face.

"I'm sorry to be late, Miss Wiles."

She wiped her brow. "Mr. Stein keeps it too hot in here."

"You're cheeks are red. Are you sure, you don't have a fever? It's going around you know. It feels cold in here."

"I'm fine."

"I still hope you'll allow me to take you home. I've bought you a sandwich from the café on the corner. Thought you'd be starved by now."

She looked at the bag in his hand. "It's kind of you, Mr. Archer. I'm afraid I'm not hungry."

"The man told me it is Maryland crab fresh from the bay this morning."

"Oh yes. It is one of my favorites. Thank you."

He reached for her box of belongings. "Here, let me take that."

She waited. He stared. "Aren't you hungry a little?"

"I had some bad news," she said, handing him the box. "I don't suppose Mr. Stein told you."

"Told me what?"

"The academy has closed. We've all lost our jobs."

Nathan frowned. "I'm sorry. You must be. . ."

"Upset, devastated, taken off guard?"

He set down the box and took her by the elbow. "Come sit down."

"We really should do as Mr. Stein wants," she said.

"It won't hurt him to stay a few more minutes."

She sat down and set the bag on her desk. Deciding it necessary to eat, she pulled out the sandwich, wrapped tightly in waxed paper. The aroma did entice her. "I'm surprised by your gesture. Usually a woman brings food to a man, not the other way around."

He smiled. "Am I right in assuming you're disappointed?"

"I'll prove to you I am not." She bit into the succulent sandwich and shut her eyes. "You got this from the Belvedere Hotel didn't you?"

"I'm staying there, temporarily of course. I had one of those for supper last night and figured everyone in Baltimore likes them."

"They make the best seafood. I'll miss it."

"You're leaving town?"

"It depends. I need to make a living." She broke the sandwich in two, waved half in front of him, then held it out. "Go on."

"I already had one on the way over. I couldn't resist. Seems a lot of things in this town are not easy to ignore."

They both smiled, and a little laugh came from Karien. Who was this man who made her feel happy when her world had just fallen apart?

"I'm curious," she said, "why you're staying at the Belvedere."

"A little business. Are you interested in horses?"

Her eyes widened. "Indeed I am, not for pulling wagons and carriages, but for riding. I've seen riders in the park. I've never had the chance to ride, but I think I'd be a fast learner."

"Too bad you don't live in Refuge. I could teach you."

"I've never heard of Refuge. Where is it?"

"Virginia. I've a place along the Shenandoah."

"Are you near Harpers Ferry, where the Civil War began?"

"Yes, and across from Point of Rocks in Maryland."

"I've lived in Baltimore all my life and have known nothing but city life. It must be wonderful to ride across the fields where you live. The park has trails, and people see the same things over and over. I think it would be more interesting to explore new places."

"I ride all the time. I own a stallion named Matador."

"Matador." Karien sighed. "That's a lovely name for a horse. You said you are here on business. Does it concern your horse?"

Nathan crossed his legs and settled back. "I've purchased a mare from Ireland." He leaned forward. "Now you know I'm not a city fella."

She lowered her eyes. "I try not to assume."

"I don't have a Baltimore accent."

"True, you do not."

He settled back again. "Neither do you, Miss Wiles."

"I know. Everyone notices."

"I suppose I'm right in saying you are a mystery to me."

"It's no mystery, Mr. Archer. My mother insisted I learn good diction, and she forbids slang to be spoken in the house."

"Does your father agree?"

"He and Mother always agreed. He's not with us anymore."

"I'm an orphan."

She looked at him. "Are you?"

"Long story. Well I suppose we should be going."

"How will you transport your mare, Mr. Archer?" She laughed. "Surely you cannot fit her into an auto."

He pulled on his coat. "Right you are, Miss Wiles. By train is the best way." He paused and looked at her. "You know, now that you are free, perhaps you'd consider coming with me to meet Matador's lady."

Before she could reply, a shadow crossed the floor. Mr. Stein stepped through, his face reddening. "Miss Wiles, you should have left by now. Have you collected your things?"

Karien gathered her box of books and music. "Yes, Mr. Stein. I apologize for lingering."

Nathan stood and took the box from her. "It's my fault. We were just about to leave."

Mr. Stein relented, signaled by the sudden ease of his brow. "It is easy to fall into conversation with Miss Wiles. Do not be much longer, please."

Stein walked out, Karien surprised by his leniency. She laid her hand across the top of the piano. "I would take it, but I can't afford it, not on a music teacher's salary, which I've lost."

"I'm sorry. It is unfortunate." Sympathy spread across Nathan's face, and his eyes locked onto hers. "Have you any prospects?"

"Not as yet. Mr. Stein suggests I advertise."

Archer nodded.

"I should give private lessons."

"But if you advertise in other city newspapers, you could leave Baltimore and start afresh."

"It's not so easy to start over. But I'm capable. Maybe I should become a missionary. Surely there are mission churches that need someone like me."

Nathan set the box outside the door, turned back inside, and opened the piano lid. "Would you mind playing something?"

"Oh. . .I don't know."

"How good are you?"

She stared at him a moment. The tone of his voice challenged her. "It is a matter of opinion, Mr. Archer."

He folded his arms. "I don't know anything about music. Nevertheless, I have a good ear and can appreciate it. So would you?"

She touched the keys. "I suppose I could one last time." Pulling the bench closer, she dusted it off and sat down. "Chopin. A short piece and then it's over."

Chapter 7

Sunday, February 7

Clutching her hymnbook, Karien made her way out the massive oak doors of the Church of the Messiah to the redbrick sidewalk. She breathed in the chilly air, blinked her eyes, and picked up her pace to get home. Her mother and Liza hurried alongside her.

"I'm glad we went to church early," her mother said. "Let's hurry home."

"I'm all for a hot cup of cocoa, Mrs. Wiles. This wind is brutal." Liza kept up beside Karien.

The three stopped at a street corner. "We'll take a shortcut across Liberty Street," Karien said. She wrapped her mother's arm through hers, and they crossed. A few carriages were parked along the curbs that morn, and a biting northwest wind blew down the streets, carrying the blare of a train coming into the station. Tugging at the brim of her hat, Karien shivered. The musky scent of the harbor and the salty fragrance of the Chesapeake seemed heavier than usual.

"I've never experienced wind like this," her mother said. "It's likely to blow shingles off roofs."

"And the hats off our heads," laughed Karien. She held her gloved hand firmly against the top of her own.

Her mother glowered and questioned why she found it funny. "It goes straight through my coat into my bones," she said. "And it's whipping my hem tight around my ankles."

"I don't think it is funny," Karien told her. She had to raise her voice to be heard. "I laugh at the challenge it's made of getting home. It keeps pushing us back."

They weaved through crowds of other people leaving services. All bent their heads against the fierce gusts. A policeman sheltered from the icy blast in a doorway on the windward side of the street. A watchman in a thick wool coat checked locks.

"I'm frozen stiff," Liza said moments later. "Thank the Lord we're home."

"I'm dying for a cup of hot coffee." Karien could taste honey, cream, and her favorite cocoa stirred into her mother's freshly brewed arabica.

After heading up the steps to the front door, they ducked inside. Liza pulled off her coat and plopped down in an overstuffed chair near the fireplace. Karien set kindling in the hearth and lit it, while her mother left for the poky kitchen in the back of the house. Soon a tray with cups and saucers, a blue delft creamer and honey pot, a tin of cocoa, and a plate of cinnamon toast was set on the serving table. Karien smiled at the way her mama drew her blue woolen shawl over her shoulders and folded her hands in her lap with an attentive gaze.

"So glad we're home. What did you think of the service?"

"I've always loved the story of the good Samaritan." Karien replied.

"Me too," said Liza. "I just wish one would come along and take care of me. If I don't find a job soon, I don't know what I'll do."

Karien sat on the settee across from her mother and spooned cocoa into a cup, then honey and cream. Pouring the coffee, a whiff of steam caressed her face. "Don't worry, Liza. Something will come up. You're too good a teacher to be wasted on anything else."

"What would I do without my optimistic friend?" Liza yawned. "Beg your pardon. Have you plans for the day?"

"Mr. Archer's horse is due in."

"He's a nice young man, Karien," her mother said. "If he proposes, you should consider accepting."

Liza sipped her drink. "She can't, Mrs. Wiles, not if she wants to teach."

Every time that odious rule came up, sadness filled Karien. She realized that loving Nathan Archer had become a reality she could not deny. But she could hide her feelings—at least for a time.

She kicked off her shoes and warmed her toes in front of the fire. "Mr. Archer and I are merely friends. He knows my desire to keep teaching. I doubt he would ask me to marry him, Mother. You really must put the idea out of your mind."

"I can't help it. To think of my only child being a spinster. I want to be a grandmother." She set down her cup on the tray. "I know it sounds selfish of me, but I do. It's not the only reason I'd like to see you married. I want you to be happy like I was with your father."

Karien scooted over to her mother and kissed her cheek. "I know how much it means to you. Let's not forget the silver lining to every cloud. The rules may change one day."

"When is Mr. Archer coming by?" Liza asked.

Karien smiled. "He should be here any minute to take us to see the mare. I bet she's beautiful."

Liza's brows lifted. "You mean we're all going?"

"Don't you want to go?" Karien said.

"It's so cold outside, and I want to finish reading Mr. Wister's novel *The Virginian*. I'll pass it on to you when I'm finished. It's a western with a strong, silent hero and a pretty schoolteacher from the East."

"In other words, a romance, and of course the heroine has to be a teacher. Let me know how it turns out, and I'll consider it. At the moment, I'm—"

"Busy with Mr. Archer. You're such a romantic, Karien, and so sensible about it."

Shocked that Liza would imply all her time was taken up by Nathan, she looked at her wide-eyed. Then she caught the approving smile of her mother.

Liza set her cup aside and stood. "You'll excuse me, won't you, Karien, from going with you?"

Karien nodded. "Enjoy your book, Liza. If your room is too cold, there is a quilt in mine you can use."

After Liza breezed out of the room, Karien's mother said, "Irish bred horses are noted to be among the best in the world. I used to ride bareback on my grandfather's farm. That's how I met your father. I have days when I drift back to those times. I miss County Cork."

"It must have been romantic, Mother. You haven't changed the subject a bit. I'm wondering what this is leading up to."

"You know I think Mr. Archer is the romantic type, don't you?"

A smile had become habitual whenever someone mentioned his name. "I don't know. I only met him recently."

Her mother gave her a sidelong glance. "He's taken you to lunch and dinner, to the Music Hall and art galleries, and to Lexington Market. I will thank him for the fish he gifted us. You've enjoyed yourself, haven't you?"

"I have. We've enjoyed each other's company, and we agree on almost everything."

Her mother sighed. "You don't need me tagging along today."

"Yes, I do. You don't want to miss seeing Contessa do you?"

"He's named her already?"

"He asked me to name her."

"Do you know what that means?"

"Her name? Yes, it means countess."

Her mother shook her head. "No, no, Karien. What I meant is do you know what it means when a gentleman asks a lady to name a horse he owns?"

"I haven't any idea, but I'm sure you're about to tell me."

"It means he trusts you, that he admires you greatly. It is a romantic gesture on the man's part. And when a lady does give a name, it means she reciprocates the gentleman's devotion to her."

"You really believe that, Mother? I've never heard of such a thing."

"Well, it's true. It was a custom in County Cork. At least that's how my mother explained it to me."

The knocker on the door tapped twice. "It's him."

Karien rushed from the seating room and opened it. Nathan smiled and swept off his hat. His rich brown eyes glowed looking at her. The wind ruffled the light brown locks that brushed along his collar. She had noticed at times when they were in a restaurant that he'd gotten snide looks from gentlemen about the length of his hair. It never seemed to bother him. She loved it and at times wished to touch the tips of it.

"Am I too early?"

He jolted her back from her thoughts. "No, your timing is perfect." Karien grabbed his coat and pulled him inside. A corner of Nathan's mouth lifted with surprise.

"Sorry to be so forward, but it is freezing and the air is rushing in." She shut the door.

He leaned in. "I didn't mind you forcing me inside."

She narrowed her eyes and crossed her arms. "I wouldn't call it forcing. Can I take your coat?"

"No thanks. I've come to tell you the ship has docked. I hope you don't mind if we head out. It's a cold day, but we have carriage blankets."

"Where are we going?" Karien's mother called from the other room.

Nathan stepped through. "Brisk morning, Mrs. Wiles. I was telling Karien I have a carriage waiting with warm blankets. We'll first go to the harbor and then on to the livery where I've arranged the mare's boarding until I can get her on the train. She'll be happier in my fields."

"Will that be soon, Mr. Archer?"

"Yes, in a few days. I plan to head home at that time. My mare was supposed to arrive two weeks ago, but the ship sent a telegram that they were delayed and would be late. First by a repair needed to the engine, and then ice. That's why I've been in Baltimore so long…longer than I expected."

Karien knew that once Contessa was on her way, Nathan would return to Refuge. A pang ran through her to think he'd leave so soon. Her face felt cold all of a sudden. She moved closer to the fire. "Must you leave us so soon?"

"I've responsibilities at home, Miss Wiles."

"Don't forget your dear friends here, Mr. Archer," Karien's mother said. "You will come visit us, won't you?"

He nodded. "I don't easily forget my friends, Mrs. Wiles."

How Karien wished she could force down her feelings. His reply to her mother's question seemed vague. He'd not forget but made no promise to return.

Her optimism failed her, and her heart ached to think of him gone, wondering if she'd ever see him again. She swallowed the lump in her throat. "We have to leave now, Mother."

Her mother put her hand on her forehead and moaned.

Karien rushed over to her. "Mother, are you all right?"

She lifted her hand enough to peek at Karien. "No, dear girl. That migraine I had during the night has suddenly befallen me again."

Karien frowned. *Befallen?* What was her mother up to? "Really? You were fine a moment ago."

"But I'm not fine now, dear. Oh, my head does ache something fierce. I cannot go out in the cold. I need to go to bed." She pinched the bridge of her nose and sighed.

With a swift turn, Karien faced Nathan. "Mr. Archer, I cannot possibly leave my mother. She's in awful pain."

Nathan looked disappointed at first, but then the tightness in his face softened. "Of course you can't."

Mrs. Wiles sat up and gave him a pleading look. "Yes, she can, Mr. Archer."

"Are you really ill?" Karien leaned down. "You're not pretending?"

"All I need is a dark room and my cozy bed."

"And me to look after you."

Mrs. Wiles waved her hand frantically at Karien. "I don't need you hovering around me, opening and closing my door, while all I want is rest. I insist you go with Mr. Archer."

"I'll help you upstairs and give you an aspirin."

Mrs. Wiles stood from the chair with her fingers rubbing her temples. "I can do it on my own, and besides, Liza is here if I need anything."

Nathan turned his hat in his hands. "Miss Gable is not coming with us?"

Karien set her mouth. "She says it's too cold."

"Don't forget your gloves, Karien dear." Her mother walked past

Nathan. "Have a good time."

Karien followed her mother into the foyer with Nathan. Together they watched her climb the staircase and head down the hallway to her room.

Karien narrowed her eyes when she heard the door shut. "I know what she's doing."

Nathan smiled. "Hmm, so do I."

Chapter 8

Baltimore's Inner Basin glistened under a cobalt sky. Seagulls whirled and screeched above the murky water. Karien raised her hand to her eyes and looked up. Some of the birds dove for fish, while others perched in the shrouds of the tall ships. The piers and docks were less busy than on the other days of the week when skipjack watermen unload their bushel baskets of oysters and buyers haggled over the price of blue crabs and rockfish.

Karien watched sailors unburden the ships. Bales wrapped in muslin. Wooden crates of fruit from the South. Barrels of molasses, passenger trunks. Nathan took her by the hand and led her to the edge of the dock where a tall ship shadowed the wharf. Down the gangplank, a sailor led a restless brown mare. She whinnied and shook her mane. Her ears twitched, and she pounded her hooves.

"There she is," said Nathan.

In awe of the mare, Karien squeezed Nathan's arm. "I didn't think she'd be so tall."

"Come on, let's welcome her to America." Nathan hailed the sailor. The horse snorted and flared her nostrils. Then she reared up, twisted, and kicked. "Whoa. Steady, girl." Nathan spoke softly as he held out his hand to her. She stood still and sniffed.

"You take her, sir. I'm better at unloading cattle than this wild beast."

"She's not wild, just nervous. She's been cooped up and wants to run." He took the reins, touched her muzzle, ran his fingertips up her head and then along her neck. The mare snorted and bobbed her head. Nathan stroked her ears, and she pushed against him. "Good girl. You'll be okay."

Karien watched fascinated. How did he win the mare over so quickly? Nathan glanced over his shoulder. "You want to meet her, Karien?"

She twisted a lock of hair between her fingers. "I'm not sure. She's so large."

A stout, barrel-chested man in a flop hat approached. His bowed legs caused his gait to sway side to side. "Sure you and your lady would like time with this fine animal, sir, but we've got to load her into the wagon." He stopped and patted the mare's back and ran his hands along her legs. "An ocean voyage made her stiff, sir. We'll be sure to rub liniment on her legs and walk her." He stretched out his hand. "Kelly, at your service."

Nathan shook Kelly's hand. Kelly swept off his hat and gave a clumsy bow to Karien. "Ah, this must be Mrs. Archer."

Even though she felt heat rise in her cheeks, Karien liked the sound of that. *Mrs. Nathan Archer*, or would she always be *Miss Karien Wiles*?

"You're mistaken, Mr. Kelly," Nathan said. "This lady is my good friend Miss Karien Wiles."

"Beg yur pardon, miss." He looked at Nathan and wrinkled his nose. "Yur a lucky man to have such a pretty friend, sir." He led the way to a wagon parked on the other side of the dock. Contessa offered some resistance. She stamped her hooves and shook her head at the plank being used as a ramp. Karien walked over and stood apart from the plank. "It's all right. Be calm."

The mare turned her head, looked at Karien, and blew out her nose.

"Hold out your hand to her," said Nathan. Karien held out her hand, and the mare nudged it.

Her hand trembled until she stroked the velvety nose. Contessa made a low rumble in her throat. "Soon you'll be safe in a warm stall. Go on. Go inside."

Kelly let out a soft chuckle. "I'm amazed, Miss Wiles." He shut the back of the trailer once Contessa was onboard. "You've a way with horses."

"Every creature responds to a soft voice and a tender touch, and they respond to music too."

"Music? Never thought of that, miss." Kelly leaned forward. "Should I give her an apple or two at your say so?"

"Please do. She deserves anything she wants."

Nathan's hand fell over Karien's shoulder. "Spoiling her already?"

Karien turned to him. "Would it be wrong of me, Mr. Archer?"

He raised his brows. "Not at all."

"Good. What do you think of my theory?"

"My uncle plays fiddle. I've seen what an Irish reel can do." He took her arm. "The stable is outside the city. It's a bit of a jaunt, so we best be on our way."

Karien looped her arm through his, and they walked over to the carriage. Dry leaves whirled around her feet, and a rare wild mulberry tree growing against one of the buildings shook bare branches in the wind. She drew closer to Nathan. The cold nipped at her cheeks.

His wool coat against her gave her a sense of safety more than it did warmth.

Before opening the carriage door, Nathan looked up at the sky. "The wind has gotten worse since I got up this morning. Is it always like this in February?"

Karien shivered. "Not that I remember."

To her delight, Nathan handed her inside the carriage and laid a carriage blanket over her knees. The heavy feel of the wool gladdened her. She could not recall the last time she had traveled in a hired carriage.

Nathan pulled out his watch and cleared his throat. "After we settle my mare, I'm taking you to—what do society people call it? Brunch?"

"You always want to feed me, Mr. Archer." She tucked the blanket around her waist. "Are you feeling sorry for me because I'm out of a job and practically broke?"

"What if I said partly? Would that change anything?"

"As long as you don't pity me."

"A little empathy never hurt anyone. Besides, I think I know you well enough to know you won't let what's happened get you down. You'll rise above it."

She slipped her hands inside her coat sleeves for more warmth. The wind strengthened and pushed against the carriage as the minutes passed.

"I know it might not be easy finding another position," Karien said. "But I have faith all will be well."

"I admire your attitude."

"Do you?"

"Well, certainly. You're not a crybaby, that's for sure."

She gave him a small laugh. "I might be in private."

"I don't mind when you share with me how you feel. Don't keep things bottled up, Karien. It's not good for the heart."

"The same applies to you, Mr. Archer."

He returned her smile. "Are you getting hungry?"

She tossed back her head. "There you go again, wanting to pity me."

"No pity. Caring, yes."

"Well, I'm glad it's you giving it and not the Salvation Army. Although I have heard they serve very good soup and bread."

Touching her chin, he turned her face to him. "Has it gotten that bad?"

She lowered her eyes. "No, not yet."

"I'll never let it get to that point, Karien."

The carriage hit a bump, and Karien squealed. She threw her hand on top of her hat when it shifted. "Sorry," she said. "I didn't mean to cry out."

Nathan pulled up in the seat. "It's all right. I think it was meant to move us apart. I was close to asking a question at the wrong time."

The carriage turned and lumbered down a dusty side street. The plodding of the horses echoed between tall redbrick buildings that blocked the sun. The interior of the carriage darkened. "What are the roads like where you're from?" she asked.

He put his boots up on the seat across from him. "Muddy when it rains. Rock hard in summer."

"And with no tall buildings to block the sun. The last time I was not overshadowed by brick and mortar was in the spring when I took students to Fort McHenry. We had our annual picnic on the grass. We have them every spring. . .or rather, we did."

"Too bad it's cold. I'd take you on a picnic."

"If I were teaching, I'd be forbidden to go on a picnic with you unless there were other people and no one could say you were courting me."

"You know how I feel about women teachers not being allowed to court or marry. Give me a hall to speak in, and I'd win the debate hands down."

Karien drew out her right hand and pointed her finger upward. "Don't forget the lunches we've had together would be cause for gossip, and. . .and being alone with you now would be cause for dismissal."

Nathan smiled back at her. "I have something else for you to think on. I received a letter yesterday from my Aunt Celia and Uncle James. I was going to wait to tell you about it, but now is as good a time as any."

Karien engaged his eyes. "It sounds intriguing, but private. Are you certain you want to share it with me? Surely I have nothing to do with it."

"You might. Let me explain." Nathan pulled the letter from his coat pocket. "Much of it is how they are, how my homestead is. Uncle James is looking after the place while I'm gone."

"They are in good health, I hope."

"I've never known a time when they weren't."

"I believe the country air has a lot to do with it." She sighed and looked out the carriage window. "The air here is thick with coal smoke some days. It cannot be good for a person."

"The air in Refuge is clean."

"Like smelling honeysuckle all year round, I bet."

"You like honeysuckle?"

"If I could, I'd grow it in my mother's yard."

"Honeysuckle grows in the hedgerows in the spring. You'll come, won't you, and find out for yourself?"

Her heart quivered. "To Refuge. . .to visit you?"

"Bring your mother. But I warn you, neither of you will want to return to the city after spending time in Refuge."

He pulled the letter from the envelope and opened it. "My aunt writes, 'The Women's Society has reopened a school funded by donors. Your uncle and I are determined to convince the committee to bring more than the conventional studies to the school. Children should experience the arts as well as the three Rs.' "

Karien's heart leaped within her. "Such as music appreciation?"

"Yes. You'd fit the bill, and Miss Gable might be ideal for teaching the other subjects."

"You think they want teachers who are accustomed to teaching in a big city? I'm sure their views are more traditional than ours. Their rules might be unbearable."

Nathan's mouth twitched. "Come up with excuses and you'll talk yourself out of it."

"You're thinking I'm ungrateful, aren't you?"

"No, you're not ungrateful, just uncertain. I've heard Miss Gable say many times that you are the most optimistic person she knows, and I agree with her. Where is your optimism? Where has your trust in the Almighty gone?"

Karien turned to him. "I have wanted to leave for a long time, except I didn't want to quit the academy. I have considered going West, taking my mother with me. They need teachers out there, you know."

He crossed his arms over his chest. "That you'd consider the West surprises me."

"There's more to the world than Maryland and Virginia. They say out in the Midwest the prairies go on for hundreds of miles, nothing but grass. And out in the Northwest there are volcanoes. Did you know that?"

He nodded. "I do know it. Traveled by rail once and crossed the Rockies and the Cascades."

"You came back. Why?"

"Oh, family mostly."

"I would forget the West if I had good cause to stay in the East, and I would miss my friends, like you and Liza." She lowered her eyes, hoping he'd say what she longed to hear.

She felt him stiffen next to her. She looked over. He set his hand on the casement of the carriage window and then knocked it with his fist. "Confound it, Karien Wiles. You can be the most frustrating woman when it comes to hints I'm trying to send. I guess I'll just have to come right out and say it."

"Sorry to frustrate you, Mr. Archer."

He moaned. "When will you call me Nathan?"

"Now, if you like."

"I would."

"All right. I'm listening. . .Nathan."

"I don't like it when you refer to me as just a friend."

"You don't? I wasn't aware it offended you."

"I know why you do it, but I can tell when I look in your eyes that you don't mean it."

Karien smiled. "When I say you are my friend, I mean it with all my heart."

"Your heart?"

"Yes, my heart."

"Doesn't your heart feel something more, something intense and deep?"

She lowered her eyes. "Well, I. . ."

"You won't say?"

"I don't know what to say."

"You'd rather be silent, lead me on, and let me figure it out?"

"No, that would be cruel." She looked at him.

"Then answer me this. Who has the right to deprive you of love? Who has the right to say you cannot have a husband and a family and still teach music? Who has the right to condemn you to a lonely life?"

She did not wish to sound trite, but she could not help but say, "The school boards do, if I want to make a living."

He leaned forward and raked his fingers through his hair. Then he straightened up and put his hands on her shoulders. "How can I get through to you? I fell for you the moment I saw you. I have deep feelings for you. I think of you night and day, and it pains me to think of you staying behind in this crowded, smoky, hellish city. You saw how the buildings we went between blocked the sun. You know just from crossing a street how risky it is. And the cost of living here is through the roof. If you can't think of leaving and living in a quiet town, think of your mother."

"Oh–h," Karien groaned playfully. "Well played to mention my mother."

He breathed out a weary sigh. "I'm not playing games with you."

"I'm sorry. I guess I sound smug. Forgive me?"

He tugged at her chin. "If you keep looking at me like that I will."

The carriage driver opened the window on the roof and called down. They were about to reach the stable. Nathan drew in a deep breath. "I guess we'll continue this later."

"I will sit here and not get out until you tell me—"

He narrowed his eyes. "That I love you?"

She looked at him. "Do you?"

He pulled her close. "I don't just love you. I adore you."

She looked into his eyes. He was silent a moment, and she breathed out. His mouth came close to hers. She longed to feel his kiss, to snuggle against his shoulder.

"It's been quite a day so far, hasn't it?"

"Quite a morning." Breathless, she inched back.

Tense silence fell between them. Karien did not move when Nathan's hand touched hers. "Your hand is cold," he said.

"Not with my gloves on."

"I want to kiss you."

"When?"

He touched her lips with his. Sweet, gentle, it gave her plenty of goose bumps. She pressed her gloved hand against his cheek and returned his tenderness.

"Are you warmer. . .with the blanket?" he asked when he drew away.

Her eyes remained closed. "I am. Thank you."

"Open your eyes, Karien."

When she did, tiny lights darted in front of her eyes. "I feel. . .light-headed."

"Take in a deep breath," he whispered in her ear.

Breathless, she settled against the seat while the carriage moved over the dirt road and up a hill. Had she returned his kiss properly, it being her first? She wanted to ask Nathan but decided against it. He'd tell her if he wanted to. One thing she knew was that this kiss meant they were more than friends.

The carriage came to a halt in the stable yard. Mr. Kelly had led Contessa out of the horse wagon, and when Nathan climbed out and handed Karien down, the mare turned her head and blew out her nose. The stables were set in a U shape, the doors painted green, the walls whitewashed.

She watched Nathan take the mare's reins in hand and walk with her toward an open entry. What kind of miracle had brought them together? They never had meetings on Saturdays, and he could have purchased a mare in any state in the union.

For the first time, as she watched him lead the restless horse, she felt stronger and more committed to finding a way to have what her heart desired, with the kind of help only Heaven could give.

Chapter 9

The wind pushed against the walls, and the horses stirred. A fire blazed in a large potbelly stove in the middle of the stable. Nathan drew a bench forward, and Karien sat down. Her eyes studied the beams above and the brass lanterns hanging on posts. She drew in the scent of hay and leather. It all came back to her, those wonderful times with her papa when he would hand her a sack of apples and tell her he'd bring her to see the horses.

"I remember this place. I came here as a child."

She saw something rare grow in Nathan's eyes. It was a kind of knowing and remembrance. He moved forward and looked down at her. "You're sure? It wasn't another stable?"

"I'm positive. I remember Papa holding my hand. I was fixated on the horses and begged him for one. He could never have afforded it, so he'd bring me down here to visit and we'd pretend I owned all of them." She looked up at Nathan. "It's funny that you brought me here and stirred that memory."

"Do you remember me?" Nathan spoke gently. She gazed into his eyes and held his telling look. "We met before. I'm sure of it."

"Here?"

"I was about sixteen, a stable boy, my father the stable master." Excited, he knelt down in front of her. "I remember you and your father. During the spring and summer, he'd bring you here on Sunday afternoons. You had a favorite—a chestnut gelding with a white streak on his head."

Karien's eyes widened. "The tallest horse in the stable."

"You loved the stable cats too."

"I did."

"And you pleaded with your father to let you take one home. My father was more than willing and. . .it was an orange tabby, wasn't it?"

"It was, and she was as orange as her name Marigold!" A charge rushed through Karien, and she widened her eyes as she remembered the frail little kitten being put in her arms by a lad with sandy hair and sparkling brown eyes. "You were the stable master's son who wanted to give me riding lessons."

Karien pressed her hand against her throat. She wanted to tell him how she felt about him, that she had more than fondness for him. She blinked, swallowed, and shook her head. She drew in a deep breath and then freed it. "I'm stunned. I can't believe we knew each other. Why did it take so long for us to know?"

"It was so long ago." Nathan's smile grew wider. "I think we've both changed since then." He picked up her hands. "Although, I can remember those eyes of yours, and how the color fascinated me."

Amused, Karien tapped her finger on her chin. "I remember a scamp of a boy. You had sandy blond hair, and you wore a cap made out of brown corduroy—and your boots were always muddy. You used to give me such a look that I'd toss my head at you."

"Oh yes. You were a proud one for so young. My father rarely let me speak to you. . .had me mucking out stalls whenever you came."

"It is a happy memory." Karien stood from the bench and put her hands on his arms. "I'm so happy. We are truly. . .bosom buddies."

His mouth lifted into a half smile. "A new word for it. Buddies?"

Karien looked him in the eyes, her own softening under the pull of emotion. "It's all right that you are," she whispered.

Contessa kicked against the stall. Karien went to her and ran her hand over the mare's sleek coat. "She's so spirited."

"And determined to interrupt us." Nathan leaned on one of the stall gates. "You know Contessa could be yours."

"I could never afford her."

"Marry me and everything that is mine is yours."

She swerved around to meet him. She wanted to throw her arms around his neck and say yes. "I have twenty-five dollars in the bank, and you ask me to marry you?"

"I don't care how much you have. I'm glad you aren't rich, Karien." His mouth curved into a smile. "You won't be able to say I married you for your money, now will you?"

She raised her brows. "Where on earth did you come from, Nathan Archer? You think differently than most people."

"When a man loves a woman, he doesn't care about the material things she owns. He cares about her. I know how much it means to you to teach music. Don't think for a minute that I would deny you of it. If the school board in Refuge can be convinced to change the rule, you'll have a position right away. If not, then you could teach privately."

She sat down on a bench. "Nathan, you're trying so hard to convince me. My heart needs no convincing."

Nathan crouched down in front of her. She could feel the warmth of his breath against her skin. For a moment, she thought she could hear his heart beating in his chest.

"You know how I feel, Karien," he whispered and set his cheek against hers. "At least, tell me you love me as much as I love you."

She nudged her cheek against his. "With all my heart, I do."

He drew back and placed his hands around her face. "Open your eyes."

Slowly, Karien lifted her lashes.

"Tears?" he said.

"I can't help it." She smiled. "I'm happy."

"So let's get married."

Karien drew in a breath. "You really want me?"

"What's to stop me?"

Karien cried out and threw her arms around Nathan's neck. Huddled together, she embraced him with all her might. Her faith and her optimism rose to unyielding hope. It didn't matter what lay ahead. All that mattered was she and Nathan would be together.

The horses in their stalls stamped their hooves. The mare reared her head, and her nostrils flared. Nathan and Karien stood when they heard the ringing of church bells coming from the city. These were not the peaceful sounds of Sunday bells. They were of alarm, danger, and warning.

Nathan grabbed Karien's hand and hurried from the stable out into the cobblestone yard. Stable workers gathered in a group, their mouths gaping and their eyes fixed across the grassy slopes toward the city. With Nathan's arm around her, Karien stared in disbelief. Billows of black smoke moved across the sky like thunderheads, dark, ominous, and foreboding.

Beneath the darkness, a violent red horizon flickered.

Chapter 10

The wind whipped the fire into swells of monstrous flames. Within them, fiery red tornadoes whirled and scattered. Sparks leaped from one window to another, from one roof to the next. The carriage Nathan hired to return them to Karien's home jerked to a halt. The horse neighed.

"Why has he stopped?" Karien reached a nervous hand over to the window casement.

"Driver," Nathan called. "What's happened? Why have you stopped?"

He saw a pair of firemen out in the street, one with his hands raised. The horse reared and twisted. The carriage bounced, and Karien braced herself against the walls.

A robustly built fireman stepped up to the driver, while the other snatched the halter and controlled the frightened gelding.

"We need your horse. Too many are wearing out or collapsing."

"I'll get into trouble if you take him," cried the driver. "I can't leave the carriage here."

"If you want to debate, it'll do you no good."

They argued, and in order to stop it, Nathan leaned out. "Can we go on foot?"

The fireman shook his head. Sweat had frozen into icicles on the edges of his beard. "It's a risk, sir. The fire is spreading fast. Started at the Hurst Building."

"We'll take a trolley."

"Not possible."

"Why not?"

"The electricity's been knocked out. They're going nowhere. With the way the wind is shifting and the fire moving, it's going to spread fast down Pratt Street and take out the wharfs in the Inner Basin. Too much tar and resin will feed the flames. The whole city could burn."

Frightened by what she heard and the terrifying sound of exploding glass and falling bricks, Karien gripped Nathan's arm. A great boom shook the ground, causing the carriage to tremble as if an earthquake moved under it. Her mind panicked over her mother and Liza, fearful the fire had reached them. Were they safe? Had they fled to a safe distance?

"I'm not giving over my horse," shouted the driver.

Karien knew he'd have no other choice. He climbed down as the fireman unhitched it and pulled it to the side of the street. The poor creature's eyes were wide with fright, and its ears flicked. It bobbed its head and stomped its hooves, then was led farther down the street to where a fire engine stood. She watched as the driver drew off his hat and slammed it down.

"You'll have to pay for him if something goes wrong, and the carriage too." He snatched up his hat and ordered Karien and

Nathan out. "I can't help it. You saw what they did. They took my horse. You've got to get out."

Shaken, Karien scrambled out of the carriage behind Nathan and clung to his arm. Farther down the street, flames shot up into the sky like tongues of dragons. More booms shook the ground. More terrifying sounds of falling buildings.

"They're setting off dynamite to try and stop the fire from spreading, acts like a shockwave."

"Like blowing out a candle," Karien said.

Nathan's look grew grave with each explosion. Karien buried her face in his shoulder. "Come on, Karien. We have to hurry."

Abandoned, they were on their own to reach her mother and Liza. Karien's sight blurred with the sting of smoke and with tears from fear. Nathan held her fast around the waist as he led her to the sidewalk, past a row of doomed buildings, and to the street leading home. Her heart pounded in her chest. The heat of the inferno streamed down the street, and she could feel it through her clothes. The pungent smell of burning store merchandise sickened her. She could taste the charred wood on her tongue.

Nathan unwrapped his arm from Karien's waist, grasped her hand, and ran with her down toward the old brownstone house on the corner of the next block. The wind shifted, and the smoky air shifted with it. He pulled Karien along, through a maze of people fleeing the city. Two doors from home, Karien saw her mother and Liza. They came down the steps holding on to each other.

"Mama!" Karien called, releasing Nathan's hand. Her mother looked toward her and flung out her arms.

"Karien!" They embraced and wept against each other's shoulder. "I've been so worried."

"We're all right."

"Thank God." Her mother touched Karien's face and swallowed.

"Our neighbors told us to leave, but we waited until we couldn't any longer."

"We tried to get to you as soon as we could," Karien explained.

"She's scared," Liza said to Karien. "So am I."

"Nathan." Karien's mother squeezed both of their hands. "My house is safe isn't it? It won't burn down will it?"

The heat swelled and the wind howled. "I don't know, Mrs. Wiles," he said. "But I'm determined to get us all out."

Karien tightened her hold as they hurried along. "Don't be afraid, Mother. Nathan will take care of us. Don't worry about the house." She looked over her shoulder. "Liza, keep up with us. Don't fall behind."

People heading down the street to find family and friends were ghostly figures that grew into silhouettes and vanished. Gasping, Karien wanted to fall on her knees and plead with Heaven.

A woman rushing forward stopped in front of them. Elderly and gray-headed, she bent forward, her tattered shawl slipping over her shoulders. Her eyes were large and gray, her face deep in color.

"You must move." She shook her finger at Karien. "Don't stand there. You must move, all of you."

The woman pulled her shawl over her head and hobbled away. Karien and the others moved on. "That poor soul," her mother said. "We should help her."

Karien turned. "Wait! Come with us. It isn't safe where you're going."

The woman teetered, and a breathless policeman ran up to her. "Come on, Mother," he affectionately called her. "You can't go that way. Take my hand."

"We can take her, Officer," Nathan said.

"It's my duty, sir. Yours is to take care of these ladies. I'll get the ole dear to safety."

"Where is the safest place?"

"People are going up Federal Hill. I fear the fire is spreading fast. Lots of folks praying God intervenes before the whole city burns to the ground."

The old woman did as the officer told her. Relief fell over Karien that he'd take her to a safe place. Why she'd been on the street alone or abandoned to find her own way out was beyond Karien. How could anyone do such a thing? Why hadn't hurried passersby helped her?

She looked at her own mother, and then at Nathan. Without him, there was no telling how they would have escaped catastrophe.

The slope up Federal Hill was slick from the tramping of people. Men held their ladies and helped them forward. Mothers embraced their babies and little ones. Karien's mother heaved a breath. Liza wept. Cold fear raced through Karien as she watched people flee toward safety. Some sunk down as if in a faint. Others cradled their loved ones. But no one spoke a word. A grim silence hung over the people. The only sounds were the explosions, the shattering glass, and crumbling brick buildings. Under their feet the ground rumbled.

Nathan put his hands around Karien's face. "We're not going up there. Too many people. There's no shelter, and when night comes it won't be safe." He swallowed. She kept her moist eyes on him. "Trust me."

She nodded and held her mother's hand.

"We're going to go to the stables. It's a mile walk, but we'll be out of the cold and away from the city. In the morning, we'll see what's left."

Karien's mother laid her hand across Nathan's arm. "I'd rather sleep in a mound of hay out of the wind than here."

"Me too." Still weepy, Liza folded her arms around her torso. "It's cold, and I can't bear to look down at the city."

For her mother and friend, Karien knew she had to be brave. She had to control her fear and the tears welling in her eyes. She watched Nathan in front of her, paving a way through the crowd and down through the lone side streets. She pulled her mother and Liza close on either side of her. "No more tears. Pray for the Lord to save the city."

"Do you think the academy is lost?" Liza asked.

"Most likely it will be."

Gasping, Liza slapped her hand against her thigh. "This is all so sad. I cannot bear it, Karien."

Karien looked at the worried face of her friend. "No one wants to bear it, Liza. But what other choice do we have?" Her mother caught her breath. "Are you all right, Mother?"

"Yes," her mother panted.

Nathan stopped and turned. "Give her to me."

He took Karien's mother in his arms and lifted her. Ash fell from the smoky sky. Gale-force winds plunged toward the Inner Basin and the docks. The hellish inferno roared. The sound was unearthly. The rush of wind moaned between buildings. Dynamite blasts and relentless heat caused window glass to shatter before the fire reached them. Shards fell and hit the pavement. Horses pulled fire wagons and neighed in their struggle.

The ominous ringing of a church bell echoed through the city. Suddenly it ended. Karien threw her hands over her ears as the bell fell and the church's brick and mortar tore away. She stared toward it. "The Church of the Messiah," she murmured. "Lord, help us. It's gone."

The sky turned to night. Darkness fell over rooftops and filled the streets. Blazing colors of red, yellow, and orange reflected in the shards of glass scattered on the street.

Too overcome to speak, Karien reached for Nathan's arm. They reached the far end of the city where the shanty houses and buildings were sparse. Soon the road turned into rusty dirt, and green meadows spread out aglow from the far reaches of the blaze. The wind fell away. Within seconds, it rose again, and the smell of burning came with it.

Chapter 11

By the time they reached the stables, night had fallen. Karien and Nathan made their way up the grassy knoll with her mother and Liza. The stable master and two of the stable boys rushed forward, their faces as panicked as the ones they had left.

Nathan put Karien's mother down and wrapped his arm around Karien. She walked with him to the highest point on the hill and looked down at the city aglow in the distance.

The piers jutting out into the Inner Basin were on fire. Boats and ships were bottled up in the harbor. Their lantern's swayed like stars amid the blackness.

"Jesus, help those poor souls down there," uttered the stable master.

"Yes, Lord," Karien whispered. Nathan rubbed her shoulder. She knew he felt the same.

"Thank God this happened on a Sunday. If it had been during the week. . .all those people at their jobs. . ." The stable master shook his head.

"Those in the fire's path have gone up Federal Hill," Nathan told him.

"They'll be freezing all night until help comes."

He turned to the stable master. "I couldn't let the ladies suffer. I hope you don't mind we've come here."

"Not at all. Let's get everyone inside where it's warm. We've plenty of blankets, and I'll have one of the lads bring you hot drinks."

Inside the stable, Karien's mother sat close to Karien with a blanket wrapped around her. The journey had exhausted her, and she sighed restlessly. A flood of trouble bathed her eyes and tightened her face. Karien's hand gripped her hand to comfort her.

Nathan drew close and inquired after Mrs. Wiles's well-being, and Liza, who had finally stopped weeping, drew from her coat pocket a handkerchief and a small Bible. "It was the first book I thought of taking."

Karien smiled lightly. "Not *Jane Eyre*, Liza?"

"A novel cannot give hope like the Word of God." She hugged it to her breast.

"No, dear friend, it cannot. I wish I had mine and our family Bible."

Horses sighed in their stalls. The scent of leather tack, straw, and horses overcame the smell of burning that wafted on the wind. Karien watched Nathan, her eyes following him wherever he moved.

"Nathan," she said. "Thank you. If it weren't for you, we would—"

He held up his hand. "There's no need to say it, Karien. What matters is we're safe."

Her mother eased her head onto Karien's shoulder. "Mother is exhausted."

"We should all get some sleep." He tucked the blanket up to

her chin and smiled down at her. "I'll be over by Contessa if you need me."

If only he'd stay with her, wrap his arms around her, and keep her warm. He made her feel protected. Even now as he walked away, she could feel it.

A sliver of morning sunlight fell over Karien's eyes, and she opened them. Nathan held his hand down to her. "Let's you and I go outside and see what's happened. Don't wake the others."

Careful not to stir her mother and Liza, Karien took his hand. He pulled her up out of the hay, and together they passed through the stable doors. They looked down from the top of the knoll. The devastation was enormous, and no doubt her home was destroyed.

Steam from the hot bricks of fallen buildings mimicked smoke with a ghastly white vapor. The water reflected the undulating flames of piers burning away. Black pilings jutted from the water in the hazy morning light. No longer could they make out buildings in the business district, except for jagged, blackened spears and ragged facades stripped of their opulence, size, and grandeur. Every building near Jones Falls had burned away or was still aflame.

Karien's heart ached and her throat swelled shut. She stared, her eyes moist with tears. Broken to see such devastation and loss, she trembled. "My mother's house—it must be gone." She hid her face in Nathan's shoulder and cried. He pulled her close and held her.

"By the looks of it, there's no way it could have been spared." He cradled her face with his hands. They were warm, and Karien sighed at his touch. "I'm going to saddle Contessa and head down there. That way we'll know for sure."

"You don't want me to go with you?"

"It's best you don't. Your mother needs you." He smiled at her. "It will give you the chance to tell her about us." He kissed her lips with a brush of his. "But I'll ask her permission when I get back."

His smile, his kiss, his caress made Karien return his smile. She leaned up and pecked his cheek. Then they went back inside the stable. Nathan found a saddle and bridle, and drew Contessa out of her stall.

Karien's mother stood beside Liza. "Where are you going, Mr. Archer?"

"Not to worry. I'll be back."

"Are you going to see if the house is still standing?"

"Yes, ma'am, I am."

He climbed into the saddle. The mare stomped her hooves and sidestepped. She lifted her head, smelled the air, and snorted. Nathan looked down at Karien. She saw uneasiness within his eyes. He dug in his heels, clicked his tongue, and urged the horse through the misty air. Karien watched him gallop down the knoll toward the smoldering ruins and whispered a prayer for his safety.

Chapter 12

Old things are passed away; behold,
all things have become new.
2 Corinthians 5:17

Karien tapped her fingers along her knee. She heard the music in her head. The beauty and serenity of the hymn gave her comfort and joy. She had heard the story behind the song, how it had given a wife and daughter peace during a tragic moment in their lives. And the one word from the hymn that echoed the most in her mind was *trust*. Change had come. A new start. A new life with Nathan.

Liza was napping, and Karien's mother stared in silence out the Pullman window. To Karien, she seemed far away in her thoughts, given to sorrow. She had lost her husband years ago, and now the house they had shared from the time they were married had burned down to the foundation. Karien's loss could not be compared to what her mother had lost. A teaching position could be replaced, and she had found the love of her life, love that soared beyond anything she ever could have imagined.

Nathan leaned toward her. "What are you playing, darling?"

She shut her eyes. "'*'Tis So Sweet to Trust in Jesus.'* Do you know it?"

"I know it well. It was my mother's favorite hymn."

"It is appropriate, isn't it?"

"I'd say so. Do you often play notes on your knee?"

She looked at him and smiled. "Only when there's no piano around."

"You'll enjoy the piano at the Archer House."

Her eyes beamed. "You have a piano?"

"An old one. It hasn't been played in a long time." He leaned back in his seat as the train went around a sharp curve. "I'd like you to see if it needs tuning. It'll be yours, after all."

She put her arm through his. "I'm so happy, Nathan. A piano is the best wedding present you could give me."

He pressed his brows together. "Don't you want something else, my love? Jewelry, for instance."

She shook her head. "I've no need for jewelry. . .except for a wedding band."

"That you shall have, and an engagement ring to go with it, dear girl. Would you mind one that was my great-grandmother's?"

"I would love it."

"If I'd known I'd find my wife on my trip, I would've brought it with me." He picked up her hand and kissed the top of it. "I should have gone down on my knees. Forgive me?"

"Yes." Karien blushed and drew her hand from his. "Everyone will see."

He smiled. "You have such soft hands."

"Mind yourself," she teased. "Tell me about your house. When did you buy it?"

"I didn't. I inherited it from my father."

"It has history." The thought pleased her greatly.

"My ancestor Colin Archer sided with the Yanks as one of Washington's troops. The saltbox house he built was burned down by British soldiers."

"How interesting."

"My father inherited the land when Grandad died and built the existing house. That's the reason we left Baltimore."

"My family didn't come over from Ireland until after the war." Karien sighed and looked into his eyes. "Isn't it amazing how God brought us together? I could have taken a teaching job somewhere else instead of the academy, and you could have bought a mare in Virginia or Maryland. We were meant to be."

The wheels of the train squealed, and the train slowed. It jerked as it pulled into Refuge Station. "Here we are." Nathan squeezed her hand. "Are you ready for the next adventure, Mrs. Karien Archer to be?"

"Ready and willing, Mr. Archer."

As they alighted from the train, Karien saw a woman with a broad smile frantically waving a handkerchief. She wore a hat large enough to be a tea tray, decorated with pink plumes and silk flowers. She headed toward them, her pace quick and steady, still waving but this time calling out to Nathan.

Reaching him, she threw open her arms. "Nathan, my boy! At last you're home." She looked up and down the platform. "Where is that beast of yours? The one you insisted come from Ireland. You did get her, didn't you? For all the trouble you went through, I do hope so. Otherwise, you wasted a great deal of time and money."

"Aunt, the time was well worth it. Allow me to introduce Miss Karien Wiles, my fiancée."

She bobbed her head and gave Karien a "How ya do?"

"And her mother, Mrs. Wiles."

Another smile and bob.

"And her close friend, Miss Liza Gable. Ladies, my aunt Celia Sutherby."

"So pleased to meet you ladies," his aunt said. "Nathan wrote to me about you, Miss Wiles. You are even prettier than he described."

Blushing, Karien lowered her eyes and thanked her for the compliment.

"Best wishes on your engagement, and to you, Mrs. Wiles. You're inheriting a fine son-in-law. I hope you enjoy our little community. You have been the talk of the town ever since we got word you were coming."

The three ladies smiled, and Karien said, "I know I will love it here. All of us will."

Nathan put his aunt's hand on his arm. As a group, they walked down the platform. "Have you read the papers, Aunt?"

"Your Uncle James does. I can't be bothered with all the goings-on in the world. I think I would get very blue if I didn't avoid newspapers."

"Were there articles about the great fire?"

"Oh indeed there were. Your uncle James read them aloud to me over breakfast. Your letter was very informative on how you and the ladies escaped. You should receive some kind of commendation for your heroism, Nathan."

He twisted his mouth. "I'm no hero, Aunt. Please don't tell people I am."

Aunt Celia looked at Karien. "Do you agree with me, Miss Wiles? Shouldn't he be called a hero?"

"He chooses to be unsung, ma'am. But his actions were heroic indeed. If it were not for Nathan, I dare not think what would have happened to us."

Nathan cleared his throat. "If I had the ladies stay at the Archer House, Aunt, would it be a cause for gossip do you think?"

"Yes, Nathan. It would." Aunt Celia leaned toward Karien's mother. "Improper, I'd say. Karien is his fiancée."

"I agree, Mrs. Sutherby. Have you a hotel in Refuge?"

"I was hoping to put you up."

"We couldn't possibly intrude."

"Intrude? I would welcome your company." She gave Karien, her mother, and Liza all pleading looks.

"If it isn't too much trouble, we'd love to, and it would only be temporary," Karien's mother said. "I'm a good cook, and I like to wash dishes. You must let me pitch in."

Aunt Celia stopped and threw up her arms. "How wonderful." She drew beside Karien's mother. "We've plenty of room. It's been awhile since we had guests in the house. I'm sure you aren't in the mood for fun after what you've been through, ladies, but James and I cannot do without it. I hope our lively lifestyle does not bother you."

Karien's mother smiled. "I could use a bit of fun, Mrs. Sutherby."

"Good. We can have tea in the afternoons, and Nathan and James can go fishing."

Immediately Karien liked Nathan's aunt. Her bubbly personality would lift their spirits, and she just might be the type of person to change the minds of the local school board concerning marital rules. "Do you have a piano?" she asked, moving closer.

Perpetually smiling, Aunt Celia nodded. "Yes, we do have a piano. In fact, it is the only one on our street. The church has an old one, and there's the one at Archer House. Do you play?"

Nathan put his arm across Karien's shoulder. "Miss Wiles is an accomplished pianist, Aunt."

His aunt's brows arched high on her forehead. "Wonderful! I will host a recital. I cannot wait to hear you play." She then laughed.

"I'll have to get out my feather duster and brighten up the keys."

Karien moved Liza forward. She'd been trailing behind. "Our Miss Gable taught English at the Margaret Brent Academy. She knows a great deal about the classics, especially the Brontë sisters."

"Is that so, Miss Gable?"

Liza rummaged through her bag. "Yes, ma'am. *Jane Eyre* is my favorite. I would have snatched it right up, but the Bible was more important for me to save from the fire. I grabbed it when we left Mrs. Wiles's house. I lived with her and Karien, you see, which was very convenient since Karien and I taught at the same school."

"What luck! Two teachers. We've so much to talk about." Aunt Celia paused and craned her head. "Oh, here comes James." She called to him, "Oh James. Here we are—over here, dearest." She bent toward the three ladies. "James doesn't say much, but when he does its worth listening to."

Uncle James planted his feet on the platform and shoved his thumbs into his vest pockets. "Nathan, you are in good health?"

"Yes, sir."

Uncle James bowed after removing his hat. "Ladies."

Nathan stepped beside his uncle and introduced the ladies. To Karien, he had a mild, handsome appearance. A strong jaw. His eyes a manly hazel. Karien looked away, realizing she stared at the white clerical collar around Uncle James's neck.

"I hope your journey was pleasant," Uncle James said. "I've read the papers, and I'm deeply distressed by what has happened in Baltimore. Thank the Lord it was a Sunday, else it would have cost lives. I hope you'll find our little town lives up to its name."

He held out his arm to his wife and walked with her toward the station doors. Karien whispered to Nathan, "You didn't tell me your uncle was clergy."

One corner of Nathan's mouth lifted. "I did when I read to you Aunt Celia's letter."

She set her hand on her forehead and sighed. "I forgot." She leaned closer. "Is he one of those fire-and-brimstone preachers?"

"You'll find out when we go to church on Sunday."

She pinched his arm. "Don't keep me in the dark."

He laughed. "No, he doesn't bring down the roof. But he is effective and quite good."

She hugged him close. "I don't mind some fire and brimstone from time to time. It wakes me out of my earthly slumber."

They went out of the station and to a wagon parked out front. Karien's mother set her gloved hand over her mouth and stifled a giggle. Liza smiled and shrugged her shoulders.

"It was James's idea," said Aunt Celia. "It's a hoot isn't it?"

A sway-backed nag turned its head and knickered. A blue ostrich plume fluttered between its ears. The wagon had two rows of old carriage seats in front and a long flat bed in the back with benches on each side.

"I've never seen a wagon like it," Karien said. "I like the feather."

"Polly likes it too. That's the old mare's name. We use the wagon for church outings and weddings."

Uncle James and Nathan handed the women up. "I have to see to my mare," said Nathan. "Get her out to the old place."

"We'll drive out to Archer House with you and show the house to the ladies, especially"—Aunt Celia looked at Karien—"since Miss Wiles will be living there in the near future."

Uncle James climbed into the driver's seat and picked up the reins. "I want to get a good look at your new mare, Nathan. Get her saddled, and let her run like the wind."

Chapter 13

Archer House surprised Karien. As the wagon rounded a corner shaded by forests on each side, the building came into view, and she drew in a breath at its beauty and age. It caused her heart to leap in her chest. Under the bright sunshine, standing on stretches of green grass, the house was not the clapboard building she had expected. Instead, she viewed a rough-cut fieldstone house with a crimson clay roof, green shutters and a door to match, nine mullioned windows in front, and two massive chimneys, one on each end. A portico porch led up to the door. Brass sidelights shone like gold glass in the daylight.

Aunt Celia looked over her shoulder. "Pretty isn't it?"

Karien could not help but love the house. So much room. Grass all around. Trees and shade. An open sky above. "I've only seen houses like this in books."

"The interior is plain, but it is a warm family house. I have fond memories of this place. I was proposed to by James in the yard under the wisteria arbor on the Fourth of July twenty years ago. We always have picnics here on the Fourth."

"How romantic." Liza sighed.

Karien looked for the arbor. "Nathan and I will build memories like yours, Aunt Celia."

As they drove in, a magnificent black stallion raced along a split rail fence. "That must be Matador."

Karien's mother reached over and held her hand. Liza scooted forward next to Aunt Celia for a better look. Behind them came the pounding of another horse. Karien smiled when she saw Nathan on Contessa. He pulled off his hat and waved it. "Wahoo!" he shouted.

Aunt Celia laughed. "There he goes trying to imitate the Rebel yell, James."

Uncle James grinned and snapped the reins. "I'd say he does a fair job of it."

Nathan raced past them, swinging the hat above his head, his mare running fast and free at last.

Nathan pulled rein in front of the wagon. Contessa pranced and bobbed her head. At the fence, Matador whinnied and pranced along the rails. "He wants his bride," Nathan said. He dismounted and looped the reins around his hand. "Now that she's had some exercise, I'll put her out in the field with him."

"Is it safe?" Karien shielded her eyes from the sun and studied the tall steed. "He won't trample her or anything, will he?"

"Don't worry, Karien. She's safe. She might reject him at first, but she'll come around."

She went to climb down. "I can't wait to see the house."

He held up his palm. "Not yet."

Karien settled back into the seat and blinked. Her mother and Liza questioned him. "She can't go inside until I carry her over the threshold."

Aunt Celia turned. "That's right. It's our tradition."

Karien agreed family traditions were important. Her mother also agreed and said, "I think it is extremely romantic, Karien. By the looks of the exterior, the interior will be just as beautiful."

Liza scooted forward. "Mr. Rochester never carried Jane over the threshold because he had been blinded and couldn't see her, but Jane boldly went inside and claimed it for her own."

Karien knew the story, but as she watched her beau unsaddle his mare and lead her into the field, she said to Liza, "Nathan is nothing like Mr. Rochester. He has not deceived me, tricked me, or manipulated me like Edward Rochester did Jane Eyre." She patted her friend's hand. "But I see your point, Liza."

"But like Jane and Edward, Nathan sees you as his equal. You are fortunate, Karien."

"I am, more than I can say."

Liza lifted her eyes and sighed. " 'Yet, while I breathe and think, I must love him.' "

Karien's mother tilted her head. "What is that, Liza?"

"A quote from chapter 17 of *Jane Eyre*, Mrs. Wiles."

Karien put her arm over her friend's shoulder. Nathan walked toward the wagon. "Yet, while I breathe and think, I will always love him."

Chapter 14

A week had passed since Karien arrived in the small town of Refuge with her mother and friend Liza, and she was getting used to the Virginia accent. Friends and neighbors of the Sutherbys were eager to meet her, and she attended the bring-and-buy at the church hall. Her mother spent her time writing letters to distant cousins, to her lawyer, and to the insurance company about the house. All their possessions were gone, all their clothes and mementos. With the money Karien had saved, they were able to replace them—modestly. Even her wedding dress would be simple white cotton with a transparent overlay embroidered along the hem and sleeves.

Curiosity concerning the school and the search for two teachers nagged her day and night. With her shoulders back and her head held high, she would go in for an interview in hopes the rule she could not marry would be overlooked.

Finally, the day came when the school board was to meet. She dressed in a moss green skirt and white lace shirtwaist that she'd purchased at a small local shop, on sale from last fall's fashions.

Liza paced the floor in the room they shared. "I'm so nervous, Karien. I wish I was as confident as you."

"You have no reason to worry, Liza. You have excellent qualifications. There's no reason why they wouldn't want you." Karien took from her change purse the only pair of earrings she owned and put them on her ears.

"What if we aren't the only two applying?"

"Let the best teachers win, is what I say."

Liza sat down on her bedside. "Aren't you worried they won't consider you once they find out you and Mr. Archer are engaged?"

Karien tucked a curl behind her ear and pinned her hair up loosely. "I'm trying to be optimistic. God will put me there if He wants me there. If not, something better is ahead for me."

"I really should follow your example and have more faith." Liza stood and smoothed down the front of her skirt. "I don't know what I would've done if you and your mother hadn't taken me under your wings."

Karien placed her hands on Liza's shoulders. "What makes you think you haven't done the same? Now put a smile on your face. We'll face that committee together."

Karien and Liza left through the front door and headed down the walk and through the picket gate arm in arm. Delighted with the bliss of the air and the morning light, Karien thought that worrying seemed senseless. Not a cloud floated in the sky, and a gentle breeze whispered through the trees.

"Karien, what will you tell Mr. Archer if they offer you the position, requiring you to stay single."

"I will tell him I've turned it down. There's no possibility I'll give him up."

"He's a good man, and he was so gallant to get us out safely."

"Gallant, yes, and kind. I suppose he cannot wait to learn my fate."

They paused where the old schoolhouse once stood. An open field took its place, sparse with grass and patches of ground where over the years children had played. The new schoolhouse stood beside the lot.

Liza tilted her head. By the look on her face, Karien knew disappointment had dampened her friend's eagerness. "It's not as large as the academy."

"It's perfect." Karien nudged her friend's arm. "We are, after all, in a small town. I'd say at least twenty students would fit in this school."

"Hmm, you're right, Karien. Most small towns have dinky little one-room schools. This building has two stories. I should be glad to see it won't be so cramped."

Karien sighed. "Cramped no. It certainly looks cozy with those tall windows to let the sunlight in."

A woman stepped out the door and raised her hand to them. Karien tugged Liza forward. "Remember, you're more than qualified. You've no reason to doubt."

"I haven't, have I? I got through my interview with Mr. Stein, after all."

The woman, dressed in gray and wearing heavy black shoes, came down the steps. "Ladies, you are here for interviews?"

Karien stepped forward with her hand outstretched. "Yes, ma'am. I'm Karien Wiles, and this is Liza Gable. Are we early?"

"You're right on time. Come inside."

Around a large table were gathered five people, clearly members of the school board, by the looks of them. Four ladies and one man fixed their eyes on Karien first, then on Liza. The ladies wore fashionable hats. The broad brims shadowed their faces and shoulders. The frocks they wore must have come from the latest Sears catalog. Her mother had a copy, and Karien recognized the style immediately, not that their attire mattered. Still, it surprised her, for she thought only women in the cities wore such fashions, whereas women in small towns wore calico, wool skirts, and plain shirtwaists.

Tiny wrinkles and gray streaks of hair gave them an air of dignity. The gentleman had a face much like Karien's former employer and wore large spectacles. He folded his hands and placed them on the table. Beside him lay a folder, pen, and glass of water. He opened the folder.

"We would like to speak with Miss Gable first, if you don't mind, Miss Wiles. Once we are finished interviewing her, we will call you in."

She felt a blush cover her cheeks. Why hadn't she thought of that first? "Of course. May I wait out in the hall?"

The gentleman nodded. "Please do. You'll find a chair there."

She glanced at Liza and left. The empty hallway echoed her footsteps. The chair, hard as an oak stump, stood just outside the door. A clock ticked away on the wall across from her. She could hear voices behind the door and said a prayer that Liza would rein in her nerves and pass the board's inspection.

Fifteen minutes was all it took. The door opened, and Liza stepped out and quietly closed it. She grabbed Karien's hand. "I got it," she whispered with enthusiasm. "They've accepted me. I'll be teaching every subject to a group of ten children of all ages."

Karien stood and embraced Liza. "I'm so happy for you. When do you sign the contract?"

"I already did!"

"Without reading it first?"

"It was easy. Simply the normal rules and regulations, and what my pay would be."

Before Karien could ask any further questions, the door opened and the gentleman asked Karien to come in. Liza told her she'd wait for her, smiled, and wiggled down into the chair.

Her time in the room had been brief. Now she noticed how fresh it smelled. The usual portrait of President Washington hung on the wall. An American flag stood in a corner. Windows sparkled with new glass.

"I'm Mr. Hobbs, the head of the school board. This is Mrs. Noble our treasurer, Mrs. Foster our secretary, and Mrs. Strickland our vice chairwoman. Mrs. Bullard is here to break a tie when we vote."

"Hello." Karien nodded and hoped she sounded friendly. They said nothing.

"Please take a seat, Miss Wiles."

"Thank you, sir. I cannot tell you how much I appreciate this opportunity," she said. "I'm sure you have seen the news about Baltimore and what happened there."

"We have indeed," Mr. Hobbs replied. "It's terrible."

"I saw it for myself, sir. I'm not the only teacher forced to leave the city."

"But it was not due to the fire that you are applying for a new position is it?" He opened the folder, adjusted his specs, and looked down at it. "You were fired by your former school, is that correct?"

"No, sir. I was not fired. The school closed and all the teachers were let go. We were all saddened by it. The Margaret Brent Academy was an excellent school."

"Well, you've confirmed what Miss Gable told us."

Karien lowered her head, saddened by the thoughts of the fire but also bothered they tested her in this way. "Miss Gable is an honest person, sir. I'm glad she will be teaching your children. I've never known anyone with the grasp she has on the English language and literature."

The women remained silent but kept their eyes on her. They asked no questions nor made any remark about any of the things Karien said. Mr. Hobbs, on the other hand, kept the conversation going and at a formal pace.

"Miss Wiles, with your impeccable credentials, we've agreed to have you join our school."

A rush of joy flooded her. "Thank you."

"No doubt the children will greatly benefit from the wonders of music, and it will help them to be well rounded in the arts. We are proud our school is one of the first in the state to offer music as part of the curriculum. Mrs. Strickland, would you outline the requirements?"

Finally, one of the women would speak to her. Mrs. Strickland raised her chin and fixed a pair of bland gray eyes on Karien. She had a stern, matronly face, and her clothes hung on her. Beneath them were skin and bones. Those eyes got to Karien, but she hid her uneasiness well.

"We've a list of rules that must be strictly followed, Miss Wiles," Mrs. Strickland said. "It is our understanding that you are acquainted with the rules and regulations for teachers, so these should come as no surprise. If you agree to our terms, we welcome you with open arms with a salary for a single lady who has few expenses."

Karien swallowed. She knew singleness would eventually come up. How to handle it she did not know, except that she would stand her ground. If they wanted her, they'd overlook the rule. If they were rigid, they'd let her know that they wouldn't hire her. She had no cause to fear. She'd marry the man she loved and adored who loved and adored her in return. A life with Nathan she'd not give up.

"For the moment, I'll be paying rent to Reverend Sutherby and his wife."

"We understand your mother is with you. Would a teacher's salary be enough to support her as well? Would what we offer be an impediment?"

"I'm good at budgeting, Mrs. Strickland."

"You are also accustomed to the rules for teachers, aren't you?"

"From the academy, yes."

"We abide by strict rules, the basics of course, and we expect them to be adhered to. Here is the list. You've most likely seen it before." A card was handed to her, and she looked at it. Oh yes. It was the same as what was given to her at the academy, but with one additional requirement.

"I cannot speak to. . ."

"A person of the opposite sex. That cannot be changed."

"Not even the post office clerk? How can I not speak to him when I need to mail letters?" She hoped she did not sound sarcastic. She had to lead up to the subject of having a fiancé.

"For him, we make an exception."

"What about the doctor?"

"Only when sick, Miss Wiles."

"My landlord is a gentleman."

"Reverend Sutherby is clergy, and of course you would speak to him."

"I have to be honest. This is extreme. At the academy, I could speak to a gentleman but not step out with one."

"You're not keen about this rule, obviously. You must understand we do not want our teachers tempted into marriage."

"Forgive me, for I do not mean to cause a debate. Marriage is a natural desire for a young woman, and an institution made by God. Why is it frowned upon for female teachers? Other positions do not hold the same rule."

"Such as?"

"Well. . .seamstresses, nurses, and. . ."

"Governesses, elders' companions, domestics keep to the rule." Mrs. Strickland picked up the folder and pen. "Are you holding something back, Miss Wiles, concerning this subject?"

Karien bit her lip. "I'm not holding back, Mrs. Strickland. I'm engaged to be married."

The members stared in silence. "To whom are you engaged?" Mrs. Strickland asked.

"Nathan Archer, ma'am."

Brows lifted. "The one who owns a horse farm outside of town?"

"Yes."

"I'm afraid that changes everything."

Mrs. Strickland scribbled something down and closed the folder. Then she handed it back to Mr. Hobbs. "If you change your mind, let us know, Miss Wiles," Hobbs said. "Weigh the benefits between a rewarding teaching position and the drudgery of being a housewife."

Karien set her mouth and held back an angry word. Abruptly she stood. "You're asking me to change my mind, sir. Why can't the board change theirs?"

Hobbs drew off his glasses. "Because, Miss Wiles, we are bound to the rules laid out by educators, who know better than you or this board."

Mrs. Noble swiveled in her chair. "I'm not sure I agree to this ruling, Mr. Hobbs. Miss Wiles is highly recommended."

"I agree with Mrs. Noble," said Mrs. Foster. "What difference does it make whether she is married or single?"

Mrs. Strickland pressed her lips and narrowed her eyes. "It is the rule."

Mrs. Noble shook her head. "Make an exception. I vote to hire Miss Wiles."

Mr. Hobbs twisted his mouth. "You wish a vote?"

"I do wish it."

"A vote won't change the rule. It is Miss Wiles who must change if she wants the position," said Mrs. Strickland. "Furthermore, if you cannot agree to the standards of education, ladies, I suggest you be removed from the board."

A pause followed. Karien put out her hand to Mr. Hobbs for the folder. "I would like my résumé returned, sir."

He slipped it out and handed it to her.

"I wish you all a good day and success in finding the right teacher for the school." She folded the papers and tucked the lot into her handbag. She turned to leave but stopped at the door. "I forgot to mention. Reverend and Mrs. Sutherby are hosting a recital on Thursday evening. Please come. Everyone in town is invited."

"You'll be playing, Miss Wiles?" Mrs. Noble asked.

"Yes." She opened the door.

"I don't know about the rest of the board, but I'll be there. I can't ever recall a time in Refuge when real music was played."

"I hope I meet your expectations, Mrs. Noble."

Karien opened the door to leave. Liza got up. "Did they hire you?"

"No." Karien pulled the door shut. "They cannot get past the rule about marriage, except for two of them."

Liza shook her head. "I'm sorry, Karien."

"Don't be. Remember—there is a silver lining to every cloud."

Chapter 15

Nathan arrived exactly in one hour as he had promised. He wore riding boots, and Karien smiled, knowing he must have ridden the stallion over. She went forward, and he put his hand out to her and pulled her close.

"I can't wait to see him." She pulled away, and he drew her back.

"Not until you tell me they hired you."

"They didn't. It's because of the marriage rule." She looked up at him. "I won't give you up, Nathan, not for anything in the world."

He glanced over at the door. They could hear the members talking and debating—obviously over Karien. Nathan pressed his lips together hard. Then he headed toward the meeting room.

Karien followed him. "Where're you going, Nathan?"

He turned. "I have a few words for these stiff collars."

"Not Mrs. Noble or Mrs. Foster. They were in favor of me."

"So Hobbs and Strickland are the culprits. I may not change their minds, but I'll give them a piece of mine."

When he walked in, the school board members looked up. Mrs. Strickland narrowed her eyes and frowned. Mr. Hobbs stood from the table. Nathan drew off his hat. Karien stayed in the hall, beyond the door he left opened. "Oh dear," she whispered to Liza.

"Mr. Archer. Is there something you want?" said Mr. Hobbs.

"I rode my horse over to meet Miss Wiles with high hopes you people would see the sense of hiring her." He leaned his hands on the desk. "She tells me you decided against it."

"I will handle this, Mr. Hobbs." Miss Strickland stiffened her back. "Mr. Archer, we can have a civil discourse, but only for a minute or two. We've work to do, and you're interfering."

"Your work can wait, Mrs. Strickland. I'm here to vouch for Miss Wiles's character and talent. You must give her a chance, if anything to improve the children's education."

"Society has strict rules we must adhere to, Mr. Archer."

"You mean the one about being married. What's more important? The rule or the students? The happiness of the teacher or a school having control over her life?"

"It has nothing to do with control. It has everything to do with responsibilities that would overwhelm a female teacher. We cannot afford to hire single women and then lose them the minute they marry."

Nathan paused with a lift of his chin. If Karien didn't know him as well as she did, she would say his look was arrogant. It certainly expressed a challenge.

"I've seen many a good person put aside because of an unfair rule. I care about her happiness. Teaching music is everything to her. It's her God-given calling."

"Interesting you use a religious point of view."

"And that offends you?" He waited for an answer. Mrs. Strickland narrowed her eyes, but the rest of the members could not look him in the eye.

"I see your minds are made up," Nathan said. "It's really too bad."

Karien worried Nathan would say something he'd later regret and went up to him. She tugged his sleeve. "Thanks for standing up for me, Nathan, but you must stop."

She looked at the board. "Again, thank you for having given me the opportunity of an interview. There will be no more said about it."

Mrs. Strickland gave her a smug smile. "The position is still open to you if you are willing to sign the contract and abide by the rules."

With a shake of her head, Karien set her hand on Nathan's forearm. "Thank you. But I'm going to marry this man."

Mrs. Foster stood. "Good for you, Miss Wiles. I wish you happiness. Not all of us on the board were against you."

Karien nodded and smiled. Then she tugged at Nathan's sleeve. They proceeded through the door and left the school with Liza. The stallion raised its head and snorted. Liza backed up.

"I'll go now, Karien. I'm sure you and Mr. Archer have a lot to talk about." With a swish of her skirts, Liza headed down the sidewalk.

Nathan held the stallion's bridle. "See if he'll let you touch him, Karien. Don't be afraid. He won't bite."

She held out her hand slowly, touched his muzzle, and slid her hand up the streak on his head then down his neck. Nathan lifted her up into the saddle. She savored the strength of his hands holding her waist. Keeping her leg snug around the saddle horn, she looked down at Nathan as he moved the stallion forward and out onto the street.

"So. . .are you mad at me for stepping in?" he asked.

"No," she replied. "I'm not mad. I am glad you stopped when

you did. There are some battles not worth fighting. Some minds are sealed shut."

"Are you sure you want to give up?"

Karien clutched Matador's mane. "I see where you are going with this. If you are asking if I'm having doubts about marrying you and giving up a teaching career, cast those thoughts from your mind. I'm going to marry you, Nathan Archer, come storm or high water."

Nearing the Sutherbys' house, Karien saw her mother standing beside Mrs. Sutherby outside the white picket gate. "Mother is anxious," Karien said. "I bet Liza told her."

Nathan looped the reins over a slat in the fence and helped Karien down. Her mother and Mrs. Sutherby's mouths gaped at the steed, amazement in their expressions to see Karien had ridden on its tall back. She smiled at their expressions. Was it so unusual in Refuge to see a woman seated in a saddle with her beau leading the horse? Perhaps not, but for her mother it seemed a bit of a shock. In the city, the only thing she'd ever seen Karien ride was a streetcar.

Karien gripped her arms and shivered. "Can we go inside? It's chilly out here, and I'm dying for a fire."

She skipped up the front porch steps. She felt happy and drew in the crisp morning air. The day had certainly brought with it disappointment. However, Karien knew the love she and Nathan had for each other was the silver lining she had looked for.

Chapter 16

I will sing unto the L*ORD as long as I live:*
I will sing praise to my God while I have my being.
Psalm 104:33

Tall mullioned windows faced west in the Sutherbys' sitting room. Thursday's twilight brought with it hues of pink and orange along the horizon and shone across the hardwood floor. Extra chairs had been placed around the room, flanked by Mrs. Sutherby's prized houseplants.

Beneath the window stood a baby grand piano. Karien smoothed down the front of her frock with nervous fingers. Every seat had been taken. Likely, most of the town's residents had never heard classical piano, and she wonder if it was the proper way to warm them up to her.

"How often has that piano been played?" she asked Nathan. He stood beside her outside the door.

"I can't remember hearing it played." He held her hand. "They've heard the organ at church, and that's really all, I think."

"You've heard me play. You think they will like it?" she whispered.

"I've no doubt. Why not sing something first? You know, to get their rapt attention. You've got the voice of an angel."

She squeezed his hand when Mrs. Sutherby stepped to the front. She smiled broadly and opened her arms. Over her shoulders, she wore an elegant purple lace shawl with fringe. "Well, I must say, I am pleased to see so many faces." She reached back and touched the baby grand. "This ole instrument hasn't been played in many years. Tonight is special. Our guest was trained at the prestigious Peabody Institute in Baltimore and taught at the Margaret Brent Academy. May I introduce Miss Karien Wiles."

Mrs. Sutherby led the applause. Karien looked up at Nathan. He smiled and moved her forward with a gentle hand. She made her way down the aisle and sat down at the piano.

An elderly gent in the front row dragged off a tattered kepi cap and set it on his lap. "What'cha gonna play first, Miss Wiles?"

Karien smiled at him. "What would you like, sir?"

He paused and ran his hand over his bristly chin. "Hmm. Let's see. How's about something modern, something lively we can tap our feet to?"

A lady of elder years, dressed in faded black, elbowed him. "You would ask for that, Marshal. I'd like to hear Chopin." She looked at Karien and raised her eyebrows. "Can you play Chopin, miss?"

"Yes, ma'am, and Debussy and Listz as well. But first"—her fingers tripped over the ivory keys—"I will honor the gentleman's request. It's a popular song. You may already know."

The crowd stirred with excitement. Mr. Marshal grinned and looked around the room as if he'd won a prize. The lady smiled and wiggled her head. Her hat toppled, and she adjusted it. No wonder, thought Karien. She hadn't used a hat pin, instead tying it under her chin with a string of red braided trim.

Karien glanced at Nathan. He folded his arms across his chest and winked. The moment she opened the piano lid and set her music on the stand, members of the school board arrived. Gentlemen offered their seats to the ladies. Mr. Hobbs remained in the back. Karien had no nervous flutters at their arrival or resentment toward them. Glad they had come, she could now show them what they had missed.

"This song has lyrics by Ren Shields." She lifted her hands.

"It does?" Mrs. Sutherby said eagerly. "Well, go on. Sing! Sing!"

Clearing her throat, Karien lifted her fingers above the keys. "Hold on to your hats. Here goes."

She skipped her fingers up the length of the keys, a sort of introduction. The old gent's eyebrows inched higher and he scooted forward in his chair.

Karien sang:

"I love a sailor, the sailor loves me,
And sails ev'ry night to my home.
He's not a sailor that sails o'er the sea,
Or over the wild briny foam;
For he owns an airship and sails up on high,
He's just like a bird on the wing.
And when the shadows of evening draw nigh,
He'll sail to my window and sing:
'Come, take a trip in my airship,
Come, take a sail 'mong the stars,
Come, have a ride around Venus,
Come, have a spin around Mars.
No one to watch while we're kissing,
No one to see while we spoon.
Come, take a trip in my airship,
And we'll visit the man in the moon.' "

Her mother, seated next to Mrs. Sutherby, sucked in a breath. "Dear me, Karien."

"Do you all know the rest?" Karien asked. "Sing along if you do." The happier faces were endearing. Mrs. Sutherby stood up and began to lead the group, sweeping her hands up and down, back and forth in time with the music. The room burst into singing, except for the sour-faced Mrs. Strickland and Mr. Hobbs.

"One night, while sailing away from the crowds,
We passed through the milky white way,
Just idly sailing and watching the clouds,
He asked me if I'd name the day.
And right near the dipper I gave him my heart,
The sun shines on our honeymoon,
We swore from each other we never would part,
And teach all the babies this tune."

Mr. Marshal slapped his knee and jumped up. He grabbed the lady beside him, hauled her up, and danced with her across the floor. Everyone sang the chorus:

" 'Come, take a trip in my airship,
Come, take a sail 'mong the stars,
Come, have a ride around Venus,
Come, have a spin around Mars.
No one to watch while we're kissing.
No one to see while we spoon.
Come, take a trip in my airship,
And we'll visit the man in the moon.' "

The song ended with raucous applause.

Mrs. Sutherby smacked her hands together. "What a funny

song, Miss Wiles. Imagine sailing away in an airship to the man in the moon, when there is no such person."

The remainder of the evening turned into a singalong. Toe tappers as they called it, and lively hymns. As the clock reached nine, Karien soothed the audience with Frédéric Chopin's *Raindrop* Prelude, followed by Claude Debussy's Arabesque no. 1, and Franz Liszt's *Liebestraum*. A quiet serenity fell over the room, and when she finished, ladies wiped their eyes and men stared admiringly.

She stood and bowed gracefully to her listeners. Mrs. Sutherby stepped beside her. "Any questions for Miss Wiles?"

Hands shot up. "I have one," Miss Noble called out. She rose. "It's not really a question. More like a request. Miss Wiles, would you be willing to come to my home once a week and teach my Arabella how to play? We'd pay you whatever you charge. We have an old piano in the basement, and we'll haul it out and have it tuned."

"I'd be glad to. Is there someone in town who can tune pianos?"

"I can," Mr. Marshal shot up from his chair. "It's been a long time, but I can do it. I tuned the one you played on just for this occasion."

Karien thanked him. Then Mrs. Foster stood. "I'd like you to teach my Henry."

"And I'd like lessons for my grandson," said another.

"Mine too."

A stout woman in the second row raised her hand. "People have said I'm too old to learn. I think forty-seven is all right. May I have lessons also, Miss Wiles?"

More requests circled around the room, so many that Karien could not keep up. Sourpuss Mrs. Strickland shot up from her seat, scowled, and stormed out. Mr. Hobbs shrugged, put on his hat, and followed her.

Refreshments were served, and once the last couple left and the rest had gone to their beds upstairs, Nathan drew Karien aside in the shadowy hallway.

"They loved you!" He picked her up and whirled her around. When he set her down, he lifted her face to his. "When was the last time I told you I love you?"

"Yesterday." She sighed. "Say it again."

"I love you, Karien Wiles. Still want to be Mrs. Archer?"

"As long as you take me just as I am and don't mind when I begin my own business."

"I think it's grand. How about getting married this Sunday after church?"

"Sunday would be lovely." She threw her arms around his neck and pressed her cheek against his.

"Companions and equals. Does that suit?"

"It suits very well, Mr. Archer. You won't mind hearing the piano played so much in the house now that I have lessons to teach?"

"I'm happy for you. You showed those two old snoots how much they missed. They'll never change, but maybe the rules will after this."

"Anything is possible." Then she stood back. "You've never let me see the inside of Archer House. I hope it has furniture and a pot to cook in and dishes to eat from," she teased.

"I have those. Want to learn how to train horses and care for them?"

"You told me Contessa would be mine, so yes." She put her arms around his waist. "Oh I do love her. She's so gentle."

Nathan kissed her long and soft. "I'm feeling quite passionate, dear lady. I think I should leave now."

She stepped over to the front door and opened it. "Good night, Mr. Nathan Archer. I'll need a few days to myself, so you cannot see me until Sunday. Promise you won't try."

He slapped on his hat. "Hmm, that will be hard. But I promise." He stepped out onto the porch and to the stairs. Karien leaned against the doorjamb and looked up at the stars. The sky shone black as coal with stars too many to count. In the city, she never saw them like this or felt the beauty of the heavens looking down upon her.

"Nathan?"

He made a swift turn on his heels. "Yes, my darling?"

"God has blessed us, hasn't He?"

"More than I could've imagined."

"So much was lost in February, but we also gained far more than we realized."

In the lamplight, Nathan's eyes glowed. Dragging off his hat, he stepped toward her. "If I could shout, Karien, and not wake everyone up, I would."

She laughed in time with his joy. "I know you would, and so would I."

"More blessings are on the way."

"Lots more."

"Children, dogs, cats, and horses—the whole kit and caboodle."

Karien shook back her hair and smiled. "And music. Lots of music."

Author Notes

The Great Baltimore Fire

The portion of this story concerning the fire in Baltimore is based on actual events that happened on Sunday, February 7, 1904. It began in the John Hurst & Co. Dry Goods Store in the heart of the business district. The cause of the fire was believed to be a discarded cigar.

At the time, America was experiencing an economic recession, and the building was packed with inventory, the perfect fodder for a massive fire. The building ignited, and flames spread to upper floors and up to the roof. The fire grew into a colossal inferno and sent firebrands across to nearby buildings, setting them aflame.

The Church of the Messiah, as mentioned in the story, caught on fire. The walls crumbled from the heat and fell. The bell plunged to the ground with a great sound that shook the hearts of firemen, police, and citizens in flight.

After two days, the fire had incinerated 140 acres and fifteen hundred buildings. It threw tens of thousands of Baltimoreans out of work. Businesses were lost. The piers in the Inner Basin were destroyed. People fled to ships in the harbor, and the vessels blocked the retreat. Others made their way to Federal Hill in the freezing weather.

Firemen from other towns and cities arrived, and the pumps from their engines shot water into the flames. The water froze on wires and debris. Fortunately, no lives were lost, but if it had been a workday, there is no doubt many people would have perished.

Music in *A Song in the Night*

"Come Take a Trip in My Airship" came out in 1904. The music was composed by George Evans, and the lyrics were written by Ren Shields. It was one of the most popular songs of its era. A copy of the sheet music can be found at the Library of Congress website at https://www.loc.gov/resource/ihas.100005954.0/?sp=3. Many performances of the song can also be found on the internet. Later versions of the song have slightly different lyrics.

The Margaret Brent Academy

Although the Margaret Brent Academy is fictional, Baltimore does have the Margaret Brent Elementary/Middle School, which bears no relationship to this story. I chose the name because of the significance of Margaret Brent in the history of Maryland and Virginia. She was born in Quinton, Glouceste rshire, England, in about 1601 and immigrated with her siblings to the colony of Maryland in 1638. She settled in St. Mary's City on the eastern shore as a young, ambitious woman of about thirty-seven, destined to make history.

She was the first woman in the Colonies to appear before a Court of the Common Law. Wealthy male immigrants owned vast landholdings. Mary, however, settled in and purchased her own land not only in Maryland but in Virginia as well.

Governor Leonard Calvert of Maryland appointed her as his executor in 1647. Mary helped to ensure soldiers were paid and fed and saved the colony from rebellion. Cecil Calvert, second Lord Baltimore, condemned Mary's actions. She was a woman succeeding where politicians had failed. Eventually she left Maryland and settled in Virginia where she passed away in 1671 at an estate called Peace.

God bless the teachers who influenced my life and encouraged me to follow the Prince of Peace.

Rita Gerlach lives in central Maryland with her husband and two sons. She is a bestselling author of eight inspirational historical novels, including the Daughters of the Potomac series of which *Romantic Times* book review magazine said, "Creating characters with intense realism and compassion is one of Gerlach's gifts."

810-516-7250